PENMORT CASTLE

GHOSTS AND REINCARNATION SERIES
BOOK III

KRISTEN ASHLEY

ROCK CHICK
PRESS

Penmort CASTLE

GHOSTS AND REINCARNATIONS SERIES

NEW YORK TIMES BESTSELLING AUTHOR

KRISTEN ASHLEY

This book is dedicated Mike and Gwyneth Ashley.

Knowing both is like being handed one of life's surprising gifts, the kind of gifts you know you will always cherish.

❦ I ❦

NEGOTIATION

Cash Fraser sat in the back corner of the pub. A small cranberry-red bottle of sparkling water was on the table in front of him, a glass of ice beside it.

He hadn't yet bothered to pour.

He was considering leaving.

His being there he knew was a ridiculous idea. How he'd let James talk him into it, he couldn't fathom.

But he had.

And now he was there.

And she was late.

Cash didn't have a great deal of patience for anything including, and perhaps especially, waiting.

He'd made the decision to leave when the door opened, but he hesitated at what he saw.

He knew it was her the minute his eyes hit her.

He knew this because James had exquisite taste.

And she was definitely exquisite.

She was wearing winter white. A loosely knitted, woollen, white beret was pulled down low over her head covering her ears. She was wrapped in a white, well-tailored, wool overcoat that was nipped in at the waist. You could see the winter white turtleneck hugging her throat through the soft, white pashmina tucked stylishly in the lapel of her coat. She was wearing a chic pair of very high, dangerously thin spike-heeled snakeskin boots, and on her hands were grey leather gloves. The strap of a slim, sleek, expensive bag in matching snakeskin was on her shoulder, the bag tucked under her arm.

From his distance Cash could see that, even without the heels, she was quite tall. She had thick, long blonde hair bursting out from under the beret, flawless skin, and her rounded cheekbones had been made rosy from the bitter cold outside.

Cash took in her elegant clothing and good looks distractedly.

It was her presence that captured his attention.

She was not the kind of woman you looked at twice.

No, she was the kind of woman who, when she caught your attention it didn't move away.

And she was also the kind of woman who knew this as fact.

She tugged off her gloves as her eyes scanned the patrons. They stopped when they found him.

He watched her body go still, and even though her face remained bland, he thought for a moment she was going to turn around and leave.

Instead, she moved both gloves to one hand and pulled the beret off her head, her long, shining hair exposed dramatically with the movement. She walked toward him, her fingers plunging into her hair at her forehead and pulling it back. She lifted it at the back of her head, grasping it in a fist, flicking it out and dropping her hand, her hair settling to frame her face magnificently.

It was an effective show, drawing attention to her extraordinary face, her glorious hair as well as the long length of her body.

And she had Cash's attention as well as every man's in the room.

She walked with a natural grace even in those absurdly high heels, and he stood as any gentleman would when she made her final approach.

She stopped a foot away and tilted her head back to look at him.

Her eyes, Cash noted, were a warm hazel.

He found this warmth surprised him. She was the physical definition of cool.

"Cash," she said softly, warmth also in her voice.

"Abigail," he returned.

Her full, glossed lips tipped up slightly at the ends. Not a smile, not even a grin, just a nonverbal affirmation.

That's when she leaned into him. Her fingers curled around his upper arm and he felt one of her breasts press lightly against his chest as she tilted her head back further to touch her cheek against his.

Her perfume, he noted, was complicated and sophisticated, musky, yet vaguely floral.

The scent suited her.

When she moved away she murmured, "Abby."

"I'm sorry?" he queried.

Her eyes met his. "Call me Abby."

He didn't respond verbally but lifted his chin.

She didn't look like a woman who had an uncomplicated name such as "Abby." "Abigail" also didn't fit her and he wondered if this was her real name.

"Drink?" he asked.

"Red wine. A glass of pinot noir if they have it," she replied and Cash realised she was an American.

James hadn't told him that.

He also noted she was an alto, her accented voice pitched low and soft.

"Certainly," he replied to her request and stepped away to go to the bar.

He watched her as he ordered the wine. She took off her coat and scarf and he saw that she wore a snug-fitting, thin, winter-white turtleneck and a matching body-hugging skirt that ended just above her knees and clung to her thighs, hips and bottom. She had a pair of pearl studs in her ears and a gold watch at her wrist. No other jewellery.

Again, he noted her attire absentmindedly.

What held Cash's attention were her curves. She had full breasts, a tiny waist, rounded hips and a rather generous backside, all of this with those long legs, and, he observed, superb posture.

She sat with her side toward him and crossed her legs, her head bent to her bag that was in her lap. She pulled out her mobile and he saw her expression in profile change when she hit a button and looked at the display. At first he thought she was annoyed. Then a line of white teeth were exposed when she bit the side of her lower lip as if she was undecided about something.

Cash felt another small hint of surprise mainly because, the minute her teeth caught her lip, he thought she looked rather adorable.

He watched her make her decision. She released her lip, the tip of her tongue slid out to wet the upper one as she pressed and held a button on her phone. Once it was turned off, she thrust the mobile back in her bag, tossing it on the chair with her coat.

At that instant the bartender gave him her wine, Cash paid for it and walked back to the table.

When he came close, she looked up at him over her shoulder, her shining hair gliding along her back, her graceful jaw jutting out, her full lips slightly parted, her warm hazel eyes locked on his.

She'll do, he thought as he set the wine in front of her.

"Thank you," she murmured politely.

He sat opposite her and as she looked at him he noticed there was something in her eyes. Something he couldn't exactly read. It was something deep and intriguing. Something she meant to hide but was not quite successful in doing it. Something that, Cash thought as he kept his eyes on her, looked an awful lot like pain.

Nevertheless, his decision was made and as usual he didn't waste any time.

She was taking a sip of her wine when he asked, "How much?"

His bluntness startled her and it looked like she had difficulty swallowing as she blinked at him.

"I beg your pardon?" she inquired.

"James explained things to you?"

Her gaze held his and she replied, "Yes."

"How much?" Cash repeated.

Her eyes slid to the side and Cash didn't know what to make of this. It would disappoint him if she tried to be coy. It would irritate him if she tried to fleece him.

Her eyes came back to his. "You want what James explained?"

He wanted more than what he knew James explained, but he'd get to that in a moment.

"Yes," he answered.

Without hesitation she said, "Ten thousand pounds."

Again she'd surprised him. He'd expected her to ask for more. Indeed he knew without question she was worth more. He'd definitely pay double that. He'd even consider paying triple.

Not one to let a good deal slide by, he nodded immediately. "Agreed."

He watched with no small fascination as her composure slipped and several emotions, one after the other, chased across her face.

They went by so fast he couldn't read them all but he could have sworn he caught disappointment and even alarm before she gained control so swiftly it was as if it never happened at all.

"Done." She held up her wine glass. "Shall we toast on it?"

"I'm not finished," he replied.

She regarded him a moment, her eyes shuttered. Then she took a sip of her wine, set it on the table, sat back in her chair, her gaze returning to him, and she waited.

He didn't make her wait long and he didn't sugar-coat his question.

"I'd like to know how much more to fuck you."

The minute he'd finished his query, with interest he watched her jaw get tight, as did her entire body, and her obvious negative reaction surprised him yet again.

He continued calmly with the raise of an eyebrow, "Is that not part of the service you provide?"

"I'm not a prostitute." Her low, soft voice now held a hint of displeasure.

"I'm sure James explained to you that this deal includes you sleeping in the same bed with me," Cash reminded her.

"Sleeping," was her quick retort.

Cash thought about her hesitation at the door, remembered her teeth catching her lip in indecision, the fleeting loss of poise when they started talking money, and he had an uncomfortable suspicion.

"Do you have other clients?" he asked.

"Yes," she answered promptly.

"In the UK?" he pressed.

Her eyes locked on his. "No."

"The States," Cash pushed.

"Are you needing references?" she returned, her tone slightly sharp, and he nearly laughed.

Abruptly he leaned toward her and repeated, "How much to fuck you?"

He watched as her stare turned into a glare and realised immediately there was fire behind that ice.

Cash found this very interesting.

"How much?" he asked again.

She frowned and her eyes started to narrow.

"I'll double your fee," he told her.

"I don't think so," she replied with disgust.

"Triple," Cash returned.

"Absolutely not," she snapped, her eyes fully narrowed.

She was, it appeared, getting angry.

And he knew immediately he liked it.

She was also not making a single move to leave.

"I'll give you fifty thousand pounds," Cash said.

He didn't have to wait for her response to his generous offer.

She leaned toward him and he knew she'd lost her temper even before she hissed, "You couldn't afford me."

"Then James didn't explain who I am," Cash retorted.

"I know who you are," she bit out. "Everyone knows who you are."

"Then you know I can afford you."

She didn't reply.

He got closer and she held her ground, something which said a lot about her. He was close enough to smell her perfume again and close enough to see there was a slight peach sheen to the gloss on her lips.

He wanted her.

Simple as that.

And he was going to have her.

He decided to finish the negotiation. "One hundred thousand pounds and that buys me unlimited access to you throughout our arrangement."

She made an indistinct angry noise in the back of her throat before suggesting, "Perhaps this isn't a good idea."

He pulled in breath through his nostrils and sat back.

He kept his eyes on her for a second that led to two then slid into three before he said, "Perhaps not."

He thought he'd called her bluff.

Instead she turned, grabbed her things and stood.

She looked down on him. "It was a pleasure, Mr. Fraser," she stated. However, the way she said it he knew it most definitely was not.

This amused him and Cash smiled.

She glared.

This amused him more.

She turned to leave when he stood quickly. He wrapped his fingers around her upper arm, halting her retreat.

He pulled her to him gently and his mouth went to her ear where he murmured, "Two hundred thousand."

Her body jerked then froze and she hesitated, indicating to Cash indecision.

Finally her neck twisted so she was looking at him before she said, "Two hundred thousand and we don't consummate this part of the arrangement until we go to the castle."

Cash was impressed.

She was very good.

She'd started at ten thousand and finished getting twenty times that.

"I like you," he told her.

"Well, I don't like *you*," she snapped back.

This made him smile again which also made her eyes drop to his mouth.

He decided he liked her eyes on his mouth. He liked it a great deal.

Cash ignored his body's pleasant reaction and commented, "That should make your job more difficult."

Her gaze returned to his and she replied coldly, "Don't worry, no one will suspect."

"Including me?"

Her brows snapped together. "Pardon?"

"I'm not paying you not to like me. I'm paying you to like me." He hesitated and his voice dipped lower when he finished, "I'm paying you to like me a lot."

She stared at him a moment and he wondered what she was thinking.

Suddenly she moved. Her upper body swayed into his and her hand touched him at his waist. She leaned up and her mouth brushed his softly as her breasts swept his chest.

His body reacted pleasantly to that too.

Not moving her mouth from his, her eyes open, she murmured, "You won't suspect either."

She moved back, only inches, her hand went from his waist and she did something that surprised him yet again.

She lifted her hand and used her thumb to wipe her lip gloss gently from his mouth, the whole time she watched her thumb's movements.

It surprised him because it was not something a woman did to a man she'd only just met. It was also not something a woman did for a man she did not like.

It was something a man's woman did for him.

Before Cash could react, she was walking away, swinging her coat on as she went, yanking her hair out of the collar with a casual movement of her arm.

He watched her hair tumble down her back as she walked out the door.

Yes, Cash thought as he reached for his own coat, *she'll do*.

❧   2   ❧

ABBY'S REASON

"**A**re you *nuts?*" Jenny shrieked after Abby told her the unusual turn of events that occurred at the pub an hour before. Abby watched as her friend shook her head forcefully before shouting, "I didn't sign up for *this!*"

Abby pulled her bare heels up to the edge of the couch she was sitting on and wrapped her arms around her jeans-clad legs (she'd changed out of her Ice Queen outfit upon arriving home). The whole while she did this, she kept her eyes on her irate best friend.

Jenny was probably right. She *was* nuts.

She had to be.

What was she thinking, agreeing to have sex with someone for money?

It wasn't nuts.

It was *insane.*

However, there was the not-so-insignificant fact that she was going to be two hundred thousand pounds richer.

Two hundred *thousand* pounds.

She still couldn't believe it, and when she thought of it she wondered what on earth Cash Fraser was thinking.

Cash Fraser; the man, the legend.

He'd become known to the human populace just over a year ago when someone leaked that he was the real man behind the story of a box office topping action movie. The movie was about a brilliant industrial spy ring breaker (who even knew there *was* such a job in real life) that all the big multinationals turned to and paid millions upon millions of pounds (so they could save billions) when they had a problem.

It was then that the dangerous, thrill-seeking, *gorgeous* Cash Fraser was uncovered.

Once he was exposed the media went nuts.

This was mainly because he looked like a movie star, but also because he acted like a dangerous action man.

Uncommonly tall, dark and handsome, standing at six feet four (and she discovered this afternoon that was *tall*), he had a lean, muscled, broad-shouldered body and a thick head of so-dark-brown-it-was-nearly-black, almost-but-not-quite-curly hair he wore in a way that was far too long for any other man but looked messy and sexy on him. He had the most unbelievable black eyes she'd ever seen. They were liquid black, their colour shocking in its depth and intensity.

And he had a way about him that translated in print when some journalist described it (and she'd witnessed it firsthand) and in pictures when the paparazzi captured it. This was probably due to the fact that he was not the kind of man who wanted people to write about him, take photos of him and print them in papers. And he made that pretty clear in a variety of dangerous action man ways.

This behaviour only threw fuel on the fire.

For instance, a couple of times he made it clear by ripping a camera out of some photographer's hands and destroying it (and on one occasion, giving the photographer a broken nose).

He'd had some trouble with that. Something about which he also didn't care.

He had enough money to pay fines and attorneys and buy new cameras. His job, due to its rarity and danger, paid well. At least it did in the movie. The way he dressed (the navy suit with the deep lilac, expertly tailored shirt and expensive tie he wore that afternoon was *lush*) and the easy way he could spend a couple hundred thousand pounds on a prepaid girlfriend proved this as fact.

There were probably some women out there (maybe not just some, maybe scores, maybe *thousands*) who'd pay Cash Fraser that amount of money for just one smile directed at them. Abby had already had two—she'd counted—and they were *good*.

And, Abby figured, these women would no doubt pay a whole lot more to have a shot at servicing him in his bed.

The very idea of Cash Fraser paying *them* wouldn't even be considered.

And she had to face it. The bottom line was, Abby needed the money.

Further, she no longer had anything to lose. Jenny knew that. Everyone knew that. Even her neighbour—nosy, crazy, maddening "keep your cat out of my garden" Mrs. Truman knew that.

Yes, Abigail Butler had a lot to gain from this deal—two hundred *thousand* pounds to be exact.

At least this was what she preferred to focus on. Not the fact that she'd just become a very highly paid prostitute even if it was to a good-looking, wealthy, industrial spy ring breaker who had an action movie based on his life.

Abby pushed these thoughts aside and said softly, "Jenny, calm down."

Jenny's dark-brown eyes grew wide.

"Calm? You want me to be calm?" she asked, then yelled, "You just agreed to sleep with a man for money!"

Abby let her legs go and stood, taking a quick step across her living room to get close to her friend.

"Be quiet!" she snapped. "Pete's here!"

"I don't care!" Jenny snapped back, but thankfully quieter this time. "Since you've apparently lost your ever-loving mind, I'm considering this a one-woman intervention. If Pete wants to join in all the better!"

Abby had known Jenny since they met as roommates their freshman year at university twenty years ago. Over the decades, even when there were sometimes thousands of miles between them, they'd stayed very, *very* close.

Regardless of her auburn hair, Jennifer Kane was usually pretty mellow and laidback.

Unless she was inebriated or angry, then she was pretty crazy and very loud.

Like, for instance, now.

Abby tried to use logic. "Tell me what's changed since Kieran went to James and offered my, um..." Abby hesitated then forged on, "services."

"Well," Jenny started, her voice dripping with sarcasm. "When I overheard James talking to Cash Fraser at that party and came up with my wild scheme to pretend you were a high-class, very discreet escort...after thinking about my stubborn, silly, stupid best friend not letting me and Kieran help her. Even though we can. Even though we don't mind. Even though we both love her like crazy and we *want* to help. I thought my *brilliantly stupid* idea may be a good way for you to earn some quick money to get you out of a pickle. At the time I talked you and Kieran into the idea, and Kieran into approaching James, which I'll remind you he really didn't want to do, as in *really*—"

"Jenny—" Abby began with a warning in her voice that her friend was digressing to oft-gone-over ground.

"At the time," Jenny continued, ignoring Abby's warning, "you were just going to be a paid escort, wearing fancy clothes and eating fancy dinners and being on the arm of a hot guy."

She flipped out her hand in an angry, dismissive gesture and kept ranting.

"So you'd have to pretend to be his girlfriend and sleep in bed with him at a spooky castle. It was supposed to be platonic! It was supposed to be easy money! It was supposed to be a reason for us to go shopping for fancy clothes! But *no*..."

Jenny drew out the "no" with exaggeration and kept right on going.

"Now, you've agreed to have sex with him while in said spooky haunted castle where, I will remind you, over the centuries five, that is *five*..." she held up five fingers, "women, all of them blonde, which you also are in case you hadn't noticed, and all of them the lovers of the man of the house, which you will be if you go through with this, God help you, and all of them were murdered by a malevolent ghost!" she finished on a shout.

Abby had heard the story of the famously homicidal ghost of Penmort Castle. Everyone had. It was lore.

Though many people had claimed to see the ghost of the raven-haired woman floating around doing nasty things to guests and servants, no one had proof that she actually killed anyone.

And she never did anything to family. Unless that family happened to be sleeping with the man of the castle, as in, say, his wife (which it was always his wife, only on one occasion was it his mistress).

Of course, all the possible witnesses were dead.

"There's no such thing as ghosts," Abby told her friend.

Jenny threw up her hands, stared at the ceiling and exclaimed, "Huh!"

Her eyes moved back to Abby and she kept going.

"Excuse me, but weren't you with us when we used that bizzar-O board with the magnifying glass in a plastic heart to call up the ghost of Wendy's grandma our sophomore year? Wendy's grandma knew Wendy had slept with Kathleen's boyfriend Brian! Who would know that but Wendy, Brian and a being from beyond the veil? Kathleen *freaked* when Grandma spilled the beans. You believed in ghosts then!"

Abby had to admit, Jenny wasn't wrong. Everyone had freaked. Though it had to be said, no one had freaked more than Kathleen. That had been an interesting night.

Abby tried a different tactic. "Cash Fraser isn't the man of the house."

"No, he isn't, *officially*. What he *is*, is the illegitimate son of the now-dead man of the house. If things were different, if Anthony Beaumaris had married Cash's mum, that castle would be his. I don't know if ghosts can tell the difference, but you probably won't have the opportunity to explain this detail before she pushes you down a stone stairwell, plunging you gruesomely to your death."

After that dramatic statement was uttered, before Abby could get a word in, they heard a throat being cleared.

Both women turned to the door and Pete, Abby's handyman, was standing there.

Since Abby returned to England, Pete had been a fixture in her life. She liked Pete. She liked him a lot.

She still wished she didn't see so damned much of him.

On the far side of fifty, Pete was stocky and medium height. He had a weathered face, a shock of dark hair peppered with grey and a gentle manner.

He'd been a trusted friend of Abby's grandmother and now he was a trusted friend of hers.

"Abby love, sorry to interrupt but..." he hesitated and Abby braced for bad news.

For the last year Pete had been the bearer of many a bad tiding. The roof needed to be re-tiled. The windows needed to be replaced. The insulation needed to be ripped out and re-installed. There was mildew and damp. It never ended.

Now he was there looking at the bath, for every time Abby took a shower it rained in the vestibule. This, Abby, even not being very *au fait* about such things, didn't think was a good sign.

"Just sock it to me, Pete," Abby encouraged on a pretend smile.

He shifted on his feet. "I think I'm gonna have to bring a man in."

Abby sighed.

It was *never* good when Pete had to bring a man in.

"Or two," Pete finished.

Abby's stomach clenched and she turned and looked at Jenny, an *any more questions?* expression on her face.

She looked back at Pete and said, "Call them in."

Pete looked uncomfortable. "We're talkin' plumber and electrician. They might be pricey, but I'm not qualified—"

"Call them in, Pete," Abby repeated.

"You probably shouldn't take a shower for a while," Pete went on.

"Okay," Abby replied.

"Or a bath," Pete continued.

Abby stared.

She only had one bathroom. Well, she had three. It was more to the point that she only had one *working* bathroom.

"No bath?" she whispered.

"Water damage to the floorboards. You fill up that roll top tub and get in it, it could go through the floor," Pete explained.

Visions of Abby, naked and bathing, crashing through the floor of her ancestral home did not make Abby feel warm all over.

"Call in the guys, Pete," Abby said quietly.

Pete nodded, looking about as happy about his errand as Abby was. He gave a chin lift to Jenny and backed out.

When Abby turned back to Jenny she thought her point had been made. She also thought it was time to fire up her computer and check her bank balance.

James, who Abby had met only once through Kieran, who Abby had known for twelve years because he was Jenny's husband, was playing Abby's...she hesitated because the word "pimp" didn't sound nice, so she decided to think of him as her business manager.

James was supposed to tell Cash to transfer a quarter of the agreed amount into her account. He was also supposed to give Cash her phone number so she'd be reachable by Cash. The down payment would be augmented the day they went to the castle when Abby would get another quarter of the money. The last half would be transferred at the end of the arrangement.

Fifty thousand pounds would go a long way toward paying a plumber and electrician. It would also pay off what she owed Pete, who allowed her to pay an instalment on a monthly basis, but she had an ongoing and growing balance that she owed him. It would also allow her to bring current the two loans she'd had to take against the house. Not to mention the two credit cards that were maxed out. And her line of credit with the bank that was over the limit.

When she opened her mouth to make her point to Jenny, Jenny got there before her and asked softly, "I still don't know why you don't just sell this house."

Abby closed her mouth and her eyes.

When she opened them again, she replied, "You do know."

"It's just a house," Jenny returned.

"My mother grew up here. My grandmother grew up here. My grandmother inherited this house from her father who died before she was born. It was the only thing he was ever able to give her that would keep her safe, warm and protected. And *he* grew up here, as did his father and his father before him. I can't sell it. It's the only thing I have left of them. It's the only thing I have *at all*."

A look of pain crossed Jenny's face before she could hide it, but her next words explained it, "You have us, Kieran and me. You have friends. You have—"

Abby's voice turned harsh in order to hide the hurt of the invisible hand that always squeezed her heart when they had this conversation. When the reminder came, yet again, of all she *didn't* have.

"You don't understand. You have Kieran. Ben's gone, Jenny, *dead*."

Abby spit out the last word that she didn't need to use. A word she didn't need to remind her friend was attached to Abby's husband. Jenny knew all too well and Abby watched her friend flinch.

She kept talking through her friend's flinch.

"There will never be another Ben. I'll never have that again. Most women don't get that kind of love even once in their life. I had it and now it's gone and it hurts every day. Even after all this time it hurts every *single* day. Mom's gone. Dad's gone. Ben's gone and now Gram's gone. I need this house. I need the memories I have in this house. I'll never give it up. Never. I can't. Gram wouldn't understand. Mom wouldn't understand. Hell, even Ben wouldn't understand if I let this house go. They all loved it just like I do. You don't get it. You *can't* get it. And I hope to God you never do."

Jenny started to speak but Abby shook her head.

"If I have to do something you don't approve of to take care of myself, my life, my home, then I'm sorry. You can't take care of all my problems. I can't lean on you and Kieran for everything. You've been there every time. Mom, Dad, Ben, Gram and all the crazy, stupid stuff I've done in between. Now it's high time I stepped up. I got myself in this mess, I'll damned well get myself out."

"Abby, please—" Jenny started.

"No," Abby cut her off. "No. *You* please. Please just support me and help me. One month, then I can start over. I can get the house back in shape and get my life back on track. One month and then we can put it all behind us." Abby put her hands on her petite friend's neck and bent her face toward her. "I need you to support me with this, Jenny. Please."

Jenny's face gentled but she didn't give up. "Abby, honey, I know how you feel about this house and I love it too. You know I do. But I think you're focusing on this house and fixing it up and keeping it as some weird way to keep hold of your family, of Ben. I promise you, Abby, I *promise*, you won't lose the memories of them if you give up this house."

She was wrong.

Sometimes, if Abby was out somewhere and the memory of Ben decided to travel through her mind, she'd forget what he smelled like. She'd forget what it felt like to have his hands on her body, his fingers finding hers, his knee brushing hers under a table. She'd forget what his voice sounded like, his laughter, his familiar chuckle when she'd done something he considered "adorable."

Sometimes she'd even forget what he looked like and she'd have to drop everything and rush home.

In this house, she'd remember.

She'd remember him at the kitchen table drinking coffee and chatting with her grandmother or playing cards with her mom and dad. She'd remember him decorating the Christmas tree in the living room. She'd remember him teasing her grandmother that she had way too damn many rose bushes in the garden that Gram would ask him to prune. She'd remember hearing his laughter coming from the study mingled with her father's as they drank whisky and tried to outdo each other telling rude jokes. She'd remember him making love to her in the same roll top tub that was now the bane of her existence when her grandmother was on holiday in Germany and they were watching the house.

Abby could never, *ever* sell this house.

"You don't understand," she whispered, feeling the tears pricking her eyes.

"No," Jenny whispered back. "I don't." She paused and then sighed before speaking again, "But if this is what you've got to do, girlfriend, then this is what you've got to do."

Abby swallowed back her tears and nodded her gratitude.

"I'm just not going to tell Kieran," Jenny finished.

"That's probably a good idea," Abby agreed.

Jenny's reaction had been dramatic enough.

Kieran would probably shout the roof down.

And Abby had just had it re-tiled.

❧ ❧ ❧

An hour later, with both Pete and Jenny gone, Abby sat at her grandmother's writing desk in the living room and stared at the transaction that beamed grand and glorious from her bank statement, which was displayed on the computer screen.

Abby felt relief sweep through her.

All right, so she was a very highly paid prostitute.

But at least now she could pay off that unbelievably expensive outfit she wore today that maxed out credit card number two.

Her mobile on the desk sounded.

Abby picked it up and looked at the display, fear that word of her new job as whore had leaked out to Kieran and he was going to give her what for replaced the short-lived relief she'd felt the moment before.

The display said UNKNOWN CALLER, and since Kieran was very known, Abby engaged her phone and put it to her ear.

"Hello?"

"Abby."

Oh dear Lord, it was Cash. She knew it immediately. She'd never forget his deep, rough voice with the more-than-subtle hint of Scottish burr.

What did she say? What did she do?

"Yes," she replied.

"James explained your terms," he told her, his voice just as deep, just as rough and just as sexy over the phone as it was when he leaned close and calmly asked how much it would cost to fuck her.

She'd never forget that either. She'd wanted to hit him when he'd done it.

She also had the very weird desire to kiss him.

She hadn't had the desire to kiss anyone since Ben. It had been four years. Four very long years.

Then again she'd never been your normal girl next door.

Abigail Butler had always been a little weird, a little headstrong, a little crazy, and more often than she cared to admit (like today), a lot stupid.

But there was also the fact that Cash Fraser was an unbelievably handsome, shockingly sexy man.

Abby's eyes went to the computer screen. "I see he did."

"You have the money?"

"Yes," she replied.

"Tomorrow night. Dinner. It won't be casual dress."

What did he mean, *It won't be casual dress*? Did that mean formal? Did that mean evening gown? Or did that mean a nice pair of slacks?

Hell, she couldn't *ask*. He thought she was an experienced escort. That was what Kieran said when he'd talked to James and she'd even lied to Cash herself that day that she had other clients. Any experienced escort to the rich and famous would know what to wear to dinner.

"Fine. What time?" she asked, sounding even to her own ears like she knew what she was doing. It appeared she was actually *good* at this stuff and she didn't know if she should take that as a positive or negative sign.

"I'll pick you up at seven," Cash told her.

"No," Abby replied immediately, luckily sounding brisk rather than panicked, "I'll meet you at the restaurant."

"You aren't going to meet me at the restaurant," he returned in a very firm voice.

The panic deepened but Abby fought it. "I'm sorry, Cash. Part of the deal is you don't get to know where I live."

"You live at number twenty-two Eton Road."

Oh dear Lord, how did he know that?

If James told him then James wasn't being a very good business manager. He was only supposed to give him her phone number.

Now what did she do?

Time to put her foot down.

"You aren't coming here. I'll meet you at your house."

"I'll be at your place at seven," he repeated.

The panic was now full blown.

How would she cope with Cash Fraser and his charismatic presence forcing his way into her home? She didn't need memories of him here. He'd ruin everything.

She forced her voice to go cold. "You'll not come to my house."

"Seven," was his reply.

Then he disconnected.

She disengaged and whispered, "Bloody hell."

THE FIRST DATE

Abby was already in the vestibule when the ancient bell in the door clanked discordantly as Cash Fraser turned it.

Not wanting to be taken unaware, nor give him any reason to enter her home, she'd been ready for half an hour.

She'd watched for his arrival at the window while alternately pacing the living room. All that time she wondered if he could track her down if she took his money and escaped to the wilds of the Brazilian rainforest (and, as he was an industrial spy ring breaker, she figured he could).

On that dismal thought she'd seen his car pull in the drive. She watched his tall, powerful body knife out of the car as if he was being born anew from its sleek depths before she dropped the curtains she was peeking through. She took a long calming breath (which failed to calm her incidentally) and ran to the entry, the echo of her heels clattering against the large black and white diamond-tiled floor rang through the cavernous hall as she moved.

Her cat, aptly named Beelzebub (because the fluffy, black furball was a little devil), chased her, weaving around her high-heeled feet, nearly tripping her (part of the reason he was a little devil for he did this often and sometimes succeeded in his efforts).

She was wearing her grandmother's clothes.

With only a day to prepare and her life in its usual—if quite a bit more dramatic—turmoil, she hadn't had time to shop for anything new.

However, for her first date as paid escort to handsome Cash Fraser, she knew she needed something special. Something she and Jenny would refer to as Clothing Courage.

And as ever, Gram, even dead for over a year, did not disappoint when her granddaughter was in need.

That day, the plumber and electrician became a plumber, electrician *and* contractor because once the bathroom suite and tile were ripped out, the rotting floorboards had to be replaced and there was the small fact that two walls of plaster fell down.

Therefore that day had been spent not at the mall but in the tile shop where she bought what seemed like—and cost as much as—acres of expensive replacement tile.

She'd also sent out cheques paying off her credit cards. She settled her debt with Pete and significantly drew down both of her loans. Lastly, she'd gone to the grocery store and bought enough food to feed an army.

This final errand for some reason gave her a glorious sense of freedom.

She hadn't been able to afford to go nuts at a grocery store or any store or in any way shape or form in so long, she forgot how it felt not to have to watch every single penny.

Knowing her day would be full, the night before Abby had gone rooting through her grandmother's things to find something "not casual."

Abby's grandmother kept everything. There were four bedrooms in the house, and when Gram died and Abby moved in, the wardrobes in all four, as well as boxes stuffed full in the loft, were filled with clothes from the many decades of her grandmother's, and her mother's (and her great grandmother's), lives.

It was a veritable clothing museum and definitely any clotheshorse girlie-girl's dream.

Tonight Abby was wearing a dress she'd carefully unpacked, hand washed and allowed to drip-dry overnight and that day she'd steam pressed it.

It was vintage '40s, made of aubergine silk crepe. It had a bloused boat-neck bodice that fell gracefully to a slim body-hugging waist that had a three-inch band of intricately-designed black beading. The straight skirt came to just below the knee and had a slit up the back. It had short, loose sleeves and an elegant drape that exposed Abby's back to just above her bra strap.

Abby kept her hair down but blew it sleek to frame her face. And she'd done her makeup in what she referred to in her wide array of makeup looks (an array she'd once enumerated to Ben while he nearly choked himself laughing even though she was *not* being funny) as "Smoky Evening."

She wore the antique dress with a pair of sheer black stockings with a seam up the back and her own black velvet, high-heeled shoes that had a rounded closed toe, bare sides and an intricately designed heel made of a multitude of slender velvet bands leading up and into a delicate ankle strap.

The shoes were designer and expensive and Abby had owned them for six years.

They were bought in the days of Ben. When he was, obviously, alive. When they'd both had good jobs (but Ben's was better and higher paid). When they'd lived in a two-bedroom townhouse in the Georgetown area of Washington DC. When Ben had managed their money, setting aside a modest amount for their retirement, with two savings accounts he carefully monitored—a small one for a rainy day, a larger one for the extravagant vacations they liked to take.

Ben didn't mind that more than occasionally Abby bought expensive shoes or designer clothes or exclusive pieces of jewellery. Back then, they were only just beginning to talk about starting a family. It was still just the two of them. They were young. They had all the time in the world to think about the future.

On that heartbreaking thought, Abby swung her grandmother's heavy black velvet cape around her shoulders, shoved her arms through the holes and fastened the silk frog at her throat.

She had to stop thinking about Ben.

At least for tonight.

"Be good, Zee," she told her cat, who meowed in return and

performed a downward-facing kitty-cat stretch as Abby grabbed her grandmother's velvet evening bag and her own black leather gloves.

She allowed herself a moment to bend and scratch her cat's behind, her newly-manicured, pearlescent-pink-tipped nails sifting through the fine, soft, black fur just above her cat's tail right where Zee liked best to be scratched. When she did, as usual, Abby heard him start to purr.

After she gave Zee his customary goodbye, Abby positioned herself strategically at the door so she could push through before Cash got any ideas about coming inside. She opened the door only as far as it needed to go watching the ground so she could step out without tripping, then shoving her body through. She came very close to Cash, who for some reason didn't move out of her way.

She immediately smelled his cologne, not because it was overpowering, but because she was that close to him.

She'd smelled his cologne when she'd met him. It was subtle. Slightly woodsy, slightly spicy, *very* male.

It entirely suited him.

Abby ignored her brain registering she very much liked his scent.

She pulled the door until she heard the latch catch and twisted, tilting her head questioningly to see that, although his body was facing her and the door, Cash's head was turned to the side.

Abby looked in the same direction to see what caught his attention.

Then her stomach did a nosedive of dismay.

Mrs. Truman from next door was on her front doorstep, a shawl wrapped around her shoulders to protect her against the damp, bitter, late-January cold. The light from the vestibule illuminated her (and her short, tightly-set blue hair) and two of her three King Charles spaniels were dancing around her ankles and yapping noisily at Cash.

I don't need this, Abby thought and opened her mouth to say something before Mrs. Truman could *do* something. Something crazy or snooping or irritating or all three.

But as usual, Mrs. Truman got there first.

"Who are you?" she snapped at Cash, as if she was entitled to know and also as if she knew beyond all doubt that whatever his answer, it was going to cause her great misery.

Abby again started to respond, but it was Cash who spoke first, his deep, throaty Scottish brogue sounding through the dark night.

"Cash Fraser."

Mrs. Truman leaned forward, giving Cash a sharp look both of them could see even across Abby's stoop, drive and hedge and Mrs. Truman's hedge, drive and stoop.

"So you are. Thought I recognised you. Seen you in the papers. What are you doing with Abigail?" Mrs. Truman asked tartly, clearly feeling that she was owed this information as a privilege of her very existence, when she most definitely was not.

Again, Cash answered, "Taking her to dinner."

"On a date?" Mrs. Truman inquired as if this concept was foreign to her. Foreign and abhorrent like they lived in a time when women were sequestered until marriage and anyone breaking this time-honoured rule should be tarred and feathered.

"Yes," Cash replied and Abby's head tilted back to look at him because she could hear a hint of amusement in his voice.

She saw up close (as they were only inches away) in the light, which was shining from the stained glass window over her door, that he was, indeed, amused.

And Cash Fraser's handsome face amused was better than it was unamused, and unamused he was spectacular.

Abby felt her jaw get tense.

"Abigail does *not* date," Mrs. Truman informed Cash authoritatively and she would know. She kept a close eye on Abby, everyone in the neighbourhood and likely everyone in the entire county.

Oh dear Lord, Abby thought.

"She does tonight," Cash returned.

Abby almost laughed because this was all so absurd, it was hilarious.

At the same time she almost screamed because this was all so absurd, it was scary.

Instead of doing either, she moved to the side, linked her arm through Cash's and called, "We've a booking, Mrs. Truman. We don't want to be late. Have a lovely evening."

Cash, Abby was happy to note, moved with her as she manoeuvred him toward the grand expanse of stone steps that led up the side of her house to her front door.

Her torture at the hands of her demented neighbour, however, was not quite over.

"Abigail Butler!" Mrs. Truman yelled to their forms descending the staircase, and Abby turned her head to look at the old woman when she continued, "I'll not have him racing his fancy car down the street, waking me up at all hours. You tell him that," she demanded, even though Cash was right there beside her.

"We'll be quiet," Abby called back.

Mrs. Truman was still not done. In fact, she'd saved the best for last.

"And no necking on the front stoop. This is a nice neighbourhood," she declared.

At that, but most especially at Cash Fraser's highly amused, soft laughter, Abby didn't know if she wanted to die or if she wanted to kill Mrs. Truman.

She decided to kill Mrs. Truman. The woman was old and had lived her life. Abby was also relatively certain her sentence would be light if some of her other neighbours testified about Mrs. Truman at the trial.

"Good night, Mrs. Truman," Abby called firmly.

They heard a loud "humph," which travelled the distance between Abby and Mrs. Truman's house as Cash led Abby to the sleek black car in the drive.

All thoughts of Mrs. Truman fled as Abby stared at the car, not having taken it in when Cash arrived.

It was a Maserati.

Ironically, since he'd died in one, Ben loved cars. All cars. Indeed anything with wheels, but most especially fast cars. They'd only ever been able to afford a Nissan Z car for him, which he loved, nearly (but not quite) as much as Abby, and that had been used when they bought it.

This was brand new.

Ben would have adored this car.

Cash took her to the passenger side and opened the door for her, and Abby found she couldn't stop her breath from catching.

She'd dated frequently before Ben (not at all after him) and every once in a while her suitors would open the car door for her and only the first few dates.

Throughout their time together Ben had always opened her door for her even if they were going to the grocery store. Abby used to tease him about this show of gallantry, explaining she was a healthy girl, she could open her own doors. He'd always ignored her and did it anyway.

She'd secretly loved it. It was one of the many ways Ben took care of her, protected her and showed he loved her.

With a guiding hand on her arm, Cash steered her to her seat and waited courteously as she shifted her legs into the car before he slammed the door.

Abby took deep breaths to calm herself.

She had to stop thinking about Ben, especially now. Now was *not* the time to think of her beloved, but very dead, husband.

She tried to appear outwardly calm as she buckled herself in and Cash slid in beside her.

After he'd secured himself and started the car, he faced Abby and remarked, "Your neighbour is interesting."

Abby kept her body facing forward, only turning her head to look at him, her mind whirling in desperation to explain away nosy Mrs. Truman.

Not only that, she wondered what he thought of her living in a huge, rambling, four-storey, Victorian semi-detached in a quiet seaside town in an even quieter, old, settled and sedate neighbourhood where the average age of her neighbours was four hundred and twenty-two.

Abby reckoned that Cash probably thought that high-class call girls would not live in such places. Not, Abby thought somewhat hysterically, that she knew where Cash or even she would think a high-class call girl would live.

To his remark, Abby replied coldly, "Mrs. Truman is a raving shrew."

And she watched as Cash Fraser laughed.

And when he did something profound happened to Abby.

His laugh was deep, throaty and rich. So much so it was almost physical, filling the car and reaching out to her like a caress.

The feeling was so pleasant, the sound of his laughter so arresting,

Abby found herself stunned, wanting it never to end and frightened of it at the same time.

Frightened because *she* made him laugh and she had the feeling he didn't do it often. Her being able to make him laugh felt like some kind of victory.

She knew in a flash that she'd want all of that again, and fleetingly, against her will, she had the bizarre wish that it didn't happen like this with her, his paid escort.

Instead, for the first time with any man since Ben, she wished this was real. That she was there because Cash wanted her to be, not because he'd paid for it.

She turned to face forward, tucking her purse in her lap and starting to put on her gloves in an effort to focus when she said, "You can, of course, think it's funny. *You* don't have to live next to her."

His laughter died to a soft chuckle through which he asked, "Is she always like that?"

"No," Abby replied serenely. "Sometimes she can be worse."

He burst out laughing again, and even though she didn't want to, Abby turned to watch, liking the look of his handsome face in laughter, again feeling the sense of triumph mingled heavily with fear.

If she wasn't seated (and it was anatomically possible), she would have kicked herself.

Because she knew she was trying to make him laugh.

She most definitely *had* to get control of herself.

She had to endure the next month being seen publicly on his arm and going with him to his ancestral home (which wasn't *officially* his ancestral home) to help him make the statement that he was quite assuredly unavailable. Thus protecting him against his unofficially official uncle's determined, and unwanted, attempts to get him to marry one of his wife's daughters by a previous marriage.

Abby did not know why dangerous action man Cash Fraser didn't just tell his uncle to go jump in a lake. She also didn't know why dangerous action man Cash Fraser didn't utilise one of the many women at his disposal for this errand instead of paying for one.

Neither of these things were any of her business. She had a job to do and it wasn't a job she should *enjoy*.

It had become quickly and blindingly apparent that it was also very, very, *very* important for her always to keep her head screwed on straight when she was dealing with Cash Fraser.

Since her crooked head had for thirty-eight years directed her down many a wild, winding, screwy path, Abby knew this was going to be a difficult task.

Luckily, he got control of his hilarity, put the car in gear and reversed expertly—and somewhat alarmingly quickly—out of her drive.

Then he raced down the street.

After that, he turned left and raced down the next street.

After *that*, he turned right and raced down the next.

And *then* he turned left again and raced down yet another street.

Abby clutched the door handle as he manoeuvred skillfully (and rapidly) through a roundabout at the edge of town and raced down a dark secluded straightaway.

She was about to say something before she *did* something, something embarrassing, something like shriek in terror, when she looked over at him and saw that he was driving with his right hand on the steering wheel, his left casually resting on the knob of the clutch.

Just looking at him, she knew instinctively he had complete control of the powerful car.

Her body relaxed and her fingers loosened from the door handle, her hand moving back to join her other one in her lap.

He didn't speak. Neither did she.

This lasted for a while.

Finally Abby started to get uncomfortable.

So she asked, "Where are we going?"

"To dinner," was his uninformative answer.

She looked at him. "I know. But where?"

"A restaurant," was his equally uninformative answer.

Abby sighed and looked straight ahead. "Will photographers be there?"

"Yes," he replied.

"Is there some kind of event happening?" she pressed, wanting to know what to expect.

"No. I've arranged a tip-off call to be made. They'll hear we're there and they'll show," he answered and went on, "They'll be fed the information about you tonight."

Abby blinked in surprise and again turned to look at him. "What information?"

He glanced at her before his attention returned to the road and he negotiated a winding turn at approximately five hundred miles per hour faster than she'd ever contemplate while he replied, "Your back story."

"My back story?" she repeated stupidly, not having the first clue what he was on about.

His voice dipped lower, deeper and throatier (and therefore quite a bit sexier), when he responded, "Abby, it wouldn't exactly serve my purpose for them to know what you are. James has arranged for them to be fed your story."

Abby felt like he'd slapped her across the face.

She was, of course, providing him a service at a fee. However, she didn't exactly like to be reminded of that.

She shirked off the hurt and went on, "And what's my story?"

It was an altogether different but immensely more painful reaction she had to his answer.

"You're an American widow. You used to work at the Pentagon in a civilian position for the United States Air Force. Your husband was a lobbyist on Capitol Hill for a large healthcare not-for-profit. You have dual citizenship, American father, English mother. You moved to England from DC some time after the death of your husband when you inherited your grandmother's property."

Abby felt every muscle in her body seize up.

Kieran had given James her real story.

Why would he do that?

Why, she had to repeat in her head, on God's green earth would he *do* that?

She tried to steady her rapidly beating heart and mentally forced her body to relax. She did this by thinking of all the gratifyingly horrific ways she was going to make her good friend pay for his betrayal.

"There's quite a bit of detail in that story," she said softly, for lack of anything else to say and trying to throw him off the fact that the air in the car had suddenly grown thick and she was the reason for it.

"Your husband's name was Benjamin Butler," he informed her and hearing Ben's name come from Cash's mouth made instant tears burn the backs of Abby's eyes.

"That's a nice name," she whispered while she worked very hard at controlling her tears. She continued when she had herself together, "And what if they check?"

Cash glanced at her as he rounded a bend, the car gliding smoothly down a steep winding hill.

"You sound surprised," he remarked.

Abby didn't reply.

Cash carried on, "I've been told your people have taken care of this."

It was then she realised why Kieran had divulged her story and Abby stopped considering her varied forms of torturous retribution.

Part of the plan was that she and Cash would be seen together, photographed together and talked about before they attended his aunt and uncle's Silver Wedding Anniversary celebrations at the family estate, Penmort Castle.

Seeing as he was Cash Fraser, dangerous international spy hunter, people would be curious to know who the hell *she* was.

She hadn't exactly covered her tracks, given a false name, had plastic surgery to modify her features or even changed her hair colour. If they checked, it wouldn't be hard for them to find out.

She looked out the passenger window, and hoping she sounded bored with the details, stated, "I don't involve myself with those things. My..." she hesitated then used his terminology, "people do."

"You work alone," was his strange reply.

Although it was a statement, it was also a question and she didn't know how to answer, mainly because it was obvious she would work alone.

He hadn't asked to look like Hugh Hefner with five escorts dripping off his arms.

"Of course," she replied.

"For yourself," he went on.

She looked at him again. "Yes."

"Not with an agency," he persevered and she finally got it.

"Not with an agency," Abby repeated.

"How many people take care of you?" he asked.

"Two," she replied honestly, not thinking to include James, who was Cash's friend and for Abby just a go-between. Or Pete who took care of her in a way but not *this* way.

"Do they work for others like you?" Cash pushed and Abby pressed her lips together.

This was none of his business.

And furthermore, him saying the words "like you" made her feel cheap and dirty even though she was expensive and had showered that evening at Jenny's for fear of her tub crashing through the floor.

"Cash," she said softly, but she hoped her meaning was clear, this information was not his to have.

It was and it wasn't. He changed the subject, but not really.

"May I ask a personal question?" he requested.

"And the questions you've been asking aren't personal?" she returned.

When he replied there was a hint of surprise in his voice. "No, Abby, they're not. Business is not personal."

Damn, damn and double damn, but she'd given something away. *He* didn't know her "back story" was real. *He* didn't know that her "people" were her two best friends in all the world. *He* didn't know that the reason behind her prostituting herself was very, very personal.

She covered by acquiescing. "Of course, ask me anything you want."

She noticed that they'd reached the city and he'd negotiated the bridges to turn back across the river. He now paused their conversation to parallel park on the street outside a restaurant she knew. One she'd always wanted to go to but couldn't afford. One that Kieran and Jenny wanted to take her to (and pay) but she wouldn't let them.

It was exclusive because it was pricey. She looked and saw that the décor through the big windows facing the river was simple. The lighting soft and romantic, the tables draped in white cloths with white buds blooming from small, glass vases. Flickering tea lights lit the tables and she could see a roaring fire was burning in an ancient hearth against the back stone wall.

Cash, having parked and turned off the car, interrupted her perusal of the restaurant with one word, and that word startled her because there was a low vibrating harshness underlying it.

"Why?"

Her eyes moved from the restaurant to Cash. "Pardon?"

"Why?" he repeated.

"Why what?" she asked, confused and wondering if she missed something.

"Why are you what you are?"

Abby blinked then swallowed. Then she had the desire to cry which was mingled with the desire to flee, which was also mingled with the desire to reach out and slap him as hard as she could thus punishing him for something for which she should be punishing herself.

She didn't do any of these things.

She also didn't answer.

He didn't read her silence correctly, as in that she refused to answer.

Instead he went on, "You could get the same things you want without doing what you do to get them."

Her body grew tight and her voice was cold when she asked, "And what, after knowing me all of perhaps thirty minutes, do you think I want?"

"You live in a three-quarters of a million pound house in an exclusive town. You wear five hundred pound shoes and you knew the value of my car just glancing at it," he informed her, and she had to admit she was shocked he knew these things.

Though he didn't know the state of her house, which likely would decrease its value. That said, its location would guarantee a very good asking price.

Still she was taken aback that he knew how expensive her shoes were. What man knew something like *that*?

She kept silent and he carried on, "And you know your value."

"What does that mean?" she snapped, not knowing his inference but knowing she didn't like it whatever it was.

"It means that you know a man would pay a great deal to possess you."

She hadn't known any such thing until he'd proved it yesterday.

Still, she replied swiftly, "That's the point."

His answer was soft. "Fucking hell," he muttered and he sounded annoyed. "Abby, you're a clever woman. You know you can sell yourself without having to sell yourself."

"What I do with myself is no business of yours, Mr. Fraser," she replied, her voice ice cold.

The effect, even on her, was chilling.

They sat in the car staring at each other, Abby trying not to shiver. As each moment passed the air started to grow heavier and heavier.

Abby didn't entirely understand it but she had the vague feeling he was angry and she couldn't imagine why.

When she could stand no more, hiding the fear she had at what he might answer, she offered, "Would you like to back out of our arrangement?"

"Fuck no," was his immediate if somewhat curt response, and Abby felt herself relax.

Without delay, the edgy conversation obviously over, he turned and exited the car.

As he rounded the back to come to her door, she felt her relaxation disintegrate and got tense because she had the nagging suspicion that she'd hoped that would be his answer but not simply because she needed the money.

Which would indicate that she was failing—somewhat spectacularly —at keeping her head on straight.

And at this realisation, she thought, *Oh, bloody hell*.

☙ ☙ ☙

"Our coats," Cash commanded the waiter after he paid the bill.

"Of course, sir," the waiter replied.

Cash's eyes moved back to Abby, who was sitting across from him, her elbow on the table, her head in her hand. Her fingers had sifted into her thick hair at the side and her gaze was turned to the boats bobbing at their ropes on the river.

She, he thought, looked pensive.

He, Cash knew, was angry.

There were a variety of reasons for his anger.

First and foremost, he was angry because he'd agreed not to have her until three weeks later when they went to Penmort.

He couldn't imagine, considering the price he was paying for her, what made him agree to that ludicrous caveat.

He wanted her tonight.

He was also angry because she was what she was.

When a woman looked like her, talked like her, smelled like her, dressed like her, had warm hazel eyes that contradicted her cool composure and hinted at something deeper and more intriguing and had wildly varying, easily readable, if puzzling reactions, that woman should not be a whore.

He was also angry because it was clear she intended to keep herself distant, which was likely a necessary professional detachment, when he wanted to know her story.

That wasn't exactly true. He knew her story.

She'd given it away in the car with her reaction to what he thought at the time was a fabrication.

Abigail Butler, body for sale, had a dead husband named Benjamin who used to be a lobbyist. She used to work for the US Air Force. Now she lived in her grandmother's home and sold herself to men who could afford to pay top price.

What Cash meant was he was angry that she kept herself distant when, for some baffling reason, he wanted her to share. He wanted her to admit her story and explain why a successful woman would turn to prostitution on the death of her husband.

This was not in his experience a normal reaction to grief.

He wanted to know why she would do such a remarkably stupid thing. He wanted to know why, when it was clear she could attract another man and live a very comfortable life, undoubtedly earning her keep on her back but at least not debasing herself in doing it.

Lastly, he was angry at himself for giving a fuck.

Abigail Butler had a purpose in his life for one month only.

She was going to cushion him from his uncle's idiotic intentions while Cash extricated himself from that messy situation at the same time rubbing his uncle's nose in his many failures and securing what was rightfully his.

And she was going to satisfy him in bed as many times as he could manage in the one week she was available to him.

And then she'd be gone.

Dinner, it went without saying, had not been enjoyable.

Not that the food wasn't delicious, because it was.

Not that her company wasn't enjoyable, because it was. Both innately (she continued to be a bundle of contradictions—cold and unapproachable mixed with warm and amusing), as well as conversationally (she was clearly well-read and well-travelled with a capacity to listen actively and share, if only superficially).

Not that she wasn't earning her pay because no one in that restaurant witnessing her behaviour (her soft, enticing smiles, the times she'd touch his hand while speaking, when she'd lean toward him with avid attention as if his terse, impatient responses to her soft conversation were utterly fascinating) would think she was anything less than a woman clearly smitten with her dinner partner.

He'd paid six thousand, six hundred and sixty-six pounds for that night with her not including the exorbitant bill for dinner, and she'd earned every penny.

The waiter came with their coats, and Cash stood relieving the waiter of his burden and throwing his overcoat on his chair. He shook out Abby's cape and moved around her so she could remain where she was. Once behind her, he positioned the heavy garment on her shoulders as she moved slightly back into his body, getting closer to him. This was not to make his task easier but a show to those watching, including the three photographers he earlier saw positioning themselves outside, that this was an act of intimacy between a man and his lover, not one of chivalry.

She wasn't just good, Cash thought with growing disgust, she was superb.

And this made Cash even angrier.

She fastened the cape at her throat and put on her gloves while he donned his overcoat then gripped her elbow, leading her out of the restaurant with all eyes on them.

He could visualise them together. Abby was blonde, tall and elegant, but tonight in that alluring dress that hinted at the body beneath it rather than brazenly displaying it as her clothing did yesterday, she showed she had a unique, individual style. Cash was dark and much taller, but not overpowering her with his height as he did with most women. And men, for that matter.

He knew they made an exceptional-looking couple. It was part of the package he'd paid for.

They were out into the night and he was not looking forward to the drive to take her home.

He would want to come in and make two efforts. The first would be getting her to open up to him. The second would be getting her to sleep with him.

Neither, Cash knew at this juncture, would succeed.

And Cash was used to success. Failure was unacceptable. But he knew that would be what he'd face if he pressed her.

And he didn't like this either.

They'd only taken two steps on the pavement when Abby, as if oblivious to the now descending photographers, curled into him. She put her hand to his stomach and he stopped at her bold touch, his head tilting down toward her.

She was smiling at him.

Not one of her composed, controlled smiles. This one was radiant and lighting up the night, as if she was happy, carefree and deeply in love.

At the sight, something in his gut clenched and it was a feeling he'd never felt before in his entire life.

The feeling wasn't painful, instead it was supremely pleasant.

Unusually caught off guard by her smile and his response to it, he didn't react as she came up to her toes, leaning into him, her breasts pressing against his arm as she tipped her head back. Her eyes were slightly closed, her lips lightly parted, her entire face an invitation.

Without willing himself to do it and completely unable to stop if he'd tried (which he didn't), his head bent, and as she intended, doing the job he'd paid her to do to put on a show for the photographers, his mouth met hers.

The minute their lips touched hers relaxed under his, her scent filled his nostrils in an overwhelmingly intoxicating way and her body melted into his, bestowing on him a goodly amount of her weight as if she'd lost the ability to stand on her own two feet.

He accepted her obvious if somewhat surprising invitation and deepened the kiss, his hand moving from her elbow in order to wrap his arm tightly around her waist, hauling her closer to him.

Her body went rigid as his tongue touched hers.

She tasted, he realised with acute clarity, as complex and exquisite as everything else that was Abby, and he felt his body begin to heat in response.

His head came up at her reaction and he belatedly saw the camera flashes around them.

Her guard was down and Cash could easily read the strange mix of wonder and alarm on her face.

Instinctively he recognised that something had changed. She might have begun this show for the photographers, but it didn't end that way.

He attributed this to the brief but remarkably affecting kiss and the cameras, which she had to know where there.

The former of the two reactions he saw on her face served to please him, dissipate his anger and bring him to the swift decision that he would not wait to have her. Instead, he'd coax her to break her own rule and sleep with him before they reached the castle.

The latter reaction was understandable, he knew the cameras could be disconcerting if you weren't used to them.

Cash gave a glare to the photographers even though it was he who called them there in the first place. They'd managed to interrupt some-thing that had turned into a moment Cash most definitely did *not* wish to be interrupted.

One called out a question that Cash didn't bother to hear. When he started leading Abby to the car, his arm firmly around her waist rather than at her elbow, he unconsciously moved his body to shield her from the cameras. It was a natural instinct at complete odds to the whole point of this exercise.

And he didn't give a good God damn.

For comfort's sake, her arm stole around his waist though her hand never left his stomach. When he looked down at her again, she was peering around his body at the calling photographers.

Cash saw that she had not managed to compose her expression. Her customary aloofness had disappeared. The alarm was still there (the wonder, unfortunately, gone), and Cash again found himself thinking she looked rather adorable.

"It'll be all right," he murmured his assurance.

Her eyes shifted to him, and still unguarded, he read immediately that she most definitely didn't believe him.

And it was right there for him to see, there was no thinking about it.

Abigail Butler, the woman who very much wanted him to believe she was a remote, impersonal, accomplished call girl was instead downright adorable.

Taking in her endearingly disgruntled look, Cash couldn't, if under torture, have stopped himself from throwing his head back to laugh.

So this was exactly what he did.

❦ ❦ ❦

And that was one of the pictures printed the next day, along with one of the kiss.

Abby with one hand on Cash's stomach, the other arm around him, her upper body curled into his side, but she was walking forward even as her head was tilted back. She was regarding Cash with what looked like loving irritation. Cash's arm was around her waist, his head was tipped back, his attractive face full of laughter.

❦ ❦ ❦

Fifty miles away in a cold, sturdy, ancient castle situated on a steep cliff, its parapets facing the waters of the Bristol Channel, Alistair Beaumaris sat amongst the used china and silver of the breakfast table, looked at the picture and it put him in a very bad mood.

Alistair was brother to the true heir of Penmort, Anthony, who had, to Alistair's way of thinking, foolishly sired an illegitimate son to a Scottish beauty but never wed her. Nevertheless, upon his brother's death, Anthony bestowed the Beaumaris fortune on her as well as the castle.

After his brother committed this heinous act, Alistair had spent thousands of pounds in the attempt to convince the courts it was impossible to bequeath "outside the family" as well as convincing them the fortune went with the castle.

And, fortunately, he'd succeeded in these endeavours.

Now, unfortunately, Alistair Beaumaris needed Conner Ewan "Cash" Fraser.

He needed him to marry one of his stepdaughters.

Not that he liked Cash Fraser. Indeed, he hated the man. In fact, his preference would be to see him just as dead as his father. And if he didn't need him he would make his preference a reality, just as Alistair had done with Cash's father.

Not even that he liked his stepdaughters and wanted them to make an excellent match. He didn't hate them. They could be tolerable some of the time. However, most of the time they were wholly annoying and he had no problems telling them so and explaining exactly and in some detail how they were.

No, he needed Fraser's money.

And that reminder put Alistair in an even worse mood.

❧ ❧ ❧

The ghost of Vivianna Wainwright floated two inches from the high ceiling directly over the cluttered table, not, for now, allowing her presence to be seen or felt.

She looked down at the picture in the paper and her spectral eyes moved lovingly over the tall, dark man.

They grew hard as they shifted over the cool, blonde woman.

Vivianna's mood was not bad.

It was murderous.

❧ 4 ❧

THE PHONE CALL AND THE PICTURE

Abby heard the phone on her bedside table ring, ripping her from a deep, fitful sleep, and Zee made a mew of disapproval as he stretched his four legs out, arching his back into Abby's belly.

She peered at the clock and saw it was just after eight in the morning.

Cash had her home before ten with no necking, likely much to the disappointment of Mrs. Truman, who Abby saw peering through her draperies when they arrived. Though he walked her to the door, he didn't attempt to come in, didn't attempt to give her a goodnight kiss, but also didn't leave until she'd made her way safely inside, closed the door *and* had turned on the light in her bedroom.

Still, even though she was in bed early, she didn't get to sleep until the wee hours.

This was because she spent hours tossing and turning with the realisation that she'd, again, done something thoroughly and completely stupid.

Although there were other stupid things she'd done in the last thirty hours (many, *many* of them), her Latest Stupid Abby Act Obsession currently centred around that kiss.

When she'd kissed him the day before at the pub it had been to make a point and it was under her control.

However, wiping her lip gloss from his mouth had been habitual. It was something she'd done for Ben countless times. She was, of course, a girl who liked her lip gloss.

She didn't know why she did it to Cash. She just had and she'd kicked herself for it before burying the memory deep in the recesses of her mind.

But she couldn't bury that kiss. It was right at the surface.

The smell of Cash, the feel of his body against hers, his hard mouth, and finally, the sweet touch of his tongue.

He tasted of brandy which he'd drunk after dinner. Brandy and the rich chocolate torte with clotted cream he'd had for dessert.

Good God, but he tasted good.

She'd felt the touch of his tongue from her mouth, through her body, to the tips of her curled toes.

She'd never felt anything that luscious or that strong.

Not even with Ben and Ben had been a fabulous kisser.

And that meant her exasperation with herself was mingled with the guilt she felt at betraying her dead husband.

She shoved these thoughts aside. These weren't waking-up thoughts. These were beating-yourself-up-in-the-middle-of-the-night thoughts.

She reached to the phone and pulled it out of its receiver.

She was not big on mornings, though she was usually up well before now. Exacerbating her usual morning mood was the weight of her current predicament.

Therefore, when she said, "Hello?" into the receiver, her fresh-from-sleep voice sounded peeved.

"Abby."

It was Cash.

What was *with* this guy?

Could he not leave her alone for even a moment?

"Cash," she said, her voice sounding breathy.

There was heavy silence before he said softly, his burr trilling deliciously in her ear sending an uncontrollable shiver down her spine, "I've woken you."

She tried (and failed) to ignore the shiver and then tried to decide what to say.

She couldn't tell him she had trouble sleeping. That would expose too much.

She also couldn't lie and say she hadn't been asleep, her voice made it obvious.

"I like my sleep," she said instead, something which was not a lie.

There was more silence and this was heavier.

When he didn't break it, she called, "Cash? Is there something you want?"

"Yes," came his immediate reply.

She got up on an elbow and Zee looked up at her, blinking (Zee, being feline, liked his sleep too).

When Cash didn't expand on his answer, Abby was forced to ask, "Well? What is it?"

There was a hesitation, then, "Do you cook?"

She blinked at Zee and repeated stupidly, "Cook?"

"Yes. Pots. Pans. Spoons. Ovens. Cook," he spoke in one word sentences, sounding like he was trying not to laugh.

Abby felt her blood pressure rising.

This was not because he seemed to be amused at her expense.

This was because him seeming amused made her feel funny and not in a bad way. It was a good way. It was a way that put her vow to be faithful to her dead husband in heart, mind and soul (if not in deed, obviously) until the she day she died in peril.

With effort she controlled it. She knew she let on way too much last night. Somehow she had to keep her distance without being unfriendly.

How she was going to manage that, though, she had no earthly clue.

"I know what cooking is," Abby answered. "What I'd like to know is why are you calling me at eight o'clock in the morning and asking me if I know how to do it?"

"Because, if you do, you're cooking for me tonight at my place," he replied.

Abby's heart lurched at the very idea of cooking a meal for him at his home. The lurch was both fear and excitement, something else, with effort, she controlled.

"I fail to see how that's going to get our picture in the paper," she returned.

"What will be seen, and perhaps photographed, is you coming in my front door," Cash explained, though she could tell he was no longer amused but attempting to be patient.

She had to admit he was right, and Abby pushed up to rest her back against the headboard as Zee got to his feet and stretched.

"Wouldn't it be better if we went out?" she queried.

"Abby, if we always go out, they're going to think we're dating. If you're at my place, they're going to think we're together. The object of this is to make them think they missed the first part and that we're well into the second part," he informed her, and again, annoyingly, he was right. "Now, do you cook?" he repeated.

She gave in ungraciously on a sigh, "I cook."

When he spoke again, he was back to sounding amused. "My assistant will call you and make certain whatever you need is at the house."

"Fine," Abby replied, deciding that giving in also had the additional benefit of bringing her closer to the end of this weirdly intimate conversation.

Her anticipated relief was short-lived when Cash said, "Bring a bag."

Abby's lungs seized.

"Pardon?" she wheezed into the phone.

"A bag," Cash repeated.

"Why?"

"You're spending the night."

Oh my Lord, she thought.

"What do you mean, spending the night?" she asked, the breath coming back into her lungs with a burning *whoosh*.

There was a pause before he asked, this time back to sounding like he was attempting patience, "I'm not certain which part of 'spending the night' you need me to explain."

Her blood pressure rose again, this time for a different reason, and she failed at controlling it. "The part, Mr. Fraser, where you don't remember that the deal is I don't sleep with you until we go to the castle."

His voice was low, rough, vibrating and unbelievably effective when he replied softly, "Darling, the deal is I don't fuck you until we go to the castle. I can sleep with you whenever the hell I want. And tonight you're spending the night."

Was that the deal?

The preliminary deal was, she pretended to be his girlfriend including sleeping in the same bed with him. The point was that she'd share a room with him at the castle, thus proving to his uncle that she was, indeed, his very attached and devoted girlfriend.

However, there were no restrictions noted on that and she'd stupid, stupid, *stupidly* not made any.

He'd amended the deal with the sex part, which she'd only restricted to after they went to the castle, not getting into the sleeping-in-the-same-bed-with-him part.

Which meant, yet again, he was right.

But why would he want to sleep with her?

What, she asked herself again, was *with* this guy?

"Bring a bag," he repeated.

"Fine," she snapped.

"Enough to leave things you may need there," he demanded.

Oh dear Lord in heaven above, she cried in her head.

Through her teeth she gritted out loud, "Fine."

"Moira will give you my address and make sure you get in," he told her.

"Who's Moira?" she clipped.

"My assistant," he answered.

For some reason that took the wind out of her sails.

"Oh," she said softly.

More silence, then she heard his voice, far less authoritarian, much gentler and definitely sexy, say, "What are you making me for dinner?"

"Fillet steak marinated in arsenic," she returned acidly.

She heard his quick bark of laughter. It was nearly as delicious as his soft burr sounding in her ear and she knew she'd done it again.

Unconsciously, she meant to make him laugh.

"Are you done with me?" she continued, far angrier with herself than she was with him and wondering if she could find a hypnotist who could stop her from being funny and charming.

While she was contemplating her first move of the morning (directly to the phonebook to look up hypnotists), the soft burr was back, trilling lushly through the phone and throughout her system, when he answered, "Not even close."

Then she heard the disconnect and he was gone.

Zee stared at her, likely wondering about breakfast.

Abby stared back and muttered, "Bloody, *bloody* hell."

❧ ❧ ❧

"What is *with* this guy?" Jenny exclaimed as she snapped hangers across the rails of a clothing display at Harvey Nichols.

It was early afternoon, they were shopping, and Abby had shared her plans for the evening.

"I'm learning that during negotiations I should be very detailed in what I will, and will not do as an escort," Abby replied, snapping her own hangers.

Jenny stopped snapping hangers and stared in disbelief at Abby.

"What?" Abby asked her friend on raised brows.

"Do not even *joke* about the possibility that this will become your profession," Jenny hissed.

"That's not what I meant," Abby replied, and it wasn't.

"Well, it sounded that way." Jenny went back to snapping. "This whole situation is flipping me out. I've got a perpetual headache. Kieran's not getting his usual servicing, which is flipping *him* out *and* pissing him off. I'm not sleeping. I'm on edge. I *hate* this and I hate it more because it was my idea in the first place."

"Jenny—" Abby started, her heart going out to her friend, the depths of her guilty feelings digging to new lows.

Abby had a lot of friends, a lot of very good friends, but Jenny was the best by a mile.

Jenny had been there when Abby's mom got cancer. Even though she and Kieran lived in Amsterdam at the time, until the bitter end (and it was bitter, ugly and painful for everyone, especially Abby's mom) Jenny came to Virginia every few months and stayed weeks. Not only for Abby but for Abby's mom who was known as "Mom Deux" to Jenny.

Two years later, when Abby's dad had the heart attack that killed him, she and Kieran (living in California then), had dropped everything and flown to DC.

Abby had been inconsolable and Ben had all he could do to take care of her, cope with his own grief and deal with a situation at work that was demanding his attention. Jenny and Kieran had arranged everything, the funeral, the memorial service, and the food and drink for the gathering at Ben and Abby's afterward.

A year after that, one minute after Abby woodenly closed the door on the police officer who stood in her foyer telling her that Ben had been killed instantly "at the scene" of a car crash, she'd picked up the phone and called Jenny.

Again, Jenny had dropped everything, flew out and stayed with Abby for two months, even going so far as sitting on her knees beside Abby in the bath and washing her hair when Abby was too exhausted from grief to bathe herself. Jenny cooked and she cleaned. Jenny held her when Abby sobbed. She poured the tequila when they sat around and got drunk while remembering all the many wonderful things about Ben. In the middle of the night, she crawled into Ben and Abby's big bed and held Abby tightly while she rocked, trying to get to sleep without her husband at her side. And before she left, she helped Abby pack up his belongings, tucking away the precious mementos and sending away the things she didn't need.

When Kieran and Jenny moved to England, Kieran's promotion and transfer took him to Bristol, a city close to Gram. Gram had grown a bit unsteady on her feet, far weaker and definitely in need of routine visits. So Jenny and Kieran bought a house in the same seaside town so Jenny could look after her grandmother.

And when Gram died, it had become clear after three years facing a mountain of debt, on her salary, that Abby could not (and had not for a very long time) maintain the home she shared with Ben.

Jenny came out and helped her get Ben and Abby's house ready for the market. She helped her pack. She helped her arrange the shipping.

She helped Abby close down the tattered remnants of the life she'd loved and then Jenny had helped her leave it behind.

At Harvey Nicks, Jenny kept on snapping hangers and ignored Abby's pleading tone.

Without looking at Abby, she asked, "Did you see the picture?"

Abby knew exactly what she was referring to and she had. One of the workmen who came in that morning to work on her bathroom had looked at her strangely, and when she'd asked in a teasing way why, he'd showed the paper to her.

Seeing the picture had been a shock.

She had hundreds of pictures of her and Ben.

Ben had been tall too, though not as tall as Cash.

But he'd been blond, like Abby (but darker), blond and blue-eyed with the big stocky body. Jenny said Ben gave the best bear hugs because he was a human bear, and Jenny was right.

Abby had not seen herself with another man since Ben because there were no other men since him. She'd never expected to see herself with another man. She hadn't anticipated the pain she'd feel when the pictures of her and Cash started appearing.

She hadn't anticipated a lot.

Including the fact that she thought—somehow weirdly detached— that she and Cash looked good together. It was almost as if she was looking at two other people, not herself and Cash.

Her mom, dad, gram, Ben, Kieran and Jenny had, for years, teased her that she was some kind of bizarre mutant.

She'd not been a very pretty baby (to say the least) or a darling little girl.

She'd been passably pretty in high school, not ugly enough to get bullied, not pretty enough to get many dates.

In college, though, as she matured and let her wild nature loose (or looser, as her father would say), things had changed.

A few years after college she met Ben, and she didn't think about it much until later. Until they all started commenting on it.

Even the day before he died, Ben had mentioned it.

"I married a pretty lady," he'd whispered in her ear that morning, his voice husky because it was right after they'd made love. "What'd you do with her?"

Abby had twisted her head and kissed his neck.

"What do you mean? She's right here," she'd whispered back, tightening her arms which were wrapped around him.

He'd lifted his big body up on his elbows and framed her face with his hands.

"No. What I got right here isn't a pretty lady." His face was serious, then his mouth descended to touch hers and against her lips, he said, "She's a beauty."

He hadn't been joking and to that day, standing in Harvey Nichols with Jenny and knowing it was one of the last things he ever said to her, Abby treasured that memory. She equally treasured knowing, before he died, that her husband thought he'd been married to a beauty.

But the picture with Cash was something else.

After Ben, Abby *really* didn't think of the way she looked. She couldn't care less.

But wearing her "Smoky Evening" look and her expensive shoes and her grandmother's elegant cape, she looked like she belonged on movie-star-gorgeous Cash Fraser's arm.

And if Jenny was flipping out, Abby was *freaking* out.

"It's a good picture," Jenny whispered, and Abby felt her throat get tight.

"Yeah," Abby agreed.

Jenny cleared her own throat and commented, "He's hot."

Her friend didn't know the half of it.

And for the first time in their friendship, Abby didn't share.

She was terrified of what Jenny would say if she knew the confused, illicit, guilt-ridden feelings she had about Cash.

Feelings she shouldn't have.

Feelings she wasn't entitled to have.

Feelings that would lead nowhere because firstly, her heart belonged to a dead man and secondly, she was the other man's whore.

And Jenny, who adored Ben, would never forgive her for betraying him.

Maybe with someone she met in some normal way, at a pub, at a party, walking down the street.

Not with Cash Fraser.

Instead, Abby asked, "Okay, so what does a girl wear to make dinner for an international hot guy, spy hunter?"

Jenny kept slapping hangers, staring down at the clothes with a discerning, determined eye, clearly on a mission, and muttered, "No clue."

Abby started to move to another rail. "We'll figure it out."

And they would.

Because they always did.

SLEEPING WITH CASH

U pon opening the door to his home, Cash smelled the food and it was instantly apparent that Abby could cook.

He also heard the music.

It was hard not to. The neighbours could likely hear the music.

This was because it was loud.

He threw his overcoat around the newel post and headed to the back of the stairs, rounded the wall and then down the back stairs toward the kitchen, which was at garden level.

He was late, tied up at work. He'd called and told her this fact. She was already at his house when he'd phoned and she didn't seem to mind that he'd be home at nine rather than seven, as he'd told Moira to tell her he'd be.

He did mind.

Further, he minded that she obviously didn't.

Now it was a quarter after nine and it sounded like she was having a blowout party attended by rock stars, groupies and their various and assorted roadies and hangers on.

He made it to the garden level of his three-storey townhouse to see, thankfully, she was not having a party.

Instead she was reading a magazine.

When he'd bought his house in Bath and started renovations, he'd had this level torn out so most of it was open plan. Then he'd hired an interior designer who designed the space for him.

Against the back wall there was a modern black, chrome and stainless steel state-of-the-art kitchen that several women he'd brought to his home had been in gales of ecstasy about, but Cash himself rarely used.

At the foot of the stairs separated from the kitchen area by a wide counter with tall stools was a comfortable seating area he never used.

Across from the stairs and extending from the kitchen there was a modern black-lacquered dining table that seated twelve that he sometimes wondered why he'd purchased because he'd never sat there.

There was a cloakroom under the stairs and the only interior door, off the dining area, led to a workout room with a rowing machine, elliptical machine, weights and weight bench that, outside of his bedroom, was the room he used most in the house.

The wall to the garden shared by the kitchen and seating area had been fitted almost entirely with floor to ceiling windows including a set of French doors.

Abby was lying on her stomach on his enormous scarlet-red couch.

She was, he was surprised to see, wearing a pair of bottom-hugging jeans, high-heeled shoes with what looked like a number of thin, sexy straps at the ankle and a taupe jumper woven in such a way that it was see-through. Visible underneath was a creamy camisole.

Her back was to him and her hair was in a ponytail at the back of her head. She had her knees bent, ankles crossed, feet swaying in the air, and she was flipping through the pages of a magazine.

She looked like the stereotypical American teenager, and if he heard her snap some gum in her mouth, he wouldn't have been surprised.

His hand went to the knot in his tie and pulled while he called, "Abby."

He watched as her body jerked.

Then her head twisted around, ponytail flipping over her shoulder, and her eyes locked on him in stunned surprise.

She regarded him as if she was house sitting and expected him at that moment to be in a business meeting halfway around the world, not in his house as he told her he'd be.

"You're home," she announced unnecessarily.

"That and I'm starving," he replied.

"You're late," she told him, not moving from her position.

"I called," he informed her, yanking off his tie, walking deeper into the room and tossing it on the large grey chair that sat perpendicular to the couch.

"You called and said you'd be here at nine. It's not nine. It's *after* nine," she returned.

Cash shrugged off his suit jacket. It joined his tie and he unbuttoned the top three buttons of his shirt.

He was not in the mood for this.

He planned to have been there the last two and a quarter hours eating the food she'd cooked for him and exploring the sexual boundaries of their arrangement.

He had not planned to be as tired as he was, as hungry as he was, and as late as he was. Further, he had not planned to come home to smell something nearly as enticing as her ass in those jeans, enter into a loud conversation with her so he could be heard over her music and have her behave like she was his actual girlfriend, something which, for many years, he avoided having.

This was one of the reasons he did not approach any of the women of his acquaintance to perform the duties he was paying Abby for, as he had no desire to give them any ideas. And they'd get them, he was certain.

"Abby," Cash stated wearily. "I'm shattered. I need a drink, food and bed in that order."

She studied him calmly for a moment then put her hands in the couch and lifted in a push up, twisting her hips into a sitting position. She rose to her feet and went to the stereo, turning down the music to a decibel level that was almost, but not quite, normal.

"What do you drink?" she asked, her spiked heels sounding on the wood floors as she walked to the kitchen.

"Tonight, whisky," he answered, watching her move through his house.

She went directly to the cabinet where his housekeeper stored the liquor and opened the door.

Obviously she'd become acquainted with his kitchen.

"Water?" she asked.

"No."

"Ice?"

"No."

"How many fingers?"

She was also obviously acquainted with whisky.

"Two," he answered.

She took down the whisky and a squat glass and poured two fingers while he went to the stereo and turned the music down past normal straight to old woman.

When he turned away from the stereo, she was in front of him with his glass.

"I think it might be illegal in a few countries to play Foreigner that low," she declared in her soft voice.

"I doubt England is one of those countries," Cash returned.

"I bet Scotland isn't," she replied, and seeing her mischievous grin, suddenly he wanted to kiss her.

Not touch his tongue briefly to hers but kiss her so hard, so long and so thoroughly he could smell her sex mingled with her perfume.

She didn't read his mind. Instead, she went on to tease, "Though, considering your people brought us the Bay City Rollers, maybe not."

It was deeply unfortunate, Cash thought, that she'd teased him.

That made him want to kiss her even more.

He didn't because he knew if he did, at that moment, he might not be able to stop.

He took the whisky from her and lifted it to his lips, his eyes watching her over the rim of the glass. Even dressed casually with very little makeup, she was stunning.

Before taking a drink, he returned, "My people also brought you Nazareth."

He watched her warm, hazel eyes grow even warmer.

"Touché," she replied softly.

Good Christ, he thought, taking in her warm eyes and soft tone and he found it took a supreme effort of will not to reach for her.

She seemed oblivious to his rampaging thoughts and turned, again heading toward the kitchen.

"I ate already," she informed him as she moved and he followed.

This did not please him.

He didn't respond. He leaned a hip against the counter and saw the kitchen was clean and tidy, only a glass half-filled with red wine sat on one of the counters.

Abby took down a plate.

"If I eat late, I don't sleep. My body doesn't like it," she shared.

He knew she liked her sleep. She'd told him that morning when he'd woken her to hear her sweet, soft voice sounding husky, irate and adorable.

He watched her pull out cutlery and set it beside the plate she'd retrieved.

While he did he found that he didn't like that he knew exactly eight pertinent facts about her. These being she sold her body for money, couldn't sleep if she ate late, lived in her grandmother's house, had a dead husband, liked loud music, red wine and sleep, and most importantly, she sounded unbelievably fuckable in the morning.

"I would have preferred you waited for me," he told her honestly.

Her gaze shifted to him as she pulled on oven mitts.

"Sorry," she murmured, sounding like she actually was and turned away to open the oven door.

The tantalising smell came out in a wave and she extricated an earthenware pan filled with what looked like pasta shells overstuffed with meat and sauce and covered in cheese.

"Stuffed pasta shells, garlic bread and salad," she announced. Setting the pan on a pad, she threw off the mitts with an expert flick of her wrists and her eyes went back to him. "Baked pears with cream and chocolate sauce for dessert," she told him, reaching to pull open the drawer by his hip. "I ate my dessert too," she admitted.

"If that's as good as it smells, I'll forgive you," he told her.

"It is," she smiled then bent her head, grabbed a serving spoon and shut the drawer.

"Who taught you to cook?" he asked as she served up the shells.

"Mom," she replied.

"Is your mother close?" he inquired.

"I like to think so," was her strange, and Cash thought, evasive answer.

Cash didn't let it go.

She might wish to remain distant but he didn't want that and he bloody well paid enough to have her as close as he wanted her.

Which was exactly what he was going to get if he had to tie her down and interrogate her.

Shaking off that altogether too stimulating thought, he pressed, "Is she in England?"

"No," Abby replied.

"America," he stated.

"Yes."

"That's not exactly close," Cash remarked.

She'd finished serving up the shells and was returning to the oven for the bread.

"Well, she's not exactly in America." She came back to the counter with the bread, gracefully flipping the oven door closed with her foot before she did. Her eyes stayed on her task as she went on, "It's more like she is and she isn't."

"That sounds difficult to do," Cash observed.

She tore off an enormous chunk of what looked like homemade garlic bread and put it on his plate before her eyes met his.

"She's dead, Cash."

Her quiet words felt like a blow to the stomach.

Fucking hell but he was a bastard.

"Abby," he said softly by way of an apology.

"It's okay. It was a long time ago," she told him, putting his fork on the plate and handing it to him then she moved to the fridge.

Cash carried on. He shouldn't have but he didn't know that so he did.

"Is your father still in America?"

"Yep," she said casually, head in the fridge. "Lying beside Mom."

When she turned around, hands holding a big salad bowl, her gaze came to his.

He saw her eyes were carefully guarded.

His eyes were on her, his fork suspended halfway to his mouth.

She went on matter-of-factly, "Heart attack. Dad. Cancer. Mom. Mom went first. Two years apart."

With some effort, he started to eat.

The food was, incidentally, better than it smelled.

She put his salad in another bowl, dressed it and slid it along the counter to where he was eating and watching her.

She was busying herself putting away the food when he remarked, "That must have been rough."

"It happens."

"It does, Abby. That doesn't mean it isn't rough."

She finished with wrapping foil around the shells, and head bent to the pan, she replied quietly, "Miss them every day."

He felt her four words settle heavily somewhere in his gut.

He decided to let her be, and as she put the food into the fridge, he told her, "That may be the first time anyone used that oven."

She closed the refrigerator door and came back to the counter saying, "I wondered why it was sparkling clean. I thought you might be obsessive compulsive."

"I have a housekeeper." He looked pointedly around the pristine room then back to Abby. "The jury's out on if she's obsessive compulsive."

He heard her soft laughter as she jumped up to sit on the counter and grabbed her wineglass.

"My verdict, yes," she said to him with a grin, and he was experiencing the strong desire to put his food aside and kiss her when he watched an unusual look cross her face.

She was, Cash realised, struggling with something.

He didn't wait for her to win her struggle because her winning, he thought (correctly) would mean him losing.

"What is it, Abby?" he asked.

"Nothing," she promptly replied.

"Say it," he demanded.

"Cash—"

"Abby, what is it?" He sounded just as impatient and annoyed as he was getting with her cagey behaviour.

"I just wondered..." she hesitated then lifted her hand as if to pull her hair out of her face. But she encountered it tied back and looked endearingly confused for a moment before her hand drifted down to her lap.

He waited.

She took a sip of wine.

He finished his pasta and salad and prompted, "You wondered what?"

Her eyes came to him. "About your folks." She cleared her throat. "I wondered about your folks."

Cash didn't hesitate. "My father's dead, no one knows how. Mysterious circumstances."

Her face gentled. "I'm sorry, Cash."

"Don't be. I never knew him."

He saw surprise flash in her eyes before she said, "I'm sorry about that too."

He moved to put his dishes in the sink. "Don't be sorry about that either. From what I know, he was a twat."

When he turned from the sink, she was watching him, and gently she repeated, "I'm sorry about that too."

At her words, instead of walking to her, forcing open her legs and pulling her into his arms, moulding her body to his, crotch to chest, so he could kiss her like he very much wanted to do, he leaned his hip against the sink, crossed his arms on his chest and replied, "I'm sorry about it too."

She took another sip of wine, tilted her head and asked, "Your mom?"

"Suicide. I was fifteen."

Her eyes got wide and she breathed, "Bloody hell." She shook her head and went on, "Oh my God."

"I found her." Cash, likely suffering from guilt for forcing her to talk about her own dead parents, found himself sharing a piece of information that he rarely shared with anyone.

"Oh my God," she repeated.

"It wasn't a surprise. She'd tried three times before," Cash continued.

Her back straightened and she lifted a hand that Cash saw was shaking before she demanded in a voice as shaky as her hand, "Please, stop talking."

"She wasn't a well woman, Abby. It was the reason my father didn't marry her," Cash explained because she was looking pale and for some reason in pain.

Her look intrigued him.

Women looked at him in many different ways, all of which he could read. Cash knew Abby was horrified by what he'd shared, but he didn't quite understand the pain.

"Still," she whispered, breaking him out of his thoughts. "You found her?"

"It was expected. Every time I came home, I expected something. She was bipolar, amongst other things, and refused to take meds. When she was high, she was brilliant, funny, beautiful, smart, full of energy. When she was down, she was suicidal. It's not as tragic as it sounds if it's your life. It's only tragic when it's not," he stated calmly because he was calm. He'd long since learned this lesson and he'd learned it very well. "She was the one who called me Cash, came up with it during a high. I was very young and it stuck. I don't remember ever answering to anything else."

Latching on to a change of topic, Abby asked, "What's your real name?"

"Conner."

She observed him for a moment.

"Yeah," she said softly. "That fits too."

He moved toward her and stopped in front of her. He leaned in and put his hands on the counter at either side of her hips.

He watched as her body tensed and he ignored it.

"When I met you, I thought the name 'Abby' didn't suit you," he told her.

"Really?" she asked, leaning away from him but, he noted, trying to look like she wasn't.

This nearly made him laugh.

"Really," he replied and moved closer. "But tonight, you're an Abby."

"I'm always Abby," she returned then, with her voice slightly breathy and higher than normal, she asked, "Do you want pears?"

"Not right now," he answered.

"More whisky?" she queried.

Cash shook his head.

She bit the side of her lower lip just like she did the day he met her.

He'd been right.

It was adorable.

With his eyes still on her mouth he said, "Right now, it's time for bed."

❧ ❧ ❧

Abby opened her eyes to a feeling of warm unfamiliarity mingled with the realisation that it was early morning and dark.

For a moment she was pleasantly confused.

Then her brain woke, her senses cleared, her vision adjusted and panic ensued.

In the shadows she could see a wide expanse of chest and a bedside clock that said it was twenty past five.

Both the chest and the clock belonged to Cash.

Her body froze as she took in her position.

She was lying tucked tight to his side, her thigh thrown over one of his. She was curled so deeply into him that her calf had fallen between his legs. Her head was resting heavily on his shoulder, a good deal of her body doing the same down the length of his and her arm was wrapped around his waist.

She found this position disturbing in a variety of ways.

Firstly, she had not slept in a bed with anyone other than Jenny since Ben died, and she couldn't believe she'd had any sleep at all beside Cash much less almost on top of him. But it appeared she had.

Secondly, she'd never cuddled with Ben in sleep. Not because she didn't want to but because Ben didn't like it. He'd gently told her early in their sexual relationship that he preferred to be unhindered while sleeping.

This had always secretly disappointed her and after he'd died she yearned to go back in time with the knowledge of what would befall them and coax him into learning how to sleep with her pressed against him.

Lastly, she barely knew Cash Fraser. She'd been in his company only three times. Yet she felt comfortable and snugly warm cuddled up to Cash's long, hard body in a way that wasn't forbidden or wrong (as she thought it should feel), but instead in a way that seemed perfectly natural (as she thought it was *not*).

Last night, after he told her it was time for bed, Abby had been close to hysteria.

It took all her energy and concentration not to let on this was the case.

Indeed, their very short evening together took a lot of energy and concentration.

There was something weirdly intimate passing between them regardless of the fact that they barely knew one another.

She thought it had a lot to do with her being in his home, cooking for him and waiting for him to get home from work. These were things you didn't do on a second date. These were things you did for someone you knew well and cared about.

She was also trying to be friendly without being too friendly, and she thought this might be working though she found it immensely taxing.

Cash made it harder by deciding, freakishly (to Abby's way of thinking), to deepen their conversation past the trivial to the very personal. Pressing her for information and openly sharing the horror stories of his mother and father didn't help. It was impossible to stay distant from someone who told you he didn't know his father outside of the fact he was a "twat" and found his mother after she'd committed suicide.

In fact, any human with a modicum of compassion was forced by all the rules of *being* a human with a modicum of compassion not to stay distant when such a story was shared.

Even though nothing about him invited it—indeed he seemed entirely adjusted to his hideously sad history—Abby had wanted to put her arms around him. She found it almost painful not to give into this instinct.

But then he'd said they were going to bed and everything else flew out of her head.

He'd moved away from her on the counter (thankfully) and asked where her bag was. She told him, they went upstairs and he retrieved it from the lounge and took her to his bedroom.

All the while, Abby's sense of doom intensified.

He had an enormous master suite on the second floor, replete with a huge king-size bed covered in a deep-grey comforter with six big, fluffy pillows stacked at the head—three to a side, two in black pillowcases, two in midnight blue and the top in a matching grey sham.

The furniture in the room was heavy, dark and uber-masculine. The look, like everything else in his house (and everything about him) was powerfully male, sleek, expensive and modern.

He showed her to the adjoining bathroom. It was immaculate white, looked brand new and fitted with what appeared to be a top-of-the-line bathroom suite. It had grey accent tiles and thick, luxurious towels in the colours of his bed sheets.

He'd left her in the bathroom. Abby had closed the door behind him and changed.

The search for a casual but classy outfit in which to cook dinner for Cash Fraser, International Spy Catcher, was nothing compared to the search for what to wear to his bed.

She didn't want to give him any ideas by wearing anything alluring. But she also didn't want to step out of her role of Cool Paid Escort to the Rich and Famous by wearing what she'd normally wear (a pair of comfy PJs).

She and Jenny had settled on a dusty-blue nightgown made of super-soft, stretchy cotton that hugged her upper body and fell to a line of charcoal-grey lace at the hem just above her knees. Thin, grey, satin straps held the nightgown to her shoulders but there was no other adornment. It was fitted and graceful without being overtly sexy.

She donned the nightgown, brushed her teeth, washed her face, applied moisturiser, pulled out her ponytail, and taking a deep, calming breath (which didn't work in any way), she walked out to the bedroom.

Cash had turned on the overhead light to the room when they entered, but now only a soft light shone from the sleekly lined lamp on the bedside table that had a black shade and a glass base. He was standing by the bed, his phone in hand, his thumb moving over the screen, wearing nothing but a pair of dark-grey cotton, drawstring pyjama bottoms, the quality of the material demonstrated by a low sheen.

His chest and feet were bare.

Abby (and her rapidly beating heart) noticed immediately that Cash's clothing was *not* costly camouflage.

Cash Fraser had a great body.

His chest was all smooth muscle leading down to the planes and contours of strong abdominals. His collarbone and the tops of his hip bones stood out in sexy relief. His biceps and lower arms had well-defined muscles, his veins slightly jutting.

She found herself thinking (at that moment descending into a kind of dazed madness) that a man with a body like that could climb mountains, fight wars, battle opponents hand to hand in bloody combat and, no matter the challenge, always come away the victor.

This alarmed her.

Greatly.

Even as it captivated her.

Even more greatly.

"Abby?" he called and her body jerked at his deep brogue saying her name.

Her eyes flew from him to the bed and she stared at it in desperation like it was going to form a mouth and start telling her a fascinating tale.

"Sorry," she muttered. "Tired," she muttered again, not trusting her own voice.

"Which side?" Cash asked, and as she was studiously regarding the bed at the same time trying to ignore her thoughts and feelings, she didn't know what he was talking about.

Her eyes shifted to him.

It was a mistake.

He was too gorgeous for his own good (and hers).

"Pardon?" she inquired.

"Which side of the bed?" he asked and she started yet again.

She slept on the left with Ben. She'd taken to sleeping in the middle without him.

"The middle," she blurted.

Another mistake.

This made him smile.

He had a great smile.

Oh dear Lord, she thought.

He twisted his torso and placed the phone on the bedside table then strolled to her.

He got up close and his chin tipped down to look at her.

"Relax, darling," his burr was a soft rumble, "I don't bite."

In desperation, Abby tried to be flip. "That's a relief."

"Though, I don't mind if you do," he continued and she could do nothing but swallow.

He saw her nervous reaction and it made him grin.

Then he walked past her to the bathroom.

She scrambled to the bed, getting in on the left side. She pulled the covers high and curled into herself, making her body as diminutive as she possibly could.

She didn't know if she could do this. In fact, she was pretty certain she couldn't. In fact, she was extremely certain she was giving it all away by acting like a frightened virgin.

She couldn't give it all away. She'd dug this hole for herself, now she had to live in it until the time when she could dig her way back out.

She forced herself to relax, uncurl and assume a sleeping position that normal people might use, on her side, hands tucked under her face, knees crooked.

Minutes later, he came out of the bathroom.

She didn't watch as he turned out the light and got into bed.

But her body was tense as he turned to her. She felt his hand come to rest on her hip and his mouth went to her ear.

"Good night, Abby," he said softly.

"Good night," she replied chirpily.

She could swear she heard him chuckle.

Normally this might annoy her. At the time, she was too flipped out to let it register.

He kept his hand where it was but settled behind her. She could feel his body, though he kept his distance.

She waited.

He didn't move and he didn't try anything.

She waited more.

He stayed where he was and she felt his hand get heavier as his breathing got steadier. Moments later, his hand slid away as he fell to his back.

She waited more, hoping he'd start snoring which would give her a valid reason to find somewhere else to sleep.

He didn't.

Eventually her body relaxed and shortly after she fell asleep.

Now this.

How she'd snuggled into him, she had no idea. But she had to move and fast.

Carefully she rolled to her back.

Unfortunately, Cash rolled with her.

His body was pressed to her side much like hers was to him moments before (except, of course, the head to the shoulder bit), and she felt his hand come to rest on her belly.

His voice was husky when she heard him ask quietly, "Abby, are you awake?"

She decided immediately to feign sleep.

Cash was not deceived.

"Abby," he called.

"Mm?" she mumbled, hoping he would think she was *mostly* asleep.

Cash was still not deceived.

His hand slid across her belly to curl around the top of her hip and she felt his face in her neck before he murmured, "Darling, I know you're awake."

There was, she had to admit, something about him calling her "darling" that she liked way too damned much.

However, when he said it into her neck while they were in bed, she liked it a whole lot better.

Which made it worse.

A lot worse.

"Not entirely," she muttered her lie.

She was completely awake and totally panicked.

She felt his body laugh even though she didn't hear it. His face came out of her neck and his fingers put pressure on her hip to roll her to her side and into him.

She lifted her hands and pressed them against his chest as his face went to the other side of her neck.

"Let's see," his voice rumbled against her skin, "you sleep like a dead weight pressed into me all night and all of a sudden your body jerks and freezes and you pull away. I'm thinking you're pretty fucking awake."

Abby was stunned and not about the fact that he knew she was lying. "I slept like that all night?"

"You rolled into me five minutes after you drifted off and stayed there."

Abby was even more stunned. She'd been certain he'd fallen asleep before her.

"Sorry," she mumbled.

His face went away, and although she couldn't see him she felt his eyes on her.

"Sorry about what?" he asked.

"Sorry if I bothered you while you were sleeping," she told him. "And sorry if I woke you."

His mouth came to hers and he murmured, "Don't be. I'm not."

Then he brushed his lips against hers softly and after, his mouth trailed down her cheek to her ear.

It occurred to Abby at that moment that something was not quite right.

Then she felt his tongue touch the skin under her ear.

Her belly dipped.

"What are you doing?" she asked, her voice breathy, her hands putting light pressure on his chest.

"Tasting you," he whispered in her ear and she felt a happy tingle slide from her ear downward.

Her hands on his chest pressed harder.

"Um, Cash, we have a deal," she reminded him.

"Yes," he murmured, his mouth moving to trail along her jaw. "We do."

She found breathing was becoming difficult. "Cash, stop it."

"No," was his surprising and terrifying answer.

She'd been correct, something was definitely not right.

"Cash!" She gave him a shove and his body stayed where it was but his head came up.

"Abby," he returned patiently.

His mouth had gone away but his face was close and his hand at her hip had somewhere along the line become an arm wrapped tightly around her waist.

"Are you reneging on the deal?" she asked, her voice sharp.

"No."

She pushed at his chest again. "What do call this?"

At her push, his arm got tighter and his other hand forced itself under her, travelling up her back to sift into her hair and cup the back of her head.

What Cash said next made all the breath force itself rather painfully out of Abby's lungs.

"I agreed not to fuck you until we went to the castle. I didn't agree not to do anything else."

Abby thought immediately this was not a fortuitous turn of events.

"Well I didn't agree to anything else," she retorted angrily.

Anger, she hoped, would hide her fear.

"You didn't stipulate against it either," he replied.

This was true.

"Then I do now," she told him.

His fingers twisted in her hair.

This was not painful. It was gentle and highly effective as it caused a pleasurable tremor to slide from her scalp all the way through her body.

"Abby," he said softly. "So far I've paid nineteen thousand nine hundred and ninety-nine pounds to spend approximately eleven hours with you, the majority of that sleeping. Do you honestly believe I'd pay that much to take you out to dinner and chat with you in my kitchen?"

She had to agree that sounded absurd.

Then again, everything about this situation was absurd.

"I'm not comfortable with this," she declared even though she wasn't entirely certain what "this" was. She was, however, relatively certain she was uncomfortable with it.

"Do you want to back out?" he asked even as his arms grew tighter.

"I think I do," she responded, even though all of a sudden she wasn't certain she did.

"Then you can pay me back thirty K and we'll call it off."

Her body seized and her mind flew through quick calculations of the money she'd already spent and the money she likely needed.

The original ten grand she'd asked for was the bare minimum of what she needed to take off the pressure of her debt and get current (and this was before she knew she needed major work done to the only usable bathroom in the house). She'd intended on selling some heirlooms, finding a job and hoping to stay on top of things.

The fifty thousand he'd already paid her would get her entirely out of debt as well as allow her to do some much needed updating to Gram's house.

The two hundred thousand would allow her to fix up the house so it was thoroughly restored. It would allow her to keep Gram's lovingly conserved collections of vintage clothing and priceless (to Abby) family heirlooms. And it would give her a generous nest egg allowing Abby time to decide what she wanted to be when she grew up.

She had, she knew, no choice.

She couldn't back out.

Her hands gentled on his chest but her body stayed tense.

"All right, Cash," she said softly. "But I want to know, in detail, what you feel you've paid for."

She didn't really *want* to know. But she knew she *had* to know.

He rolled to his back, taking her with him and reached out an arm to turn on the bedside lamp.

She blinked at the sudden brightness even muted by the black shade, and as she was doing this he rolled back. This time into her so his body was mostly on top of hers, his weight settling into her but somehow not all of it.

Their position meant his strong, heavy legs tangled naturally with hers and the intimacy of this was not lost on Abby. It felt strange and wonderful at the same time it felt very wrong.

His hand came up to rest against the side of her head, the tips of his fingers sifting into her hair at the temple.

Lying atop her she saw his hair was messier than normal, his black eyes sexier than normal and his face held a frighteningly determined expression.

This, she knew, did not bode well.

"In detail," his voice came at her quietly but his words were ruthless, "I've paid for the right to put my hands and mouth on you. To kiss you, taste you, touch you, anywhere I like, everywhere I want, and do whatever the fuck else I want with you."

Abby stopped breathing.

Cash kept talking.

"I've also paid for the right to expect that you'll do the same to me."

After he said that, Abby fought against hyperventilating.

Cash on the other hand was completely calm. "I've paid for the right to make you come with my hands and my mouth as often as I like, whenever I like, wherever I like, given reason. I've also paid for the right to expect you to return the favour."

"Cash," Abby breathed.

Cash ignored her. "I've paid for the right to be familiar with you when I want, where I want and I'll give detail to that too."

She decided she didn't want any more detail.

She didn't have a choice. Cash kept going.

"I'll be touching you, kissing you, holding you and whatever the hell else I want to do with you in private and in public."

Abby was back to pressing against his chest.

Cash was back to resisting her efforts.

He went on, "If I ask you a question, you answer it honestly. You don't hold back and you don't evade. I've paid quite generously for you to play the part of the devoted, adoring girlfriend. I've paid for you to play it convincingly, when we're alone and when we aren't, in all that being my girlfriend entails in these modern times. I've paid for it and I expect to get it and it's what you're going to give me."

Abby stopped fighting because she was concentrating on breathing.

"Do you have any questions?" Cash asked, his tone polite, the underlying firmness of it resolute.

Abby, no longer having a voice, shook her head.

He'd been, she thought, pretty thorough.

"I'm giving you the chance to back out now, transfer the thirty K back into my account by close of business today and you'll never see me again," he told her, paused for a second then continued, "If you don't back out, that means you agree to these terms for the length of our arrangement and we'll not discuss this again. Is that understood?"

Abby, still not having a voice, nodded her head.

Cash, still calm, his face still hard, watched her.

Then he asked, "What's your decision?"

Abby found her voice and whispered, "I need some time."

"You've got two minutes," Cash returned.

Abby felt her eyes grow round.

"That isn't time!" she cried idiotically, because it was, just not much of it.

A muscle in his jaw leapt and Abby watched it with concern because it was an indication that he was not at all happy and she had a feeling that an unhappy Cash was a very bad thing.

He spoke.

"We've already set the plan in motion. You back out now, I'm fucked. I don't have time."

She had thought two days ago that she'd done something immensely stupid.

She'd been wrong.

It was catastrophically stupid.

But the truth of the matter was she needed the money. It meant security and freedom and it meant that she could keep hold of the only things left in her life—outside of Kieran and Jenny—that meant anything to her.

And if she backed out now, Cash was, indeed, fucked.

And for some bizarre reason she didn't like that idea either.

She made her decision.

It terrified her but it was the only choice she had.

She asked so quietly her voice was barely discernable, "Do we have to start right now?"

Something intense and unfathomably deep flashed in his eyes at her words, and Abby felt a corresponding emotion in the region of her heart.

"Yes," he replied, her heart sank and he dipped his head to touch her mouth with his. "And no," he went on, speaking against her lips and her heart leapt.

"What does that mean?" she whispered.

"Put your arms around me," he commanded, his throaty, deep voice had grown gruff.

She did as he asked, sliding her hands from his chest, around his sides to wrap them around his back.

"Now, Abby," he started. "I'm going to kiss you and you're going to kiss me back. Then you're going to go back to sleep and I'm going to work. Tonight, after you make me dinner again, we'll begin."

Without giving her a chance to reply, he did as he said he'd do, his head slanting and his mouth opening over hers.

The minute his tongue touched her own, her body liquefied, and even though she didn't will herself to do so, she kissed him back. One of her hands slid up his spine to plunge her fingers into his thick hair, the other arm wrapped tighter around his waist.

The kiss was shattering, tearing through her, hot, sweet and wet. It was long, it was hard and it was unbelievably, delectably thorough.

She'd never experienced anything like its fiery intensity.

Never.

Not with Ben.

Not in her dreams.

Not in her whole, damned life.

When his mouth disengaged, the only thing Abby could think was that she wanted more.

A lot more.

Everything.

But she didn't get it. Instead, his eyes moved over her face and they were blazing as fiery hot as his kiss. Something he found in her face made his expression shift to a soft satisfaction before his head bent and he kissed her neck below her ear.

"Go back to sleep," he murmured there.

And without another word, he was knifing away from her out of bed. He flicked the covers back over her, turned off the light and headed to the bathroom.

Abby lay in stunned silence, listening to the shower and knowing that there was a very good possibility that she'd never sleep again. She thought there was a slim chance she might spontaneously combust. And she realised with a flash of guilt that, mixed with heady longing, she felt wetness between her legs and an arousal the intensity of which she'd never experienced in her life.

And if you told Abigail Butler that she would turn and curl her arms around Cash Fraser's pillow, tucking it to her body and smelling his cologne combined with the scent that was all him, and she'd fall promptly to sleep after her latest drama, she would have laughed in your face.

But that was just what she did.

❧ ❧ ❧

Dressed and ready for work, Cash walked into his dark bedroom, his eyes on Abby's form in his bed.

He was very pleased to note that she'd not lied during the negotiations in the pub.

It was abundantly clear that Abigail Butler may sell her time and her presence, but she most certainly never sold her body.

He sat on the bed in the crook of her lap, half hoping to wake her, half glad he didn't.

He bent low and kissed the skin of her exposed shoulder. Then he lifted his hand and slid the hair from her neck and he kissed her there.

She twisted her head in sleep, not to dislodge his touch but to deepen it.

He smiled against her skin.

He got to his feet, pulled the covers over her shoulder and left the room.

He didn't give a fuck if that very day any of his clients' entire multinational conglomerates were stolen out from under them.

Cash would not be late home that night.

❦ *6* ❦

MRS. TRUMAN

Abby sat at the big, battered farm table in her grandmother's huge kitchen. The Aga stove, aided by a merry fire burning in the stone hearth of the fireplace, warmed the space so thoroughly, even the huge chunks of slate that formed the floor felt heated.

She was drinking coffee with Pete and listening to him tell her about plumbing, electricity, new boilers, chimney pots and so on down to re-plastering and paint, all of which her house needed to be put back to rights.

"That's just what I see, love, but I'd get someone in to do a survey," Pete advised, before draining his mug. His gaze came back to her as he put down his cup. "I know someone if you want me to set it up."

Abby nodded. "I can't do this anymore, Pete. Every week it's something new. I need to know what I'm up against."

He grinned at her with approval. "Smart girl."

She smiled back and grabbed his mug. "Another cuppa?"

"Supposed to be bringin' the boys up in your bathroom one, so make it three," Pete answered.

Abby stood and went to the kettle.

She'd decided on the way home from Cash's that now the deed was irrevocably done, she was setting the plans in motion to get her life back in order.

She was not going to delay.

When her arrangement with Cash was over, she was going to begin anew and she was going to hit the ground running.

Over a year ago, Jenny had negotiated a good deal on the sale of Abby and Ben's home. Selling her furniture, her car and their other belongings allowed Abby to pay off her mountain of debt and left her with enough to rest comfortably as she started her new life in England (or so she thought).

Abby had decided to take a month or two off before starting work. In hindsight, of course, this was not the most sterling idea. She already knew her grandmother's home needed attention. Gram was a packrat, she kept everything. Abby had visions of spending her days sorting and tidying, maybe slapping some new coats of paint here and there, making Gram's home her own.

However, a week after she'd moved in, it had rained, as it had a way of doing in England, rather heavily outside.

Unfortunately, it had rained rather heavily *inside* too.

Abby had spent the night rushing around with pots, pans and bowls to place under the drips.

She'd spent the next day listening to Pete tell her she needed a new roof and that the leaks had been around awhile, there was water damage. Gram, who'd spent most of her time on the first floor, probably didn't know it (or didn't want to).

After paying the taxes, Gram's inheritance didn't come with a boatload of money. The roof and repair of the water damage dug deep into Abby's reserves, but she had no choice, and even if it was expensive, it certainly didn't bankrupt her.

She had time to make it up and get her life rolling.

At least that was what she thought.

Deep into December, about a month after she'd moved in, England was gripped by an arctic cold snap. Gram's home was also gripped by it. The house was huge, big rooms, tall ceilings, wide stairways and lots of open space in the halls. The boilers were in overdrive and older than

Mrs. Truman. Abby kept the fires in the rooms blazing with wood and coal and still could barely keep out the chill.

Unfortunately, some of the rooms had chimneys that needed work and Abby learned the hard way she should have had them looked at before she built fires in their grates.

Pete came after the smoke cleared (literally), telling her not only did she need her chimneys serviced, she needed new windows and insulation for her insulation had been installed during the Boer War (this was not Pete's estimate, it was Abby's).

She lived in a conservation area so she couldn't buy cheap but effective windows. She had to buy expensive timber-framed ones.

At the time Abby had found a job. She was working. She liked her job and the people there, but her pay was a fraction of what it used to be. Since she didn't have a mortgage (although her gas and electric bills were staggering), she thought this would be okay and she could live the standard of life she was used to.

Also, considering she had a goodly amount of money in the bank and not knowing what would soon befall her, she'd sold her gram's old estate car and bought herself a brand new, sporty BMW 118. Not going over the top (she thought) but it suited her and Ben would have loved it.

This had dwindled her reserves further.

To pay for the chimneys, insulation and windows, she'd taken out a loan.

Then, in a shocking turn of events, she and four of her colleagues had been made redundant. To their credit, her employers were nearly (but not quite) as upset as Abby and promised if things improved they'd call her (so far, obviously, they hadn't).

Out of work and nearly out of money, Abby soldiered on.

She spent her days alternately working at high-paid but short-lived contracts or clearing out her grandmother's piles of magazines and newspapers, the plethora of books and knickknacks, and a kitchen full of equipment that was broken, rusty or hadn't been needed since cavemen were starting fires by striking together flint rocks.

Then one bathroom groaned to a halt, which Abby ignored (and shouldn't have). Then another one did (ditto the ignoring bit).

Then the window men found the damp, the fixing of which led to her second loan. And the insulation men found the dry rot, the fixing of which led to Abby being broke.

Kieran and Jenny had offered help on numerous occasions, but Abby had refused.

They'd done enough.

There were no jobs in sight, contracts were growing thin and Abby's desperation was increasing.

It was the evening after the day Abby sold one of her brooches—a gold and pearl antique one that belonged to her great-grandmother— that Jenny went to the party.

Jenny knew about the brooch, knew that Abby hated selling it and then she overheard James and Cash talking. She heard James's suggestion of a discreet escort to deflect attention off some business Cash was involved with regarding his uncle (business Jenny didn't hear). And further protect him against his uncle's increasingly frustrating efforts to throw Cash in front of one of his three stepdaughters.

And Jenny came up with her idea. She talked Abby into it. Then Kieran.

That morning, showering in Cash's bathroom and attempting to ignore the fact that Cash's naked body had been in the same space but hours before (and also trying not to think about how much she liked his shower, it was *lush*), Abby thought instead about what her family would think of what she was doing.

The answer she came up with was not much. They wouldn't like it, not one bit.

Then again, she couldn't imagine Gram, or Abby's mother for that matter, ever allowing anything to happen to the house or allowing it to go out of the family.

Desperate times, desperate measures.

She couldn't think about what they'd think. She'd learned the hard way after Ben died and she tried to hold on to what they had that she had to live in the here and now, keep herself fed and keep her legacy safe.

The bell in the door clattered, taking her out of her thoughts just as the kettle flipped off.

"Can you see to the drinks, Pete?" Abby asked as she headed out of the kitchen.

"Sure thing, love," Pete replied.

Abby walked through the house, pulled open her huge front door and on the stoop stood Mrs. Truman with her three spaniels on leads.

Abby tried not to groan.

Instead, she greeted, "Mrs. Truman."

"Well?" Mrs. Truman snapped.

"Well what?" Abby asked.

"Well, what was it like?" Mrs. Truman snapped again.

"What was *what* like?" Abby queried, confused and hiding impatience.

"*Your date!*" Mrs. Truman shrieked then shoved her way in, bringing her dogs with her, something that Zee would not like at all. "Making an old woman stand out in the cold," she muttered. "What's with young people these days?" Mrs. Truman went on to grouse, bending down to detach the leashes from her canines who scattered to the four winds upon release.

"Mrs. Truman, my cat—" Abby started.

"Pah! Your cat can take care of himself. Little Georgie learned *that* the *hard* way," she announced as she unbuttoned the big fabric-coated buttons of her granny coat. "I need tea," she declared.

"I'm kind of—" Abby began again but Mrs. Truman had her coat off with a nimbleness of someone at least three hundred and forty-two years younger and threw it over the antique, oak, mirrored coat stand in Abby's vestibule.

Abby heard her old lady shoes squelch on the tiled floors as Mrs. Truman headed toward the kitchen.

With no other choice, Abby closed her front door and followed but she did so after heaving a deep sigh.

By the time she'd made it to the kitchen, Mrs. Truman was opening and closing cupboards, reaching high on her tiptoes to do so as she was about four feet tall. Pete was carrying three full coffee mugs with a packet of biscuits tucked under his arm.

Abby gave him a "save me" look but he was rushing toward the door. However he had the decency to look sheepish about it.

"Did you see the papers, Peter?" Mrs. Truman called, finding herself one of Abby's grandmother's delicate and irreplaceable (thus never used) china teacups with saucer and the box of tea.

Pete, his escape foiled, turned to the older lady.

"The papers?" he asked.

Mrs. Truman jerked a thumb at Abby and said, "Our girl here out on a date with an international playboy."

Abby didn't know when she became Mrs. Truman's girl and for a moment she considered it more terrifying than what her life had become.

"Is that so?" Pete asked, already knowing about her date because he had, indeed, seen the papers.

"They look good together," Mrs. Truman grumbled, dropping a teabag in the teacup and sounding like she didn't believe her own words. "Though he's way too tall," she said this last as if Cash could and should do something about his height.

"I've got to take these to the boys. If you'll excuse me," Pete said and started to head out, giving Abby an apologetic look.

"Yes, Abigail's having work done *again*." Mrs. Truman poured water into her tea. "Banging, knocking, banging, blah, blah, blah. It's enough to kill an old woman."

Because it made her a very bad person, Abby tried to stop herself from thinking that might be a wish come true, but she couldn't quite do it.

"I'll just be heading up," Pete said.

Mrs. Truman waved him on his way at the same time she spooned three sugars (a fact Abby found unbelievable, there was *nothing* sweet about Mrs. Truman) into her tea. "Go, go, go. Abigail's got some talking to do and it's not for men's ears."

Abby rolled her eyes to the ceiling. As she did this Pete disappeared.

When she mentally came back into the room, Mrs. Truman was helping herself to some biscuits.

"I've just made a decision," she proclaimed and Abby braced.

"What's that?" Abby asked, not wanting to know and going to the kettle to make herself another cup of coffee.

"I'm having you and your new man over for dinner with those two friends of yours. The Australians," Mrs. Truman told her as she teetered to the table balancing her cup and saucer, which held four biscuits, and Abby sucked in breath in horror at the very idea of Cash, Jenny and Kieran sitting down at any table much less Mrs. Truman's table.

"That's very nice of you but it isn't necessary, Mrs. Truman," Abby replied.

"I *know* it isn't necessary. If it was *necessary* I wouldn't do it." Then she contradicted herself. "But someone has to size this fellow up, and with your grandmother out of the picture that someone is *me*."

Abby desperately tried a different tactic. "Cash is a pretty busy guy. He's—"

"Pah!" Mrs. Truman burst out and Abby waited for her to say more but apparently she felt that summed up her argument.

In another demonstration of just how bad her luck could get, at that very moment Abby's mobile, lying on the table in front of Mrs. Truman, sounded.

Abby, all the way across the kitchen and with her hands full, couldn't get to it as fast as the heretofore unknown agile Mrs. Truman could.

She snatched it off the table and studied it briefly as Abby dropped the spoon and coffee and hurried across the room.

"Mrs. Truman—" she said as the older woman touched the screen and put the phone to her ear.

"Abigail Butler's phone, Edith Truman speaking," she announced grandly.

Abby halted and hoped to all that was holy that there was a salesman or someone else she didn't care about on the other end.

"Yes, Abigail's here and I'm glad you called," she said tartly, sounding as if she was *not* glad and furthermore the last time she was glad was 1943. "Abigail and I were just talking about you and we've decided you're both coming to dinner at my house tomorrow. Seven o'clock."

Abby's heart sank as she realised Mrs. Truman was speaking to Cash.

What was next? Would the sky fall? The oceans boil? Tidal waves on the Bristol Channel?

The lady sat and listened and then snapped, "Well, change them!

I'm an old woman. I don't know how many dinner parties I have left in me."

Abby watched as Mrs. Truman paused and listened some more, then went on, "The stories say you're a clever boy. They even made a movie about you. You'll think of something. Now bring a bottle. White. Chilled. And some flowers. I like roses. And some chocolates. None of that stuff from the grocery stores, decent chocolates." Then she finished, "Abigail's right here."

With that she held out the phone to Abby.

Abby stifled the urge to strangle her to death and took the phone, mumbling, "Excuse me."

With all due haste she left the room, walked down the hall and shut herself in the living room.

Once there, she put the phone to her ear and with no further ado said, "I told you she could be worse."

She heard Cash's rich laughter through the phone and at the sound her belly dipped.

When he'd stopped, she asked, "How much do the English authorities frown on homicide of blue-haired ladies?"

Cash didn't answer, instead he told her, "I'm considering hiring her. She'd strike fear in the hearts of half the bastards I have to deal with every day. How old is she? My pension people will want to know."

"Nine hundred and ninety-two," Abby answered and heard his lush laughter again and knew she'd tried to make him laugh on purpose, *again*.

When his laughter died, she asked, "Why are you calling? Is something up?"

There was still amusement in his voice when he responded, "I'm calling because that's what women expect men to do. You expect us to call at least once a day, proving we're capable about thinking of nothing but you when we're not. We're thinking about work."

Abby smiled to herself, walking to the window where she saw Jenny parking her new Mini outside. "So you're calling me to tell me you're not thinking about me?"

His voice changed when he replied. It got that deeper, throatier, sexier that she was beginning to like way too much.

"You? No. Your ass, your smile, your hair and that fucking kiss this morning? Yes."

She was inordinately thrilled he was thinking about the kiss. When she wasn't thinking about her screwed up life, her troubles, her house and crazy Mrs. Truman, that was all she could think about.

"Mostly," he went on, "I wanted to make sure you got my note."

She'd gotten it. It was sitting on the kitchen counter by his espresso maker with a set of keys beside it. The black ink was a manly scrawl on the sheet telling her to take the keys, leave a grocery list for his housekeeper and that he'd be home at seven.

She'd made a grocery list but she'd also met Aileen, his housekeeper, by bumping into her while going out the front door.

To Abby's surprise, Aileen acted like she didn't run into a woman every time she came to see to Cash's house.

They'd chatted for a bit and Abby decided she liked her. Then again, there were few people Abby didn't like. She could count only one and at that very moment that particular person was sitting in Abby's kitchen.

"I got your note," she told Cash as she walked toward the door.

Jenny was about to come in and Jenny was Abby's best friend in the whole world. She didn't want her to meet Mrs. Truman without warning. No true friend would let that happen.

"Good. What are you making me for dinner?" Cash asked in her ear as Abby opened the door to find Mrs. Truman outside it eating a Bourbon biscuit and unabashedly listening.

"Mrs. Truman!" she cried instead of answering Cash.

"You need to speak up when I'm eavesdropping," Mrs. Truman told her. "I'm not as young as I once was and that includes my ears."

At that moment, Jenny walked in stomping her feet and slamming the door, shouting, "It's fucking cold out there!"

"Language!" Mrs. Truman snapped and Jenny swung around, her face getting pale.

Jennifer Kane was the kind of woman who didn't let anything faze her. Kieran had a great job that paid really well but he also had to move from country to country. Without a peep, Jenny went with him. She said goodbye to friends. She bought and sold homes and cars and shipped belongings. She found new friends and renewed acquaintances. She travelled to far lands with her husband on business and pleasure.

She could even change her own oil.

What she couldn't do was live without fear of nosy, maddening Mrs. Truman.

Jennifer Kane was a strong woman but she wasn't Superwoman.

"Cash," Abby whispered, "I think I have to—" she was going to say "go" but Mrs. Truman was speaking.

"You and your Australian husband are coming with her," she pointed a bony finger at Abby, "and her new man, to my place for dinner. Tomorrow night. Seven."

Jenny's pale face swung to Abby and she asked, "I am?"

"You are," Mrs. Truman declared, moving toward her coat, "Bring a bottle. White. Chilled. And some dog treats. They're having company too."

With that she let out a piercing whistle. Abby winced at the shrill sound nearly dropping the phone and she could hear little spaniel feet thundering through the house. Mrs. Truman turned her attention to Abby.

"Tell your man I won't take any last minute excuses. I don't care if he's got fancy schmancy friends. If Marlon Brando himself asks him to dinner, he's going to say no. Understood?"

"I think Marlon Brando is dead, Mrs. Truman," Jenny, now standing (or more accurately huddling, protection in numbers as it were) beside Abby, informed the old woman.

"Is not," Mrs. Truman shot back.

"I think he is," Jenny, unwisely, pressed.

"He is *not!*" Mrs. Truman snapped loudly and Abby could hear Cash chuckling in her ear so she knew he could hear every word. "I would have heard," Mrs. Truman went on.

"Maybe I'm wrong," Jenny mumbled toward Abby (and Abby's phone), and Cash's chuckle became laughter.

The dogs had arrived and Mrs. Truman was clipping their leads on them.

"Tomorrow. Seven. Don't be late," she said and then she was out the door.

Abby rushed forward to close (and lock) it behind her.

"I'm sorry, Cash. That was—"

"Stop saying sorry, darling." His burr sounded softly in her ear, her body experienced a top to toe shiver and he finished, "See you tonight."

Then he disconnected.

Abby dropped her phone from her ear and saw Jenny was staring at her.

"What just happened?" she asked, and Abby had a fleeting feeling of fear that Jenny knew about the top to toe shiver.

"What?" Abby asked, trying to look innocent.

"Are Kieran and I really having dinner with you, Cash Fraser and *Mrs. Truman*?" Jenny queried as if she wanted above all else in the world for Abby to say "no."

Abby was forced to disappoint her friend. "I'm afraid so."

"My God," Abby breathed. "We're going to have to pretend he's your new boyfriend. He doesn't know about us."

This was true.

"Oh my God," Abby whispered, a new feeling of fear gripping her.

"Don't worry," Jenny rallied first. "I'll talk to Kieran. Everything will be fine. Right?"

Abby nodded, as ever sucking courage from her friend in a time of need.

Abby and Jenny walked to the kitchen together.

"Was it okay?" Jenny asked, "Last night?"

Abby nodded, went to the kettle and took it to the sink to refill it.

She was going to lie.

If there was ever a time to lie, this was it

Jenny already felt responsible enough. She didn't need to know what happened this morning.

"He was really late," Abby explained to her friend. "We just talked and then went to bed. He didn't try anything."

"How weird," Jenny mumbled to herself before her eyes focused on Abby. "What'd you talk about?"

"Music." That wasn't a lie, really. "Food." That also wasn't a lie, as such. "Not much, he was really late." That was a total lie (well, not the last part).

Jenny looked at Abby closely and Abby figured her friend knew she was telling tall tales (or short uninformative ones), but Jenny's face cleared and her eyes got soft.

"He's being okay with you?" she asked quietly.

"Yeah," Abby replied, setting the kettle on its charge and flipping it on. She turned back to her friend and rested her hips against the counter. "He's a..." She hesitated and then went on, sharing just a little bit, "Jenny, I think he's a good guy. He thinks I'm funny and..." she stopped.

"And what?" Jenny prompted.

"And that's it. It's weird sometimes because he's so hot, and, well... he's rich and paid for me to be with him, but when I forget that, it's okay," Abby told her.

"You're sure?" Jenny asked and when Abby nodded, she watched her friend's body relax and realised just how much Jenny was shouldering this burden.

She'd been right.

Definitely right.

Abby wasn't going to share any of the things that were *not* okay with Cash.

Further, Abby wasn't going to share any of the feelings about Cash she felt relatively certain Jenny would *not* think were okay.

Jenny walked to a cupboard and pulled down a mug asking, "So, what does Hot Guy, International Man of Mystery, Spy Master General wear to bed?"

At that, Abby knew, for now, everything was okay.

❧ 7 ❧

LATE

Abigail Butler was stupid.

Stupid, stupid, *stupid*.

She thought she was being smart. She'd had it all planned. Then, as usual, it all went awry.

She'd decided, since tonight was the night the use of hands, mouths, touching, tasting, etc. was going to "begin," she'd delay it by spending part of the time together with Cash cooking.

What she wanted to make for dinner would take a half an hour, more if you counted cooking time.

So she decided to arrive at a quarter to seven and still be cooking when Cash got home. He'd have to wait to do...whatever-it-was-he-was-going-to-do...until after she was done cooking, the food was done grilling and steaming and they were done eating.

She lived in Clevedon. He lived in Bath. It was a forty-five minute drive.

What Abby didn't know since she usually took the train or travelled during non-rush-hour times, was that it was a forty-five minute drive on a *good* day.

On a *bad* day (which Abby seemed to be having a lot of lately, or perhaps for the last six years) and traffic was heavy and an accident meant the cars were crawling on the motorway, it took a whole lot longer.

Furthermore, it was against the law to talk on your mobile in your car in England so when Cash called at seven twenty-five, she couldn't answer.

Even though she turned up her music very loudly so she couldn't hear the phone beeping to tell her she had a voicemail message, it rested on her passenger seat in a threatening way like a coiled snake waiting to strike, freaking her out throughout her journey.

Last, but not least, it was a veritable *impossibility* to park in Bath. She'd discovered that the day before, but somehow forgot it in the twenty-four hours since driving there last.

She was a half hour late to be there for Cash's arrival. It became forty-five minutes late by the time she parked and *fifty-five* minutes late by the time she hoofed it in her high-heeled boots to his home from her parking place, which she was sure was closer to Sri Lanka than his townhouse.

She listened to his two word voicemail message on her walk to his house.

"Call me," and he sounded not happy, to say the least.

At his door she fumbled clumsily in her purse for the key (which she should have extracted on the walk there, but she hadn't thought of that), found it, unlocked the door and rushed through into the hall.

There were welcoming lights on and she had to stop when she saw them, the pain in her stomach was so acute.

If it was dark and she got home before Ben, she lit the house (just here and there, not anything blazing and environmentally unconscious) so he wouldn't have to grope around in the dark to find the lights.

She'd never told him to do it but he must have realised her intent, and a while after they were married, Ben started to do it for her too.

She thought of them as "welcoming lights" because they said someone was home, someone who cared about you, someone who didn't want you to walk into a cold, dark house after a rough day and grope around to find a light.

It never occurred to her that Cash Fraser was the kind of man who wouldn't want her to grope around to find a light.

She recovered herself with a deep breath and walked on leaded feet down the hall, around the corner and down the stairs toward the sound of jazz (not new-age, gross jazz but old-age, fantastic bluesy-jazz).

By the time she made it down the stairs, Nina Simone had started singing, "Tell Me More and More and Then Some."

She saw Cash was in the kitchen, a tumbler of Scotch in one hand, the other hand clenched in a fist that was on his hip. He was wearing a pair of dark-brown suit trousers, a dress shirt, the colour of which was an attractive blend between dandelion yellow and burnt orange that had a subtle sheen, it was unbuttoned at his throat and the cuffs were turned back.

His eyes were locked on her.

And he looked *less* happy than his voice sounded on her phone.

"Cash—" she started.

At the same time he demanded, "Where the fuck have you been?"

"There was an accident on the motorway and then—" she began.

He cut her off. "Do you have your mobile?"

"Yes," she answered.

"Did it occur to you to phone to let *me* know it wasn't *you* in a fucking accident on the motorway?"

Two things came to Abby at once.

First, the reminder that she knew *exactly* how it felt to learn someone you cared about had been in an accident on the highway.

Second was the shocking knowledge that Cash wasn't angry because he was losing time with her, valuable time he'd paid dearly for.

He was angry because he was worried about her.

She knew how she felt about the first. It tore at her soul every day. The second she didn't know what to do with.

Cash didn't give her time to figure it out.

"Abby, answer me," he clipped.

"No," she started and when his eyes narrowed dangerously, she hurried on, "I mean, yes. Of course it did. But it's illegal to talk on your mobile in the car."

"Next time you're going to be an hour late, darling, rest assured in the knowledge that *I'll* pay the fucking fine if you get pulled over for talking on your goddamned phone," he returned, and Abby thought it was safe to say that Cash Fraser, International Hot Guy Extraordinaire, was *pissed off*.

"Cash—" she began again.

And again he cut her off by demanding, "Get over here."

She gave a start. "What?"

"I said, get...over...here."

This, Abby decided, was not going well.

She briefly considered running for her life.

She then figured Cash would catch her. His legs were longer, and even though he was standing behind the counter and she couldn't see, it was unlikely he was wearing high heels.

So, with no other option open to her, she moved toward him and as she did so he leaned forward and set down his tumbler with an angry *clunk*.

When she got within arm's reach, he snatched her purse from her and tossed it unceremoniously on the counter even though it was Coach and no one should treat Coach like that. But she wasn't going to share that morsel of knowledge with Cash at that moment.

When he was done with that, his fingers wrapped around her wrist, he gave it a sharp tug and she fell into him. Her hand came up to cushion her fall and it landed on his chest. He dropped her wrist and she tilted her head back and opened her mouth to say something to diffuse his anger when she saw his head descending.

Then he was kissing her, hard, hot, open-mouthed and hungry, his arms wrapping around her, crushing her to his solid body.

Her hand not trapped between them went to his shoulder, not in a loving embrace but to hold herself up as her knees had turned to mush.

She felt his kiss burn from her mouth, through to her breasts, down past her belly, straight between her legs, and when he lifted his head, she was nigh on panting and her body was on fire.

"I don't like waiting," he growled low.

"So noted," she breathed.

"You're going to be late, I don't give a fuck if it's five minutes, you call," he demanded.

She nodded.

He glared at her.

She stood still and took it silently, not wanting to throw any fuel on the already scorching fire.

After a while of standing in the kitchen crushed to Cash, his arms still holding her tight, she braved the wild beast.

"Do you want me to make dinner?"

"No, I don't want you to make fucking dinner," he shot back.

Obviously, she'd spoke too soon.

"We're going out," he announced.

"But, Aileen went out and bought—" she started.

His arms got tighter, interrupting her word flow by squeezing the breath out of her. "We're going...fucking...*out*."

"Okay," she wheezed.

His arms loosened and he let her go, reached out, grabbed his whisky and threw it back in one gulp. Down the glass went with another angry *clunk*. He seized her purse, tossed it to her and took her hand, dragging her to the chair where his suit jacket was. He snatched it from the chair then hauled her upstairs, hand still in hers.

They were at the front door. He'd put on his suit jacket and was shrugging on his overcoat and Abby was watching him.

His silence was flipping her out. So she broke it.

"You say 'fuck' a lot when you're angry," she informed him for lack of anything else to say.

His eyes sliced to her. "Abby, I'm not in the mood for you being cute."

At his words, she felt the room pitch crazily.

"You think I'm cute?" she whispered.

His eyes skewered her to the spot and she decided not to speak again.

Then he opened the door, took her hand and marched her through.

❧ ❧ ❧

Abby stood at Cash's bathroom sink, hands curled around the edge of the basin, deep breathing to stop herself from hyperventilating.

It was time for bed.

This was going to happen now.

She'd agreed to it. She was going to have to go through with it.

She wasn't only near to hyperventilating because she was terrified.

She was also near to hyperventilating because she was terrified about what it said about her because, deep down, she wanted it.

That night after dinner, after walking the romantic streets of Bath with Cash, after they came back to his house and ate the leftover pears with cream and chocolate sauce, she'd rinsed and put the dishes in the dishwasher.

While she was doing this she realised if this was real, if he had asked her out and this was their third date, even though (before Ben, obviously) she had a strict six-dates-before-sex rule, she would be doing something just like this with Cash.

And looking forward to it.

She might have even done it on the second date.

Earlier that evening Cash had nursed his anger on the short walk into town (he lived in a townhouse just off the Circus). He'd nursed it through the *maître d'* of the impossibly busy, posh restaurant scurrying to find the Fabulously Rich and Famous Cash Fraser a table (a prime spot two-top at the window out of which the *maître d'* rushed a couple enjoying the final sips of their coffee). He'd nursed it through a glass of neat whisky that he drank while they contemplated the menu and ordered. And he'd nursed it through their starters.

Abby learned two things the hard way. The first being that Cash Fraser did, indeed, not like to be kept waiting. The second being that Cash Fraser was formidable when he was angry, and thus one should do all in their power not to let that happen.

Once he'd thawed (somewhere in the middle of them consuming their mains), he was replenishing Abby's wine, when she quietly said, "I'm sorry I was late, Cash."

His eyes went from her wine glass to her. He finished his task, put the bottle on the table and Abby held her breath as he got out of his chair, throwing his cloth napkin on the table by his plate.

She had no idea what he was going to do and she watched him round the table and stop beside her.

At his height, her head was tilted back at an impossible angle to look up at him and not a single thought entered her paralysed mind.

Suddenly he leaned down, wrapped his hand around the back of her head and touched his lips briefly to hers.

When he was finished, he said against her mouth softly, "Don't do it again."

"I won't. I promise," she whispered back.

He lifted up, kissed her forehead and then walked back around the table, sat down, shook his napkin out and laid it in his lap.

He calmly resumed eating.

After the shock of this tender act had worn off, Abby became aware that people were watching.

Some of them were trying to hide the fact that they were watching the fascinating show of an internationally famous man eating dinner with his partner.

Some of them weren't trying to hide anything, they were watching openly.

Abby felt a sense of desolation that there was a possibility that Cash's action was a performance for their benefit, not a demonstration of affectionate forgiveness.

But she'd never know because she could never ask.

She'd hidden her disappointment and drawn him out by asking about his music. He very much liked old jazz. Not just Nina Simone but also Louis Armstrong, Ella Fitzgerald, Sarah Vaughan, Duke Ellington and the like. She'd asked him about his work. He couldn't tell her much, it was confidential. But he'd gotten into the business while he was attending Oxford, working at a summer internship and he discovered the possibility someone was stealing and selling company secrets. Instead of whistle-blowing, he'd quietly investigated, found it to be true, presented his evidence and it all started from there.

They passed the rest of dinner in companionable conversation and decided against dessert in favour of the pears at the townhouse.

However, when they left the restaurant, instead of turning toward his home, Cash turned her toward Bath.

It was cold. She thought at first too cold for a stroll through an ancient city.

She'd decided (luckily, considering they ended up in a posh restaurant, unfortunately, considering they took a walk after) to wear a slim, black pencil skirt with a black, long-sleeved T-shirt, black, high-heeled boots and finishing the outfit with her hip-length, black wool coat that closed only by a tie-belt (her makeup that evening was her "Sophisticated Casual" look).

At first, he held her hand then, noticing she was cold, he held *her*. His arm going around her shoulders, he tucked her into his side as they strolled.

They didn't talk. They just walked, letting the beauty of Bath tell its tale as they did so.

Then something strange happened.

A flash of light, which could only come from a photographer, caught them, jarring them out of their silent, comfortable cocoon and back into the real world.

Considering this was what Cash wanted, what Cash was paying for, his reaction to the photographer was bizarre.

He looked, at a glance from Abby, for all the world *angry* at the intrusion. He immediately turned them toward his home and he seemed to be shielding her with his tall frame as they went.

When they arrived at the short flight of stairs in front of his house, he even tucked her in front of him, his arm around her waist, his other hand opening the door as he sheltered her with his shoulder from the lens of the cameraman. Cash pressed her inside and blocked the view as he shut the door.

Without a word, and Abby decided not to ask, they'd gone downstairs.

Abby fixed the pears and made decaf coffee, which she told him, even though he could probably care less, she had to drink as she never drank caffeinated beverages after noon or she'd never get to sleep.

They ate and drank while Abby sat on the counter and Cash stood close, his hips resting against a corner in the counter, one of them also resting against her knee.

When they were done, she'd rinsed and put the dishes away and was standing at the sink, turning off the faucet, thinking crazy thoughts, when she felt him behind her back.

His hand came to her hip, his mouth to her neck, and he murmured, "Time for bed."

At his words her stomach did a queer little dip that wasn't unpleasant in the slightest.

Now there she was, wishing for the first time since Ben (and drowning with guilt about it) that she was experiencing the scary but thrilling anticipation of connecting with someone whom she found handsome and compelling.

Not about to perform the services for which she was being very generously paid.

"Bloody hell," she whispered to her reflection and walked out of the bathroom.

The lights again were dim, only the lamps on either side of the bed were lit.

Cash was lying on top of the covers slightly to the middle of his side, wearing his pyjama bottoms. His back was to the headboard, his long legs stretched out in front of him, ankles crossed.

He held a sheaf of papers in his hand and there were several small piles of papers fanned out on Abby's side of the bed.

Abby stopped at the sight of him.

"Was I in the bathroom a year?" she asked, referring to his swiftly taking over the bed with paperwork.

His head lifted from his study of the papers in his hand and she noticed immediately that he was wearing a pair of attractive silver-framed reading glasses.

She also noticed that he looked really good wearing his attractive silver-framed reading glasses.

"You wear glasses," she told him unnecessarily.

"Yes," he replied.

"They look good on you," she blurted, feeling like a fool.

Slowly, he smiled. Abby's stomach did that queer thrilling dip again.

In his throaty brogue, he ordered, "Come here."

Her stomach did the dip yet again. She ignored the dip and headed to her side of the bed.

Cash stopped her by saying, "No, Abby. This side."

She did a stutter-step, confused. Her eyes went to him and she saw he was watching her. While she stood frozen and undecided, he patted the area on the bed beside him.

She changed directions and went to his side of the bed. He put the papers in his lap, leaned up and his fingers curled around her wrist. He pulled her down to seated on the bed then settled her at his side, her body resting the length of his, her head on his chest, his arm around her, her hand on his bare midriff.

"I have to go through this before the morning," he muttered, his fingers curving around her shoulder. "It won't take long."

She was a little surprised, a little disappointed, and a lot relieved.

"Okay," she replied quietly.

It felt weird, lying beside him while he read in bed. Weird and wonderful and warm and sweet and comfortable and a lot of other things it shouldn't feel.

Moments ticked past as he read and she lay there.

For a bit, she tried to read the papers. Then she realised what little she read made no sense to her.

He shifted papers around, dropped some, picked up others, somehow never disturbing her.

More moments passed and he started stroking her shoulder.

This made her realise she was tense and her body, of its own volition, began to relax.

More moments passed and the tips of his fingers slid up her shoulder, up her neck and his fingers started to play absently with her hair.

She'd always liked it when anyone played with her hair.

Lying in Cash's bed, his warm, strong body against hers, made it all the better.

In fact, she thought dreamily, it was *the best*.

More moments passed and Abby fell asleep.

8

CASH'S REASON

Somewhere in a dream, Abby heard, "Abby, I have to get ready for work."

To this, her response was to curl her limbs more tightly around the dream Cash Fraser's body. This had the added benefit of the front of her dream body pressing deeper into the front of Cash's.

"Darling," his low, deep brogue was husky and sounded, weirdly to Abby considering it was a dream, vaguely disappointed.

Then her body, not of its own volition, moved and the heat of Cash was gone.

Abby curled into his pillow and fell back to sleep.

❧ ❧ ❧

Abby felt her hair slide off her neck and then the words, "Abby, I'm leaving," semi-penetrated her unconsciousness.

Her eyes fluttered open and focused on Cash, who in the dark she could see (just barely) was sitting, fully dressed, in the crook of her lap.

"What?" she asked sleepily.

"I'm going to work," he replied softly.

"Oh."

"I'll be at your house just before seven," he told her.

"Okay," she said, settling deeper into his pillow, then mumbled, "Will you call me today?"

"I'll call," he answered.

She snuggled into the pillow and whispered, "Good." But before he could move she kept talking, "Last night, I thought we were going to begin."

"Begin what?"

She let out a soft sigh and said, "You know...*begin*."

His voice held a smile when he replied, "We did, Abby. Couldn't you tell?"

She pulled his pillow to her chest and whispered, "Not really."

"Then you weren't paying much attention," he muttered.

She was still not paying much attention. She'd started to drift back to sleep when she felt the covers pulled up over her shoulder, and after that, fingers trailed softly down her jaw.

Suddenly out of nowhere something hit her and panic seized her chest in an angry claw.

As Cash's hand moved away, her own shot out and caught his wrist in a vicelike grip.

She quickly got up on an elbow and her eyes flew to his shadowed form.

"Abby—" Cash started, sounding surprised and pulling at his wrist.

But before her mind kicked into gear and she could think what she was saying (or doing, or *feeling*), she interrupted him.

"You be careful in that car of yours," she demanded, her voice hoarse with sleep and emotion.

She couldn't see it but she felt Cash's body go completely still.

She knew his eyes were on her but since she was having trouble breathing (oxygen, she felt, took priority), she didn't care.

His other hand came up and he pried her fingers loose from his wrist. After he succeeded in his task, he took her hand in his, palm cupped to palm, and brought the backs of her fingers to his lips.

She felt him kiss her lightly there before he murmured, "Abby, nothing's going to happen to me."

"Just promise you'll be careful," she whispered.

"Darling, I promise," he replied, his voice lower, deeper, throatier, and she felt it glide through her system, calming her bizarre panic before he went on. "Go back to sleep."

She nodded and settled back into the pillows as he kissed her hand again and let it go.

Then he was gone.

And Abby lay in his bed and wondered what just happened, why it happened, how she let it happen and what he thought about it.

Even though she considered all of this for a very long time, she never came up with any answers.

✗ ✗ ✗

Cash Fraser was in a good mood.

This wasn't entirely unusual but it wasn't commonplace either.

One of the reasons for his good mood was that he had a call from his uncle that afternoon.

Normally a call from his uncle would have the opposite effect on Cash's mood.

But the call meant that Alistair Beaumaris had seen the most recent picture of Abby and himself in the papers. The picture of Abby and Cash walking the dim, street-lit pavements of Bath, his arm around her, her body folded neatly into his side.

Since the idiot who leaked the story about Cash being the man behind the movie, Cash had many pictures of himself with women printed in various publications.

Not in one of them was he taking a romantic moonlit stroll.

Alistair, not being one for common niceties, hadn't led into it or danced around it. He simply proclaimed to Cash that he was aware there was a woman in his life, and as the head of the family, he wanted to meet her.

Alistair invited them for dinner next week.

Normally a decree like this from his uncle would lead to Cash attempting to find a diplomatic way to tell Alistair to go fuck himself.

This time, Cash accepted.

He liked the idea of Alistair Beaumaris, his oddly sweet wife and her remarkably tedious daughters sitting down to dinner with Abby.

And he didn't care which Abby was in attendance, the cool, sophisticated Abby or the delightful, hilarious Abby.

Either Abby would be perfect.

Cash saw this as an advantageous turn of events.

In their minds it would solidify Abby's place in his life even before he and Abby arrived at Penmort Castle for the anniversary celebrations.

It might even have the added bonus that he would stop getting e-mails, texts and drop-in visits from his annoying step-cousins.

Or, to be precise, it might stop the aggressive, relentless pursuit of one of his infinitely more tiresome step-cousins (for the other two were simply just tedious and tended to leave him alone, when he wasn't at the castle that was).

Further, Cash very much liked the idea that he'd get the opportunity to rub his revolting uncle's nose in his frustration.

Just over a year ago, Alistair Beaumaris approached Cash Fraser in an attempt, Alistair said at the time, to heal "the family breach."

Cash had never had any relationship with his father's family. Except, of course, when Cash was in his teens and Alistair's wife, Nicola, asked Cash to stay at Penmort a couple of times. And when she'd sent him birthday and Christmas cards, all of them he received when he was younger and far less affluent, all of them containing monetary presents, however, Cash suspected, Alistair knew nothing of the latter.

Further, Cash had never wanted any relationship with his father's family.

Even further, Cash had no desire to heal the breach.

Until he discovered the true reasons behind his uncle's advances.

And after that, he discovered other things about his uncle.

And after *that*, Cash had formed a plan.

Cash had now spent months stringing his uncle along with the ambiguous possibility that he, as a Beaumaris by blood, if not in name, might help his uncle save Penmort from the creditors to whom Alistair had foolishly fallen into debt.

Cash had also spent months being purposefully vague about the idea of marriage to one of Alistair's stepdaughters. A marriage Alistair wanted because it came with Cash's money. However, mostly, it was a marriage that came with the undeniable fact that any offspring (offspring that would inherit Penmort Castle) would be a true Beaumaris.

And that was most important of all to Alistair Charles Beaumaris.

However, Cash had no intention of doing either of those.

Instead, he intended to walk away from Penmort after the silver wedding anniversary of his aunt and uncle telling them, and their daughters, that they had exactly one month to remove their personal belongings.

Cash would be moving in.

He already owned it. Or he owned the notes against it.

In three weeks, he was going to foreclose.

Abby was just a distraction.

The addition of stunning, sultry, stylish, sophisticated, smart Abby was callous and even cruel, but Cash didn't care.

Alistair Beaumaris had made his mother suffer.

And the bastard had murdered his father.

He was going to pay.

The other reason Cash Fraser was in a good mood was Abby.

If he'd been a mad scientist and could build from scratch a woman to be on his arm when he walked into Penmort Castle for the first time as its true owner, both as a privilege of his birth (which had always been the case) and legally, he couldn't have done better than Abby.

And Abby, Cash decided the minute he heard the door open upstairs heralding her safe arrival last night, had ended her career as a paid escort.

He would be the first client she sold her body to and her last client, period.

He would make it worth her while to retire and they would remain as they were for as long as that lasted. When he moved on (some time from then, Cash imagined), he would leave her in circumstances where she could live in comfort *and* the style which she obviously enjoyed without her going back to her now-former occupation.

The only thing that could darken Cash Fraser's mood that day was Abby's behaviour that morning.

Not when, in semi-sleep, she'd trapped his body with her long limbs so he couldn't get out of bed without carefully extricating himself from her.

Not when she'd engaged him in drowsy conversation which included making sure he'd phone.

No, it was when she'd panicked about him driving his car.

One second she was adorably somnolent, the next her fear hit the room like a thunderclap.

It didn't take a clairvoyant to read a car accident was how she lost her husband.

On the one hand it had been a very long time since Cash had anyone who gave a damn if he arrived where he was going safely. Her demanding he be careful made him feel something he'd not felt since his grandfather had been alive. It was a time before Cash fully understood his mother was ill, for Hamish Fraser, his mother's father, had shielded him from it. But when his grandfather had died when Cash was nine, Cash learned swiftly his new role was a caregiver, not one to be cared for.

Abby's anxious demand had brought those long-dead feelings of safety and nurture back and they were far from unpleasant.

On the other hand, there were three things he did not like.

At all.

First, he didn't like the feeling behind her outburst. It was embedded in pain and Cash didn't like the thought of Abby experiencing pain.

Second, he didn't like what her pain meant. It meant she'd once had a man in her life that she deeply cared for and Cash found he disliked that idea intensely.

Further to this second point, Cash found the concept of being jealous of a dead man both ridiculous and abhorrent.

Nevertheless, he couldn't deny he was.

Third, he didn't want her to form an attachment to him.

What they had, even though they hadn't known each other long, Cash knew was good. And if the kisses they'd shared were anything to go by, it was going to get better, much better.

But it wasn't going to last.

He liked coming home to her. He liked being home knowing she was going to come to him (although he did *not* like waiting for her).

He liked her energy. He liked her company. He liked all that she embodied.

Abby was the kind of woman that Cash Fraser—forgotten and denied bastard son of an aristocrat—lived his life knowing he was neither entitled to nor could he expect to be by his side.

Like everything else in Cash's life, he'd had to earn such an opportunity.

After Alistair Beaumaris had won his court battles, regained the family fortune Anthony Beaumaris bequeathed on Myra Fraser, and in so doing bankrupted Cash's mentally unstable mother, Alistair had left Cash and Myra with very little. When Cash's grandfather died, there was even less. When Myra slit her wrists, there was even less.

Cash had fought his way out of poverty and into Oxford and spent many years shaping himself into a man on whose arm a woman like Abby belonged.

Even if he had to pay for her.

Perhaps *especially* since he had to pay for her, considering the astronomical amount he'd paid.

But he wasn't going to get used to Abby being in his life and he certainly couldn't allow her to do it.

He liked her company but he'd been alone a long time. He preferred to be alone and there wasn't a woman in the world, not even Abby with all of her beauty and humour and contradictions, who could change that.

On that thought, Cash turned into Abby's street and saw her lights on.

He was half an hour early but he wanted time with her before going to dinner at her neighbour's. With his work and her being late the night before, they hadn't had a lot of time to get to know one another, and Cash intended to rectify that.

As he parked in the drive behind her BMW he decided he'd take her away somewhere after he'd claimed Penmort. Somewhere they could be alone, no curious neighbours, no traffic delays and no work. Somewhere warm, where all she needed was a bathing suit.

He was considering his options (and leaning toward an island in Greece) when he turned the bell on her door.

It clanked discordantly.

He looked at it and noted it had to be as old as the house, and by the sound of it, desperately in need of servicing.

He waited impatiently for her to open the door. She had to be home, her car was in the drive and the lights were on in the front room and upstairs.

He turned the bell again.

He waited again.

When he was about to knock, or more to the point hammer on her door, he saw the light in the vestibule switch on and the door opened.

Abby stood there wearing an old, faded-blue flannel man's dressing gown that was far too big on her. Her hair was held back in a wide pale-pink band, her feet were bare and her eyes were surprised.

He watched as the surprise disappeared and the shutters came down.

"You're early," she told him, not moving from the door.

At her non-greeting Cash's good mood disappeared instantly.

Firstly, because she appeared to be barring him from the house.

Secondly, because she didn't seem happy to see him.

And lastly, and most importantly, because she was wearing another man's clothes.

"I finished early," he replied.

"You work until the wee hours, how did you finish early tonight?"

Having lost his patience, with artificial politeness Cash inquired, "Are we going to hold this conversation on the doorstep?"

She gave a start then her eyes darted away and she seemed to hesitate.

For a moment Cash thought she wasn't going to let him inside. Then she stepped back, opening the door.

"I'm sorry. Come in," she murmured.

He stepped in and was immediately surprised.

It was as if stepping over her threshold took him a step back one hundred and fifty years in time.

The vestibule was large. In fact it was huge. It, and the hall leading off of it, had black and white tiled floors that seemed to stretch on forever. Both rooms were cavernous with tall ceilings. Heavy pieces of antique furniture, all of which were well kept and high quality, were positioned here and there in the vestibule and hall. The furniture indicated either Abby's grandmother had good taste or Abby had given him a significant discount on the first quote for her fees.

"I'll take your coat." He heard her say.

He shrugged it off and ignored her outstretched hands, hanging it on the mirrored coat stand in the vestibule himself.

She watched him do this then her eyes moved to him before she said, "Come into the living room. I'm not ready yet. I'll get you a drink and then I'll finish upstairs."

He followed her into the front room that was the same as the hall. Enormous and well-furnished in quality antiques.

A tassel-bottomed, inviting, maroon velvet couch faced a large stone-mantel fireplace, two matching armchairs at its sides. There were handsome tables placed strategically around the seating area for comfort of use and aesthetic purposes.

The heavy, maroon velvet draperies were pulled back with silk cord tassels. The windows were dark, exposed to the night.

The couch sat in the centre, leaving a wide expanse of floor space available to the room. Most of it was empty except for a delicate writing desk, angled in the corner, facing the room.

The desk was not for show, it was obviously in use, the brown leather desk accessories filled with pens, upended notepads and bits of paper. The desktop held a tidy stash of stationery under a tasteful, round glass paperweight in which there was a swirl of colour. Also on top was an antique brass desk lamp, now lit, the lamp's shade a pink glass globe. The desk had a delicate chair upholstered in plum velvet.

There were several bookshelves standing around the room filled with books and displaying objects d'art, all of the pieces interesting, some of them, Cash noted, highly valuable.

Cash couldn't help but think that this was not where he saw Abby living. Although it was refined, yet warm and inviting, with silver-framed photos on the mantel, on the desk and dotting the shelves and tables, Cash felt it somehow didn't suit her.

He didn't know what would but this was just not it. It was too vast, too old, and it didn't have even a hint of her playful personality or her cosmopolitan flair.

"Whisky?" she asked when he'd stopped behind the couch and his gaze moved to her.

She'd barely entered the doorway. She was standing too far away and she looked preoccupied.

"Abby, come here," he demanded and her body went still for a moment before she seemed to force herself to move toward him. When she arrived within reach, he lifted his hand to curl his fingers around her neck. "You haven't even said hello," he told her, trying not to let her see that her behaviour was displeasing him.

She blinked, looking confused, then asked, "I haven't?"

Cash shook his head.

"I'm sorry," she whispered and she sounded like she was.

This went a long way towards dispelling Cash's irritation.

"Is there something on your mind?" he queried softly.

"I…" she started, then stopped, took a deep breath and continued, "You just surprised me, being early." Her hands came out at her sides. "I'm not ready yet."

The tension left Cash's body.

Women, it was his experience, liked to make an entrance. Even when Abby left his bathroom, her face cleaned of makeup, she still managed to make an entrance (mainly because she looked damned sexy in her clinging blue nightgown).

He bent his head to touch his lips to hers as he gave her neck an affectionate squeeze.

"Tell me where to find the whisky. I'll get it while you finish getting dressed," he told her.

She nodded while saying, "In the kitchen, I'll show you."

"I can find my way."

She seemed to be considering this, her eyes darting anywhere but him.

Finally she swallowed, her gaze came to his and she nodded again. "The cupboard by the—"

He brushed her lips with his again to interrupt her. "I'll find it. Go."

Her white teeth appeared as she bit the side of her lip but she gave another short nod, disengaged from his hand and walked from the room saying, "I won't be long."

Cash watched her go, or more to the point, Cash watched her ass sway as she walked away.

He found his way to the kitchen, even more ancient-looking (and warm and welcoming) than what he'd already seen of her house. He located the whisky, a heavy, cut-crystal tumbler, poured himself a drink and walked back to the living room.

Upon entry to the room, Cash saw a black cat with yellow eyes and long, silky fur sitting on the back of the couch, its tail swaying. Instead of the pert nose of a domestic feline, it had the nose of lion. This feature significantly increased the usual catlike disdain. It regarded Cash, blinked, jumped off the couch and trotted smartly from the room.

Cash ignored the cat and looked around.

There was an empty Denby mug on a coaster on the table in front of the couch, the stringed label of the wet tea bag still in it indicating it was a cup of some complicated herbal tea. Next to that was a cookbook with an excess of multi-coloured Post-it tags sticking out the sides, a plastic row of the Post-its sitting on top of the book, a Waterman pen resting at the book's side.

Cash went to the mantel and looked at the photos. Most of the pictures were older and in black and white. All of them were candid and in every one the subjects were smiling.

When Cash turned away from the mantel, his eyes caught on a large, silver-framed photo sitting ensconced on a bookshelf, and he froze.

It was Abby's wedding photo.

He stared at it from his place several feet away and it felt like the image depicted was burning itself in his brain.

In slow motion, his body came unstuck and he walked to the photo. His fingers curling around it, he brought it to him for closer inspection.

She'd been a young bride and a beautiful one. Her beauty hadn't matured to her current magnificence, but her obvious happiness made up for it.

And she was definitely happy.

The photo wasn't posed. Abby, wearing a complicated but not over-done strapless gown made, it appeared, entirely of lace, wasn't smiling.

She was beaming.

Her head was tilted back and her arm was wrapped around a tall, brawny, good-looking blond man who was smiling down at her. She was curled into him, her arm around his back, and Cash saw the man's arm was around her waist. Her fingers were touching his face and—the photo was black and white, so colour was not discernible—but it looked like she was using her thumb to wipe lipstick from his mouth.

The intimacy of the gesture, their shamelessly unhidden joy, Abby glowing in a way she had not even come close to giving him, coupled with the memory of Abby wiping his own mouth the day he met her, all of this made Cash feel like he'd swallowed a mouthful of acid.

The intensity of his reaction vaguely disturbed him, but he resolutely set it aside, put the photo down and threw back the whisky. It took him two drinks to drain the glass.

He headed to the kitchen to refill it and was back in the front room standing at her window, sipping at his whisky, lost in thought (most of these thoughts centred around when he would find the time to purchase a dozen new dressing gowns for her), when she returned.

"I'm ready," she announced and he turned to look at her.

She was wearing a body-hugging, jade-green jersey dress. It covered her completely from wrists to hem which touched her knees.

Even if it covered her almost fully, it left nothing to the imagination. The only expanse of skin that was exposed, outside of her legs, was at the wide, low-cut, V-neck. She was wearing strappy stiletto sandals in patent-leather, a shade darker than the green of her dress. She had on a pair of gold hoop earrings, her hair down around her shoulders in a sleek fall, her makeup more dramatic than the night before, but less than it had been the first night they went to dinner.

She wore no other adornment.

She looked, as ever, exquisite.

"I wasn't sure what to wear to a dinner party at crazy Mrs. Truman's. I've been thinking about it all day," she told him as she walked into the room.

This was the wrong thing to say.

Except for his enjoyable conversation with his uncle and when work intruded, he'd thought about nothing but her all day.

"I was thinking armour but I'm not sure a suit of armour goes with these shoes," she finished when she'd stopped in front of him, a small smile playing at her glossed lips, her head tilted back to look at him.

She meant to be amusing.

For the first time, Cash didn't laugh.

Her smile faltered and her head tilted to the side.

"Cash?" she called.

He didn't answer.

Instead, he looked to the window and caught their reflection in the glass.

She was standing close, head still tilted back to look at him but she wasn't touching him.

Even in the indistinct reflection of the glass he could see they complemented each other. It wasn't the first image he'd seen of them together and it wasn't the first time he recognised they looked good.

He liked the look of them together. They matched. She looked like she belonged with him. She looked like she was the kind of woman that would belong *to* him. If he was honest with himself, it aroused him, thinking of her as his.

But she wasn't his, no matter how much he'd paid for her.

She belonged to the man in that photo.

Her hand came to rest lightly on his arm, taking him out of his thoughts, and she asked, "Cash? Is everything all right?"

He threw back the remainder of his whisky, looked down at her and replied, "Fine."

"You're behaving funny," she told him.

"I have a lot on my mind," he returned.

She regarded him a moment and then asked, "Do you…" she paused then went on, "want to talk about it?"

"No," he answered truthfully.

She hesitated before she asked quietly, "Is it me? Have I done something—?"

Cash cut her off with a lie, "It isn't you."

Her brows came together and she bit the side of her lip again. As Cash watched her teeth sink into the flesh, he realised just how much he enjoyed the endearing vision of Abby biting her lip and his hand tightened around the glass.

At her next words, his body went still.

"You're lying," she accused.

He stared at her.

He had lied many times in his life. Either no one had ever figured it out or they'd never had the courage to call him on it.

"I'm not lying," he lied again.

She ignored his words, her hand moving away as she continued, "It's what happened this morning."

"Abby—" he started, but she shook her head and took a step away.

"I freaked you out," she informed him.

"You didn't."

Her arm came up and her fingers sifted through her hair in agitation. "I don't know what came over me. I don't know why I did what I—"

Cash cut her off. "I know why."

She blinked before she breathed, "What?"

"I know why," he repeated. "Your husband died in a car accident. This morning, for whatever reason, you had a panic attack. It happens," he dismissed it, not wanting to speak of it further, not wanting to speak of it *ever*.

"My husband?" she whispered.

"Abby, let's move on from this," he suggested, but it wasn't a suggestion as such but a gently worded demand.

She wasn't listening. "What do you know of Ben?"

That was when Cash lost his patience. When she said the man's name.

Therefore, when he spoke again, his voice was abrupt to the point of being harsh. "I know you married him in a lace dress. I know you loved him when you married him. And I know he died in a car accident. That's all I want to know, and, darling, this is the last time we'll speak of *Ben*."

She kept silent and they stared at each other for a long time. Finally, her eyes broke from his and she glanced away.

His desire to arrive early and get to know her better had succeeded.

He just didn't like what he'd learned.

Cash looked at his watch and saw they still had time before they had to be next door.

Regardless of the friction palpable in the room, he decided to make an effort to salvage the night.

"We have time," he told her. "I'll get you a drink."

"I'll get it," she replied and started to move to the door but Cash caught her arm.

"Abby, I said I'll get it."

She looked up at him and took in a breath before saying, "Okay."

It was then he realised he had no idea, outside red wine and herbal tea, what she drank.

To his displeasure, his voice sounded as aggravated as he felt when he asked, "What do you drink?"

Her eyes never left his even as her lips twitched. Cash recognised the humour of the situation and his body relaxed.

Slowly the tension slid out of the room.

Abby leaned into him, wrapping both hands around his upper arm.

"It's complicated. I'll teach you," she offered and led him to the kitchen.

It *was* complicated, including hammering some ice between tea towels to crush it (because she didn't like "big ice," whatever the hell that was), using only *chilled* diet cola, a shot of amaretto, a dash of cherry juice and three cherries.

The drink itself sounded disgusting. The exacting way she desired it was hilarious.

As she was sipping, her hip against the counter, Cash got close to her.

"You're particular about a lot of things," he remarked.

She awarded him with one of her mischievous grins. "Is that a nice way of saying I'm picky?"

Cash chuckled but didn't answer because she was right.

"That's okay," she announced. "I *am* picky."

This time, he laughed and through his laughter he saw her grin turn into a smile. Cash's good mood returned once it became clear they were over their current awkwardness.

As she took another sip, his arm slid around her waist and he brought her body to his from belly to thigh.

"You didn't call today," she told him as his hand slid from her waist, up her back, pressing her closer to him.

"I'm sorry, darling. I got busy," he replied as his other hand took her drink and placed it on the counter.

"That's okay," she whispered, staring at her drink.

Her head turned and he kissed her.

Immediately, and rather gratifyingly, her body leaned into his, one of her arms going around his waist, the other hand up his shoulder to slide along his neck and into his hair.

As disgusting as the drink sounded, on Abby, it *tasted* brilliant—fresh and sweet.

He deepened the kiss and she responded, pressing closer.

His body began to react. He felt it, he liked it, his arms crushed her to him and the kiss became even deeper, hotter and therefore less in his control.

In an effort to keep hold of his slipping control, he released her lips and slid his across her cheek to her ear.

"You're coming home with me tonight," he demanded.

Her neck twisted, turning to face him at first, he thought, to say something. But when he lifted his head to look at her, her face was flushed, her eyes were half-closed and she sought his mouth with her own.

When his tongue entered her mouth, he heard her low, soft moan.

Even though he hadn't asked her a question, he liked her answer.

They were, incidentally, late to Mrs. Truman's.

9

DINNER AT MRS. TRUMAN'S

Abby fixed her lip gloss with a trembling hand in the vestibule while Cash waited and watched.

Thoughts about what happened that night were colliding in her head and her legs were wobbly from the colossal (and very effective, Cash was a really good kisser, as in *really* good) make-out session in the kitchen.

She didn't know which to focus on first so she decided to ignore both of them and carry on with the evening. She'd think about it later. Much later. When Cash was gone, her house was fixed up and she was back to her normal existence.

Then she thought she didn't want to go back to her normal existence, but she didn't want to focus on that either so she decided to ignore that too.

She wrapped her pashmina around her shoulders, tucked her bag under her arm, grabbed the wine (Cash had the roses and chocolates, both of which Abby bought from two different exclusive shops in Clevedon so as not to put Mrs. Truman in a bad mood that they were trying to pass off rinky-dink hostess gifts) and put her hand on the latch.

"Ready?" she asked and Cash's eyes narrowed on her.

She didn't get a good feeling from his narrow look. She also didn't need another reaction from Cash that would freak her out. In an effort to stop him from giving into whatever had peeved him this time, she turned the latch and tugged open the door.

She'd barely stepped over the threshold when she came to a jarring stop. Cash's hand was on her arm waylaying her.

She looked down at his hand then up at him. "Cash, we're already late."

His hand went away, he placed the hostess gifts on the seat of the coat stand and he shrugged off his overcoat, murmuring, "It's freezing out there."

She realised his intent and her body got tense.

"We're only going next door," she told him, hoping he wouldn't put his overcoat on her. She didn't want him to keep being so sweet (when he wasn't angry at her that was).

She was pretty sure that most paid escorts didn't have intense conversations about their dead husbands nor did they cuddle up to their clients in bed late at night while their clients looked over papers.

She figured she wasn't doing her job very well.

The problem was Cash didn't seem to mind *at all*, which of course made it all worse.

She noticed with frustration that he wasn't listening to her. He swung his coat out and settled it on her shoulders.

"That's really unnecessary," she finished.

"Abby, it's below freezing," he told her.

She looked up at him and exclaimed, "We're walking next door!"

"And you're not going to get cold while we're doing it," he retorted.

"This is ridiculous," she grumbled. "What are *you* going to do? Now *you* don't have a coat."

"What I'm not going to do is stand out in the cold arguing," he declared with annoying logic.

"All right, fine," she muttered and turned toward the steps but something made her look to Mrs. Truman's and she halted at what she saw.

Kieran and Jenny were standing at the door, Mrs. Truman in the door, and they were all watching her and Cash.

Illuminated by Mrs. Truman's light, both Jenny and Kieran were wearing comically identical stunned expressions. Mrs. Truman was scowling.

"It's seven o seven," Mrs. Truman announced loudly. "Did I say dinner was at seven o seven? No, I did *not*. I said it was at seven o'clock." She paused and Abby saw her eyes snap to the bottle Abby was carrying then Mrs. Truman demanded to know, "Is that wine chilled?"

"Yes, Mrs. Truman," Abby called, deciding to ignore Kieran and Jenny's stunned looks as well as the fact that she was swimming in Cash's warm, heavy overcoat that smelled way too much like him.

With a hand at the small of her back, Cash led her down the steps and to Mrs. Truman's house. Kieran and Jenny were inside by the time they got there and Mrs. Truman slammed the door behind Cash.

"Cash, this is—" Abby started the introductions but Mrs. Truman interrupted her.

"Take off your coats. Give me that wine," she ordered then, for some demented reason, she shouted, "Marco!"

When everyone stood around waiting and nothing happened for a few moments, Jenny leaned toward Abby and asked under her breath, "Are we supposed to say 'Polo?'"

Abby felt a hysterical giggle start welling up inside her that she managed to tamp down when a young, dark-headed man wearing a white shirt and black trousers appeared.

"This is Marco," Mrs. Truman proclaimed with a flick of her wrist in his direction. "He's seeing to us tonight." Abby didn't know what that meant and didn't have a chance to ask. Mrs. Truman continued speaking, "Marco, take their coats. I'll take the wine to the kitchen. Then they need drinks." When Marco didn't move fast enough (though he did somewhat immediately move toward Jenny), Mrs. Truman snapped, "Chop chop! I'm not paying you to stand around and ogle pretty women!"

Marco took the coats, divested them of their gifts, and Mrs. Truman bustled them into her front room before she disappeared with her two bottles of *chilled* white wine.

Abby quickly performed the introductions, feeling acutely self-conscious as Cash shook Kieran's hand and bent low for Jenny to touch his cheek with hers.

Kieran Kane was Abby's height, thus shorter when she was wearing heels. He was slim, straight and had blond hair that looked highlighted but was actually his true colour, made thus by being streaked by the sun while he jogged and cycled like a madman. He had a permanent tan because when he wasn't working he was always outdoors or taking his wife on holidays where there were beaches.

Both Kieran and Jenny were trying to study Cash without appearing as if they were studying him (and, incidentally, they were failing).

For the first time in her life, Abby was in a social situation where she had no clue what to do.

How did one go about making what amounted to her "john" and her two best friends comfortable at a dinner party?

Luckily (or unfortunately, depending how you looked at it), Mrs. Truman forged into the breach.

She charged into the room carrying a vase filled with Abby's roses that had been quickly yet artfully arranged. She placed it on a table and demanded to know, "What are you doing standing up? Sit!"

They didn't sit because Marco followed Mrs. Truman and asked their drink preferences. When he got to Abby and she slowly explained how she wanted her amaretto and Diet Coke, Marco stared at her in horrified confusion.

"Diet Coke and amaretto?" Mrs. Truman snapped. "What kind of drink is that? And who *crushes* ice?"

Cash took pity on Marco at the same time tactfully ignoring Mrs. Truman.

While sliding his arm along Abby's shoulders, he said, "I'm sure Abby will settle for a glass of red wine."

To which Mrs. Truman retorted, "We're having *fish*. You don't drink red wine with *fish*." Then she turned to Marco. "Get her a white wine. Go on, go."

Marco quickly left (or more appropriately, *escaped*) and Mrs. Truman settled them into her furniture.

Abby looked at her surroundings and noted that Mrs. Truman was a packrat like her grandmother. Although she didn't have piles of books, newspapers and magazines, she had an overabundance of knickknacks, toss pillows and throws. This was all squeezed in between a crazy mix of furniture that dwarfed the room (even though Mrs. Truman's house was the exact same as Abby's and the room was huge).

The effect was claustrophobic.

Or maybe, Abby thought, it was all that was her *life* that was claustrophobic.

When Abby settled into the couch between Mrs. Truman and Cash, she caught Jenny's eye. Cash had placed his arm along the couch behind her, and as Abby looked at Jenny, Cash's fingers curled in to stroke her neck.

Jenny's eyes moved to his fingers and they widened.

Abby couldn't help it. It felt so nice she shivered.

Cash felt the shiver. He must have misinterpreted it as her being cold and his arm moved to rest around her shoulders, pulling her into the warmth of his side.

Jenny's eyes bugged out.

Abby's heart skipped a beat.

Unaware of any of this, Mrs. Truman asked, "Well? Isn't anyone going to speak?"

Surprisingly it was Cash who entered the conversational void by asking Mrs. Truman, "How long have you lived here?"

"Forty-five years," Mrs. Truman answered. "Morty moved me in on our wedding day."

"Morty?" Jenny asked.

"My husband, God rest him," Mrs. Truman replied.

Abby looked at her neighbour, who she'd known (and feared) for as long as she could remember, "You've never mentioned him before."

"You never asked," Mrs. Truman retorted smartly.

And Abby realised she hadn't. She'd never made any friendly overtures to Mrs. Truman at all, not when she was young, not since she'd been living next door. She'd just put up with her.

She knew her mother, father and Ben thought she was hilariously cantankerous and thus also never engaged her in simple conversation.

Abby's grandmother, however, often had Mrs. Truman over for tea or dinner which was how Abby got to know her, and Gram liked her very much.

The rest of the family never understood it.

Something about Mrs. Truman's reply made Abby feel uncomfortable.

"When did he pass?" Kieran asked softly and Mrs. Truman's eyes moved to him.

"Thirty-six years ago. He married me when I was twenty-five and we were together for nine happy years. Then one day, he was gone. Hit by a bus," Mrs. Truman answered matter-of-factly but her voice was far less severe than normal.

Even though she noticed this, Abby didn't process it.

Mainly because she'd been married to Ben when she was twenty-five and she'd had nine happy years with him before he died.

"I'm sorry, Mrs. Truman," Jenny said gently, her eyes shifting between the older lady and Abby because this coincidence was definitely not lost on her, and Mrs. Truman's back went up.

"I'm sorry too, been sorry for thirty-six years. As I'm sure you could tell. Now, let's not talk about maudlin things. You," she pointed at Kieran, "why are you so tan? It's January, no one should have a tan in January. Don't you work?"

At that, Kieran explained his love of cycling and holidays with his wife while Marco served their drinks. Conversation, shockingly, flowed easily from there.

And this was because of Kieran and also Cash.

Both men politely asked questions of Mrs. Truman or politely answered her nosy ones.

For her part, Mrs. Truman remained crabby and curious but she was unexpectedly forthright. Therefore Abby learned more about her neighbour in half an hour than she'd known in thirty-eight years.

She also learned about Cash.

Not that he shared more than absolutely necessary when asked questions. More that he was polite and solicitous to the older woman. It wasn't something she expected from the dynamic, imposing, impatient Cash Fraser. She didn't know what she expected. Brooding silence maybe, or perhaps edgy tolerance. Not a man relaxed and at ease with his company and surroundings.

At this, Abby felt the tension ebb out of her body and she started to enjoy the evening.

Mrs. Truman wasn't a gracious host but you couldn't say she wasn't an interesting one. As the conversation flowed Abby realised that the old woman was enjoying herself, and it was clear she was blossoming under the men's attention, especially Cash's (as would anyone, Abby had to admit). She was still grouchy, but humorously so.

Abby also realised that because of her reputation it was unlikely Mrs. Truman had a lot of dinner parties. She mentally kicked herself for being so lost in her own troubles she didn't notice that, when Abby's grandmother died, her lonely neighbour had lost her old friend who'd lived next to her for forty-five years.

By the time Mrs. Truman announced it was time to eat and demanded they all go to the dining room, Abby felt Cash deserved some gratitude for his efforts.

While Mrs. Truman headed out to see to the meal, Abby grabbed Cash's hand, delaying him as Kieran and Jenny moved from the room.

He stopped and his chin tipped down in order that he could look at her inquiringly.

She smiled up at him and told him in a whisper, "You...are...the...*master*."

His eyes lit with humour at her words but he asked, "I'm sorry?"

"Mrs. Truman. You're handling her like a master. I know you can't tell because, well, she's Mrs. Truman, but I think she's half in love with you," Abby informed him.

The light in his eyes stayed there but it grew warmer just as his head descended and his face disappeared in the hair by her ear.

"I hope, when we're alone later, you'll still think I'm a master," he murmured teasingly, and Abby's body gave a delicious tremble right before all the tension that had ebbed out of her came slamming right back.

What did *that* mean?

She decided instantly that she did *not* want to know.

Cash felt her body go solid and apparently her reaction amused him. She knew this because he chuckled before he led her into the dining room.

The minute they entered, Mrs. Truman bossily informed them they were switching partners, and as the men made their way to their assigned seats, Jenny grabbed Abby's forearm and tugged.

When she had Abby's ear close to her mouth, she hissed, "What on earth is going on?"

Abby knew what her friend was referring to but she decided to play dumb.

"What do you mean?" Abby whispered.

"I mean you and Hunky International Spy Chaser, that's what I mean," Jenny whispered back.

"I don't know what you're talking about." Abby was still playing dumb and still whispering, not wanting anyone to hear.

Jenny's fingers tightened on Abby's arm. "Bickering on the front step like an old married couple. The finger action on the couch. *Snuggling*," she hissed. "*In company*," she went on. "You're supposed to be his girlfriend but this is..." she hesitated. "I don't know what it is!" she finished.

"Jenny—" Abby started, but Mrs. Truman was getting cross at the delay.

"What are you two ninnies whispering about? Come on, share with the group," she called.

Abby turned toward the table, thankful for once at Mrs. Truman's interference, and answered, "Nothing, Mrs. Truman."

"Women problems," Jenny, for some momentarily-possessed-by-Satan reason, explained.

"Oh dear, you aren't pregnant are you?" Mrs. Truman asked Jenny as Abby took her seat next to Kieran and Jenny slid into hers next to Cash.

"Um, no," Jenny answered and her eyes moved to Kieran.

It was an insensitive question even though Mrs. Truman didn't know that (and probably wouldn't care). They'd been trying now for three years with no luck.

Mrs. Truman speared Abby with her eyes, "Please tell me *you* aren't."

Abby was taking a sip of her wine when the question was asked and she choked in horror and disbelief before saying, "Me? Pregnant?"

Mrs. Truman rolled her eyes to the ceiling and for some ungodly reason started talking to Abby's grandmother. "I tell you, Meg, children these days. There's no controlling them." Mrs. Truman looked back to Abby but jutted a thumb at Cash. "I don't care how handsome and charming he is. Don't let him get you into trouble."

Kieran burst out laughing, Cash turned a devastating smile in Abby's direction and Jenny stared at her speculatively.

Abby hoped the floor would form a mouth, open up and swallow her whole.

"Mrs. Truman, why don't you stab me with your butter knife?" Abby requested.

"And why would I do a fool thing like that?" Mrs. Truman shot back but even as she did so her lips were twitching.

"Because it'd be less painful," Abby returned blandly, and for the first time ever, Abby saw Mrs. Truman laugh.

Although she was trying to be funny, and she was weirdly pleased with herself for making Mrs. Truman laugh, Abby didn't think anything was amusing.

Instead, she thought, with everything that had happened over the past six years, and everything that had happened recently, and everything that was *going* to happen, it was high time to get drunk.

❧ ❧ ❧

"Abigail, you're inebriated," Mrs. Truman remarked jovially—yes, jovially!

"Am not," Abby returned cheerfully, but this was a lie, because she was.

It was after their delicious four-course meal (not including the cheese tray), served by the silent Marco. They were having after-dinner drinks in the living room.

Jenny had gotten over her freak out at Abby and Cash's behaviour and also conquered her fear of Mrs. Truman. Once she entered the conversation, drawing Cash out more, familiarly teasing Kieran and amusingly going head to head with Mrs. Truman, the evening became fun.

Abby joined in and through it all she had more wine than was prudent.

But she didn't give a good God damn.

She didn't like what had happened to her life, but she weirdly *did* like what was currently happening to it, even though she knew she shouldn't. It wasn't sensible.

Further, she was scared silly at what was *about* to happen at the same time she couldn't wait.

If all that didn't make you want to get drunk, indeed *deserve* to get drunk, Abby didn't know what did.

"I hope you can handle sick. Men, it's my experience, can't handle sick. Or poo," Mrs. Truman, who likely was also a little intoxicated if her new conversational gambit was anything to go by, said to Cash. "Sick and poo and men do not mix," she declared. "If you need me later, call me. I can handle sick. My dogs get sick all the time." She paused and added as an informational afterthought, "They also poo."

"Where *are* your dogs?" Jenny asked, leaning toward Mrs. Truman as if her answer would cure world hunger, proving it was highly likely she, too, was less than sober.

"They're locked in my room. Probably *pooing* on my bed," Mrs. Truman answered then cackled loudly as if this comment was the height of comedy.

Abby and Jenny agreed because they giggled right along with her.

"Why are we talking about poo?" Kieran muttered to Cash, and Cash's response was to shake his head.

This caused more gales of laughter from the women.

At that Cash got to his feet. He did so with his hands on Abby's waist, pushing her up in front of him.

Once they were standing, Abby gazed up at him and asked, "Are we leaving?"

"Yes, darling, before you get any more wine in you and pass out on Mrs. Truman's floor, we're leaving," Cash replied.

"Ooo, he called you 'darling,'" Jenny burst out, drunkenly forgetting that Abby's place in Cash's life didn't exactly garner endearments. Then in a colossal mood swing, she turned a glare at Kieran. "Why don't you call me 'darling,' darling?"

"Because you're not my darling," Kieran replied on a grin. "You're my pumpkin."

Jenny's glare darkened ominously. "I don't want to be a pumpkin. A pumpkin is a vegetable. A darling is..." she faltered then declared, "A darling!"

"How about 'sweetheart?'" Kieran suggested.

Jenny appeared to be considering this before she grumbled, "Darling's better."

Kieran's grin didn't waver as he explained, "I'm not a darling type of guy, pumpkin."

"Well, I'm not a pumpkin type of girl, *darling*," Jenny shot back.

"Time to call it a night," Mrs. Truman decreed, slowly getting to her feet. "Marital tiffs always herald time to call it a night."

At this Abby burst out laughing.

Cash started to manoeuvre her laughing form from the room but Mrs. Truman interceded.

"You men, get the coats. We'll wait here where it's comfortable," she ordered bossily.

Kieran got to his feet muttering, "Your wish..." and he bent to kiss the top of his still-irritable wife's head.

With a smile on her lips Abby watched this, but her attention was diverted when Cash's hand came up, curled around her neck and he gave her an affectionate squeeze before he left the room.

She had to admit, she really liked it when Cash did that.

Abby watched him leave, then forgetting her audience, she sighed.

"He's *luscious*," Jenny proclaimed, her eyes on the door Cash just went through.

For one beautiful moment, forgetting herself and her circumstances, in the direction of her friend Abby breathed a very girlie, "I *know*."

Mrs. Truman broke into this exchange by starting, "When Morty died," and Abby and Jenny's eyes turned to her, their drunken glow slipping at the older woman's words, "I promised myself never again. Never again."

Abby and Jenny kept watching as her face changed to an expression neither of them had ever seen, not just from Mrs. Truman, but on anyone. It was forlorn, full of regret and difficult to witness.

Abby watched as Mrs. Truman's attention focused on her.

"After your man died, Meg and I talked about you. We talked about you all the time. She worried so much. She told me how grief-stricken you were. She thought you'd never recover. Meg worried you'd end up just like me."

Abby's throat closed and Mrs. Truman's voice got soft when she carried on.

"I like him, this new one. Your grandmother would be pleased, Abigail." Her voice dipped to a whisper. "So very pleased."

Abby felt tears well in her eyes as guilt tore at her heart because, even though it wasn't her idea to have this dinner, her "new man" wasn't her new man at all.

The entire situation was a deception and she was inadvertently making a fool of her new friend.

Her voice was hoarse when she started, "Mrs. Truman—" but she didn't get to finish, not that she knew what to say.

The men came in bearing coats and the mood and moment was broken.

It was broken further when Abby tried to give Mrs. Truman a hug, not only as a thank you for dinner, but as a gesture of newfound camaraderie.

Mrs. Truman was having none of it.

"I do *not* hug," she announced, rearing away from Abby and putting her hand up at the same time to ward her off. "Americans *hug*. Englishwomen kiss cheeks and even then they do their very best *not* to *touch*," she said her last word as if the thought of touching was repugnant.

Abby was for the first time not offended or irritated by her cranky neighbour.

She simply said, "Very well, Mrs. Truman. You get the English way in your house. But when you come over to my house, you have to hug me goodbye."

"I think not," Mrs. Truman snapped.

"I think *yes*," Abby retorted.

"No," Mrs. Truman returned.

"We might hold hands too," Abby threatened on a tease and Mrs.

Truman made a "humph" sound, but Abby was guessing there wasn't a lot of feeling in that "humph."

Abby smiled at her and said softly, "Good night, Mrs. Truman."

Mrs. Truman's face ever-so-slightly warmed. "Good night, Abigail."

Cash settled his coat on her shoulders, more farewells were exchanged and she and Cash led the way, Kieran and Jenny following, out of the house.

On the pavement in front of Mrs. Truman's house they said their goodbyes with Jenny grasping Abby's hand and whispering a firm, "We have to chat. *Call me.*"

Abby pulled away and with false brightness in the face of impending doom, declared, "Will do."

Cash steered her to her house, took the keys from her, opened the latch and pressed her inside, following her.

He then closed the door behind them and took his coat from her shoulders, hooking it on her coat stand.

Abby watched him doing this.

Then it dawned on her drunken mind that the night was over.

It was then it hit her that they were in her house. Something she didn't want. Something she needed to protect herself from. Something that she could just come to terms with if he stayed in the hall, living room and kitchen—common areas that didn't intrude too much on her precious memories.

However, Cash wasn't staying in the vestibule. He snapped off the light switch and grabbed her hand.

Then he led her to the stairs.

Panic beginning to pierce her drunken state, she pulled at her hand (which didn't stop him) while asking, "What are you doing?"

"Taking you to bed," he replied calmly, turning at the stairs, and he had her up three of them when she came to a dead halt and he stopped with her.

"I can get to bed on my own," she told him.

"You aren't sleeping on your own," he returned.

The breath squeezed out of Abby's lungs and the beginning panic bloomed like a mushroom cloud.

She forced it back and said, "I thought we were going to your place."

He was one step up and looking down at her. "We were, until you got drunk. But then you got drunk. Now we're staying here."

He turned away and started to move forward, but she stayed where she was and declared, "I'd prefer to stay at your place."

His torso twisted and he looked back down at her. "And I'd prefer to stay here."

"Why?" she asked, her voice, she heard with irritation, sounding slightly shrill, hinting at the panic she felt.

With a firm tug on her hand, he forced her up to the step where he was standing. Then he dropped her hand and both of his came to rest on her neck.

"Because it's late and you're inebriated. You get in the car you're likely to fall asleep. I don't want you intoxicated, asleep and in a car. I want you intoxicated, awake and in a bed. This is the closest one available, unless you'd like to ask Mrs. Truman if she has a guest bedroom."

"Cash—" she started to protest but his thumb came to rest on her lips, effectively silencing her.

Once there, it slid across her lower one and she found she liked that so much she couldn't speak, much less protest.

"All day," he said in that deeper, sexier, throatier burr that she liked so much, "I've been thinking about what I'd do to you tonight. All... fucking...day."

His thumb disappeared from her lip, his fingers slid into her hair to cup the back of her head as he got closer at the same time her heart started beating faster.

"And after our time in the kitchen," he went on, "all night, I've been waiting to get you to bed." The thumb of his hand still at her neck put pressure on her jaw to tip her head back farther. "And I think you know how I feel about waiting."

She couldn't say anything. She'd lost the ability to speak. Even if she could, she still couldn't.

Because he kissed her.

And it wasn't like any of the times before. This one was different. She knew it immediately. This one was not in her control and neither was it in his. This one was sweltering from its start, burning through her.

This one was leading somewhere.

And Abby wanted to go there.

She felt a thrill race through her that was only partly fear (a *small* part), but mostly it was something else entirely.

Her mouth opened under his, his tongue slid inside and the minute it did she was lost.

She didn't care they were in her house. She didn't care that she didn't want him there. She didn't care that her feelings were confused. She didn't care that losing control put her on even shakier ground. And lastly, she didn't care that she was supposed to be keeping her head screwed on straight and she most assuredly was not.

She didn't care about anything but his lips on hers, his tongue in her mouth and the amazing things her body was feeling.

She melted into him, her arms going around his back, her body pressing against his.

At her uninhibited response, his hand fisted in her hair, sending tingles from her scalp straight down her spine (and other areas besides). The fingers of his other hand tightened on her neck as he leaned into her, bending her back, deepening the kiss.

She felt this new intensity surge through her system, making her knees go weak.

Somewhere in the back of her mind it registered that it had never been this good.

Never, never, *never*.

And she wanted more.

She let him take the weight of her as she concentrated less on remaining upright and more on the pleasant, heady sensations rushing through her.

His mouth tore from hers, his hands disappeared and she teetered a moment before he bent and lifted her in his arms. She made a noise, half of surprise, half from desire. Her arms curled around his neck, his mouth came back to hers and he kissed her while carrying her to her room.

And Abby liked that he carried her, the strength of him, his mouth on hers. It made her world tilt. She felt wonderfully dizzy and hoped the world would never come right again.

He set her at her feet beside the bed, and mouth still on hers he shrugged off his suit jacket, dropping it to the floor.

Then he leaned into her and she was falling back onto the bed, his heavy solid weight on top of her.

She forgot how this felt, having a man cover you, and she realised she missed it. The warmth of it, the safety of it, how it could shut out everything else and make just the two of you be the whole world.

But even though this thought sifted through her brain, Ben didn't enter her mind.

It was all Cash, his long, hard body, the smell of his woodsy, spicy cologne, his weight, his mouth. All of him.

Every single inch.

She found she craved him. All of a sudden she couldn't get enough, pulling his shirt from his trousers, her hands slid up the hot skin of his back as he kissed her and she kissed him back.

He rolled, taking her with him, yanking her skirt up around her hips as he did so. He sat up, forcing her to straddle him. His mouth broke from hers and he pulled at his tie. The knot coming free, he slid it from his collar and tossed it aside.

All the while Abby's mouth was at Cash's neck, tasting his skin (and liking it), gliding along his strong jaw and her hands were at the buttons of his shirt, shaking with desire as she undid them.

While she was at her task, he grasped her dress, pulling it up and forcing her up with it. She happily lifted her arms as he tugged it off and threw it aside.

Then their mouths collided, his hands roaming, skin against skin, and it felt as if every centimetre he touched was connected straight between her legs.

His mouth disengaged and he pressed into her, arms around her, torso twisted and she heard his shoes hit the floor. He pulled back and she finished with his buttons, tugged the shirt over his shoulders, down his arms, dislodging his hands from her skin. Quickly, because she wanted them back, she yanked the shirt free of his body and tossed it away.

His arms came around her, crushing her as he fell back, then rolled, mostly on top of her. His mouth glided down her jaw, her neck, her chest, then it was closing on her nipple over her bra.

"Cash…" she breathed, her hands sliding slowly into his hair.

She gasped as he pulled her nipple sharply into his mouth.

It had been so long since she had this, her body so deprived, Cash so warm and heavy, his hands causing shivers, his mouth talented, the heat shot from her nipple to between her legs and she felt herself quivering.

It was early but she was ready.

She was ready *now*.

Her hand travelled down his arm, fingers finding his wrist, she brought his hand to the heat of her and pressed it in right where she needed it.

"Jesus, Abby," he growled against her nipple and even his voice, rougher than ever, made her wet.

His lips came to hers, and needing no more coaxing, his fingers took over. As his tongue slid inside her mouth, his hand slid inside her panties and he was touching her.

She gasped at the sweetness of it, arching her back, straining her hips against his hand as his finger found her and started to move.

It was great.

No, it was awesome.

No, it was *amazing*.

So much so she had to tell him.

"Cash," she breathed. "Don't stop. That's amazing."

She felt his smile against her mouth and luckily he didn't stop. He kept going. He kept going until she was squirming against his hand and she felt it. It was coming and she knew by the feel of it that it was going to shatter her world.

But something wasn't right. She couldn't do it alone.

No, she could.

She just didn't *want* to.

"You," she said urgently, her breath coming in pants.

His mouth had gone away but he hadn't. When her eyes partly opened she saw he was close and watching her.

"You," she repeated, turning into him, losing control, coming close to letting go and letting it happen.

"Abby," he murmured and her hand went to his stomach, sliding down, feeling his hardness, hearing his soft groan at her touch and she knew she wanted all of him.

If she had a choice between breathing and having Cash inside her at that moment she would have chosen the latter.

"Cash," she breathed, tugging at his belt. "Stop."

He gave a short, harsh laugh at her words. "Darling, I *can't* stop."

"No, don't stop. I mean…" She pressed her torso deeper into his and before sanity could invade or she lost herself in what his hand was doing, she whispered insistently, "I want it to happen with you. Please, I want you inside me."

She no sooner got out the words then his hand went away and so did he. She blinked in the darkness at the sudden cold, opening her mouth to object, but then her panties were pulled down her legs and he rolled over her.

She felt his hand between them working at his trousers right before his mouth crushed hers in a mind-boggling kiss.

Her legs opened in invitation, his hips slid between, his tongue touching hers, and then he was inside her, buried to the hilt, filling her completely.

And *that* felt *beyond* amazing.

"Yes," she whispered as he moved, not slowly but fast, hard, hot, her body jolting lusciously with his thrusts.

She wrapped her arms around him as he pulled one of her legs around his waist, her other thigh he pushed up against his side, giving him better access so he could go deeper, thrust harder, and she liked it.

No, she loved it.

And she felt it. She knew it was back, ready to overwhelm her.

"Cash," she gasped and his mouth moved from the skin below her ear as his head came up so he could look at her.

"I want it." His words were a demand uttered in a husky rumble that so affected her, Abby slid over the edge.

"Cash," she repeated on a soft cry as it started.

His fingers drove into her hair, tugging it gently, pulling her head back so her neck arched even further than it did naturally with her climax.

His mouth went to her neck, she felt his lips there, his tongue touching her, his body moving inside hers, but it was mostly the scrumptious, momentous, earth-shattering explosion of her body she was feeling.

And it *was* scrumptious, momentous and earth-shattering, pounding through her body as Cash pounded inside her.

After, when Abby was coming down, her body tight around his (both her limbs and other better places), was when she heard him pull in his breath. He drove into her one last succulent time and she knew she had him.

And that was earth-shattering too.

When they were done, his weight relaxed into her. Her arms flexed, her thigh tightened at his side and her leg curled deeper around his waist, and she found, stupidly and ridiculously, she wanted to hold on to him. She wanted to hold on to the man who lit welcoming lights, who worried about her when she was late, who showed patience with an old, lonely woman, who found his mother after she committed suicide and was brave enough to talk about it.

She wanted to hold on to Cash Fraser and the magic of this moment forever.

Then sanity, as it had a way of doing, invaded.

And she wondered what, in all holy hell, she was doing.

She'd just *given* herself to him.

This wasn't supposed to happen.

Then, heartbreakingly, she remembered Ben.

There had been no one since him. When she was with him, she never even considered another man.

Now, she'd just let Cash fuck her.

In fact, she'd practically begged him to do it.

What was the matter with her?

Cash's face came out of her neck as his hand released her hair.

"Abby."

She tipped her chin down to look at him in the shadows, wondering how she was going to get out of her latest, stupid, stupid, stupid Abby behaviour.

She was thinking, hysterically, she'd blame it on the drink before he spoke.

"Don't fucking shut down on me." His voice was a warning, holding an edge of anger, making her scarily aware that, even in the dark, he could read her.

"I'm not shutting down," she lied.

"You fucking well are," he clipped and since he was using the word "fuck" a lot, she knew he wasn't edging toward anger. He was there. Before she could process this (as in let it freak her out), he went on. "What just happened was good."

"Cash."

"I don't give a fuck about whatever fucking rules you have. That was *you* that you just gave me. I wanted it. You gave it. I took it and I'm not fucking giving it back."

"Cash—" she started again.

"No, Abby. You're mine," he declared and genuine fear started edging out the beginnings of panic, the despair at her reckless behaviour and the full-tilt guilt.

"What does that mean?" she whispered, and his hand came to rest against the side of her face.

"Five days ago, I paid for a part of you. Just now, you *gave* me all of you. And I'm not fucking giving it back."

She pulled in breath at what he said and what he might mean but he kept talking.

"This is mine," he said, moving his hips and she couldn't help it. He was still inside her, it felt good and her own hips pressed into his in response.

Then his mouth came to hers.

"And this mine," he murmured before he brushed his lips against hers then his hand left her face to trail down her side. "And this is mine," he went on, his hand coming back to her face, his thumb gliding along her cheek. "And, darling, this is mine."

"Cash, I think it's safe to say you're freaking me out," she informed him softly and honestly, her voice proving her words true.

She saw in the dark his white teeth flash in a smile as his anger disappeared.

Then he whispered, "Get used to that feeling, Abby. Because when something's mine, it's *mine*, and I never give it up without a fight. And even if someone's fool enough to fight me, they never win."

"Cash, you can't have me. I'm not yours to have," she told him, her voice now sounding a wee bit desperate.

His mouth came back to hers and she *felt* that he was still smiling.

"Oh yes, darling, you are," he said there and he kissed her.

And right before his tongue touched hers and she lost herself again, Abigail Butler thought, *Oh bloody hell. Now what have I done?*

❧ 10 ❧

THE MORNING AFTER

Cash woke to find Abby curled beside him on the bed in the curve of his outstretched arm. Her knees were touching his calf, one of her hands resting lightly on his stomach, her head was on her other hand on the mattress, forehead pressed into his side.

Though it was an odd position, it felt both intimate and poignant.

He felt something else and glanced down to see Abby's cat was curled between their bodies, snug in the crook of her lap.

He rarely slept the night with a woman, preferring his own bed and the statement it made when he left them to theirs.

However, every once in a while, particularly if his partner had satisfied him, he'd break this rule.

But he'd never shared a bed with a cat.

He looked to his left and saw her clock announcing it was four thirty.

Staying at her house added an hour to his commute. He liked to be in the office by seven at the latest.

He needed to get up, get home, showered and to work.

He didn't move.

He listened to the silence of Abby's house and allowed himself a moment to process the conflicting emotions of triumph and disquiet that he felt.

Cash Fraser had had many women in his life.

Two of them were long-term relationships.

Neither of these ended well. They didn't like his work schedule which left little time for them. They didn't like his travel and he wouldn't take them along as he didn't like distractions. And they tried to impose restrictions on his life and activities which Cash would not abide.

Therefore, both times, he ended it.

The other women, often enjoyable, sometimes disappointing, were mostly acquired to satisfy him in bed.

None of them were even close to what he had from Abby, out of bed, and now in it.

Last night, with her abandoned response, Abby had taken him somewhere no woman had shown him. He'd never had a woman who let the barriers down so thoroughly, inviting him inside, not just to experience fucking great sex ending in a staggering orgasm, but something far deeper.

He didn't know he wanted it. In fact, if he'd been asked before he had it, he would have said he didn't.

But once it was his, he claimed it with a ferocity that surprised even Cash.

Since the day they met, Cash wondered which of her responses was genuine and which was an act for which she'd been paid.

Last night wasn't an act.

The arrangement was he could fuck her only after they'd gone to the castle.

She'd almost begged him to take her last night, giving him herself for free.

Now she was his, even more than when he'd paid for her.

The second time was nearly as good as the first. He'd taken off the rest of their clothes and he'd taken his time.

He searched for her sweet spots, found them and manipulated them ruthlessly until she was writhing underneath him and begging for release.

While he was doing this, she was doing much the same, her hands and mouth on him, her long limbs tangling with his, her touch bold. She was open and giving of herself and her responses while offering pleasure in return for what she took.

Like everything else about her, it was exquisite.

This was why he felt triumph.

The disquiet he felt was twofold.

Firstly, and less importantly, was his overwhelming desire to possess her. He wasn't certain what he wanted from her and there was nothing in Cash's life of which he wasn't certain.

He knew it was cliché, his intent to conquer the professional escort, break through her façade, force her response, make her his.

He thought little of this. There were many things Cash Fraser had desired in life, things others would have thought unobtainable, and with single-minded purpose, he got them.

Abby would be no different.

And the minute she told him she wanted him inside her, he decided he wanted *all* of her.

And that was what he would have.

Secondly, from the beginning something didn't strike true about Abigail Butler, Paid Escort.

She'd hid it better at first, but he felt, especially looking back, there were signs that what she wanted him to see and what was real were two different things.

She had the bearing, the coolness, the clothing, the car, all the trappings.

But her home, her cat, her friends, her nosy neighbour, her heartbreaking history and the way she behaved with him didn't quite add together.

Not that anyone in her business wouldn't have a life outside the job. It was just that she let him in so quickly.

Cash felt something was not quite right.

And it disturbed him.

On that thought, deciding to concern himself with this later and start his day, he slid away from her carefully, not waking her, but her cat gave a tired mew.

He strolled into the hall and saw what he didn't see last night. There were boxes and tools everywhere, which he found surprising. The rooms on the first floor were clean, tidy and uncluttered.

He dodged them as best he could in the dark and headed toward where he guessed (rightly, in a way) he'd find the bathroom.

He pulled on the light and stopped dead.

Except for the toilet, the room was gutted. Bare floorboards, no tile, no tub, no sink. The back wall looked like it had been set with new plasterboard, the floor underneath had new boards.

Clearly Abby was having some work done on her house.

Leaving those unappealing facilities, he turned out the light and walked up the stairs to the top floor. The house was huge, there had to be another bathroom.

He located it but discovered that the only thing that worked was the light.

He walked back down to her room, pulled on his boxers and headed down past the ground floor, where he knew from his movements last night there was no bathroom, to the garden level.

He found another bathroom, as ancient as the one on the top floor.

It, too, was not functioning.

"What the fuck?" he muttered, annoyed. He retraced his steps, using the only facilities available to him and went back to her room.

He got fully dressed and sat on the edge of her bed. Her cat's head came up and he gave an inquiring meow but kept his place.

Sometime after Cash's departure from the bed, she'd moved up and curled into Cash's pillow, her arms tight around it.

Cash shifted the hair off her neck and bent to her ear.

"Abby, I'm leaving."

She stirred slightly and her head turned toward his voice, but she stayed silent.

"Abby," he called when she didn't have a further response.

She sleepily got up on her elbow, her hand pulling her hair out of her face holding it there as her eyes moved to the clock.

Then her head turned to him.

"Do you always get up this early?" she murmured in her soft, sexy, very effective, early morning voice.

"Yes," he replied, his mind doing a scan of his schedule and finding, to his disappointment, that he didn't have time to do what he very much wanted to do to Abby before he needed to be at his first meeting.

Dropping her hair, she fell back to the pillows and told him, "That would suck."

He smiled at her quiet, amusing words, and then asked, "Abby, what's going on with your bathrooms?"

He felt rather than saw her body go still.

And he also thought this was an unusual reaction to a simple question.

Her head turned on the pillow to look up at him. "I'm having a few problems with the plumbing."

It would appear, even to someone who knew nothing about such things, with three bathrooms out of commission, she was having more than "a few problems."

She was back to withholding from him and Cash didn't like it.

"Do you need me to call someone to come and look at it?" Cash inquired, attempting patience in order to control his irritation that after all they'd shared last night she'd fallen back to earlier habits.

She got up on her elbow again and replied, "No, it's under control."

"Under control is having at least one working shower," Cash returned. "Not under control in a house this size, or any house for that matter, is having only a working toilet."

"It's being taken care of," she told him.

"When?" he pressed.

Abby sat up fully, holding the covers to her naked body and replied, "They're working on it."

Cash was finished with the conversation.

"I'll make a call," he declared. "I'll send someone to have a look at what's happening and keep them on target. You'll have a working bathtub by tomorrow night."

When she spoke again, her voice had lost that early morning sweetness and he knew she was getting angry.

"Cash, I'm taking care of it."

"No, you *were* taking care of it. Now *I'm* taking care of it."

"Cash!" she snapped.

"I'm not discussing this," he finished.

"Well I bloody well am," she retorted.

"Abby," he stated in a way that made it clear this conversation was over.

"Cash," she mimicked his tone.

At her words and her tone, Cash wanted to laugh at the same time he wanted to shout.

She was quite often unbelievably adorable, even when she was angry.

And there weren't many people who would go head to head with him. In fact, at that moment he couldn't think of a single soul who would be that stupid.

Or that brave.

Instead of laughing or shouting, he decided to try a different tack to get her to submit.

His hands went under her arms and he pulled her naked body out of the bed and across his lap. She pressed her palms against his chest and tried to pull away, but he wrapped his arms around her, crushing her to him, her hands caught between them.

"What do you think you're doing?" she snapped right before he kissed her.

At first she struggled. It took a while for him to break through but finally she started melting. Her hand forced its way from between them up to his shoulder, his neck and into his hair, her other arm going down and around his back. She pressed her torso to him and kissed him back.

He reacted instantly to her capitulation, his body started to heat, and he felt himself begin to get hard.

His lips slid from hers to the expanse of skin on her neck below and just behind her ear that he knew was highly sensitive. He wasn't disappointed. She trembled in his arms and he liked the feel of it.

"Cash, please," she whispered in his ear, her voice back to soft, sweet and effective as her hands moved on him and he felt another strong surge of desire.

"Abby," he said against her skin.

Both her hands moved into his hair and she held it in gentle fists as her head twisted and her mouth moved to his.

"It's my house," she whispered there. "My responsibility, my mess. I have to take care of it on my own this time."

The words "my mess" and "this time" registered in his brain for a brief moment before she kissed him, her tongue touching his, and she moved in his lap to straddle him.

Then nothing was in his head but the scent of her.

She wanted him, he could smell it.

His mouth moved to her jaw, down her neck, to her chest, and as he pressed his hands between her shoulder blades to arch her back, he found himself agreeing, "All right, darling."

Then his lips closed around her nipple and he sucked in hard, hearing her soft moan as he did it.

Shortly after, when he had her on her back, him on top, his clothes were gone and his mouth was moving down her chest, between the valley of her breasts, down her belly, Cash dimly realised three things.

He was, for the first time he could remember, going to be late for a meeting.

And he had, for the first time he could remember, relented on something he fully intended to do.

And he didn't give a fuck about either.

Then his hands spread her legs and he tasted her.

When his mouth touched her, he heard her gentle, rasping sigh, his mind erased and he thought about nothing except Abby.

11

THE FIGHT

Abigail Butler was in a tizzy.

No, that wasn't correct, she was in *three* tizzies.

Firstly, and probably least importantly (but at that particular moment it was the one that was most flipping her out), she had no clue what to wear to dinner with Cash's family that night at Penmort Castle.

Abby's mom was English and growing up Abby had spent most of her vacations in England. After Abby married, she and Ben came to visit Gram as often as they could. There was also the fact that she'd lived there for over a year. And England, being England, had its fair share of castles.

Therefore Abby had seen a great number of them. She'd even visited several. Some of which had given tours.

She had, however, never eaten dinner in one of them.

And therefore she had no earthly clue what to wear.

The second tizzy was caused by the distressing phone call she'd received that day from a friend of hers in DC.

Abby, being tremendously stupid, hadn't thought about what people she knew would think if they saw pictures of her and Cash in the press.

In fact, it hadn't even crossed her mind.

But then Lori phoned from DC, breathless and excited to hear Abby's spectacular news. News about the new man in her life. News about the new man in her life who happened to be a famous, super-sexy international industrial spy hunter. And lastly, news that Lori felt entitled to seeing as she was Abby's friend.

This distressing phone call had the disturbing information that Lori had seen a photo of Cash unsuccessfully shielding Abby from the camera while letting them into his house the night of their moonlit stroll in Bath.

Abby's luck, indisputably bad, meant that Lori didn't see a picture of them walking or talking or eating dinner.

No.

It had to be a photo of them at night, Cash protecting her gallantly from the camera's glare while letting them into his home. It had to be a photo that served Cash's purpose, showing the world that they'd already passed "the first part" (the casual-dating, getting-to-know-you part) and were well into "the second part" (the not-casual-at-all, spending-the-night, clearly-lovers part).

Lori had been in throes of ecstasy about the very *idea* of Abby with famous, wealthy, unbelievably gorgeous Cash Fraser.

But what made matters worse was that she was beyond thrilled that Abby had "finally moved on" from Ben and was clearly starting the next exciting chapter in her life.

Abby didn't know what to say. In fact, she didn't even know what to *feel*.

In a lucky twist, she didn't have to say much of anything since Lori would not shut up.

Which brought Abby to her last tizzy.

The Tizzy to end all Tizzies.

That morning she and Cash had had a fight.

Not just a fight but a rip-roaring, voices-raised, unpleasant-words-spoken *clash*.

She should not, she figured, be fighting with her client. She reckoned most experienced escorts avoided doing that.

But it had happened.

And now she was both angry and worried.

Angry at what Cash had said. Though, if she was honest with herself (which she found excruciatingly difficult to be at that juncture), none of it was untrue.

And angry with herself for feeling anything at all.

And worried about so many things she couldn't count them all.

She didn't like to fight with anyone and she found that fighting with Cash hurt. It hurt a lot. Their fight had been ugly and she'd caused it, so that made it hurt more.

She also worried that they wouldn't get past this even though they had to carry on with their arrangement.

And she worried what it meant that she felt too much—*way* too much—for Cash.

Enough to get in a passionate verbal battle in the first place much less feel the hurt after it had happened, and further to feel pain that the reason it happened was because she may have wounded him.

Abby reviewed her situation.

On a Sunday, she'd met him at the pub to negotiate "the arrangement."

Their first "date" was on a Monday.

And they'd made love on Thursday night.

Then on Friday, after she'd stupid, stupid, *stupidly* had sex with him, breaking her own rule and altering their arrangement, everything changed.

It changed for Abby and she was relatively certain it also changed for Cash.

Friday, his assistant Moira had called and said he'd be working late but home by eight. Moira told Abby that Cash wanted dinner in. Moira also informed her that Abby would be spending the weekend at Cash's.

Abby didn't like Moira calling her instead of Cash. It scared her, especially having her "orders" come from Moira right after Abby had (stupidly) allowed their relationship to get intimate.

Abby worried about it all day while the bathroom fitters were banging away and she was wandering the rooms with little paint pots, painting patches on the walls so she'd know what shades she wanted when the time came to decorate.

While slapping paint on the walls, she worried that now that he had her, the challenge had been won and he'd lost interest.

He *was* Cash Fraser, she reminded herself. He could have anyone, undoubtedly very easily, even her (as he'd proved).

She worried—as it was the best sex she ever had (okay, so it was the best *three* sexual experiences she'd ever had), both in the pleasure-sense and in a way that seemed weirdly more profound, a way Abby refused in her current state of turmoil to fully explore—that Cash hadn't felt the same.

Further, she worried that it *was* the best sex she'd ever had and what that said about her. And also what that said about how she felt about Ben.

Ben and Abby had had a full, satisfying and happy sex life. Ben had been a very good lover, at the time Abby thought he was great.

But what she had with Cash transcended great, going straight to *amazing*.

Further to *that*, she worried about worrying about Cash not thinking it was amazing and what *that* said.

Friday night, she made sure she was at his house in plenty of time to make him dinner. She was careful to make something nice, better than pasta shells, but not too nice, which would say she was trying too hard. She also went back to her Dinner at Cash's House Look—jeans, a nice sweater, and for courage, her makeup was done in "Carefree Splendour" (casual with a hint of glamour).

She heard the door open upstairs at ten past eight and she found to her agony that she was as nervous as a teenager on her first date.

She was listening to Billie Holiday turned down low and freaking out about her decision to buy, and bring, a few scented candles which she had lit.

His home, although gorgeous, had zero personal touches and she thought it could use some. Furthermore, she liked candles and knew the scent would soothe her.

But as she heard Cash approach, she looked around and it seemed like she was both being way too familiar in adding anything to his house when this was not her place *and* that she looked like she was trying to strike a mood.

Before she could dash through the room, blow them out, toss them in the rubbish and turn off Billie singing the blues, she saw his legs on the stairs.

Bloody hell, she thought as he came into view wearing a charcoal-grey suit, a forest-green shirt and a great tie, which made her wonder (somewhat frantically, but also not for the first time) if he just had good taste in clothing or if he had a personal shopper.

He was carrying a large glossy bag containing various-sized thin but wide boxes.

She didn't think about the bag. She thought instead about how to stop herself from fainting.

He stepped off the last stair and, eyes on her, walked to the comfy seating area off the kitchen and put the bag on a chair. Then he shrugged off his suit jacket and that joined it. He tugged off his tie and that joined it as well.

He was turned to her and in the process of unbuttoning the top three buttons of his shirt when he spoke.

"What's the matter?" he asked and her body jerked when his deep voice hit the room.

"What?" she queried, her mind blank.

His hands, finished with his buttons, went to rest on his hips.

"What's the matter?" he repeated.

Her brain decided to function, and trying to sound calm (and fearing it didn't work) she replied, "Nothing's the matter."

"Then why are you standing across the room staring at me like I'm a dread serial killer and you're in my clutches?" His voice was bland, his words filled with dry humour.

Abby, however, didn't laugh.

"I am not," Abby returned, but his words told her that she'd failed at sounding or appearing calm.

She watched in fascination as his face took on a warm, soft look.

Normally, he looked amazing.

When he smiled, he was breathtakingly handsome.

When he laughed, the world seemed to stop.

That look beat all of them.

"Abby, come here," he said gently.

On shaking legs she did as he commanded.

When she got close enough, his arms went around her loosely and he held her close but not too close.

In his deeper, throatier, sexier brogue, he demanded, "Now, tell me, what's the matter?"

And for some unhinged reason, Abby blurted, "You had Moira call me."

His head gave a small jerk then tilted slightly to the side. "I'm sorry?"

"Moira, your assistant?" she said on a question as if he didn't know his own assistant's name. "She called me today," she explained and went on, "You didn't."

Cash stared at her a moment and Abby held her breath.

Then she watched as he threw his head back and let out a deep, rich bark of laughter before his arms closed tightly around her, crushing her body to his. His head came down and he buried his face in her neck.

Still laughing against her neck, he muttered, "I see."

She pushed her body back and twisted her head to look at him. "You see what?"

He was still smiling when his head came up and his gaze locked on hers. "I see you're pissed off that I didn't call."

"No, I—" she started but his arms gave her a gentle squeeze, effectively silencing her.

"I was in meetings all day. Unfortunately what I do means I have a lot of meetings. Even though I'd vastly prefer to be on the phone talking to you, or listening to the crazy shit that goes on in your house, sometimes I won't be able to call." One of his hands came up and gave her neck that gentle squeeze she liked way too damned much. "Abby, you're going to have to get used to that."

She felt a tremor slide through her body at his words and it wasn't a tremor of fear.

"Get used to it?" she whispered, wondering what he meant.

His lips touched hers before he said, "Yes. You're going to have to get used to it." And he obviously wasn't going to say any more, as in explain what *on God's green earth* he was talking about, because he let her go and casually walked into the kitchen while saying, "I'm getting a drink. You open your boxes."

For what seemed like years (but obviously wasn't) she stared at his back as he moved around the kitchen pouring himself a whisky.

Eventually she looked at the bag with the boxes.

She looked back to him.

"My boxes?" she asked.

Back still to her, he took a sip from his whisky while standing in front of an attractive, modern, stainless steel wine rack, pulling out bottles and inspecting them, before shoving them back, and he said, "In the bag. Those are for you."

She sucked in breath and her eyes went back to the boxes.

"For me?" she whispered but he didn't answer. He'd found what he was looking for and went about the task of opening a bottle of red wine.

On legs that felt like they were made of wood, Abby moved to the boxes and found there were three. She pulled them out, opened them up and one by one unveiled three robes.

One was tailored in a man's style but it was made from a sumptuous pink silk so pale it was almost, but not quite, colourless. The next was a long, cream cotton waffle-weave but its lapel was smooth. The last was also long but this one was made of the finest dove-grey cashmere, luxuriously soft to the touch.

Abby stood frozen, the lush cashmere in her hands, and she didn't wonder why Cash was giving her presents. She also didn't wonder why those presents were all robes.

All she could think was that she'd always wanted a cashmere robe.

Always.

During the good times with Ben, in all her spending, she'd never bought herself one. She could explain away purchasing expensive shoes, handbags and pieces of jewellery with a variety of womanly excuses. But spending hundreds of dollars on a robe you wouldn't wear out of the house seemed over the top.

She knew exactly how much it cost. She'd looked covetously at many of them and not one had cost less than multiple hundreds.

And the one in her hands was of a superior quality to any of the ones she'd seen.

"Abby?" She heard Cash call and her head shot up.

He was standing at the end of the counter, his weight resting on one hand, the fingers of his other hand curled around his whisky glass, his eyes were on her.

"I—" She felt her throat close which she thought at that moment was a good thing as she had no idea what to say. She cleared her throat, the pertinent question springing into her head, and she asked, "Why?"

His face went hard and for one frightening second, she thought he was angry.

But when he spoke, she realised it wasn't anger but a very scary resolve.

In a voice harder than his face, he declared, "I take care of what's mine."

Abby felt it was safe to say that he hadn't lost interest in her and instantly she had something new to worry about.

She opened her mouth to speak but he got there before her.

"Do you like them?" he asked.

She blinked and repeated, "Like them?"

His head moved to indicate her presents and he prompted, "The dressing gowns."

Still slightly dazed, and certainly not thinking, she shook her head and said, "No."

She watched as his face went blank, guarding his reaction, but she kept talking.

"No, I don't *like* them, Cash. Any woman in her right mind doesn't *like* cashmere." As if unable to stop herself, Abby babbled on, "Any woman in her right mind wants a *room* made out of cashmere with a bed made out of cashmere, a bed with cashmere sheets and cashmere pillows and cashmere *blankets*. So she can *roll around* in cashmere. No, Cash, I don't *like* them. I love them." She paused. "But especially the cashmere."

As she was talking, for some bizarre reason sharing her honest reaction instead of keeping it from him (as she should), his mouth went from hard to soft, his lips twitched, and finally he grinned.

When she finished speaking, he was smiling while he commanded gently, "Darling, come here. I want you to show me how much you love cashmere."

Without hesitation, Abby did as he asked.

When they surfaced from their mammoth-post-cashmere-robe make-out session, his arm still around her (propping her up as her legs had gone weak), Cash poured her a glass of red wine.

He handed her the glass while murmuring, "I don't have pinot noir so you'll have to make do with a Bordeaux until I can get some in."

And she sipped her Bordeaux while thinking that Cash Fraser not only lit welcoming lights and gave great presents, he also was thoughtful enough to remember her preference in red wine even though she'd mentioned it once, in passing, on their first meeting.

It was then Abby knew she was seriously in trouble.

And it was then that Abigail Butler went deep into denial.

Suffice it to say the evening went downhill from there (one couldn't top cashmere), though it was still very nice with them eating dinner while listening to Billie Holiday.

Cash took her to bed and proved that the night before and that morning wasn't a fluke created by Abby ending a long, dry spell. But instead that he was very good with his hands, phenomenally good with his mouth, earth-shatteringly good with his tongue and she couldn't even describe how good other parts of him felt.

The next day Abby discovered Cash had a different schedule for the weekends.

On Saturday, he got up wickedly early (per usual), worked out in the room off the dining area while Abby slept in and then he went into the office.

He came home in the early afternoon and told her he was taking her into Bath.

They meandered amongst the tourists, poked around some of the more exclusive shops and had a coffee before they went back to his house. There, Cash guided her downstairs and made love to her slowly, thoroughly and satisfyingly on the couch in the area off his kitchen after which, in his arms, she fell asleep.

When she fell asleep, she was tucked between the back of the couch and Cash. She didn't know Cash left her, covering her naked body with a throw, until she woke to see him seated in the armchair across from her, fully dressed, feet up on the table, his sexy glasses on, reading through some papers.

Before he noticed she was awake, she watched him for a while, maybe moments but it felt like hours.

She liked watching him, the look of him, the way he seemed to emanate energy even sitting and reading.

As if sensing her eyes on him, his gaze moved to her and she saw his mouth move up slightly at the ends.

She tried to pretend he didn't catch her watching him and busied herself getting her clothes back on while still under the throw (and not doing a very graceful job of it, she was sure).

While he worked, she made them dinner.

After they ate, Cash led her upstairs where he made love to her again (and again) before Abby, exhausted even after her nap, fell into a deep, blissful sleep.

Sunday, Cash woke up, worked out, went into the office but got home late morning. They didn't meander around Bath. They didn't even leave his bed except for her to make them cheese on toast for lunch and for Cash to go out and pick up their dinner of takeaway curry (both of which they ate in bed).

They didn't talk very much.

Instead they learned about each other in nonverbal ways.

All day they touched and explored, getting to know each other's bodies, and Abby really liked getting to know Cash's. He had a great body and she liked what she learned and the power she felt when he responded, which was a lot.

She also liked being with someone who could just be. Who didn't talk all the time and who didn't expect the same from her.

And when they weren't exploring, they dozed. Or Abby did, contentedly, like wasting a day in bed was something everyone did.

Monday was back to their "normal" schedule, with a twist. Cash woke at his usual ungodly hour but this time he turned into Abby, waking her with his hands and mouth, making love to her, leaving her smiling into his pillow, worn out and sated, before he showered and came back to sit on the bed. As he did every morning since she'd started spending the night with him, he moved the hair from her neck to give her a kiss and tell her he was going. Then he left.

It went bad when he called late Monday morning.

She was at home to find her bathroom was beginning to look like a bathroom again (but just barely) and the surveyor Pete had brought in had sent his forty-five page report.

She'd just spoken to the plumber to get him to give her a quote on updating her other two bathrooms while the boiler man who Pete had called was assessing her heating system.

During the call, Cash had informed her he had to fly to Brussels and he wouldn't be home until late that night. He also informed her that when he came home, no matter how late, he wanted to find her in his bed.

Lost in a world that was not really hers, Abby agreed readily.

But Cash being gone meant she had time to think.

Time she didn't have when he was around, his dominating charisma, gorgeous smile or vigorous sexual appetite shoving any other thought from her mind.

And time she didn't have when he was *going* to be around, which was time she spent thinking about when he'd be back.

Time she now had for thoughts to push through.

Thoughts about the fact that her stupid, confused, screwed-up mind had tricked her into thinking that *playing* Cash's devoted girl-friend meant she actually *was* Cash's devoted girlfriend.

Thoughts about the fact that he often told her what to do and where to be, which should serve to remind her of what she truly was.

Thoughts about the fact that she was not now the paid escort of a Totally Loaded, Fabulous, International Hot Guy but she was some-thing different. Something worse. She was servicing him in bed and getting paid for it, in money, food and now exorbitantly expensive clothes.

And lastly, thoughts about the fact that since sometime midday Friday, all the way to late morning that Monday, she hadn't once thought about her dead husband. The man she'd dedicated herself to on their wedding day. Then she'd rededicated herself to him on the day she put him in the ground. That day, she had vowed she would always, but always, forever and ever, be true to him, no matter what.

She'd never gone a day without thinking of Ben and most days she thought of him dozens of times.

And she'd just gone three, almost three entire days of not thinking about Ben.

Worse, except returning a few texts from Jenny (all of Abby's responses vague), she was not only avoiding her friend but keeping things from her.

Which meant for the first time in her life, Abby had no one to talk to about her experiences, her troubles and, most importantly, her guilt.

She'd always had Jenny, who, as best girlfriends do, either happily shared the burden by just listening or gave good advice.

It was then, Abby came to a conclusion.

That Monday afternoon, Abby called Jenny and asked her to come over the next day and help her find a Going-to-a-Haunted-Castle-Outfit. She also promised her friend that they'd talk.

And, Abby decided, they would because this business with Cash was done.

Over.

She would be his pretend girlfriend and she'd be his whore. He'd paid for both.

What she wouldn't do was forget what she was to him and allow herself to enjoy it.

The first would be even stupider than she normally was and the second made her feel even worse about what she'd become.

So she'd admit to her confused feelings to Jenny and Jenny would help her find strength. Jenny always did.

And Abby would somehow find a way to do what she was being paid to do for Cash but keep herself firmly detached.

As ordered, Abby had been in Cash's bed that night when he got home late and woke her briefly when he turned her drowsy, pliant body into his warm, hard one.

"You're home safe," she'd whispered, soft relief in her voice, not yet steeled against him as she was mostly asleep.

"Yes, love," he'd murmured. "Go back to sleep."

Immediately cuddling into him, she'd done as she was told.

It was the next morning that they had their gargantuan, knock-down, drag-out, fight.

Something made her wake early. Earlier even than Cash who routinely woke at what Abby considered alarming hours.

Upon waking she realised she was, as she'd made a habit of doing, snuggled into him. This time tucked into his side, head on his shoulder, arm wrapped around his stomach.

Unusually, her brain started functioning instantly. She looked at the clock to see it was just before five and she moved carefully away. She got up and went to the bathroom, going about her morning business, even to the point of brushing her teeth, washing her face and showering.

She walked out of the bathroom wearing her new cashmere robe, her wet hair combed back. She was determined to make coffee and be in the kitchen when he descended, ready to make him breakfast before he left for work.

Not be available to him for the activities in which he liked to engage when he woke. Activities she liked too. Activities that might weaken her resolve.

The problem was, when she came out of the bathroom, the light was on and Cash was awake, alert and lying on his side in the bed. He was up on his elbow, head resting in his hand, covers down around his waist, his sleek chest in full view, and lastly, his dark eyes were on her. He had that warm, soft expression on his face that he'd shown her the night he'd given her the robes.

Her firm resolve to be Abigail Butler, Skilled but Detached Full-Time Escort and Part-Time Whore slipped a notch at the sight of him and she had to quickly fortify her defences.

"You're awake," she announced unnecessarily, and he gave her a lazy smile.

At his smile, Abby's puny defences crashed down in a humiliating heap and she was forced early on to dig into her reserves.

"It looks good on you," he said instead of commenting on her inane remark.

Abby stopped at the foot of the bed and asked, "Pardon?"

His head dipped toward her but other than that he didn't move.

However when he spoke, his voice was that deep, throaty, rich that she liked so very much. "The dressing gown. It looks good on you."

Abby swallowed and replied, "Thank you."

"Why are you up?" he asked.

"I don't know," she lied.

"You should have woken me. We could have showered together," he told her.

At the thought of showering with him (which they'd done on Sunday morning and she'd enjoyed it, like, *a lot*), she found herself digging even deeper into those reserves. She also found this a little concerning considering their conversation had lasted less than five minutes and she was already losing her willpower.

Before she could announce her intention to go make coffee and politely suggest she'd bring him a cup, which she thought would be a nice touch, he pushed up from his elbow.

"Come here," he said softly as he swung his legs around and got out of bed.

He walked to the armchair by the window, grabbed his suit jacket, and when she got close, he took her hand, led her back to the bed and seated himself on it, tugging her into his lap.

His lap was definitely not where she wanted to be if she wanted to keep herself distant from him. But she also had to keep up the charade.

However, Abby's brain decided it didn't like the charade all that much and registered how nice it was to sit in his lap. Her brain also took that opportunity to remind her about other nice things about Cash that she liked.

She absently noted his hands were doing something with his suit jacket but she was deep in thought. She was digging way deep to harden herself against the fact that she liked sitting in his lap and all the other things she liked about him besides.

She came back to the room when he leaned into her and tossed his jacket so it landed back on the chair.

And she felt her eyes grow wide just as she felt her body go still when she saw the long, slim, royal-blue velvet box in his hand.

An unmistakable kind of box.

The kind of box that held jewellery.

Expensive jewellery.

"Cash," she whispered as he forced it to click open with his thumb and her breath lodged in her throat at what she saw.

He took out a delicate diamonds-in-platinum bracelet.

Not a tacky, ostentatious one. But instead it was subtle and striking with slim links separated by tasteful, not overly large (but not small by a long shot) diamonds.

He tossed the box carelessly on the bed and his fingers wrapped around her arm below the elbow, slowly drifting down to her wrist. He lifted it and placed the bracelet around her wrist as Abby stared at his hands, concentrating on breathing.

"We were going into the meeting," he murmured while working the clasp. "I saw this in a window. It made me think of you so I sent Moira in to get it."

Abby failed at concentrating on her breathing. Her lungs burned their demand for oxygen but she couldn't for the life of her remember how to give it to them.

Cash finished fastening the bracelet on her wrist but he wasn't done. He brought her wrist to his mouth and he kissed her gently, his lips brushing the sensitive skin on the inside.

For a moment Abby almost pressed her hand against his face. She almost leaned in to press her lips to his. She almost burst into tears.

His eyes came to her, they travelled over her face and he must have read her intent because his expression gentled before his arms went around her and he whispered, "You can thank me now."

The breath came back to her lungs and with it came something she didn't know she had in her.

It was something ugly, but useful, if she intended to guard her thoughts, her emotions, and if she was honest, her heart.

It was something that made her say, "And what form of gratitude does a diamond bracelet buy you?"

She watched his face go blank and his arms seemed to convulse around her.

Then she watched with no small concern as his eyes narrowed.

"I'm sorry?" he asked and his voice had an edge. An edge that said quite clearly she should be very careful with her answer.

She wasn't.

"The bracelet," she replied, shaking her wrist as if to remind him. "I just want to be certain what I owe you for the bracelet."

She watched a muscle jump in his jaw and it took everything she had not to jump off his lap.

Or worse, beg him to let her take it back.

"Would you care," he said, very slowly and equally dangerously, "to tell me what the fuck you're on about?"

Even sensing he was angrier than she'd ever seen him before, and it was not in doubt that Cash Fraser had a formidable temper, she kept playing her game.

"I'm not on about anything. I just don't want any surprises. I like to know what's expected of me. You know that."

He watched her for a moment before he stated, "Something's changed."

"Nothing's changed," Abby returned.

His arms got tighter on hearing her lie. "Something's. Fucking. Changed."

Oh dear Lord, Abby thought.

He was saying "fuck."

He didn't shy away from using that word. Except when he was angry he used it a different way.

And he was using it that way now, which Abby knew wasn't good.

She ignored his ominous use of the F-word and repeated her bald-faced lie, "Nothing has changed."

His eyes were still narrow, his brows were drawn and he watched her mouth while she was speaking as if it was fascinating in its hideousness.

"Yesterday," he said, his words still slow and dangerous as he carried on, "I left you sweet and smiling in my bed and now you're acting like a common whore."

That stung but Abby hid it and returned coldly, "I'm not a *common* whore, Cash. I'm an uncommon one. You know that too because you made it so."

At that he moved swiftly. So swiftly, her breath flew from her lungs.

She was on her back on the bed, sucking in air and he was on his side looming over her threateningly when he clipped, "You opened your legs for me, Abby. You begged me to come inside. I didn't fucking make you a whore."

"Really? Then why did you pay me after with hundreds of pounds worth of new robes?" she replied acidly.

She hoped to all that was holy that she hid the fear that shot through her when she saw his face darken.

"That wasn't fucking payment," Cash growled.

"It seemed like it to me," Abby retorted, making her awful lie sound real, and as intended, she successfully struck her target.

His darkening face turned thunderous.

"You're a fucking piece of work," he snarled, pushing off her and exiting the bed muttering, "Unbelievable."

At that point, Abby should have kept quiet.

She really should have.

But Abby often did stupid things.

So she didn't.

Instead, scrambling off the bed, she asked when she'd gained her feet, "It was a simple question, Cash. Why do you sound so surprised?"

His dark eyes speared her and he answered, "Now *that's* a good question, darling. Why *am* I so surprised?"

Abby watched, holding her ground with effort, as he came close. So close he was an inch away.

Then he dealt a deadly verbal blow. "I shouldn't be surprised. You've made it perfectly clear you're determined to hold on to a dead man. So given time to shut down, you fucking took it."

And that's when Abby lost her phony cool composure and also lost her temper. Not solely angry at Cash and what he said but also angry at herself because she was so *embarrassingly* transparent.

"I don't *believe* you just said that!" she snapped, her voice rising and becoming shrill.

"Believe it, Abby," he clipped back, his voice rising at the same time it dipped deep.

Her voice was no longer rising, it was loud when she yelled, "You don't know a thing about me!"

His face moved close to hers and he returned crudely, "I know I can make you forget him when my mouth is between your legs."

"Oh my *God!*" Abby screeched, arms straight down, hands balled into fists in an effort not to slap him.

But he carried on.

"And I know you're full of shit. I know this whole act is full of shit. You're terrified. He died and then you sacrificed yourself to him, but you didn't have the fucking courage to slit your wrists to join him, did you Abby?"

She gasped at his cruel question, but he didn't give her time to answer.

"Instead you've done the next best thing. I don't know how you've managed to so royally fuck up your life to get where you are now. I do know you're pretty fucking comfortable letting a man pay for your company. But you're scared shitless of giving it away."

"Don't think, Mr. Fraser, with all the clever skills at your command, that you can actually read my mind while you fuck me!" she shouted.

"Darling," he shot back tersely, "I didn't have to fuck you to read you. You're an open fucking *book*."

"Don't call me darling," Abby snapped.

"I paid for you, Abby. I'll do whatever the fuck I want," he bit back.

It was at that point Abby realised she was breathing heavily and so was Cash.

She stared at him, heart beating, breath coming fast. He held her glare and returned it until Abby could take no more.

She looked over his shoulder and asked with saccharine sweetness, "If you're through with me this morning, Mr. Fraser, I'd like to go home."

She let out a shocked gasp when his hand closed around her neck and he jerked her forward, her body slamming into his and his face coming within a breath of her own.

"I'm through with you, Abby, for now. But you better fucking be ready tonight. Six o'clock. I'll pick you up at your house and if you make me wait, there'll be consequences."

"I'll be ready," she snapped.

"Wear the fucking bracelet," he returned, his beautiful voice had turned ugly. "And don't wear any fucking underwear. You want to know the price of that bracelet? It's you sitting next to me at dinner and me knowing the whole time there'll be no obstacles when I fuck you after taking you home."

And on that successful parting shot, he let her go and strode to the bathroom, the door clicking sharply behind him.

And Abby didn't hesitate in dressing and slamming out of the house. She ran on her high-heeled shoes to her car and she didn't allow herself to start crying until she hit the motorway.

Incidentally, Cash didn't call that day.

Neither did Moira.

Abby went home. Upon seeing his quote, Abby gave the plumber the go ahead to fix the two other bathrooms and also gave the boiler man her approval to replace her two boilers.

And after working herself into a state about the idea that Cash would fire her as well as getting herself worked up in another way about all Cash had said to her, she called James herself. She told him to tell Cash that if he intended to forfeit on the arrangement, he could transfer fifty thousand into her account by the end of the working day and they'd call it even.

James had sounded strangely shocked and then he even more strangely suggested she talk to Cash herself.

When she refused, he stranger than strangely suggested she visit Cash at his office to "chat."

The idea of Abby popping by Cash's office to chat after their blowout was so ludicrous, she laughed straight out (not to mention she didn't know where he worked).

Then she'd flatly refused that too and demanded to know if he would pass on her message.

Although he didn't sound like he liked it, he promised he would.

And after she'd disconnected, Abby worried that calling James was a tactical error.

Then she found she didn't have time to worry about that when she had to worry about her outfit for that evening's dinner.

Now, she was standing in the guest bedroom wondering what on earth to wear to dinner at a haunted castle.

"Hello!" She heard Jenny call from downstairs.

Abby closed her eyes, tipped her head back and breathed, "Bloody hell."

12

PAINFUL LESSONS

It took Jenny what felt to Abby like a year to reach the top floor and when she finally entered the guest bedroom, Abby knew why.

Mrs. Truman was with her.

Just what Abby needed, Mrs. Truman.

"Why are you on the top floor?" Mrs. Truman demanded to know upon entry. "I never go to my top floor. I feel like I climbed a mountain."

Jenny ignored Mrs. Truman's complaining, took one look at Abby and asked immediately, "What's the matter?"

Her best friend knew Abby well, but she had to admit Jenny freaked her out sometimes.

"I..." Abby started to answer Jenny, or more to the point lie to her, but she noticed Mrs. Truman leaning toward her.

Peering closely at Abby's face, the older woman announced, "We need tea. We can't have drama without tea. And maybe sherry. This looks like it's going to be a sherry drama."

"There isn't going to be a drama," Abby told Mrs. Truman, wondering why she was even there but not getting the chance to ask.

"Drama is written all over your face, Abigail Butler," Mrs. Truman shot back, always feeling entitled to be wherever she was.

"Abby, what's going on?" Jenny asked, also leaning in.

They were both watching her, and Abby opened her mouth to say something to throw them off the scent.

All of a sudden her eyes filled with tears and she felt them spill down her cheeks. She couldn't control them and she found she no longer had the energy to try.

"Abby," Jenny said softly, but Abby ignored her.

Stiffly walking to the bed, she sat down and put the fingers of both her trembling hands to her mouth.

Jenny and Mrs. Truman followed, Jenny crouching in front of her saying, "What is it?"

"Cash and I had a fight," Abby blurted on a tortured whisper and Jenny's head jerked before her face changed to a look of stunned surprise.

"A fight?" Jenny repeated.

Abby swiped at the tears on her cheeks and nodded. "A fight. An ugly, shouting, awful, *awful* fight." She looked at Jenny then Mrs. Truman, finding she couldn't keep it in a moment longer. She knew she should, but she couldn't. "I think I hurt his feelings."

Jenny's mouth dropped open.

She snapped it shut and parroted, "Hurt his feelings?"

"What'd you do?" Mrs. Truman demanded to know.

Abby looked away from her friend who was clearly not taking this in and turned to Mrs. Truman.

"I..." she started then squeezed her eyes shut, tears sliding down her face. She opened them and admitted, "It's a long story, but I did something. Something not very nice. He was being nice. *Very* nice. And I was very *not* nice in return."

"How very nice was he being?" Jenny asked, and Abby looked to her friend.

"*Very* nice," Abby whispered, her silent tears ended, she let go of her emotions and burst into loud, wracking sobs. She covered her face with her hands and babbled from behind them, "I was so *mean*. And I hurt his feelings. I *know* I did. He asked me to explain myself and I just made it *worse*. Then he got mad and he said the most *awful* things." She pulled her hands from her face and wailed, "But they were *true*! Even though he doesn't get it. He doesn't understand. How could he?" Abby looked at Mrs. Truman, knowing she wasn't making a lick of sense and also not waiting for an answer and cried, "He was so angry. I've never seen anyone that angry!"

"Did he hurt you?" Jenny asked, her voice hard and Abby looked at her, confused.

"How do you mean?"

"Hurt you? Did he get physical with you?" Jenny explained.

"Of course not," Abby snapped, as if the idea of Cash getting physical (in that way) was ridiculous. "He just yelled at me."

"Did you yell back?" Mrs. Truman asked, and Abby's gaze moved to her.

"No, I mean, yes. I mean, it was actually me who started the yelling," she confessed.

"You forgot," Mrs. Truman told her with all-knowing finality.

Abby stared at her, not understanding what she meant.

She hadn't forgotten a thing. She was certain that fight with Cash was burned on her brain until the end of time.

When Mrs. Truman didn't say more, Abby asked, "Forgot what?"

"You forgot," Mrs. Truman repeated.

When Abby still looked confused, Mrs. Truman sat down beside her on the bed. When she spoke again, her voice was surprisingly gentle.

"When they die, you forget."

Abby pulled a sharp breath into her nostrils but Mrs. Truman ignored her reaction and carried on.

"When they die, you remember only the good things. You don't remember the bad things. The fights. The bickering. Their annoying habits that drive you mad. Like when they don't put their socks in the wash hamper, even though the hamper is only two feet away. They drop them on the floor. Morty and his damned socks. Used to drive me insane."

Abby felt her lip tremble as more silent tears slid down her cheeks.

Mrs. Truman watched her face and leaned slightly toward her.

"After he was gone, I would have paid money to pick up another pair of his dirty socks. Those socks, the blight of my life, became a cherished memory. You forget that they're just dirty socks on the floor that you have to pick up, Abigail." She touched Abby's hand ever so lightly then took her own away so swiftly it was almost as if the touch never happened. "Now, you're remembering what it's like to be with a living, breathing, *annoying* male who you yell at and who yells at you. It isn't something that you can mould into a cherished memory because it isn't in your head. It's real and it's happening. And you forgot what it felt like. Now, Abigail, you're remembering."

"Mrs. Truman—" Jenny started, but the older woman shook her head, not taking her eyes from Abby.

"But you know," she said softly. "You know something your young man doesn't. You know that even these fights, fights that hurt so much they make you cry, are something to cherish."

Abby stared at her, eyes suddenly dry, body frozen, even though her heart was beating a mile a minute.

Mrs. Truman broke her own spell by clapping her hands.

"Now!" she announced and went on authoritatively, "Tea. And cucumber. You can't sit down with the upper crust with puffy eyes. You need cucumber and a wet flannel." She pushed herself up and bustled to the door with the energy of a woman who would never complain about climbing two flights of stairs. "I'll see to the tea, cucumber and flannel. Jennifer," she turned and pointed at Jenny, "you take care of the outfit."

And after issuing her orders, she disappeared out the door.

Leaving Abby with Jenny.

"I think you got some 'splainin' to do," Jenny said, using her best Ricky Ricardo voice, attempting to inject humour where both women knew there was none.

"Jenny, I screwed up," Abby admitted quietly.

Jenny got out of her crouch and sat on the bed beside Abby, saying on a sigh, "Why does that not surprise me?"

"Jenny!" Abby cried loudly, stung by her friend's words, even though of anyone, Jenny knew Abby could screw up, big time.

Jenny turned to her. "Girlfriend, any woman in her right mind would screw up with Cash Fraser. The man is hot. He's also interesting. He's also funny. He also looks at you like you painted the Sistine Chapel on your lunch break while wearing a bikini. And let's not forget, he's hot."

"He looks at me like that?" Abby breathed, and Jenny lifted a hand to within an inch of Abby's face and snapped.

"Hello? A little focus?" Jenny asked while dropping her hand and Abby blinked before Jenny continued. "Have you slept with him?"

Abby's mouth dropped open.

Now Jenny was just plain creeping her out!

"Don't give me that look," Jenny warned. "He's hot. I was in your shoes, I'd sleep with him," she announced baldly. "How long did you wait?"

"It happened Thursday," Abby answered.

"You were always slow," Jenny remarked.

"Jenny!" Abby cried, surprised at her friend's easy acceptance of these facts. "Do you *not* see that this is a problem?"

"Yes, I do. Because you let your heart get involved with everything you do. I despair the workmen coming to your house because you'll make them all your BFFs and end up having to buy them Christmas presents you can't afford," Jenny retorted.

"I will not," Abby returned.

"You will," Jenny replied, and before Abby could get a word in, she went on, "Cash Fraser may be hot and he may be way into you, but I'm not certain his heart is involved. And I know you won't just enjoy yourself for once and keep your heart out of it. *This* is a problem."

"He bought me a cashmere robe," Abby announced and she saw Jenny's eyes get wide. "And this," Abby continued, lifting up her wrist to jiggle the diamond bracelet that even after that fight Abby could not bring herself to take off. "That's why we fought. Because of the bracelet, and kind of the robes too."

Jenny was staring at her wrist, but she breathed, "Robes. *Plural*?"

"Yes, three. Only one cashmere. The other one was silk and the other one—"

"Oh my *God*," Jenny whispered, her eyes snapping back to Abby. "Why is he buying you presents? He paid, like, a *fortune* for you."

"I don't know!" Abby cried. "He's freaking me out. It's all freaking me out. I can't keep my head on straight."

Jenny's eyes narrowed on her. "You like him."

"Well, of course I like him!" Abby clipped and shot off the bed, starting to pace. She whipped around and looked at Jenny. "He's hot."

"You don't like him because he's hot," Jenny returned.

"You can't *not* like him because he's hot. That's how hot he is!" Abby cried.

"Oh shit," Jenny breathed.

"What?" Abby asked.

"He's good in bed," Jenny whispered while she stood, then pleaded, "Please tell me a man that hot, that rich, that *everything* is also not good in bed."

Abby just looked at her friend not wanting to lie, also not wanting to share.

She didn't have to, Jenny already knew. "Shit. He is. He's good in bed."

"Jenny—" Abby started.

Jenny interrupted her, "How good?"

"Good," Abby answered quickly.

"How good?" Jenny pushed. "God-like good or just, you know, good-good?"

Abby thought about lying. Then because she was stupid, stupid, *stupid*, she decided against it.

"God-like good," she muttered.

"Oh *God*," Jenny breathed.

Going for the gusto, Abby whispered, "Better than Ben."

Jenny's face went pale and Abby held her breath.

Here we go, Abby thought.

"Really?" Jenny asked softly.

"Really," Abby replied. Her eyes began to fill with tears again and she took a deep breath to control them before saying, "We had a nice weekend, Cash and I. He's different than Ben. He doesn't talk as much, but he's more intense. He doesn't move around as much, but somehow he radiates more energy. He takes all my concentration. And," she paused then went on, "I like giving it to him."

Jenny regarded Abby for long moments and finally came closer, her voice going soft. "Abby, you've got to be careful. You have to remember what this is."

Abby closed her eyes and sighed.

When she opened them, she said, "I know."

"Are you going to be able to do that?" Jenny asked.

"I might not have to. That fight was ugly, Jenny," Abby told her. "He might not want me around anymore."

"I still don't understand about the fight," Jenny said.

"I was trying to pull away from him. I threw the diamond bracelet in his face, saying he was treating me like a whore."

Jenny sucked in a sharp breath before she whispered, "You did not."

"I was trying to maintain a distance," Abby defended.

"*Is* he treating you like a whore?" Jenny asked.

"No. Yes. I don't know! I've never *been* a whore," Abby answered, frustrated. "I've also never received cashmere robes and diamond bracelets like they were flowers and chocolates." Abby pulled her hand through her hair, bunching it in a fist at the back and looked at her friend. "I don't know what to do."

Jenny stared at her a moment and then said quietly, "Abby, you do your job. You do nothing but your job. If you like it, okay. It'd be hard not to like. If he wants to give you stuff, okay. Take it. That's his deal. But you have to remember, always, it's a job. Just a job. So when the time comes and he's through with you, you can walk away, put this behind you and get on with your *real* life."

Abby bit the side of her lip, not liking the idea of Cash being "through with her," not at all. Even after The Fight. But she nodded because she knew Jenny was right.

Very right.

It was then Mrs. Truman bustled in with a tray.

"You don't have cucumber. All you had was broccoli and carrots. Carrots don't take the puff out of your eyes." She slammed the tray down on the bedside table and turned, hands on hips, to Abby. "I had to go to my house to get cucumber," she declared, as if her house was in Bangladesh, not next door. "You're lucky I had some. Now lie down," she ordered and turned to Jenny. "Do you have the outfit sorted?"

"No," Jenny admitted.

"What have you two been doing?" she snapped and then stomped to the wardrobe grumbling, "I have to do everything."

Thus ended the drama and for the next half an hour, Abby lay on the bed with two slices of cucumber on her eyes covered in a cool, wet washcloth. She had to take them off to inspect the different outfits Mrs. Truman and Jenny brought from every corner of the house to show her.

Not one of them would do.

Mrs. Truman was holding up (and imperiously shaking) a strapless, baby-blue, knee-length dress with a full skirt made of acres of netting and a satin sash as a belt that Abby was relatively certain her mother wore to the prom (if she went to the prom) and demanding, "This is perfect!" when Jenny came in with more clothes.

"Mrs. Truman, I can't wear that," Abby said.

"Why not?" Mrs. Truman returned. "It's just the thing."

"That is *not* the thing," Jenny butted in, her lip curled in disgust, her eyes on the dress Mrs. Truman was holding.

"It most certainly is," Mrs. Truman shot back.

"It is, if Abby was going to the dance-a-thon where she'd end up doing the hand jive with Danny Zuko. It is *not* when Abby is having dinner at a castle with Famous-Worldwide Hot Guy Cash Fraser," Jenny retorted, and before Mrs. Truman could respond, she looked at Abby and stated, "I think *this* is the thing."

And Jenny held up the dress Abby wore to Ben's work Christmas party the last Christmas he'd been alive.

A taupe that was so light it was almost cream, the dress was made of soft wool, clingy in all the right places but providing maximum coverage. It had a cowl-neck and the hem fell to mid calf. Abby wore it with her high-heeled mocha suede boots and matching wide belt.

It had cost a fortune, though the boots and belt cost more, and Ben had loved it. He loved it so much, they left the party early so he could take her home and take it off.

It was perfect. Expensive, timelessly stylish, sexy-yet-demure, and best of all, it would remind her of Ben.

"That's it," Abby announced.

"Thank God," Jenny sighed.

"I still like the blue," Mrs. Truman grumbled, but it was too late. Abby had made her decision and she had to get a move on if she was going to be ready on time, which she felt at that moment was a moral imperative.

Mrs. Truman and Jenny put away the clothes while Abby did her makeup in a new look, elegant with a bit of drama (the look she dubbed "Castle Chic").

Mrs. Truman left to see to her dogs and Jenny did Abby's hair using a curling iron to give her loads of curls then smoothing it all away from her face in a barrette at her nape that burst in a riot of curls down her back, all the while giving her an "it's-just-a-job" pep talk.

Then Jenny left Abby alone with her cat, Zee.

It was a quarter to six and Abby was nervous as hell.

But, importantly, she was ready.

She was in her bedroom transferring needed items into a small, mocha-coloured, patent leather clutch when she heard the bell at the door.

Her head shot up and she stared at her bedside clock.

It couldn't be Cash. He couldn't be early again, not tonight of all nights. She wasn't yet mentally prepared to face him.

Abby left the clutch on her bed and ran down the stairs to see who it was and get them gone before Cash arrived.

Zee, having absented himself during the drama and ensuing clothes-fest, ran to the door with her, nearly tripping her twice.

Abby threw it open and stood frozen, staring at Cash.

One look at him and she knew that he wasn't over the fight.

Not by a long shot.

Abby made a mental note for possible future reference that Cash Fraser could hold a mean grudge.

"You're early," she told him.

"Do they say that instead of 'hello' in America?" Cash returned, his dry words reminding her she was being rude, and she immediately felt like an idiot.

"Sorry, come in." Abby stepped out of the way, eyes to the floor, and prattled on, "I'm ready. I need two seconds. Wait here, I'll be right back. I just have to go get my bag."

Then she turned tail and ran, Zee running alongside her.

She darted to her room, realised she forgot her lip gloss, flew to her dressing table and grabbed it. In all this activity, Zee decided to go away and come back later when Abby wasn't in a tizzy.

She bent over the bed, shoving everything into her purse and snapping it shut. She straightened, turned to run downstairs and instead ran headlong into Cash.

Her body jerked back but his hands came to settle on her hips to hold her where she was.

She tilted her head to look at him, surprised he was there and opened her mouth to speak.

But he got there first.

"I see they aren't finished with the bathroom," he remarked.

Abby stared at him.

She didn't know what to make of this. His handsome face was closed, his eyes cold and he looked remote. Abby knew, without knowing why she knew, that this meant he was angry.

Very angry.

Scary angry.

Yet his comment was bland.

And he was there. He hadn't yet fired her. Not that she'd given him a chance, but still.

"They say it'll be done tomorrow," Abby informed him.

Keen to get on with the evening and out of her bedroom, she started to move around him, but his fingers tensed at her hips and she stopped.

Her head tipped back in question. "Cash, we should—"

He cut her off by saying, "A minute."

She looked at him and his eyes held her captive as one of his hands moved lightly over her bottom.

"Cash, what are you—" she started, but he cut her off again.

"You're wearing underwear," he told her.

Abby's breath froze in her lungs.

Oh dear Lord, she forgot about the underwear.

She felt her pulse beating in her neck.

"Cash—" she began.

"Take it off," he ordered and she blinked in stunned surprise.

"What?" she breathed.

"Take them off," he repeated.

Abby felt a thrill run up her spine and it wasn't the usual thrill Cash gave her, or at least not entirely.

In a pleading whisper, she begged, "Cash, please don't make me—"

He interrupted her again, his voice patient but barely so, "Abby, take them off."

Abby felt her spine go ramrod straight, thinking he couldn't *make* her not wear underwear. And if he tried, he could have the damned bracelet *back*.

"No," she replied, her voice had grown cold.

His head tilted to the side, something dangerous flashed in his eyes, and he asked softly, "No?"

Being stupid (but brave, she told herself) in the face of obvious peril, Abby held her ground and repeated, "No."

He gazed at her for a moment, then two, before he replied quietly, "All right, Abby."

She felt her body relax.

He'd given in. He wasn't going to make her do something that made her uncomfortable. And she had the fleeting thought maybe it was all going to be okay.

She had this thought right before his head bent, his arms went around her tight and he kissed her.

It wasn't like any kiss he'd given before. It was hot, demanding and very effective, but it was also hard and claiming, taking everything but giving nothing in return.

It still, unfortunately, worked on Abby because it came with the scent of him, the feel of him and the memory of how good they could be.

When her arms went around his neck, signifying her not-very-hard-won capitulation, he shifted. They fell—him on his back, her on top of him—to the bed.

He rolled immediately, pinning her under him, not giving her a chance to think. Only feel.

His mouth was on hers, then it was on her neck just under and behind her ear, a sensitive spot that he manipulated ruthlessly.

His hands were all over her, smoothing over the wool at her side, her hip, up her midriff. His thumb caught against her hard nipple making sweet sensations shoot through her. At the feel of them, her neck arched as she gasped and his thumb stroked back, then again, and again.

When she was trembling under him, his thigh went between her legs, his knee pulling up her dress as his hand went down her belly. His fingers took over for his knee and yanked the skirt of her dress up and they were there, in her panties. She felt them sliding against her and his touch rocketed heat straight through her.

"Wet," he murmured, his mouth touching hers, his word shivering through her.

His fingers moved and all she could think of was what they were doing, how they were making her feel, how delicious it felt and finally one slid inside.

"Cash," she gasped.

She was pressing against him, her hands roaming his body urgently and then clutching at him as her hips bucked, riding his hand as his finger moved in and out, his thumb circling magnificently at the exact perfect spot.

Somewhere in the back of her head it registered that he was holding himself away even as he held her close, his hand between her legs, his other arm wrapped tight around her, his face buried in her neck.

But before this thought could intrude, Cash forced her response and it shot through her, her neck and back arching, her hips rearing against his hand. She heard the soft, low noises she made as if from far away as her body exhilarated in the glorious orgasm he'd given her.

And when she was done, breath coming fast, her hands still clenched in his suit jacket, his fingers left her, and she couldn't help it. That felt good too and she let out a soft moan. His hand glided over her hip to her bottom, pressing her against him as he held her until her trembling stopped.

"Now, darling," his voice rumbled roughly against her neck, "*that* was worth a diamond bracelet."

Her body went still at his words, but he didn't notice.

Or worse, didn't care.

He pulled away, exited the bed, leaned over and tugged her dress down. Then he grabbed her hand and pulled her to her feet at the side of the bed.

Her legs were shaky, not only from her climax, but also her emotion. Her head tilted back to look at him and when her eyes caught his, his were still cold.

And that coldness froze the heat right out of her, chilling her to her core.

"Fix your hair," he ordered. "I'll meet you at the door."

On that, without a word or touch, he turned and left.

Abby stared after him until he disappeared.

Then she stared some more.

As she did she realised throughout the time they'd been together he'd never treated her like a whore. Not once. Not with the robes. Not with the bracelet. Not with all of his orders to be somewhere or do something.

She knew this because with what he'd just done, he'd treated her like a whore.

On unsteady legs, she went to her dressing table, smoothed back her hair and re-clipped the barrette firmly. She fixed her lip gloss, grabbed her bag and walked to the light switch. She flipped it off and walked down the hall, down the stairs to the front door where she saw Cash, standing, waiting, wearing his overcoat, ready to go.

Averting her eyes, she reached out to grab her mother's deep-taupe, long, wool winter coat.

Before she could swing it around, in one of his usual gallant gestures (this one, for obvious reasons, bittersweet), Cash took it from her hands and held it out for her.

She turned her back to him and slid her arms through as thoughts began to invade, feelings began to press in and Abby could feel the tears pooling in her eyes.

She took deep breaths to control them.

This effort failed.

Lifting her hand, she pulled her hair out of the collar after Cash settled the coat on her shoulders. In an effort to hide her face, she kept her gaze to the floor as she walked to the door, turned the latch and opened it.

"Abby," Cash's voice called.

Only her torso twisted toward him, her eyes, tears still shimmering and unshed, lifted to his.

When her gaze met his, Abby could swear she saw his nearly imperceptible flinch, but this didn't penetrate the aching fog that shrouded her.

"I'm ready," she said softly, turned and walked out into the bitter cold.

She didn't feel the chill.

13

PENMORT CASTLE

Cash was furious.

He'd been furious all day.

No, strike that. He'd been furious that morning.

In the afternoon, after James spoke to him, he'd been livid.

But those feelings had been directed at Abby.

Driving his car down the dark motorway toward Penmort Castle, Abby at his side, silent and staring at nothing out the passenger window, Cash was, at present, furious with himself.

That morning after she'd accused him of making her a whore when it was *she* who sold her body for two hundred thousand pounds, and after she'd told him she considered the dressing gowns he'd bought her a payment for services rendered, he'd felt a fury unlike anything he'd felt in his life.

Then he'd spoken to Abby in a way he'd never spoken to a woman in his life.

Indeed, it was not lost on Cash that over the last week, Abigail Butler had made him feel, and do, many things he'd never felt or done in his life.

When he'd come home on Friday night to a light burning in the hall, Billie Holiday's voice coming at him only to walk downstairs and see candles flickering, dim lights shining and Abby in a kitchen surrounded by cutting boards topped with chopped vegetables and something on a grill pan covered with foil, he'd felt something strange.

It was something he couldn't remember ever feeling, but perhaps he'd had it once when he was a child before his grandfather died.

It was contentment.

Even though she'd appeared anxious, coming home to her still made a strange ease settle over him.

And throughout the weekend, this ease grew.

It grew when he caught her eyes on him after her nap, her gaze soft and almost awed, as if he was a god, not a man. It grew simply because she was sleeping, exhausted by him, naked on his couch. It grew the next day when he'd done something he'd never done before—spent most of a day in bed with a woman. It grew as he discovered her body, was stirred by her touch, pleased that she seemed just as happy to do nothing but the same. And then she dozed while he held her and sometimes he'd slide his hands along her skin, familiarising himself with her even while she slept.

Lastly it grew the night before, when he came home and turned her into his arms and she'd muttered in sleepy relief that he was safe at home.

Cash knew it was *him* that she was happy was safe. It was *him* she looked at with awe. It was *him* on whose couch she slept naked. It was *him* whose body she put her mouth on, smiling against his skin when she made him groan.

It was *him*.

Not *Ben*.

And Cash began to feel more than content.

He felt peace.

And he'd never, not once, felt peace in his life.

Knowing as a child does that something was not right with his mother, with his father's family, Cash had not even felt it when his grandfather was alive.

Abby gave that to him. He felt it. He understood it. And he meant to keep it.

But that morning, Abby had upset that peace.

And that afternoon, when James had come to deliver Abby's message, she'd annihilated it.

James had seemed surprised, confused and even concerned at the message he had to deliver.

James had been at Cash's side on the pavement when Cash made the unprecedented move to peer through a shop window and pause in his daily business to buy a diamond bracelet for a woman.

Cash had never done such a thing. Not for any woman.

James, for years a colleague and a friend, had attempted to ask tactful questions but Cash didn't bite.

James didn't need the answers. Cash's actions told the story.

And Cash couldn't care less.

Abby was his. She'd given herself freely. Not just the first time, every time, all weekend, with her response to his touch, her reaction to the cashmere dressing gown, her gaze on him while he was reading.

Everything.

And as he told her, he took care of what was his.

And being Cash's meant she'd wear cashmere and diamonds.

That was simply the way it was going to be.

But the message she relayed to James said quite plainly she wanted to end things.

And that idea, Cash found, he could not tolerate.

It was so intolerable it caused the slowly ebbing burn, which had been reducing all day, to re-ignite.

For a moment he'd even felt actual rage.

Therefore, by the time he stood at Abby's door, he planned to teach her a lesson. He planned to make it perfectly clear the difference between being his and being his whore.

Spurred by fury, he'd carried out his plan.

And after, at the door when she'd looked at him with deeply wounded eyes, the intensity of hurt in them caused Cash to feel a sharp pain in his gut.

It was then he realised that this plan had *not* been his most stellar.

He turned off the motorway and navigated the winding roads of Devon, heading for the coast.

He knew he was going to have to do something else he'd never done and he had no earthly idea how. And he was furious that he'd put himself in that position. He was even more furious that he'd been the cause of her pain.

Over the distance, Cash considered his options.

However, before he came to any conclusions, Penmort Castle loomed in front of them, its lit towers and turrets a daunting vision against the dark night.

Cash barely registered the vague thrill he normally felt when he saw Penmort.

He'd been there only two times as a teen, when Nicola had invited him to stay. Both times had been, despite her best efforts, unsatisfactory. He'd been there relatively often since Alistair had offered his artificial olive branch.

This time he would be entering as its owner, a goal that he'd spent a year doing all in his power to achieve.

It should have been a triumph.

Cash didn't give it a thought.

He drove up the steep hill at the side of the castle and stopped at the arched, gated doorway set into the thick, stone wall that surrounded much of the castle.

He pulled the emergency brake, switched off the car and noted Abby's hand was already on her door handle.

In an effort to forestall her, his own hand went to the area above her knee. But at his touch, she instantly jerked away. Whether this was anger, hurt or revulsion, he didn't know.

He also didn't care.

"Abby," he called as she continued her efforts to exit the car, partially opening the door.

They had only moments before their arrival would be discovered. He had to get this done now. He had no time to waste.

Swiftly, he leaned across her, his fingers curling around the door handle, and he slammed it closed.

Her head turned so she could look at him. He could see her face dimly lit in the outside lights of the gate.

She didn't look angry, hurt or revolted.

She looked blank.

Fucking hell, he thought.

He lifted his hand to her neck and held her there.

"Abby…" he started softly.

"Yes?" she asked, her voice as expressionless as her face, and Cash wondered how long it would take to achieve his new goal of winning Abby back.

As usual, he didn't delay.

"James talked to me this afternoon," Cash told her.

She stayed silent, but he felt her body grow stiff.

"In future," he went on quietly, "if you have something to say to me, you contact me yourself. Is that understood?"

Her body stayed stiff but she gave a short nod. Her neck tugged against his hand, trying to pull away and he gave her a gentle squeeze indicating he wasn't done.

She went still.

"You made me very angry today," he said, trying to keep his voice gentle. She sat silent, eyes on him. "Tonight, instead of simply being angry *at* you, I took that anger out *on* you." He paused and gave her neck another squeeze. "It won't happen again."

She remained silent, her eyes on his, and he waited for some sign she understood. But he didn't get it.

Instead, all of a sudden her eyes moved to the side.

Surprising him, she leaned in, her hand coming to rest lightly on his shoulder and she pressed her lips against his.

He thought for a moment this was an act of forgiveness. But before relief could fully form, mouth still on his, she whispered, "We're being watched."

Then her head tilted, she pressed closer, her fingers curled into his shoulder, and she opened her mouth under his, the tip of her tongue touching his lips.

He knew it was an act, a show for whatever audience they had.

And he didn't care about that either.

He accepted her invitation and the opportunity it offered, opening his own mouth and drawing her tongue inside. One arm went around her to haul her soft body closer, his other hand fisted in the curls of her hair at her back, gently tugging down to manoeuvre her mouth so his would have better access.

He deepened the kiss, and gratifyingly her hand moved from his shoulder, sliding up his neck and into his hair as her body yielded to his.

He knew then he had her.

Pressing his advantage, he kissed her until he heard that low, sexy noise she made in the back of her throat. A noise he discovered on Sunday that corresponded with a rush of heat between her legs.

And when he knew he could still reach her, his mouth broke from hers, slid down to her neck and Cash breathed in her perfume.

He heard her soft but heavy inhalations in his ear and he smiled against her skin.

"We'll finish talking later," he murmured.

She had no time to reply. There was a sharp rap on the passenger side window and Cash felt Abby's body jolt in surprise.

"Is everything okay?" his step-cousin, Fenella, shouted, and Cash saw her small face peering through the glass.

"Fuck," he muttered right before Abby pulled away.

With no other choice (although he would have preferred to start his car, drive to Abby's, take her back to her bed and finish what they'd started in the car—this time, with *both* of them finding release), Cash began to exit the car, but he was intercepted by Abby's hand on his arm.

He turned back to her and her hand came up toward his face, it hesitated, then pulled back but stayed suspended and her finger circled.

"Lip gloss," she whispered and two intensely unpleasant sensations hit him at once.

One was loss.

The other was remorse.

"Hello!" Fenella called from outside.

"Take care of it," Cash demanded, ignoring his cousin, his brief sense of relief fading back to irritation, again directed at himself.

He may still be able to reach her in one way, but in another she was very far away.

"What?" Abby asked, her head turning from the direction of Fenella back to Cash.

"Take care of it," he repeated. When she hesitated he continued with a note of warning in his tone, "Abby—"

"Oh, all right," she gave in, her voice soft but annoyed.

Cash was illogically pleased to hear her exasperation. It wasn't a good reaction but it *was* a reaction and he felt that boded well.

Therefore he smiled when she leaned in, reached up, her hand resting on his cheek as her thumb wiped the gloss from his mouth.

"Who is that?" Abby whispered while her finger slid across his lips.

"My cousin." Cash's mouth moved under her thumb.

"Are you two okay?" Fenella yelled in the window.

Abby's hand fell and she gave him a look he couldn't quite decipher before her head twisted toward the window and she called, "We're fine. Be out in two seconds!"

With nothing for it, Cash sighed his displeasure that the moment was lost before he knifed out of the car and slammed his door. He rounded the bonnet, his eyes on Abby who had extricated her lip gloss and was fixing her lips in the mirror of the sun visor.

"I was worried that you two were fighting," Fenella announced as he arrived at Abby's door where Fenella was standing.

Cash looked at his cousin.

Fenella Fitzhugh was Nicola's firstborn daughter and she looked like her mother. Blonde, petite and pretty, but unlike her mother it was in a sharp, pointy-faced way. She was too short for Cash's liking and far too thin.

She was also, as had been evidenced in the last few minutes, unbelievably irritating in an obtuse, coy way.

How two people who were kissing passionately in a car could appear to Fenella to be fighting, Cash had no idea.

Instead of commenting, he simply greeted, "Fenella," and moved around her to open Abby's door.

He bent in and took Abby's elbow, guiding her out and firmly positioning her free of the door before he slammed it.

"You must be Abigail," Fenella stated the obvious.

"Abby," Abby replied, her quiet voice warm and friendly.

Her hand came out to take Fenella's as she leaned in to touch the other woman's cheek with her own.

When Abby pulled away, Fenella exclaimed, "We've all been waiting with bated breath to meet *you*. Cash has *never* brought a woman to Penmort."

Abby looked at him from under her lashes as she murmured, "Really?"

"Really!" Fenella nearly screeched, and Cash winced at the shrill noise. "Mummy is in a dither. An...actual...*dither*," Fenella declared.

"Um, is a dither a good thing?" Abby joked.

Fenella waved her hand in front of her face, Abby's quip flying right by her. "Oh, Mummy's always in a dither about something or other."

In all of his memories of Nicola Beaumaris, Cash had never known her once to be in anything close to a "dither."

Cash, finished with this ridiculous exchange, decided to intercede.

"Perhaps we can move this conversation out of the negative three degree weather and somewhere warmer?" he suggested drily.

"Oh yes! What was I *thinking*?" Fenella cried, and then motioned to them to follow. "Come inside."

Fenella led the way and Cash and Abby trailed, Cash's fingers curling idly around hers, his thoughts on Abby as well as what that night would bring.

Outside of Nicola, who would give Abby a genuine warm welcome, Cash couldn't begin to guess how his uncle, and Nicola's two remaining daughters, Suzanne and Honor, would behave.

His thoughts were not positive.

He was taken out of them when he felt Abby's step slow and his head turned to her.

She was looking up, her lips parted, her face registering wonder.

Cash's gaze followed hers and he noted they'd entered the gate, climbed the steep path and up the steps into the common, turned left and were headed straight toward the castle.

Brilliant beams of light were shining from the ground up toward Penmort illuminating it brightly against the night sky.

The castle was a rambling L built around the side of a tor. It had thin bands of terraced gardens containing meandering paths running along its outer edge. It had a jagged roofline, some of its towers and turrets rising five imposing stories from the ground. There was another level built below into the face of the tor. It had a jutting rectangular entrance at the bend of the L and was built of a mellow red-brown stone.

The land had been occupied, and fortified, since the time of William the Conqueror when the sea, long since receded, had reached to the bottom of the tor. The castle that stood now was built during the Jacobean era, over four hundred years before. The entirety of its interior décor had been painstakingly, with no expense spared, refinished during the reign of Victoria.

Since the property was granted to its first Beaumaris master, Henry, by Richard the Lionheart, generations of men—men whose blood flowed in Cash's veins—had built and rebuilt the manor and then fortified, defended and possessed it for over eight hundred years.

"It's beautiful," Abby whispered, her voice filled with awe.

He looked down at Abby and then up at his ancestral home.

She was correct. It was beautiful.

He took her hand and tucked it in the bend of his arm, effectively pulling her body closer to his side as he led her forward.

Moments later, with the smell of Abby's musky, floral perfume in his nostrils, the feel of her against his side, Cash stepped through the enormous door and over the threshold of Penmort for the first time its owner, not only by birthright, but as the victor of a bloodless battle.

As his and Abby's feet hit the stone floor of the entrance lobby, it wasn't only Cash who felt the floor slant beneath him.

Abby swayed, her body twisting so her front was pressed into his side, her other hand coming around to clutch his shirt at his stomach.

In front of them, halfway up the short flight of stone steps, Cash saw Fenella's frame pitch awkwardly, and she threw her arms out to steady herself.

For a moment they all seemed suspended.

When the sensation ended, Fenella whirled toward them and cried, "What was *that*? Are we having an earthquake?"

Cash looked down to Abby and saw her face was pale. She was still grasping his shirt in her fist, her other hand gripping his biceps tightly.

"Are you okay?" Cash asked.

Her head tipped back to look at him, her hazel eyes wide and frightened as she whispered, "Did you feel that?"

"I felt it," Cash answered. Pulling Abby closer to his body, his head turned to Fenella and he asked, "Has that happened before?"

"No!" Fenella cried and pressed her hand against her stomach. "That was *weird*."

"Cash!" Nicola's voice greeted from straight ahead and Cash lifted his eyes to his aunt.

Arriving in the entrance lobby was Nicola Beaumaris and her youngest daughter, Honor.

Nicola was nearly sixty years old but she looked ten years younger. Tonight, as usual, her blonde hair was pulled back into an elegant bun at her nape, her clothing was understated yet stylish, and her bearing was graceful but friendly.

Honor was the only one of Nicola's daughters that Cash could remotely endure. She was not rail-thin like her sisters but curvy to the point of being plump. When she wasn't being silent, sullen or superior, she could be quite clever and on rare occasions displayed a sense of humour.

"Did you feel that?" Fenella asked when her mother and sister entered the hall.

"Feel what?" Honor returned.

"I don't know what," Fenella replied. "It felt like an earthquake."

Nicola came to a dead halt one step down and stared at her oldest daughter. "An earthquake?"

"Yes, the room pitched and—" Fenella started.

Honor interrupted her sister, her voice weary. "Fenella, don't be dramatic."

"I felt it!" Fenella cried, and then spun toward Cash and Abby. "You felt it too!"

"We did," Abby's soft voice confirmed Fenella's story.

Fenella pointed a finger at Abby and squealed, "*See!*"

"Fenella, don't point," Nicola's voice was gentle but firm. "And don't tell tales." Nicola descended the stairs to come close to them, but her kind eyes were on Abby. "You must be Abigail." At Abby's nod,

Nicola went on, "My eldest has a vivid imagination," she explained. "She swears Penmort is haunted."

Cash heard Abby's indrawn breath and felt her press closer to him.

He had, of course, heard about the famous ghost of Penmort Castle. It was the spirit of the raven-haired beauty, supposedly named Vivianna Wainwright, who was also the spurned lover of one of Cash's ancestors.

Legend told that Vivianna was a practicing witch and once her love was thwarted, she'd put a spell on her soul before hurling herself off the tallest tower of the castle, falling down the side of the tor to a gruesome death.

She'd done this not to kill herself, but to live eternally within the castle as a malevolent phantom, wreaking vengeance by causing intermittent havoc and murdering the true loves of Penmort's male line.

In all the castle's history, this had allegedly happened only five times. Not generation to generation, but the tale dictated each time the victim had been Penmort's master's one true abiding love.

It was, Cash knew, complete rubbish.

His fingers covered Abby's on his biceps and he murmured, "It isn't true, darling."

"Then what just happened?" Fenella demanded to know.

"I'm sure spooky Vivikums has better things to do than ruin Mummy's dinner party," Honor retorted.

Fenella's face blanched before she whispered, "Don't call her that. She doesn't like it."

"Hogwash," Honor returned on a sharp hiss.

Nicola's hand came out to touch Abby lightly. "Abigail, what must you think of us? Let's take your coat and get you a drink."

Cash escorted Abby up the steps and into the foyer, took her bag and then her coat from her shoulders, motioning with his chin that Abby should follow Nicola.

He saw Nicola take Abby's arm in her hand and guide her toward the drawing room saying, "I'm Nicola, Cash's aunt. You've met Fenella, this is my youngest, Honor."

Fenella and Honor trailed them and Cash watched as Abby cast a tremulous grin over her shoulder at Honor.

They disappeared into the drawing room and Cash took off his coat and tossed his and Abby's belongings over a wide window seat before he traced their steps.

They were gathering in the drawing room, Alistair and Suzanne already there. When Cash entered, Abby was greeting Suzanne.

Suzanne was Nicola's middle child and the only one of the three that Cash actively detested. Far prettier than both her sisters, she knew it. She had the same sultry aura of Abby, but where Abby's was simply a part of her, Suzanne's was a weapon she used.

And Cash had learned over the last year she used it aggressively.

As pretty and alluring as she was, she was no match for Abby's striking beauty and casual glamour.

The minute his eyes fell on Suzanne's face, which was turned to Abby and filled with unconcealed spite, Cash saw that Suzanne knew that too.

Cash felt his body tighten, instinctively going on guard at the malice he saw in his cousin's eyes.

"Abigail!" Alistair boomed, and Cash turned from one opponent to another.

His uncle did not look like a Beaumaris, at least not any of the former occupants of this house whose portraits hung in the gallery upstairs.

He was not tall, but of average height. He was not dark-headed with black eyes, but had light-brown hair and faded-blue eyes. He was not lean, straight and broad, but paunchy, slightly stooped with narrow shoulders.

And his eyes were mean.

He'd apparently decided to play the effusive host. Cash knew this because Alistair approached Abby, planted his hands on her shoulders and gave her a kiss on the cheek.

This was not Alistair Beaumaris's normal manner.

"Delighted you're here. Absolutely delighted," Alistair proclaimed as Cash positioned himself close to Abby's side. Alistair looked up at his nephew and smiled a rusty smile. "Cash, my boy."

"Alistair," Cash replied shortly and with considerable effort controlled the desire to curl his lip in loathing.

"Sit, sit," Alistair motioned magnanimously to one of the two facing sofas. "Where's Trevor?"

"Here, sir," Trevor, one of several Penmort servants that Alistair had long since lost the ability to afford, came forward.

"Abigail, what would you like to drink?" Alistair asked and Abby opened her mouth but Cash spoke for her.

"Amaretto and Diet Coke, only if it's diet and only if it's chilled. Crush the ice. A splash of cherry juice and three cherries," Trevor, Alistair, Nicola and her three daughters stared at Cash as he went on, "For me, whisky. Neat."

All eyes moved to Abby when she said quietly, "Or, if that's a bother, a martini would do."

Trevor looked relieved and asked, "Gin or vodka?"

"Vodka," Abby replied, hesitated and then went on, "Up, no ice." She hesitated again and queried, "Would you mind chilling the glass?" On Trevor's shake of the head, she hesitated yet again and added, "Olives, no onions." And then she paused and completed her exacting litany, "Three of them, on a toothpick, please."

The minute she was finished, he couldn't have helped it and didn't try, Cash burst out laughing.

When he was done, he slid his arm around her, curling his fingers on her shoulder. He pulled her to him and gave the side of her head a kiss.

When he moved away, Abby's head tilted back and she stared up at him, her face soft but stunned, her eyes shining in a way he'd never noticed before.

Her gaze felt like a physical thing, light and sweet, almost like a caress.

Cash noticed something move in his peripheral vision and with regret he tore his eyes from Abby, looked to his audience and saw they were all watching.

Alistair looked angry.

Fenella looked bewildered.

Suzanne looked irritated.

Honor looked astonished.

Nicola looked pleased.

Cash shared Nicola's mood and guided Abby to the sofa, seating them both, crossing his leg and tucking her close to his side with his arm around her.

"So tell us, Abigail, what do you do?" Alistair asked, positioning himself at the fireplace, close to the mantel, assuming a Man of the Castle pose.

"Call me Abby," Abby invited.

Alistair's face cracked into a false grin. "Abby."

"I used to be an interpreter and translator," Abby answered, and Cash felt his body go still as she unveiled this crumb of knowledge that he didn't know. She appeared not to notice his reaction and continued, "I can read and speak four languages, well five, if you count English."

"Really? How interesting," Nicola put in. "What languages?"

"French, Spanish, Italian and Portuguese," Abby answered. "It's been a while. I'm a little out of practice."

"It's probably like riding a bike," Nicola assured on a smile.

"I hope so," Abby replied, smiling back.

"You said 'used to.' What happened?" Suzanne, seated opposite them next to her mother on a sofa, asked, and Abby's head turned toward her.

"Oh, life," Abby stated vaguely and went on, "You know how it is."

"No, actually, I don't," Suzanne returned, her voice not containing curiosity but hints of acid. "How is it?"

"Suzanne," Nicola muttered in a warning tone.

"How did you two meet?" Fenella entered the conversation, changing the subject and Cash felt rather than saw Abby turn her head to look at him, but his eyes were on Suzanne.

"In a pub," Cash answered, his gaze moving to Fenella, who was seated on the arm of the sofa.

"A *pub*?" Honor inquired as if the very idea of meeting someone in a public house was not only common, but foul, and Cash's eyes sliced to her.

"A pub," he repeated firmly and watched as Honor, under the heat of his glare, took a small step back and behind her mother. His eyes moved to Abby, his voice growing softer, and he continued, "You were wearing white."

Abby stared at him a moment and Cash watched as warmth seeped into her hazel eyes. Her hand came to rest lightly on his thigh.

"Yes, I was," she replied with gentle surprise as if it was ten years since they met, not just over a week.

Alistair cleared his throat and Cash felt Abby's body start against his side as the all-too-short spell was broken.

"You're obviously American," Alistair observed when Abby turned to him. "What brings you across the pond?"

Abby didn't hesitate in answering. "I inherited the family home when my grandmother died just over a year ago."

"Oh, Abby. I'm sorry to hear that," Nicola murmured and Abby smiled at her.

"So you just dropped everything and moved to England? That seems a bit extreme," Suzanne remarked, and both Cash and Nicola opened their mouths to say something when Abby spoke.

"Yes, well," she said on a friendly smile. "There wasn't much to drop."

"Pretty girl like you? Didn't leave a man behind broken-hearted, did you?" Alistair queried half in jest, and Cash felt Abby's body go solid.

"No," Abby answered.

"I find that hard to believe," Suzanne commented and Cash decided he was done.

In a low voice he ordered, "Suzanne. Enough."

Suzanne widened her eyes in mock innocence and asked, "Enough what?"

"Enough of the third degree," Cash responded instantly.

"Well, she's very pretty, Cash. I can't imagine you're the first man in her life," Suzanne retorted. She had, Cash surmised, sensed something and she honed in on her target with lethal ease. Suzanne's eyes, as hard as her tone, moved to Abby when she continued, "Cash is family. We're just trying to get to know you."

Abby's chin lifted but she smiled politely at Suzanne when she agreed, "Of course. And you're right. Cash wasn't the first man in my life."

"Well, of course not. That'd be ludicrous. You have to be at least thirty," Fenella put in and Abby's head swung to her.

"Thirty-eight," she informed Fenella, and Fenella's mouth dropped open.

Suzanne ignored her sister's second change of subject and pulled it back to one she preferred. "So you did leave a man behind."

"Not exactly—" Abby started as Cash's body got tight in order to control his temper.

Nicola leaned forward to intervene, but unfortunately Alistair got there before anyone.

"Well, you've outdone yourself now. You're with Cash. And he's a Beaumaris. Whatever idiot let you leave him behind is no match to Cash," Alistair declared with false pride.

"Alistair!" Nicola snapped but Abby spoke at the same time.

"I was married," she stated.

"Oh dear, a divorcée," Honor muttered in mock horror, and Abby's head turned to his cousin.

But Cash was finished.

"Abby isn't divorced. Her husband was killed," he clipped, his abrupt, angry tone ending the ridiculously inappropriate conversation.

Nicola's sharp intake of breath was audible and Cash watched the blood drain from her face. Fenella, Honor and even Suzanne had the good grace to look uncomfortable.

Alistair, however, looked strangely snide.

But Abby clearly didn't read Cash's tone and continued, her voice low but strong, her eyes locked on Suzanne.

"Seven car pileup on the highway. Two other people died too, but not like Ben. Ben died instantly. He was the only one to die instantly," she paused then went on, the words innocuous, her tone making them heart-wrenching, "at the scene."

Cash felt his chest tighten, and ignoring their onlookers, he used his arm to curl her into him before murmuring, "Darling, you don't have to talk about this."

Abby moved her hand from his thigh to his chest, her pale face lifted to his, her eyes, he saw, held unconcealed pain.

He knew exactly what it cost her when she whispered her lie, "It's okay. They're your family. They should know."

He realised that she was playing her part and playing it beautifully.

He also realised he hadn't once regretted his decision to pay two hundred thousand pounds for her.

Until that instant.

She pulled away, her hand leaving his chest, and looked back at Suzanne. "I loved him. He died four years ago and there hasn't been anyone since." Her back straightened before she said, "Until Cash." Cash watched her head tilt inquiringly, her eyes never leaving Suzanne. "Do you have any more questions?"

"Not right now," Suzanne returned coolly, but she shifted on her seat in a way, Cash thought distractedly, that made her look uncharacteristically uneasy.

"You'll let me know when you do," Abby replied politely but pointedly.

Suzanne had no retort.

Abby's body stayed tense and only when she felt Cash's fingers squeeze her shoulder did she relax against him.

At that moment Trevor walked in with their drinks.

Cash watched Nicola lean toward Suzanne before she hissed angrily under her breath, "We'll talk later."

Trevor served their drinks and as Abby took a sip, Cash used Trevor's distraction to catch Abby's attention.

When her head tilted back to look at him, he murmured, "Are you all right?"

With uncustomary openness, she whispered, "No."

"I'll explain things about my family later," he promised.

She gave him a look that said clearly she really didn't want to know. Her look was so adorable, he couldn't help but laugh.

He dipped his face, rested his forehead against hers, and muttered softly, "You're exquisite."

She blinked as her lips parted, and Cash thought that was adorable too.

"I hope you two are hungry," Alistair boomed, again breaking the moment and Cash had to bite his lip to halt his angry retort.

But the moment was gone. Abby pulled away, turned to Alistair and Cash lost her yet again.

And from there the night progressed with no more turmoil. No "earthquakes," no offensive interrogations and Abby handled herself beautifully.

By the end of dinner it was clear Nicola liked her. Fenella seemed taken with her. Honor thawed enough to be slightly charming. Even Alistair wasn't a match for Abby's unique blend of candour and humour, and to all appearances, began genuinely to enjoy the evening.

They were walking back to the drawing room for after-dinner coffee and liqueurs when Abby asked the direction of the restroom and Fenella guided the way.

Upon entry to the drawing room, Suzanne absented herself immediately, not partaking in coffee and not waiting to bid Abby farewell.

Fenella joined them as Suzanne exited the room and was settling herself on the arm of the sofa with her cup of coffee when they heard Abby's piercing scream.

At the hideous sound, Cash felt his blood run cold but he didn't hesitate.

Slamming his brandy on the table, he knifed off the couch and sprinted to the bathroom, threw open the door and halted at what he saw.

Abby, her right arm bloodied, was lying unconscious on the floor surrounded by reflecting shards of mirror.

14

SPECTRE

"Call an ambulance." Abby heard Cash's deep, terse voice order from very close.

"Get some towels." Nicola's voice came from farther away.

"Oh my God. The blood. I think I may be ill," Honor remarked from even farther away.

Abby felt herself being carried and knew she was in Cash's arms before she opened her eyes to see his rigid jaw up close, her temple resting on his shoulder.

"Cash," she whispered and his head jerked to look at her.

"She's awake," Fenella noted gratuitously.

"You're all right, love," Cash murmured his soft assurance but his troubled expression belied his words.

He turned to face forward again as he carried her into the drawing room.

"Honor, I said get some towels." Nicola was closer, crowding Cash as he laid Abby on the sofa.

"What happened?" Alistair asked, looming over the back of the sofa, brows drawn, his strangely unsettling (and not in a good way) eyes locked on Abby.

"Give her a moment," Nicola demanded as Cash sat next to Abby's hip, carefully took her wrist in his hand and slowly pushed back her torn, bloodied sleeve.

Abby watched him do this and it was then it came back to her.

She'd been at the sink drying her hands, looking in the mirror in the bathroom, wishing she had her lip gloss handy (because every girl knew in any intense, gruelling, overly-emotional situation, which that night had been from the start, you needed lip gloss) when through the mirror she'd seen the vision behind her.

Seen it and seen *through* it.

A woman: dark hair, beautiful, pale face, her long hair streaming as if caught in a fierce wind and her old-fashioned violet dress floating in tatters around her.

Her expression was filled with blatant, frightening, *evil* hatred.

Abby had had no time to react when the vision moved toward her so fast it was shocking.

Abby screamed the terror that suddenly gripped her just as she felt a sharp thrust between her shoulder blades. She just got the chance to lift her hand to cushion her fall, but the push was so strong, her hand went through the mirror. The mirror shattered around her wrist, the shards cutting her and the sudden pain mixed with some water on the floor and being off-kilter made Abby slip. She went down, her forehead, with her weight and momentum behind it, slamming against the basin.

And then everything went black until she was in Cash's arms.

And at that moment, lying on the sofa, Abby knew she had to get out of there.

Now.

"Cash," she whispered urgently, and his eyes went from her arm to her face.

"Quiet, darling," he muttered, his gaze lifted to her forehead and narrowed.

His hand left her arm and came to her face, his palm resting against her cheekbone as his thumb cautiously tested the bump on her forehead.

At his tentative touch, Abby winced at the pain and jerked her head against the cushion of the sofa. Cash's hand moved away immediately and his eyes locked on hers.

"Fucking hell," he swore.

Abby didn't have time for her possible concussion. There was a haunting afoot and apparently the ghost in residence did not like her.

At all.

"We need to get out of here," she demanded, not caring about appearing rude in front of her audience because she thought it was more important to exit the premises immediately since the place was fucking *haunted*.

Cash had no time to respond for Honor arrived, announcing, "I've got the towels."

Cash's head came up. "Get me a bowl of warm water. Gentle soap." Clearly whoever he was addressing hesitated because he barked, "*Now!*"

Abby's eyes moved and she saw Honor scurry from the room as Nicola turned to Fenella.

"Get a flannel, dear. With some ice," Nicola requested.

Abby's hand came to Cash's arm and she tried to lift up.

"Cash, really, we have to go," she said, but Nicola was at the side of the sofa.

The lady leaned in, tucking a pillow under Abby's head as she pressed on Abby's shoulder to settle her back.

"Just be still, Abby. Let Cash have a good look at you," Nicola cajoled.

Abby's eyes went from Nicola to Cash, who was wrapping her arm in a towel. On the way there she caught Alistair staring daggers at her from his place behind the couch.

It was then Abby realised that she was going to have to be clever.

This was not good. At the best of times, Abby was far from clever.

However, clever at that moment included not informing them she'd just seen an actual ghost, much less been viciously shoved into a mirror by one.

"I'm sure I'm all right," she told Alistair.

"You're not going to sue me, are you?" Alistair demanded to know, and Nicola gasped.

Then she snapped, "Alistair! What's the matter with you?"

His eyes moved to his wife. "She's American. They sue."

"I'm not going to sue you," Abby assured him and pushed up on her free elbow. "I'm really all right. I just slipped on some water and fell."

Cash's eyes pinned her and he commanded, "Lay back."

"Really, I'm fine. I just feel a little silly, that's all," she told Cash.

"Abby, lay back," Cash repeated.

"Cash—" Abby started.

"Abby, fucking...lay...back," Cash clipped, eyes narrowing and since he was using the F-word in *that* way, Abby felt it prudent to do as he commanded.

She lay back.

"Here's the water," Honor arrived with a glass bowl of soapy water and a tea towel, Trevor at her heels. She laid the bowl on the table by the sofa and Cash turned to it immediately.

"Do you need me to call the ambulance, sir?" Trevor asked Alistair.

"No!" Abby cried. An ambulance might take forever and she needed to get out of there before the black-haired phantom came back, dragged her up the nearest steep stairwell only to send her plunging back down to her grisly death. "I'm fine. Honestly."

"Call the ambulance," Cash ordered Trevor.

"Cash, I said I'm fine," Abby butted in as Trevor left the room.

Cash's eyes came to her. "You lost consciousness."

"I know but—"

"I want them to look at you," he went on.

"Well, I understand that, but I can tell you I'm—"

"Abby, this isn't up for discussion," he finished, and the way he spoke those words said plainly he was *finished*.

"Oh, all right," she muttered, but she didn't even attempt to do it with good grace.

At that, Cash's face changed, went soft, his black eyes grew warm and he murmured, "*Now* I'm beginning to think you're fine."

Abby jumped at her chance. "Good. Then can we—?"

"No," he cut her off shortly.

She gave him a glare.

He accepted it calmly then turned back to the water.

"*Here's the ice!*" Fenella, for some reason, shrieked upon entry and rushed forward.

Nicola took the ice and sat on the arm of the sofa, holding it lightly to Abby's forehead while Cash deftly but cautiously cleansed her arm.

Abby rolled her eyes up and looked at Nicola. "I'm so sorry I ruined your lovely evening."

"Hush, dear. This didn't ruin anything. Let's just get you seen to," Nicola replied kindly.

Abby went silent and decided to spend her time not thinking about her imminent death at the hands of a see-through spectre, but instead, contemplating her evening.

Abby liked Nicola. She would be hard not to like. Nicola was lovely.

Abby also thought she might like Fenella and Honor. They were both a little unusual, but in entirely different ways. Fenella was kind of cute, in a drama queen, slightly grating way. Honor was harder to read, but Abby got the weird sensation that her prickly demeanour was a defence mechanism, against what, Abby didn't know.

Alistair was a contradiction. Instinctively upon meeting him, Abby didn't like him. His eyes were strange, definitely calculating and almost cruel. But his manner was welcoming and friendly. Abby didn't buy it and she had the feeling Cash didn't either.

On the other hand, Abby disliked Suzanne intensely. The woman was not nice in any way and she was also rude. How Suzanne could be borne of Nicola's loins was beyond Abby.

And lastly, there was Cash.

And that evening she'd been given yet something else to worry about.

Because, stupidly (as usual) she'd not thought about the time when circumstances would necessitate Cash playing the devoted, adoring boyfriend back to Abby's devoted, adoring girlfriend. The thought hadn't cross her mind.

Therefore, she'd been unprepared to experience Cash acting like her loving boyfriend.

Even though she knew it was pretend. Even after what he'd done at her house. Even after she'd insanely almost forgiven him for his callous behaviour in her bedroom when he'd been so sweet to her in the car. Even after all that, she hadn't been ready.

She hadn't toughened herself against how it would feel to have him do such things as casually hold her hand, kiss the side of her head and call her "exquisite"—a compliment said in Cash's rough, deep burr that far exceeded any Abby had ever received.

But it was fake.

It wasn't real.

It wasn't what she'd had with Ben.

It wasn't what her mind told her it was, which was that it was something far, far better than what she had with Ben.

That would be an impossibility.

For what she had with Ben was real and it was wonderful.

And what she had with Cash was make-believe, even if it felt fantasyland remarkable.

And she had to remember that.

This was a job, her job, but Cash also had to play his part.

And it was clear that in the meantime he fully intended to enjoy that for which he'd paid handsomely.

And it was also clear that he wouldn't allow Abby to stand in the way of him getting that. He'd taught her that lesson earlier. He was quite content to live his part of the pretence as long as Abby lived hers.

If Abby stepped out of the role for which she was paid, she would be punished.

And therefore she renewed her oath to keep her head screwed on straight and remember, always, always, always, this was a job. Just a job. And one day soon, he'd walk away and she'd get on with her life.

Firm (she told herself even though she didn't believe herself) in her resolve, she watched Cash place the bloodied towel in the bowl. He wrapped her arm in a clean, dry towel and when he was done his eyes came to her.

"The cuts aren't that bad," he said.

"I told you," she returned.

"I still want them seen to," he went on.

She rolled her eyes on a sighed, "Whatever," and heard Cash's chuckle.

Her eyes rolled back only to see his face close to hers. Nicola removed the ice, and Abby made a mental note always to pay attention right before his lips touched hers.

He moved away a scant inch and remarked quietly, "We're going to have to talk about those heels you're always wearing."

Abby blinked, confused at his declaration and asked, "Why?"

His face didn't move away while he explained patiently, "Because, darling, they've become a health hazard."

He couldn't be serious.

Could he?

Abby tried honesty.

"It's been so long, I don't think my body can readjust to wearing flats. My spine might collapse and I'll become crippled," Abby told him, not joking in the slightest, but even so, Cash chuckled.

"We'll take that chance, shall we?" he suggested, but in a way that was more a command than a suggestion.

"Cash, I can't wear flats. You'll be, like, towering over me *all the time* if I wear flats," she told him.

He moved back and his hands came to rest on either side of her as he said, "I like that idea. If I'm towering over you, it might have the additional bonus of intimidating you so you'll do what I say instead of arguing all the time."

"I don't argue all the time," Abby argued.

His brows went up, making his point nonverbally.

Abby glared.

The sound of approaching sirens filled the room.

"Saved by the paramedics," Abby breathed dramatically, and watched Cash's devastatingly effective smile before his fingers came to curl around her neck to give her an affectionate squeeze.

With that he moved away.

When he did, Abby's eyes fell on Alistair and she sucked in breath.

Alistair was looking at Cash and the way he was doing it was *exactly* like the ghost had looked at Abby.

His face was filled with wicked, murderous hatred.

A terrified shiver raced up her spine and it was worse than the fear she'd felt at seeing a ghost.

This man, she knew, intended Cash harm and for some reason that was worse than the thought of harm coming to Abby.

Before she had a chance to process this new worry, the paramedics arrived.

They'd shone a light in her eyes, asked her silly questions about day, time, current location, bandaged her arm and declared her fit, but they gave Cash warning signs and symptoms of concussion.

They left and Alistair was back to his good-humoured self (probably because he was walking Cash and Abby to his front door).

Cash settled her coat on her, handed her bag to her and Abby embraced Nicola, Fenella and even Honor while Cash donned his own.

She touched her cheek to Alistair's as he asked, "You'll be at the celebrations?"

Abby pulled away and nodded, and Alistair's eyes took on a happy but devious look that gave Abby a bad feeling.

"Good," he muttered, but Abby didn't think it was good at all.

Abby shook off her thoughts of doom telling herself that her first encounter with a real, live (well, dead but still existing) ghost was making her see things that weren't there and looked at Nicola.

"You'll tell Suzanne we said goodbye?" she requested politely.

"Of course," Nicola assured, but her embarrassment at her daughter's rude behaviour was evident and Abby felt for her.

Abby smiled, leaned in and gave her arm a squeeze. Then Cash took her hand and they left.

As they walked, Cash threaded his fingers through hers and lifted their hands to press them against the side of his chest.

Abby's brain, making clear where it stood in Abby's battle to guard her heart, registered that it was nice walking with Cash that way. So nice, Abby's brain decided it would walk that way with Cash anywhere. To his car after a dinner party or through the very fires of hell, it didn't care.

When they made it to his car and he'd beeped the locks and opened her door, Abby had control over her wayward thoughts and she turned to him.

"I'm sorry about this evening."

Cash's chin dipped down to look at her.

"Why are you sorry?" he asked.

"Well," Abby began, pointing out what she thought was obvious. "Because I was snotty to their daughter then broke their mirror, fell and lost consciousness in their bathroom and ended their evening with a visit from an ambulance."

His arm went around her, his other hand coming up to fist in her curls, pulling her head gently back farther to look at him.

"Suzanne's a bitch and always has been. You handled yourself well, considering. You were within your right to walk across the room and slap her."

Abby emitted a soft gasp at his brutally honest words, but he continued, his voice dipping softer, throatier and far, far sexier.

"You handled yourself beautifully," he said, and Abby felt a rush of warmth she had to fight back as he went on. "And as for apologising for your accident, darling, I'm beginning to realise that, regardless of how charming it is, I'm going to have to teach you to stop doing it."

"What do you mean?" Abby asked.

"You apologise a lot," he replied.

"No I don't," she returned.

She saw his smile before he remarked, "You argue a lot too."

Abby stayed silent and Cash brought her closer as his face got to within a breath of hers.

"Earlier tonight I did something to you that I deeply regret. Now you're standing in my arms apologising for my family being rude and for slipping on water. Do you not see that's absurd?" he asked.

She had to admit, he made sense.

She wasn't going to tell him that.

And she wasn't going to give in to the deeper warmth that invaded the region of her heart at him admitting to "deeply" regretting his earlier behaviour.

Instead she told him, "I'm tired, Cash. Can we just go home?"

He hesitated and she got the vague feeling he was disappointed before his arms got tighter and he lifted up to kiss her forehead.

"Of course, love," he said there and looked down at her again. "Which home would you prefer?"

She wanted to go to her home and her bed and her warm, fluffy cat who was evil in a cute way, not evil in a scary, murdering ghost way. But she knew that wasn't smart.

"Yours," she answered.

His mouth touched hers lightly. He moved back and guided her safely into the car, slammed the door, rounded the hood, got in, turned the ignition and they were away.

And Abby couldn't help but feel, until Penmort Castle was lost in the distance, that the whole building watched their departure.

❧ ❧ ❧

Her body was rolled onto its back and she felt a strong knee pressing insistently between her legs.

Her eyes opened and in the shadows she saw Cash's face disappear in her neck right before his mouth slid along its length. His hand smoothed up her hip, taking her nightgown with it, then went under it and up to close with intent around her breast.

"Cash," she whispered.

At the sound of his name, his thumb slid across her nipple and his head came up.

Fire shot from her nipple to between her legs and Cash murmured, "How are you feeling?"

"I was feeling great because I was asleep," she informed him, her voice still husky from slumber.

His lips touched hers and he suggested against her mouth, "Let's see about making you feel even better."

Then he went about the business of achieving that aim.

Spectacularly.

❧ ❧ ❧

Abby was on top straddling Cash, who was deep inside her.

Her back was arched, one of his arms wound around her waist, his other one high at her back, fingers curled under the joint of her arm. His head was bent and his lips were drawing her nipple inside his mouth with a sharp, delicious pull when her hands fisted convulsively in his hair and she came.

Hard.

It was so wild, beautiful and out of control, her hips, as if they had a mind of their own, ground into his, the walls around the heart of her flexing tightly. She felt him rigid, deep inside her, and it was as if her whole being existed between her legs.

His head moved away from her breast and if she'd been aware of them, she would have wanted to halt the telltale rasping moans that accompanied her climax.

Before she was through, he twisted. She was on her back and he was driving into her, deeply, almost violently, his hand curled around the crown of her head, the fingers of his other hand going between them and she gasped aloud when he touched her. Her orgasm exploded anew, bigger, wilder and she cried out his name before her head came up and her teeth sank into the flesh at his shoulder.

His hands moved to the backs of her thighs, pulling them high against his sides and he thrust harder, faster. She heard his sharp intake of breath before one of his hands moved back to fist in her hair, yanking her head back, his open mouth sought hers and she blissfully accepted the deep sigh of his climax.

It was some time after that Abby realised this was not the way to start her first day of having her head screwed firmly on straight.

His hips pressed gently into hers as he murmured against her neck, "Exquisite."

At his word, Abby shivered before he pulled out gently, rolled them to their sides, but his hand glided over her bottom and down the back of her leg, keeping it hooked over his hip.

His fingers trailed up her spine, cupped her head, tucked her face in his neck and remained there, lazily playing with her hair.

"We have things to talk about, darling, but I have to get to work," he said over her head.

Last night on the long ride home, she'd fallen asleep.

Cash had gently woken her in the car and she'd leaned heavily against him on the short walk to his door (how he found a parking spot directly opposite his front door, she had no clue and groggily thought it unfair).

After Cash made her take two paracetamol, they'd gone straight to bed, Abby breaking one of her most closely held rules of never, but never, going to bed without taking off her makeup and putting on moisturiser.

Apparently being assaulted by a spirit from beyond the grave took it out of you.

At the current moment, she didn't know what they had to talk about.

What she did know in her post-double-orgasm addled brain was that she needed a swift retreat and a call to Jenny for another "it's-only-a-job" pep talk mixed with an "oh-my-God" strategy session on how to survive a murderous ghost.

"That's okay," she muttered into his neck.

"Do you feel like cooking tonight?" he asked, and she tilted her head back to look at him.

His chin dipped down and she felt his eyes on her in the early morning dark.

She also felt herself wishing, even though she knew she shouldn't, that his gentle concern was real.

"I conked my head and scratched my arm, Cash. I'm not an invalid," she told him, her words made soft by her voice. "Stop worrying about me."

His head dropped further, his forehead coming to rest against hers.

"Abby," he said, and something in the way he said her name made her brace, mentally throwing up walls because she knew that tone—harsh but sweet and unbelievably warm, a tone she'd never heard from him before—was akin to an emotional battering ram. "Darling, you show it, you act it, but I need you to say it."

Abby's breath caught and she forced herself to let it free.

"Say what?" she whispered.

"That you forgive me," he replied.

Her throat closed and tears burned the backs of her eyes.

She was right. The walls around her heart splintered ominously under his attack.

"Say it," he demanded.

She swallowed.

"Abby, please, fucking say it," he growled, the words were curt, their meaning anything but.

"I forgive you," she whispered, and she knew she did, and further, she knew that was stupid too.

She had no time to dwell on this. His arms went tight around her, his mouth crushed down on hers and he gave her a world-tilting kiss.

When his mouth broke from hers and Abby's mind and body recovered from his words and his kiss, she realised she was in worse trouble than she first imagined.

And she imagined it being pretty dang bad.

But she knew then this wasn't just going to be a battle over her emotions.

This was going to be the epic battle of a lifetime.

Cash broke into her thoughts. "I'm sorry, love, but you're going to have to get up with me."

Her body went still at that alarming news.

What was next? Was he going to handcuff her to his side and make her spend the day with him?

"Why?" she asked, her voice as alarmed as she actually felt, and he laughed.

Her head tilted back to look at him, not thinking one damned thing was funny.

His chin tipped down and she saw the white flash of his teeth indicating he was still smiling.

"You can go back to bed in a minute," he assured her. "I just want to check your arm."

Oh, that was it.

Abby relaxed.

"I'm sure it's fine," she told him dismissively, sliding her head down on the pillow.

"I want to check," he returned.

"It's fine," she repeated, and got a tight warning squeeze of his arms in response.

"Abby, I want to fucking check," he finished in a not-to-be-denied voice.

With no other choice Abby gave in, but not without muttering, "Geez, you're stubborn."

His arms got tighter and he said, "Yes, I am, and I'll remind you why."

Abby didn't like the sound of that.

Cash went on, "You're mine. And, darling, I'll repeat as necessary until you get it into that obstinate head of yours, I take care of what's mine. Is that clear?" he finished on another arm squeeze.

Her mind on the epic battle that lay before her which seemed to get worse by the second, Abby grumbled a barely distinguishable, "Yes."

When she did, the tension she didn't realise was in Cash's body slid away, he rolled, taking her over the top of him and pulled them up.

He knifed out of bed, Abby going with him. He took her to the bathroom and did exactly as he wanted.

Fifteen minutes later, her cuts covered with antibiotic goo and bandaged anew, Abby crawled back into bed as she heard the shower start.

She lay awake in bed long after Cash got ready, came back to bed, pulled her hair from her neck and kissed her there after telling her he was leaving.

She didn't just lay awake.

She lay awake gripped with fear.

Fear of ghosts.

Fear of Alistair's intentions.

Fear of Cash.

Fear of her own weakness.

And fear that, one way or another, either propelled off the side of an ancient castle by a vengeful spirit or conquered by a beautiful warrior, her life as she knew it was going to end.

15

BATTLE STATIONS

Abby waited until she'd gotten dressed and taken two more paracetamol to combat the nagging headache that started some time after Cash left. A headache that was only partially due to her misadventure with the ghost but mostly due to her crazy, screwed up life.

She waited until she was sitting on the train platform to engage her phone and connect straight to Jenny.

When Jenny answered, Abby proclaimed, "Battle stations."

"Oh my God. What happened?" Jenny asked.

"I'm in Bath. I should be home in an hour. Be at my house when I get there." And as an afterthought she demanded, "Bring donuts."

"Oh no, is it a donut drama?" Jenny moaned, knowing exactly what that meant.

"No, it's an ice cream and tequila drama, but it's only eight o'clock in the morning. We'll wait until ten to break out the tequila," Abby told her.

"Shit," Jenny muttered, said goodbye and rang off.

A little over an hour later when Abby turned the key in her door and shoved it open, Zee darted out without saying hello.

Abby knew immediately why.

All three of Mrs. Truman's spaniels came crashing toward Abby to give her a hearty doggie greeting.

Abby bent down to offer them strokes and Mrs. Truman appeared in the hall.

"Where have you been?" she demanded, hands on hips. "The coffee's cold."

Abby straightened.

Mentally, she cursed Jenny to perdition for letting Mrs. Truman in.

Verbally, she said good morning, took off her coat and hung it on the coat stand.

When she did, Mrs. Truman gasped.

"Is that *blood*?" she screeched and ran forward with the energy of a woman half her age.

Jenny came shooting out of the living room and her eyes widened at what she saw.

Mrs. Truman had Abby's forearm in a gentle grasp and she was pushing back Abby's sleeve to expose the bandages.

"Abigail, what on earth happened?" Mrs. Truman asked.

"Are you okay?" Jenny called, coming forward.

Abby squeezed Mrs. Truman's hand and replied, "I'm fine. I need to change. Can you warm up the coffee? I'll be down in five minutes."

It was then Mrs. Truman's eyes narrowed on Abby's outfit.

"Abigail Butler, you're wearing the same clothes from last night," she accused.

"Um, yes," Abby told her.

Mrs. Truman's narrowed eyes came to hers. "Are you engaging in hanky-panky with your young man?" she snapped, and Abby felt her face flush.

"Mrs. Truman—" Abby started to tell her this, above all, was none of her business but didn't get anything out before Jenny spoke.

"That's hardly the point. Her arm is covered in bandages!" Jenny had walked up close.

"It *is* the point, Jennifer," Mrs. Truman shot back. "A good girl doesn't do *that* before marriage."

"You were awake when we celebrated the millennium, weren't you?"

Jenny returned, and Abby pulled in breath waiting for Mrs. Truman to explode.

She wasn't disappointed.

"Well, aren't you Mrs. Fancy Pants?" Mrs. Truman asked sharply on raised voice, and one of her spaniels yapped in support of its mistress. "It's clear to see Abigail has enough emotional distress with losing her grandmother and her job and overall stress with all this banging and new roofs and men in and out of her house all day. Not to mention, her first romance after the death of her beloved. She doesn't need sex mucking up the waters."

Mrs. Truman was right about that.

Alas, it was too late.

Clearly Jenny also knew the older woman was right. This was evidenced by her lack of retort accompanied by a stubborn glare.

Abby sighed.

"Ladies, can I change?" she asked.

Mrs. Truman let go of her arm. "You change. I'll make more coffee. Warmed up coffee tastes funny. You need fresh when blood's involved," she declared with authority as if this kind of situation happened to her frequently.

Abby escaped to her room, tore off her dress, thigh high stockings and boots, threw on some jeans and a long-sleeved T-shirt and dashed barefoot to the bathroom.

She said good morning to the two workmen who were installing her basin, asked if they needed a cuppa (they didn't, Mrs. Truman had serviced them) and then she ran downstairs.

The donuts had been arranged artfully on one of Gram's china platters. It sat on the table in front of the couch with Gram's silver coffee service and china.

Mrs. Truman had been busy.

Abby perused the selection of donuts.

English donuts were different than American. There was less variety, which was disappointing. But many of them involved custard and/or cream which Abby thought was a plus.

While Mrs. Truman poured her coffee, Abby selected a long donut, split lengthwise and piped along the opening with a mixture of cream *and* custard and dropped to her couch. One of Mrs. Truman's dogs jumped up beside her and sat panting and staring at Abby's donut.

The whole time Abby felt Jenny's eyes on her.

When she settled, Jenny impatiently demanded, "Start with the blood."

"Well," Abby began, not knowing how to say what she had to say without them thinking she was insane.

"Spit it out, Abigail. We don't have all day," Mrs. Truman asked, then bit into a sugar-coated jam donut, consuming at least a quarter in one bite.

"I was shoved into a mirror by a ghost," Abby blurted.

Jenny gasped.

Mrs. Truman snapped, "*What?*" but since her mouth was full, bits of donut flew out.

Abby took in a breath and explained, "Cash's family owns Penmort Castle. It's said to be haunted and I'm here, just barely, to tell you that is most definitely *true*."

Jenny shot out of her chair and leaned toward Abby. "I *knew* this would happen. I *told* you."

Mrs. Truman swallowed and decreed, "There's no such thing as ghosts."

"There is!" Jenny shouted, clearly beside herself.

"Is not!" Mrs. Truman shouted back, never really needing a reason to raise her voice.

"Trust me, Mrs. Truman, I would have been fighting your corner, but I saw her. I knew what she was. I could see *through* her. She was there. She was real. She was angry. And she shoved me," Abby told her and looked up at Jenny. "Then my hand went through the mirror. I cut myself, slipped, banged my head on the basin and went unconscious."

"Oh *God*," Jenny breathed and collapsed back in her chair.

"What does Fraser say about this?" Mrs. Truman asked.

"I haven't told him the ghost part," Abby admitted.

"Well I can see why not considering if you did he'd rightly think you were mad," Mrs. Truman retorted.

Abby turned her body to face the older woman. "Honest, I wish it wasn't true. But I'm telling you, Mrs. Truman, she's real and she means to hurt me." Abby's attention moved to Jenny. "And, in less than two weeks from now, I'm supposed to go back there for the anniversary celebrations and stay there...*overnight*."

"You can't do it," Jenny told her immediately.

"I know!" Abby agreed. "But I can't not do it either, Cash would be—"

"You have to get rid of her," Mrs. Truman butted in, and both women's eyes moved to her.

"Get rid of her?" Jenny asked.

Mrs. Truman waved her donut in the air. "Yes, get rid of her."

"Who?" Abby queried.

"The ghost!" Mrs. Truman replied with severe impatience.

"How's she going to do that?" Jenny inquired.

"I don't know," Mrs. Truman admitted. "But we'll sort something out." Then she took another bite of her donut and calmly chewed.

It wasn't lost on Abby that Mrs. Truman said, "we'll."

Abby decided not to fight it, she wouldn't win. It seemed post-dinner-party that Mrs. Truman had decided to become a fixture in Abby's life.

Abby had to admit she didn't mind in the slightest.

"I don't think it's that easy to get rid of a ghost," Abby told the older woman.

"I didn't say it'd be easy," Mrs. Truman noted, waving the remains of her donut again. "I just said we'd sort something out." She leaned forward and took a sip of coffee before sitting back and saying, "I know a few people. I'll make some calls."

Abby couldn't imagine what kind of calls she'd make to find someone to get rid of a ghost, but she didn't have time to ask, Jenny spoke.

"Are you okay? Your arm, that is."

Abby nodded. "Yes, Cash found me in the bathroom and carried me to a couch. He cleaned me up and then demanded that the paramedics look me over before he'd even let me sit up. I had a little headache this morning but mostly head and arm are both fine."

"He's a good boy," Mrs. Truman muttered but Jenny was watching Abby closely and Abby knew why.

Abby took a bite of her donut and assured Jenny, mouth full, "It's all good."

"You're being smart?" Jenny asked.

"Yes," Abby kind of lied.

She wasn't sure she was being smart, but she was trying to be.

Mrs. Truman was looking between the both of them as she inquired, "Is there something I should know?"

Abby answered with another mini-fib, "No. Just that Cash and I made up."

Mrs. Truman made a "pah" noise and stated, "Of course you did. The papers all say he's very bright. Anyone who's bright wouldn't let a good thing like you slip through his fingers because of a silly quarrel."

Abby was processing her feelings at getting a compliment from Mrs. Truman when the bell on the door clanked.

"Who's that?" Abby asked the room at large.

"How should we know?" Mrs. Truman asked back.

Abby dropped her half-eaten donut on the tray and walked to the front door, three yapping spaniels at her heels.

She opened it and a tall, good-looking young man she'd never seen in her life was standing outside.

"Abigail Butler?" he asked.

"Yes," Abby answered.

"I'm Simon. Mr. Fraser asked me to come and see about your plumbing," he announced, then shoved inside, through Abby and the dogs, and he closed the door.

"Um," Abby started, staring at him, unable to take in what he said or his forward behaviour. "Someone is already seeing to it."

Simon had walked through the vestibule, the dogs, who he was gamely ignoring, dancing at his heels, and he was standing in the hall.

"Yes, that was mentioned," Simon told her. "I'm here to make certain the job gets finished to Mr. Fraser's standards and look into the rest of the system."

Abby wasn't certain, but it *felt* like her blood pressure was rising.

"That isn't necessary," she told Simon as she noticed both Jenny and Mrs. Truman had come to the door of the living room to watch. "I've got everything under control."

Simon looked down at her. "I was also told you'd say that. Regardless, Mr. Fraser was pretty clear he wanted a report by close of business today as to how the system could be updated promptly. He's also stated he wants me to move forward and get it done."

Abby read between the lines. Cash wanted it done even if Abby refused. And it would get done, no matter what Abby said.

Yes, Abby realised, her blood pressure *was* rising.

"You're here on a wasted errand," she explained to Simon on another kind of lie. "They're almost finished."

Simon looked toward the stairs. "I'll just have a look."

"Really, it isn't..." Abby started but Simon was on the move and Abby began to follow him. "Excuse me," she called up the steps, and he turned.

"You don't have to come. I'll find my way," Simon told her, and he kept right on going.

Abby stared at his departing back.

The bell clanked again.

Abby turned slowly to the door but looked back at Mrs. Truman and Jenny.

"Well, see who it is," Mrs. Truman prompted sharply, and Abby and the three spaniels went back to the door.

She opened it and a man three inches shorter than Abby and about twenty years older stood outside carrying a toolbox.

"Abigail Butler?" he asked.

What now?

"Yes," she answered.

"I'm Nigel. Mr. Fraser asked me to pop by and fix your bell," he told her.

Abby looked at Nigel, then at the bell in her door, then to Jenny and Mrs. Truman, who'd come out into the hall.

When she looked back at Nigel, he was bent, had put his toolbox on the stoop and was petting two of Mrs. Truman's panting, happy dogs.

"Cute little fellas," Nigel remarked.

"Um, there isn't anything wrong with my bell," Abby told him.

Nigel's head tilted back and he looked at her before he reached out and turned the bell.

It clanked cacophonously.

Abby closed her eyes.

She opened them when she heard Nigel say, "Probably just needs a good cleaning. Won't take but a minute. I'll just get started."

With that he grabbed his toolbox, straightened, pushed in through Abby and the dogs, closed the door, dropped immediately to his knees and got to work.

Abby stared at him.

Then she turned and stiffly walked to Mrs. Truman and Jenny.

"Did that just happen?" she asked them.

"Yes," Mrs. Truman said shortly and vanished back into living room.

Jenny came forward and stopped when she was close to Abby.

"Remember, it's just a job," she whispered.

"We talked about this," Abby whispered back. "Cash and I. He said he wouldn't interfere."

"It's just a job," Jenny repeated.

"But—" Abby began, and Jenny's hand grasped hers and squeezed.

"Let him do what he wants to do. It's his thing. If he's getting off on taking care of you, let him do it," Jenny said and then went on, "Just don't get used to it."

"I don't think—" Abby started again, and Jenny squeezed her hand again.

"It's his thing. Not yours. Just let it go and keep focused."

"Jenny," Abby breathed.

"Focus," Jenny repeated firmly.

Abby understood what Jenny was trying to do but she was way too freaked out to let her do it.

"It's my house. It's Gram's house. Ben loved this house. It's theirs. This house is the only place I can still be with them. I can't be thinking of Cash every time I hear the doorbell or take a shower!" she cried but under her breath so Nigel couldn't hear.

"Too late for that," Jenny said logically.

"Jenny!" Abby exclaimed.

Jenny got even closer. "I know it's tough and it's going to get tougher. But you can do it."

"I don't think I can," Abby admitted, and Jenny gave her another hand squeeze.

"I *know* you can. And anyway, you've got bigger fish to fry. There's a ghost who wants to kill you, for goodness sakes."

This, Abby thought, was true.

"Priorities," Jenny finished, gave Abby's hand another squeeze, let her go and walked back into the living room.

Abby took a deep breath then followed her friend back to the donuts.

※ ※ ※

Abby felt the hair being shifted off her neck and she opened her eyes to see a man's thigh encased in black trousers with thin pinstripes set wide.

She looked up and saw a wine-coloured shirt, collar open at a muscular neck.

Then up further and she saw Cash.

He was sitting in the crook of her lap, one hand on her hip, his eyes warm on her face. Abby was lying on her side on the couch in the seating area off his kitchen.

"Did I fall asleep?" she asked in somnolent surprise.

Cash smiled, leaned forward and picked something up from the floor. He came up with her book, which she must have dropped after she fell asleep while reading.

"I think you lost your place," he murmured, setting the book by her still full, but now probably cold mug of herbal tea on the low table in front of the couch.

Abby's eyes went from the book to the digital clock on the microwave over the stove.

When she saw it was a quarter to eight, she shot to sitting position, dodging around Cash, and jumped to her feet crying, "Oh *God*! The dumplings!"

She rushed to the kitchen, registering that her nagging headache, which she'd been keeping at bay all day with pain medication, had come back. With it being way late, and with the dumplings to sort, she didn't have time to do anything about it.

Abby hurried to the counter saying, "I meant to have everything ready for you when you got home. This is going to take at least another half an hour."

As Abby threw the tea towel off the dumpling dough, Cash's voice said from behind her, "Darling, relax." She turned to walk to the drawer to get a spoon as he went on, "Martini or amaretto?"

He was at the cupboard containing the liquor, looking at ease and unperturbed, making drinks in his kitchen while she cooked.

This she found vaguely alarming because it was not-so-vaguely appealing.

Abby decided to focus on the drink rather than the appeal of Cash and herself doing normal boyfriend/girlfriend stuff in his kitchen and replied, "Martini."

While Cash started to make the drinks, Abby opened the Crock-Pot and the aroma from the food wafted strongly into the room. Without delay, she began to spoon in the dumpling dough.

As she did, she heard him say, low and deep, "Fuck."

She froze, gooey spoon in hand, and turned to see him staring at the Crock-Pot.

"What's the matter?" she asked.

"What is that?" he asked in return.

Abby looked down at the Crock-Pot then back to Cash, worry filling her at his reaction and she answered, "Irish stew. Um..." she hesitated then went on, "don't you like Irish stew?"

His eyes went from the pot to Abby and she held her breath.

"You know how you feel about cashmere?" he asked.

"Yes," she answered.

His lips turned up slightly at the ends. "I feel that way about Irish stew."

A weird, intense, happy warmth spread through her at this news.

Then it occurred to her that she'd said she wanted to roll around in cashmere and it was on the tip of her tongue to tease him but she stopped herself.

Ben, she would have teased.

Jenny and Kieran, she still could tease.

She could even tease Mrs. Truman (probably).

Cash wasn't hers to tease.

She went back to her task and muttered, "That's good."

She felt him get close and then she felt him casually kiss the side of her head as she was at her business with the dumplings.

At his kiss, the happy warmth was joined with a short, strong, lovely shiver.

He was back to seeing to her martini before she had a chance to shrug off this reaction. It took effort but she had herself firmly in hand by the time she finished the dumplings, cleaned her hands, pulled the crock out of the heating unit and slid it in the oven to bake the dumplings.

She was closing the oven door when she heard, "Abby, we have a problem."

She looked up to see Cash close the refrigerator and turn to her, his face grave.

She felt her heart start beating faster.

"What problem?" she asked.

He walked to her as she flicked the oven mitts off her hands and onto the counter, but he didn't answer.

"What is it?" she prompted when he didn't speak.

He got close and put both hands on her neck.

"Darling," he said solemnly, but there was a strange, magnetic light in his eyes. "We don't have any olives."

She saw his mouth twitch.

Her belly dipped and her heart lurched.

But she didn't speak.

Cash was teasing her.

She could likely protect her heart from domineering, sexy, charismatic Cash, but loving, kiss-on-the-side-of-the-head, teasing Cash?

Impossible!

He squeezed her neck. "Do you think you could do without the olives?"

Abby considered this. Then she bit the side of her lip.

Because the answer was no. She could absolutely not drink a martini without the olives.

Cash's eyes dropped to her mouth before he gave a shout of rich laughter and his arms came around her, pulling her to him.

"I take it that's a no," he said over her head and she could tell by his voice (not to mention the laugh) that he found this highly amusing.

"That's a no," Abby admitted to his chest.

He kissed the top of her head and murmured there, "I'll drink the martini and make you an amaretto."

She nodded and he moved away.

She had nothing to do but wait for the dumplings to bake. Therefore Abby was at odds with how to proceed seeing as they were moving around his kitchen like an old married couple, and she shouldn't be thinking about how lovely it was to move around Cash's kitchen, with Cash, like they were an old married couple.

She decided to stand, hip against the counter, and watch him make her drink.

"Did you have a good day?" she asked, thinking that sounded lame.

"No," he replied.

"No?" she repeated, watching him work, noticing that the ingredients for her favourite drink were all ready at hand. Obviously Cash (or Moira) had a conversation with Aileen and the kitchen had been stocked with her preferences.

That gave her a warm feeling too.

He continued as Abby fought valiantly against the warm feeling. "I have to go to Germany tomorrow."

Abby watched him move to the fridge for the ice and inquired, "When will you be home?"

"Saturday."

Abby's breath caught.

Her first thought was that she wouldn't see Cash for three days.

She'd been with him every day for over a week. She was used to being with him. She was used to having dinner with him. She was used to sleeping in his bed. She was used to sleeping with *him* in his bed. She was used to doing other things with him in his bed too.

She didn't like the idea of *not* seeing him.

Maybe for a day but *three*?

Suddenly Abby's emotional warrior reared up and mentally kicked her in the shin.

This reminded her that she and Cash didn't exist in that joyful time where everything about their relationship was shiny and new. They weren't caught in those early days of discovery where you spent every moment you weren't together thinking about being together, and every moment you were together thinking life was bliss. It wasn't the beginning of something that you knew, you just *knew*, was going to be something magical.

They were nothing of the sort (even though it felt like they were).

Three days was a godsend. Three days meant she could shore up her defences and have her head screwed on properly.

Three days was a *miracle*.

Her miracle lasted two seconds because Cash carried on.

"I want you with me."

Abby's body jerked at his words.

"In Germany?" she breathed.

He dumped the ice in a tea towel but turned his head to her and she saw he was smiling. "No, darling, I thought you could go to Capri. We'll meet back here."

Even though he was amusing, Abby didn't laugh. She was busy searching blindly for a way out.

Germany meant all Cash and nothing but Cash except when Cash was working, which would be time she was alone, without workmen, paint pots, Jenny, Mrs. Truman and her spaniels, which would be time she'd be doing nothing but *thinking* about Cash, which meant zero time to get her head on straight.

She came up with a solution.

"What'll I do with Zee?" she tried.

His brows went up. "Zee?"

"My cat."

"You named your cat Zee?"

"His name is Beelzebub but that's hard to say all the time, especially when you're yelling at him," Abby explained.

Cash stared at her, then asked, "You're telling me you essentially named your cat Satan?"

"Well, yes," Abby replied as if it was perfectly natural to name your beloved pet after the Lord of Hellfire and Damnation and watched as Cash did a very slow blink that forced her to defend her choice. "You don't know him. Trust me, he's aptly named. He can be a little devil."

He watched her a moment before his face grew warm and soft and Abby struggled with her instinctive, highly pleasant reaction to that look.

He smiled and turned away, shaking his head. He then slammed the ice in the tea towel against the counter, twice.

"I've tried that, it doesn't work. You have to use a rolling pin or a meat tenderiser," she informed him helpfully, but watched as he upended the perfectly crushed ice into her drink. Then she muttered, "Okay, well, if you have the strength of He-Man, it works."

She heard his chuckle as he handed her the drink, tossed the tea towel into the sink and went back to the martini.

"Can you get someone to look after your cat?" he inquired.

She could. Jenny would do it. Pete would do it too. Hell, Mrs. Truman would probably do it.

"Yes," she replied, and tried not to sigh.

He poured the martini from the shaker into a stemmed glass, saying softly, "Make the call."

Abby blinked and asked, "Now?"

He turned to her, took a sip, his eyes on her over the rim of the glass.

Her brain noted Cash looked very sexy drinking from a martini glass.

Her emotional warrior trotted over to her brain and slapped it upside its head.

"Now," he replied after his hand lowered. "We leave from Bristol Airport at half ten."

Abby's eyes bugged out. "Ten thirty! But I have to pack."

"I'll take you home tomorrow morning to pack," he told her.

"But, I need *time* to pack," she blurted, horrified. "We're going to be gone for three days. That's six outfits. Daytime and night time. Plus accessories. Plus toiletries. Plus I need to strategise makeup. I have to be prepared for anything. That might take hours. Under normal circumstances, that would take days."

"We'll be at your house by seven. We have to be at the airport by nine. You have an hour and a half."

"Seven?" she breathed, beyond horrified, straight to distraught.

Seven meant she had to be up, showered, dressed and made up to leave Cash's at six. That meant she'd have to be out of bed by four thirty.

Abby's headache started pounding but she didn't have time to worry about it because she'd started to hyperventilate.

The only times she remembered being up and out of bed of her own accord that early were Christmas mornings when she was a kid and the time her parents took her to Disneyland.

Abby didn't do mornings, especially not super-early ones where only nurses, doctors and criminals were awake and functioning.

Cash saw her dismay and tried to calm her with promises.

"You can sleep in the car," he said.

"But—" she started.

"And on the plane," he went on.

"But—"

He came close, mouth smiling (like she was *amusing* him), and he put his hand to her neck, effectively silencing her with a gentle, affectionate squeeze.

"Abby, make the call," he demanded.

She gave it a moment, ever-hopeful he would relent.

He didn't.

Abby sighed.

Then she made the call.

❦ ❦ ❦

Abby was lying on the sofa off the kitchen, her temple resting on Cash's thigh, her eyes unseeing on the book in front of her.

She didn't *want* to be in that position (well she did, but she didn't).

But she was.

After dinner, when Cash told her he had a few things to read through before going to bed, she'd joined him on the sofa and he'd manoeuvred her into that position.

Skillfully.

He was sitting upright, feet on the table, ankles crossed, reading glasses on, going over papers while his fingers idly played with her hair.

This felt nice.

All of it did.

So Abby was concentrating on anything but how nice it felt.

She decided to concentrate on dinner, which was weird. After they sat down to eat, her headache had begun hammering and her mind inventoried her belongings in a failed effort to decide what to take to Germany.

Conversation was short and stilted, but not intentionally. Abby was miles away, namely in Germany, wondering what the weather was like.

She didn't figure Cash noted this because halfway through dinner he took a call with a murmured, "Sorry, darling, this is important," and then was on the phone the rest of the time they ate.

At his side, watching him sitting at the head of the dining table and talking business while eating was when she realised he worked like a demon.

He got up early, got home late, read through papers at night and worked weekends.

Abby asked herself, what kind of life was that?

As far as she could tell, outside of working out and the time he spent with her, he had no life away from work. There were no photos around his house, no mementos from travels, no blinking answering machine with messages from mates who wanted him to meet them at the pub.

Nothing.

This worried her. Then she got worried because she was worried. Then she told herself to stop thinking about it.

He was off the phone by the time she'd done the dishes and put the food away only for him to tell her he had *more* work to do.

Now she was on her side on the couch, head resting on his thigh, legs curled into her belly, trying to read. But there was so much in her head, she hadn't turned a page in ages.

His fingers moved to her hairline, tracing it from temple to behind her ear. The tips drifted down the length of her neck to her collarbone.

Abby's attention moved from her thoughts and focused on his fingers as she heard his rough brogue say, "You're angry with me."

In surprise she rolled to her back and looked up at him. "Pardon?"

He studied her from behind his sexy glasses.

Then he tossed his papers to the side, his eyes came back to hers and he repeated, "You're angry with me."

She stared at him a moment before she placed her book on the table, rolled back around, put her hand to the couch and pushed up to face him.

"I'm not angry with you," she told him.

His hands went under her arms and hauled her closer so she was almost sitting in his lap. She put both her palms on his chest as one of his hands dropped from under her arm, the other one came to rest on her hip.

"Abby, don't lie to me," he said, but softly, taking the sting out of his words. "You haven't been yourself all night."

She felt her brows go up and started, "I—" but he cut her off.

"It's the house."

Her brows lowered significantly, registering her confusion. "The house?"

"I'll not have you living in that house the way it is," he stated firmly.

It dawned on her that he meant *her* house.

"Cash—" she began again only to be cut off again.

"I know I told you I wouldn't get involved but, darling, it's taking too long. I don't like the thought of you there without the bare necessities. Simon's report indicated there are other significant issues. They have to be seen to promptly and I'm going to see that they are."

"Cash, I—" she began *again* only to be interrupted *again*.

"I'm not discussing this," he declared.

Abby sighed and she did this deeply and loudly.

Then she asked, "Can I speak now?"

"Only if you don't intend to argue with me," he answered.

She didn't know whether to laugh or yell.

She wanted to laugh because it felt nice, him taking care of her, seeing to her "issues." She hadn't had anyone (but Jenny) to help her along the journey of life for so long she forgot how good it felt to share the burden.

She wanted to yell because he was way too damned bossy.

Instead, she did neither. Partly because she had a headache but partly because escorts didn't argue, girlfriends did.

She was, she told herself firmly, the former, not the latter.

"I can't say I wasn't a bit…" she hesitated as she found the word she was looking for, "*peeved* when Simon and Nigel showed up today. But I got over it."

His lips tipped up at the word "peeved" but he replied, "If that's the case, can you explain why you've been distant all night?"

She answered immediately, "Yes. I have a headache. I've been fighting it all day. I—" she stopped talking because she saw his eyes narrow dangerously and she knew from experience that was not a good sign.

His hand came up and pulled off his glasses.

"You have a headache?" he asked, his voice had dipped low, toward the scary zone where it went when he was irate.

"Yes," she told him cautiously, then went on. "It's not a big deal. I get them sometimes."

"Why didn't you tell me?" he demanded to know, and she could tell by the way he did that he wasn't irate. He'd gone beyond that.

"It's not a big deal," Abby repeated, confused by his reaction.

"Normally, no. When you've slammed your head against a basin and lost consciousness, then yes. It fucking well is," he returned, tossed his glasses on his papers and reached for his phone.

Abby blinked and asked, "What are you doing?"

His eyes were on his phone and he was using his thumb to manipulate it, but he answered, "I'm calling my physician."

Abby pulled in a breath then said quietly, "Cash, you don't have to do that. It's just a headache."

His eyes came to hers and pinned her to the spot.

Not that she could go anywhere. The hand that was resting on her hip had become fingers gripping it.

"Have you felt nauseous?" he asked.

"No."

"Dizzy?"

"No."

"Problems with balance? Vision?"

"No!" she cried. "Cash—"

But his eyes moved away and he said into his phone, "Tim? Cash." And Abby stared at him in shocked, but contradictorily pleased, horror as he continued, "Sorry for the late call, but Abby had an accident last night, hit her head and was unconscious for several minutes. She was checked by paramedics..."

He went on and Abby watched him.

When it became clear to Cash that all was well and clear to Abby, from what she heard of their conversation, that Invisible Tim had given her the go-ahead to live her life *and* take the flight the next day, which was something she hadn't considered or she would have faked a full-blown concussion, Cash ended the call.

"Tim thinks you'll be okay," Cash informed her.

"I already told you I was okay," she informed Cash.

"Do you have seven years of medical training and fifteen years of practice?" Cash asked evenly.

Abby gritted her teeth before she replied, "No."

He watched her mouth as she formed the word, his own mouth forming a grin.

"All right then," he muttered, leaned forward, kissed her forehead and sat back, his eyes coming to hers. "We're agreed. We'll take Tim's word for it."

They weren't agreed on anything, but Abby didn't say that.

She continued to grit her teeth and stare at him.

This made him chuckle.

Her stare became a glare.

His chuckle became a laugh.

She stopped glaring and rolled her eyes.

He pushed up to his feet, taking her with him, announcing, "Time for bed."

On *that*, they were agreed.

❧ ❧ ❧

After Cash gave her more paracetamol, they turned out the lights and made their way upstairs.

They were in bed, Abby's front pressed to Cash's, his arm resting heavily on her waist, their legs tangled, and she felt his steady breathing stir the hair at her crown.

It was then the tears stung the backs of her eyes.

And Abby realised it hurt, it actually physically *hurt*, to want something, something within reach, something that was pressed tight to you, legs tangled with yours.

Something you couldn't have.

And it hurt because she knew it was wrong to betray Ben's memory. She knew it was wrong to have the desire to move on, not to something else, but to something that felt better than what she had before.

And it hurt because she knew she was being selfish. Most women didn't even have the beauty of what she had with Ben much less the glory of all that was Cash.

To control the tears, she allowed herself a moment of weakness.

Knowing he was asleep and she was safe to give a piece of herself away, she wrapped her arm around his waist and snuggled closer to his solid warmth.

And she fell asleep.

❧ ❧ ❧

Cash felt Abby's weight settle into him.

His arm tightened around her and he bent his knee until his thigh was pressed against the heat of her. In sleep, she accommodated him by hooking her leg around his hip.

Thoroughly entwined, Cash felt the peace invade.

And he allowed himself to sleep.

✤ *16* ✤

SÉANCE

Cash pulled his Maserati into her drive, and Abby watched as he turned off the ignition.

He got out and she did as well. She closed her door and watched him go to the trunk and pull out not only her, but also his suitcases.

He put one on the ground, slammed the trunk, picked it up again and his eyes came to hers.

Then he walked right past her to the steps that led to her front door.

I guess Cash is spending the night, she thought on a sigh and followed him.

Germany had been good, or as with anything to do with Cash, too good.

Indeed, it was exceptional, or (although Abby was trying not to think this way, she was, as ever, finding it supremely difficult) one could say it was even magical.

It hadn't started that way.

In fact, they'd almost had another row before they left.

This happened when they were both in her bedroom the morning she packed.

Cash was standing in the bay window talking on his phone, alternately watching her and looking outside, his gaze resting on her far-off view of the sea (one of the many things about her house that she loved most, and incidentally so had Ben).

She'd closed her suitcase, pleased with her efforts and the fact that she still had ten minutes to spare and proclaimed, "Done!" as if she'd just successfully climbed Mount Kilimanjaro (which it felt like she had).

Still on his phone, as calm as you please, he walked to her suitcase, opened it, dug under her clothes and took out three pairs of high-heeled shoes.

She watched as one by one he tossed each shoe into a corner of the room.

First, she stared at the shoes and made a mental note to have a word with him about how he handled her designer gear. Though she made another note to do it when her head wasn't about to explode.

Then her eyes went to his.

When their eyes caught, he put his palm over the mobile and ordered, "Flats."

Forgetting for a moment that she was his dutiful escort, not his recalcitrant girlfriend, she'd marched to the shoes, marched back to her bag and repacked them.

The whole time she was at her task, Cash watched.

When she was done, he said into his phone, "One second."

He took it from his ear, again put his palm over it and uttered one word only.

"Abby."

Without hesitation, mimicking his implacable tone, she returned, "Cash."

They stared at each other and Abby mentally prepared for battle.

To her shock, he sighed, shook his head and finally smiled.

"We'll buy you a helmet in Munich," he teased, the smile had reached his eyes and she watched as they warmed.

Abby felt the now-familiar pleasantness invade her system at being the recipient of a smile from Cash accompanied by that soft look.

Turning back toward the sea, he put his phone to his ear.

For their entire trip, that had been the only time they'd disagreed.

Everything else had been wonderful.

Ben and Abby had never travelled well together. They were great once they got to their destination, but getting there and getting home had never been fun.

Ben always complained about how much Abby packed. Further, he liked to be at the airport an hour before the hours before they actually had to be there, something which drove Abby insane. He was not fond (to say the least) of Abby's penchant for duty-free shopping. Even though he usually didn't mind her spending, when they were travelling it annoyed him that she'd blow half of their budget before they even left the country (but Abby couldn't help it, the deals were just too good to pass up).

Cash didn't care how much she packed (he just didn't like her heels), not even when he had to carry her heavy suitcase down to his car. And she didn't get a chance to duty-free shop as Cash owned his own plane.

Yes. His own *plane*.

Like everything else he owned it was sleek and expensive but not ostentatious. It was a six-seater jet, a luxurious one but not overly large nor overly-well-appointed. It was comfortable and well stocked, but he didn't have gorgeous, rail-thin, model-type flight attendants wearing mini-skirted, cleavage-busting uniforms. They had to make their own coffee. Well Abby did, Cash was on his laptop the whole trip.

With some effort Abby hid how stunned she was he had his own plane. Obviously, he was expensive-escort, diamond-bracelet, cashmere-robe loaded, but owning a jet took it to a new level.

She had to hide her shock again when, once they arrived in Munich, they went to the opulent Mandarin Oriental and were shown to an elegant suite that included a king-size bed and walk-in closet.

She wasn't surprised however when he tipped the bellman, closed the door and took Abby into his arms for a quick but thorough kiss before telling her he needed to get to work.

Thus started their time in Germany and Abby thought it would be just like home.

It wasn't.

Firstly, Cash didn't wake up at five o'clock, turn to her for a heated, but quick, mind-boggling session of lovemaking and leave.

He woke up at six, turned to her for a heated, but long, lingering, mind-boggling session of lovemaking, after which he held her for a while, asking her questions in a soft voice like what she was going to do that day and stroking the small of her back or playing with her hair.

Then he left.

She spent her days in Munich's gardens, museums and churches as well as shopping, but not buying (for herself, she got Jenny a souvenir for watching Zee).

Late afternoon, he'd call to warn her he was returning to the hotel, but he always gave her plenty of time to get back to meet him there.

They spent their nights in the city's famous beer gardens with Cash introducing Abby to her new favourite thing, Prinzregententorte, a culinary extravaganza including seven thin layers of cake separated with chocolate buttercream and covered in chocolate glaze.

The minute the cake plate was placed in front of her, her eyes hit it and rounded in greedy, exultant wonder.

Cash took in her look and burst out laughing.

After he finished with his hilarity, he partially stood, leaning across the table, one hand on its top, the other one wrapping around the back of her head, and with everyone watching and his mouth still smiling, he gave her a hard, short kiss that stole her breath.

He kissed her after she'd eaten the cake too. Since he had a piece as well, that kiss tasted better, but Cash kissing her with a smile on his face was definitely the best.

He also spent their evenings conducting gentle, but thorough, interrogations.

He asked about her mother, father and grandmother, but notably and thankfully, not Ben. He asked about her former job and where she went to school.

He also shared his history, telling her more about his mother, a bit about his grandfather and explaining that, outside a couple of visits in his youth, he had little to do with Alistair and Nicola. Indeed, until very recently, he never spoke to them.

He also shared bluntly that he didn't like nor trust Alistair (Abby had kind of guessed that) and had little patience for his cousins, particularly Suzanne (which Abby had also kind of guessed).

However, it was clear he held a fond regard for Nicola.

It was Penmort Castle that made him, as he called it, "heal the breach."

She couldn't blame him for wanting to experience his legacy, even in an unfair outsider way. If she had a legacy like that, she'd want the same.

Further, he not only asked about, but shared his own favourite books, movies and music as well as guiding them into a hilarious conversation about their *least* favourite books, movies and music.

She answered his questions because, she told herself, it was her job.

Not because she liked doing it. Not because she found it easy talking with him. Not because she was curious about his past and his family and how such a magnificent man as he fit in that strange viper's den. Not because she was fascinated to know his favourite movie was *Touch of Evil* and his favourite book was *In Cold Blood*.

No (she told herself), it was just a job. Only a job.

She wasn't in Munich with a handsome, fascinating man who not only wanted to know more about her but also easily shared more of himself.

She was there to do her job.

That was it.

After they'd eat, drink and talk, they'd stroll through night-time Munich hand in hand and walk off the beer and the Prinzregententorte.

After that, they'd go to their suite and he'd lead her to the bed (or Friday night it was the shower *then* the bed) where he again made love to her, hot, long and lingeringly.

It was different for them in Germany. He worked less, spent more time with her and all else, she found (and struggled against) could be forgotten. Their time together was more relaxed without the outside world pressing down on them. It was like being on a vacation, but with Cash's work intruding however insignificantly.

Which made it much, *much* harder for Abby to remember she was playing a role rather than living a dream.

So by the time they made it home late Saturday evening, she was contradictorily both refreshed and exhausted.

Cash had declared they were spending the night at her house because it was closer to the airport. Abby had attempted, all the way home, in a polite way, to prevent this.

As she followed him up the steps to her door, she knew she'd failed in this endeavour.

She had the keys ready and was beginning to reach around him when his hand came up and he took them from her.

In one of the myriad ways Cash was different than Ben, Abby noted that Cash had made a habit of doing things for her.

Ben would open her car door or he'd make her a drink sometimes when she didn't even ask, or do other little things here and there that were mostly random, but always thoughtful and definitely sweet.

Cash took this behaviour to extremes. He opened car doors, restaurant doors, hotel doors, *every* door. He made a point of positioning himself closest to the street when they walked along sidewalks, something she remembered from years ago when her grandfather was still alive that he told her was the hallmark of a true gentleman. He asked her preference for food and drink before the waiter arrived then ordered for her. Even though she held a hotel key card to their room, when she was with Cash, she never used it. She never once touched her suitcase. He, or a bellman, carried it everywhere.

Indeed, the only things he'd allow her to do was make him coffee, pour him a whisky or cook his food.

Abby was beginning to find this grating.

She might, if circumstances had been different, have found his gallantry attractive. She would, however, probably have explained the extent of it was unnecessary.

She might, again if things were different between them, find getting him a coffee, a whisky or dinner, something she enjoyed doing.

Instead, she found this a reminder that she was *his*. It reminded her that not only did she work for him, he owned her, and as he'd told her more than once, he took care of what was his.

She wasn't his cherished partner. She was his valued possession.

He clearly took care of his possessions, his home, his car, his jet.

She was just one of many of his expensive belongings and this behaviour reminded her of that.

"Cash, you had the bags, I could open the door," Abby stated, and even though an escort would have kept her mouth shut, Abby was tired so she didn't.

His eyes moved to her. "Yes," he replied quietly. "But you aren't going inside."

Abby blinked at him in confusion, saw his eyes move to the bay window of her living room and his chin lifted. Abby's eyes followed and she saw, just dimly, what looked like flickering candlelight shining through her curtains.

Her body froze.

No one should be there and certainly no candles should be lit.

Jenny knew they weren't returning until late and she hadn't a clue they'd be coming to Abby's. Even if she'd wanted to leave them a warm welcome just in case, she wouldn't have left a candle burning.

"Oh my God," Abby breathed. "Someone's in there."

"Stay at the door," Cash ordered. "I don't want you coming in until I tell you it's safe. Understood?"

Panic welling in her, Abby grabbed his forearm as he lifted the key toward the latch.

"Cash! You can't go in there!" she hissed. "You don't know who's there."

"Darling, you might have intruders in your house. What do you suggest I do?" he calmly returned, and Abby let him go and threw up her hands.

"I don't know. Call the police?" she tried.

He dismissed her suggestion by lifting his hand to the lock while he said, "Stay here."

"Cash!" Abby protested, but under her breath so the bad guys wouldn't hear.

Cash inserted the key into the lock but he looked over his shoulder and down at her, his eyes serious, his face hard. "Stay. Fucking. Here."

All right then.

He was using the F-word.

Abby decided it was time to back down.

However, she also decided not to give in gracefully.

So she crossed her arms on her chest and gave him a glare.

He completely ignored her, opened the door and silently entered her house.

Abby waited.

She waited some more.

Then she heard several female shrieks ending with Mrs. Truman shouting, "Dear Lord, what are *you* doing here?"

Abby grabbed the bags Cash left outside, rushed in, dropped them in the entry, closed the door, pulled off her coat and threw it on the coat stand all the while hearing Cash and Mrs. Truman's loud conversation.

"What the fuck?" (Cash)

"Language!" (Mrs. Truman)

"Would you care to explain why you're in Abby's house in the dead of night and what in fucking hell you're doing?" (Cash)

"You're early!" (Mrs. Truman)

"It's fucking midnight!" (Cash)

By this time Abby made it to her living room only to see it wasn't one candle lit, but at least two dozen of them.

And it wasn't Mrs. Truman alone who was enjoying a dead-of-night, candlelit, clandestine moment in Abby's living room, but Jenny was there, to her confusion, for some reason Fenella was there too, as was some woman Abby had never seen.

The woman was dark-haired, dark-eyed, curvaceous and either around five years older than Abby or she was ten and hid it well. She was wearing stylish, hip-hugging, faded, boot-cut jeans over high-heeled boots with a cool, heavy-buckled belt Abby would kill for, all this topped with a snug-fitting turtleneck.

Oddly, she was also wearing a silk scarf wrapped around her head, the faded, fringed ends tangled in her long hair and a webby shawl was thrown over her shoulders.

It wasn't a look Abby would be able to pull off (or, in all honesty, would want to) but the lady did so, brilliantly. She looked like a rock 'n' roll gypsy.

Abby had a sinking feeling she knew what this was about.

But what was Fenella doing there?

"What the fuck are you doing here?" Cash asked, as if in Abby's brain, his angry gaze had swung to Fenella, then it moved to The Gypsy Queen. "And who the fuck are you?"

Abby put her hand up, wrapped her fingers around Cash's biceps, leaned into his side, and in the hopes of calming him, said softly, "Cash."

"Really," Mrs. Truman scolded, foiling Abby's calming attempt, "your language is unacceptable, Cash Fraser."

Cash's furious eyes sliced to Mrs. Truman and Abby was treated to proof positive that the older woman had nerves of steel when she didn't even flinch.

"Yes. You are correct." Cash was enunciating his words with scary clarity. "Normally, it would be unacceptable. But you appear to have helped yourself to my girlfriend's house to do..." he hesitated, cast an irate glance around the living room and continued, "whatever-the-fuck you're doing and by the looks of it, it isn't fucking good."

Abby looked around and realised he wasn't wrong.

Not only were there candles burning, there were heavy scarves thrown over the shades of her lamps, muting their brightness so much Abby didn't notice until then they were switched on. More scarves of velvet and silk festooned the table in front of the couch, on which there was a variety of paraphernalia, including burning incense, more candles (dripping onto the cloth, by the way), bowls filled with dark liquid, a huge, clear, round ball on a poofy, tasselled, velvet pillow, and what looked distressingly like the bones of a small animal (or an infant, and even though neither choice was good, Abby was hoping for the former).

"You weren't supposed to be home until later," Mrs. Truman stuck with her earlier theme.

Cash rocked back on his heels and sucked breath in through his nose in an obvious attempt at patience.

Jenny looked at her watch and hesitantly entered the fray.

"Um, Mrs. Truman, I think it *is* later," she said.

Mrs. Truman looked at her own watch then up to Jenny and remarked sedately, "Oh, so it is."

"Time flies when the spirits aren't talking," the Gypsy Queen put in.

Cash spoke again and this time he had his anger in check but, you could tell, just barely.

"Let's start this again," he suggested. "What are you doing here?"

"Séance," Mrs. Truman instantly replied as if this was an entirely natural thing to be doing in someone else's living room.

Or at all.

Cash's eyes narrowed and Jenny and Fenella both took steps back. The Gypsy Queen crossed her arms on her chest, a small smile playing at her mouth and Mrs. Truman went into staredown mode with Cash.

"You're having a séance," Cash repeated in a way that said he not only couldn't believe his ears, he didn't *want* to.

"Yes," Mrs. Truman replied calmly.

"In Abby's living room," Cash went on.

Mrs. Truman glanced at Jenny then back at Cash and explained, "It would upset my dogs if we did it at my house."

"Kieran would totally freak if we did it at ours," Jenny threw in.

Cash's eyes cut to her and he gave her a look that said without words, "*no fucking kidding?*" therefore Jenny took another step back.

Bravely, Fenella spoke up, "And you know Alistair would have a fit if we tried something like this at the castle."

Cash pinned Fenella with a look. "Would you like to explain why *you're* here?"

Fenella's glance darted around the room then she took in a deep breath and tried but failed to perform a nonchalant shrug. "Well, see, I was in Clevedon the other day, um..." she glanced at Jenny and said, "shopping. And I thought I'd pop by and say hi to Abby. She wasn't here because, you know, she was with you."

When she stopped speaking, Cash prompted, "Yes. I know. Continue."

Fenella's mouth moved around like it had forgotten how to form words before she plucked up the courage to go on.

"I was knocking on the door and waiting and Mrs. Truman came out and asked who I was. We got to chatting. She invited me to tea then she told me about the séance and invited me to come. I'd never been to one and well..." She hesitated before throwing her hands out at the sides and finishing in a voice that was several octaves higher than normal, "I'm here."

Cash stared at Fenella and it was clear even to someone who hadn't spent nearly every single day of the last two weeks with him that he didn't believe a word she said. Or at least not the important ones.

Surprisingly, he let it go and turned to The Gypsy Queen. "And you are?"

She lifted her chin while saying, "Cassandra McNabb. Clairvoyant and white witch, at your service."

Cash watched her for a moment, which slid into two that slid into three as all the women stood tense, waiting.

Then he muttered, "Fucking hell."

"Obviously you're tired and want a private moment to say goodnight to Abby before you go home," Mrs. Truman said and continued pointedly, "to your *own* bed."

This comment, Abby noted with alarm, made Cash, whose anger had partially cooled, look like he was going to explode.

"Actually—" he started with deadly calm, but Abby jumped in front of him, pressed her back to his front and interrupted.

"Actually, why don't you all just go on home? I'll blow out the candles and clean up for you tomorrow."

"Works for me," Cassandra muttered, wandering toward a fringed bag that lay beside the hearth.

"I'm, um, staying with Mrs. Truman," Fenella made this surprising announcement, her eyes on Abby looking weirdly like she was trying to communicate something she could not say out loud. "Maybe tomorrow you and I could have a cup of—"

Cash cut her off by saying, "No."

Fenella's eyes flitted to Cash and she uttered a strangled, "No?"

"Tomorrow's Sunday. Abby's mine," Cash declared, and when Fenella opened her mouth to speak, Cash went on, "All day."

"But you just spent three days with her in Germany!" Mrs. Truman snapped.

"Three days where I was working. Tomorrow, I'm not working and Abby's spending the day with me," Cash returned.

"You don't *own* her," Mrs. Truman shot back and Jenny made a telltale choking noise, which brought Cash's newly narrowed eyes to her face.

Bloody hell! Abby thought.

She sought to minimise any possible future damage by quickly announcing, "It's late. You all get home." She looked at Fenella. "I'll call you. Does Cash have your number?"

Fenella nodded, eyes on Cash, and said, "I think so."

"Good." Abby smiled at Fenella, and then turned to Cassandra. "Sorry this has been heated but I hope you understand we're both kind of tired." Cassandra made no reply so Abby went on in a desperate attempt to be polite. "Anyway, it's nice meeting you."

Cassandra's dark-brown eyes looked into Abby's and Abby stood frozen, having the eerie but not entirely unpleasant feeling that Cassandra was reading the words written on Abby's soul.

She broke her own spell by saying, "We'll meet again." She walked to the door, stopped, and looked back at Abby. "You've got a great cat."

Then she was gone.

The others followed close on her heels.

Abby closed the door on them and met Cash in the hall, the faint light from the living room was gone indicating that Cash had blown out the candles and turned out the lights.

Abby flipped a switch that flooded the hall with light.

The minute Cash's eyes focused on her, he remarked, "That woman is a nut."

"Mrs. Truman?" Abby asked.

"Take your pick," Cash answered dryly, and Abby wanted to be detached and beyond finding Cash amusing but she couldn't help but laugh.

While still laughing, she felt his arm slide around her shoulders and he started to lead her up the stairs.

"Do you know why Fenella would come visit you?" he asked, and Abby could swear she read more than mild curiosity in his tone.

"No idea," she replied with all honesty.

Fenella's being there was, far and away, the weirdest part of a very weird night.

Cash may have wanted to say something else but while they were on the landing turning toward the next flight of steps the lights flickered, they did it again and the hall went black.

Cash stopped them dead on the landing and for a moment Abby feared an army of malevolent ghosts would descend.

Then she realised it was just her usual bad luck, bad timing and wiring that was likely laid during World War I.

"You have got to be fucking kidding me," Cash muttered angrily in the dark.

"It's probably just a fuse," Abby replied with more hope than certainty.

She felt rather than saw Cash turn to her. She did this because his arm never left her shoulders and she found herself pressed to him, breasts to chest.

"In all the shit we talked about in Germany, I forgot to ask about this fucking house," he commented, his tone bland, his use of the F-word a huge, waving, red flag.

"It's just old," Abby tried.

"It's old," he agreed and continued, "It's also a money pit and likely a fire hazard."

"It's not a fire hazard!" Abby felt the need to defend, even though the report the surveyor gave her indicated differently, mainly due to the wiring and, perhaps, some of her appliances. She went on to semi-lie, "It's fine. Solid. It can just be cantankerous on occasion."

Or, more to the point, weekly.

Cash moved into her, his hand curling her back to his side as he reversed directions.

"Where are we going?" Abby asked as he started to guide them back downstairs.

"My place," Cash answered.

Abby halted, too tired to remember she didn't want him in her house.

"But it's late!" she exclaimed.

Cash pressed her to moving again. "It is, darling, but I'm not fucking around with a fuse box at midnight. Furthermore, I like you just the way you are. You'd be far less attractive burned to a cinder."

"I'm not going to get burned to a cinder," Abby declared crossly.

"No. You're not," he agreed and proved himself right by guiding her firmly to the entry, helping her on with her coat, grabbing his bag and using his other hand to propel her to his car.

Then he drove them to his house.

17

ALL THE TIME IN THE WORLD

Cash woke on his back, his arm outstretched and Abby was in another unusual but exceptionally sweet position. The curve of her spine was pressed against his side, the heels of her feet against his leg and her temple was resting on the back of her hand, which was curled around his biceps.

He turned into her, sliding his hand along the silk at her waist.

She was wearing one of the nightgowns he bought her the day before—a sexy, short, revealing, grey-green silk that complemented her eyes. The clerk in the exclusive boutique in London where he'd ordered the dressing gowns, and on Monday seven nightgowns, had done her job well. Cash had told Moira to describe Abby's appearance and have them send nightgowns that would suit.

They didn't disappoint, sending Cash's request by same-day courier as they did with the dressing gowns, each one was perfect and Abby had loved them. Not as much as cashmere but, she'd informed him, silk and satin (the *real* kind) were close seconds.

The nightgowns were an answer to Abby's pyjamas, which she'd unveiled Sunday night after he'd forced her, and her cat, to move in with him. Although he had to admit she looked cute in the striped, drawstring bottoms and fitted T-shirt, Cash found later when they were in bed he didn't like the obstacles they presented.

Unlike getting her presents, it was safe to say she hadn't been pleased at his demand to move in even though she didn't utter a word. Cash had felt actual physical pain at his effort not to laugh in the face of Abby's obvious struggle against her desire to argue.

However, Simon's full report, e-mailed to Cash while they were in Germany, stated that Abby's house was what, after close scrutiny of the report, Cash considered a health hazard. It needed new wiring, new plumbing, new appliances and new bathrooms. The carpeting was frayed in places, making it easy to trip, especially if one insisted on wearing high heels as Abby did, and needed to be replaced.

The list went on.

Simon had noted that a good deal of work had already been done, the roof, windows, chimneys and repairs to damp and dry rot. But there was still a good deal left to do to make it what Cash would deem habitable.

About five seconds after the lights failed Saturday night, Abby, Cash decided, was definitely not going to live there while he saw to restoring it.

She was going to live with him and therefore likely not return home for some time.

On that thought, he buried his face in her hair and fitted his body to the length of hers, breathing in the scent of her.

Last Wednesday Cash had discovered Abby's secret.

She was not, as she wished him to believe, an escort for hire.

She was instead a woman who desperately needed money.

The day after they had dinner with his uncle, he'd investigated this himself and within hours put the pieces together.

Until he transferred the money into her account, her balance was naught. She was overdrawn and had substantial credit and loan debt. Her banking history exposed enormous expenditures, which were likely repairs on her home. She'd had a job at one point, but her salary was unbelievably low and that regular deposit had stopped some time ago. This indicated she'd lost her job and hadn't had steady employment for some time, although she'd taken intermittent contract work.

Further investigation uncovered the fact that she'd amassed considerable debt in DC. It didn't take close scrutiny to see that she should have sold the house she shared with her husband and further she had continued a lifestyle she could no longer afford on her salary alone. This left her in relatively dire financial straits when she left that life behind, which meant she was ill-prepared to absorb the expenses she couldn't know she'd face, from what he could tell, upon arrival in the UK.

Why she sold herself rather than some of the valuable pieces of furniture and art in her home, Cash had no idea.

But he intended to find out.

He felt her nestle deeper into him in her sleep and he smiled into her hair.

He enjoyed this time, early in the mornings, before he woke her. This was when he had her, when she was sleeping. He also knew he had her, all of her, when he was fucking her.

The rest of the time, she was on guard.

He'd had her once, their first weekend together.

And he fully intended to have that again.

Abby being on guard started the day of their fight and he hadn't done himself any favours by punishing her that evening. She'd forgiven him, this he knew. But something had changed, that was clear.

She was trying to hide this from him.

What she didn't know was there was a big difference between Abby being Abby and Abby being the Abby she wanted him to think she was.

There were times when she came through. For example, when she hilariously repacked her heels after he'd unpacked them, when she first laid eyes on her Bavarian torte, when she panicked at the thought of him entering her house when there was a possibility of intruders, and when she'd received the nightgowns the day before.

But mostly she maintained a cautious distance, erecting and consistently fortifying walls that kept him out.

Cash intended to break down those walls. He intended to force her to admit her secrets. He intended to find out why she'd sold herself to him. Lastly, he intended to have all of her again, no holding back.

And he didn't care how long it took.

His strategy was to be patient until the time came when that was no longer working. She was coming out more and more, fitting naturally into his life, letting that guard down more frequently, and he was carefully pressing this advantage.

He knew his end game.

She would be moving with him to Penmort. He would take care of her, giving her the life he felt she should have. And he'd be certain to maintain that life for her even after it was time for him move on.

He would, when the time was right, explain all this to her.

But not before she let him in.

Completely.

Or, of course, if he lost patience.

His hand smoothed over her, sliding up her nightgown then running down her naked hip. She hadn't replaced her underwear after he'd taken her last night, demanding first that she stand beside the bed as he sat on its edge, his hands moving over the silk of her gown, pulling it up and then tugging down her panties until she stepped out of them. He hadn't removed her nightgown when he'd fucked her last night and he wouldn't do it now. He liked the sleek feel of the expensive silk. It further aroused him that he'd given it to her.

His hand moved over her belly, then down to the juncture between her legs, and he found her.

She woke instantly, her soft morning voice breathing his name.

At the sound and its effect on his body, Cash curled his other arm around her chest, holding her captive.

Then he listened, his body slowly, exquisitely tightening in response as he brought her to climax with his hand, all the while controlling her as she alternately pressed into his hand and struggled against his arm, trying to turn to him.

When he took her to the edge, her head twisted and only then did he lift his own to press his mouth against hers and absorb her moans.

But he wasn't finished.

While she still trembled through her climax, he turned her to her back and kept at her with his hands, mouth and tongue until he could take no more and knew, from the urgency she was using her own hands, mouth and tongue, that she couldn't either.

Only then did he enter her, his strokes fierce and uncontrolled, their mouths attached, tongues duelling, alternating with teeth biting at each other's lips. He knew he was close and it would be, as it always was with Abby, magnificent.

He listened to her sharp intake of breath. Her calf, with her thigh pressed into his side, curled around his back, her other leg wrapped around his thigh. He felt her convulse around him at the same instant his mind erased and his world centred on nothing but their sweet, tight, wet connection.

Then he came.

It was moments after, when Cash's face was buried in her neck, his tongue tasting her, that his world opened. But only to allow all of Abby back in, her legs and arms tight around him, the feel of her breath against his neck, the scent of her sex in his nostrils.

It was then his life as he knew it shattered.

Because, softly, huskily, *honestly*, she whispered, "It's never been this good."

His body froze even as he felt triumphant adrenaline shoot through him, electrifying his whole system.

And under him, he felt her body freeze too.

But it was for an entirely different reason.

🐾 🐾 🐾

With body frozen solid, Cash's all of a sudden still form wrapped tight in her limbs, Abby listened to the stark silence in the dark room and wondered if she'd just done what she thought she'd just done.

That was, utter her true, supposed-to-be-buried-deep feelings out loud.

Cash's head came up and Abby's tense body grew even tenser. So tense it felt like it would splinter into a million pieces.

"What did you say?" Cash asked, his burr rougher than normal and not, Abby reckoned, because he'd just had an orgasm.

Yes, she had indeed uttered her true, supposed-to-be-buried-deep feelings out loud.

Her emotional warrior threw up her hands in disgust.

Jumping straight to damage control, Abby decided to play stupid, hoping it would fool him since she *was* stupid. Beyond stupid. *Phenomenally* stupid.

"What?" she asked.

Cash didn't hesitate before repeating, "What did you say?"

Abby stayed with her stupid tactic. "Did I say something?"

There was silence a moment then Cash's hand came to the side of her face, his thumb sliding along her bottom lip. When he spoke, his voice was even rougher, so much rougher it was harsh, yet sweet and warm, just like when he'd asked her forgiveness.

"Darling," he started slowly. "Repeat what you just said."

Abby decided playing stupid wasn't getting her anywhere so her next tactic would be escape.

She tried to move away but this didn't work either because, firstly, Cash was strong, secondly, he was heavy, and thirdly, he was still inside her.

So when his whole body tensed around her, his hips bucked and she had to bite her lip to hold back a whimper of pleasure.

When she stilled, Cash spoke, "You're not going anywhere, love, until you talk to me."

Fear started seeping into her pores and Abby decided to try a different tactic. "Don't you need to get to work?"

There was another moment of silence before he demanded again, "Talk to me."

Abby felt desperation creeping in along with the fear and therefore lied, "I don't know what you want me to say."

"Anything that's the truth," he replied immediately. "For instance, what you just said."

"Cash, I don't know what you're talking about," Abby lied again and struggled underneath him, but he contained her struggles with minimal effort.

When she stopped struggling, he spoke. "You know what I'm talking about."

Her voice was higher, but cooler, denoting her fear and burgeoning anger (directed at her own stupid self) when she replied, "I don't."

"You do," he insisted.

"I don't!" she snapped and shoved at his shoulders.

But he only moved back an inch and then pressed in again.

With what he said next, Cash, Abby noted, also switched tactics.

"What do you fear?" he asked, making it clear he knew exactly what Abby wasn't even allowing herself to understand.

Angry and now panicked, Abby ordered, "Get off."

"Tell me what scares you," Cash demanded.

"Get off!" she shouted and struggled anew.

This time he controlled her struggles not physically, but verbally.

"You said it's never been this good."

At the reminder of her words, Abby went still.

Deciding to run the full gamut of personalities in the hopes of making him think she was insane, which she told herself at that moment would be a good thing, she feigned confused innocence. "I did?"

"You did," he returned firmly, and she knew he saw through her completely.

"Well, I'd just—" she started to explain, or more honestly, lie.

But he cut her off.

"No, don't," he said, and she felt his eyes remain on her briefly in the shadows before his face went into her neck and he repeated on a whisper, "Don't."

She closed her eyes tight, but he continued speaking, and what he said next did what she thought would happen earlier.

It splintered her soul into a million pieces, in one fell swoop, taking all her puny defences with it.

"I'll wait, darling. We have all the time in the world."

At these words, Abby's mind erased.

As if someone else was experiencing it, she felt his lips touch the hinge of her jaw then his head came up. The heat of his eyes was on her and his thumb stroked her cheekbone before his mouth touched hers softly. Then he gently pulled out of her and exited the bed. He tugged the covers over her and walked across the room.

She saw a sliver of light come from the bathroom before the door shut.

Mind perfectly blank, she took hold of his pillow, curled around it, pressing her face to it and closing her eyes, willing herself into denial, telling herself she'd forget. He'd forget. What just happened didn't happen. They'd move on from here.

Against her will, Cash's deep brogue floated through her consciousness.

We have all the time in the world.

She closed her eyes tighter and Cash's scent came to her from his pillow as it did every morning she curled into it after he left her. It wasn't just his cologne. It was the scent of his hair, his skin, *him.*

We have all the time in the world.

Then she remembered.

She remembered something she'd pushed so deep, its resurfacing caused pain, like she was pulling barbed wire out of her heart.

After Ben was killed, after the police left, after she'd called Jenny, she'd walked in a fog up to their bed and curled into his pillow.

And she breathed in the scent of him.

She stayed there for over a day, until Jenny came to the front door. She didn't answer the phone. She didn't eat. She didn't drink. She often slept but she only took herself away from the bed to go to the bathroom.

She simply remained curled around Ben's pillow, eyes closed, mind blank, breathing in the scent of him.

It was the only physical thing she had left. Not one of his belongings, it was a part of *him,* still there, still within reach, still able to fill her senses.

Days later, when Jenny had Abby functioning again, Jenny had started to tidy.

In a panic, Abby had taken the pillowcase and rooted through the wash hamper, sorting bits and pieces that still held his essence, shoving them in a plastic bag and hiding them in a place Jenny couldn't find them.

And when Jenny would go to the grocery store or out on an errand, Abby would go to their walk-in closet, get the bag and pull out the pillowcase or one of his shirts. Then she'd sit in the corner of the closet amongst her shoes, his shoes and other detritus that she always promised herself she'd organise, the tangled evidence of their lives together, and she'd breathe in his scent.

Eventually, Abby stopped doing this and when Jenny came years later to help her sort through her life, Abby knew she'd found the bag Abby hadn't touched for years. She also knew Jenny had disposed of it without saying a word to Abby.

We have all the time in the world.

That wasn't true. It was despicably, awfully, unfairly, completely *not true.*

They may have years.

They could only have hours.

Abby couldn't do it again.

Never, never again.

Her battered heart beating wildly, her mind held hostage to a panic so extreme she couldn't begin to control her actions, and she didn't try.

She threw the covers off the bed and launched herself from it. She snatched her panties from the floor and tugged them on. She turned on the light and ran from the room to the guest bedroom where Cash had put her four suitcases after she'd unpacked on Sunday.

She grabbed two and ran back into the room.

Zee was standing on the bed. Still somewhat uncertain of his new surroundings he'd chosen elsewhere to sleep the last two nights.

Now, for Zee, at Cash's or on the moon, it was kitty breakfast time.

In a panic, Abby ignored her cat and threw a suitcase on the floor, one on the bed and she pulled it open.

In the flurry of Abby's harried movements, Zee took off and Abby ran to the wardrobe, throwing it open, seeing her clothes neatly hanging next to Cash's.

That was something she'd struggled with Sunday when she'd hung them.

Now it tore at her shredded heart.

But she didn't stop.

Not even taking the clothes from the hangers, she grabbed handfuls of them and hurried back across the room, tossing them into the suitcase and going back. And back. And back.

The door to the bathroom opened and Abby, with an armful of T-shirts from the dresser, halted, as did Cash, just steps from the bathroom door.

His hair was wet and he was wearing nothing but a towel around his hips. His eyes moved from her, to the bed, back to her.

It seemed, to Abby's terror-clogged mind, this happened in slow motion.

"What the fuck are you doing?" Cash asked, his voice hitting the room like a whiplash, and Abby's body jerked out of its temporary paralysis.

She walked to the suitcase and threw the clothes in.

"I quit," she declared, heading back to the dresser. "I don't know if you owe me or I owe you, but whatever it is, we'll just call it even."

She was heading back to the suitcase with an armload of underwear when Cash's fingers curled around her biceps, bringing her to an awkward stop.

Her eyes lifted to his and she demanded, "Cash, let me go."

He didn't respond to her demand, instead he asked, "You quit?"

She yanked at her arm but his fingers only grew tighter so she ceased this endeavour.

"Yes, I quit," she told him.

His fingers squeezed deeper into her arm. "You quit what?"

"I quit being your escort," she explained. "Your pretend girlfriend. This isn't working for me. Therefore, I quit."

"My pretend girlfriend?" Cash repeated, eyes narrowed, and Abby was too much in a state to register that the air in the room had grown dangerously thick.

"Yes, your pretend girlfriend. I quit. Now, let me go." She jerked at her arm but he still didn't release her.

Their eyes held and she didn't feel anything. So caught up in her act of self-preservation, the house could crash down on them and she'd rise from the rubble and continue packing.

Suddenly his hand released her arm.

"All right, Abby," he said quietly, and she immediately walked to the suitcase, threw in her underwear, and seeing it was over-full, she hefted the top over and attempted to zip it closed.

"Would you like to tell me why you quit?" Cash's voice came to her from behind.

No. No, she definitely would *not* like to tell him that. Hell, she wasn't even allowing herself to *think* of that.

"No," she replied shortly.

"I see," his voice said and Abby's desperation increased as the zipper refused to budge against the gap created by her clothes.

Abby's body was gently moved away as Cash murmured, "Allow me."

Abby took a step back and watched him bend to her bag. He was still wearing his towel, the muscles in his back worked and she watched them with a detached fascination.

Therefore, at first she missed the fact that he wasn't going for her zipper. He was picking up her bag. When he had it in his hands, he turned and tossed it to the floor. It landed, went skidding and slammed against the wardrobe, her clothes flying out in different directions.

"Cash!" she shouted, but her breath left her in a whoosh as his arm hooked around her mid-section, and she found herself on her back on the bed, Cash coming down at her side then rolling over the top of her.

She blinked rapidly several times and when he came into focus, he noticed and started speaking immediately.

And he used a voice she'd never heard before. It was somewhat like the hard voice he'd used when he first told her he took care of what was his. But now it held an edge of unbendable steel that sent her spiralling into a terror that made her recent demented panic seem like an insignificant tizzy.

"All right, darling," he declared. "I'll tell you how this is going to go."

Abby went solid as she stared into his eyes, which were hard and glittering and very, very scary.

He continued, "I'm pleased you don't want to be my pretend girlfriend, considering you haven't been that since you begged me to fuck you the first time. I'll not be paying you the next instalment on Friday as agreed, nor will I be paying the remainder you're due at the end of our arrangement. Instead, I'll be setting up a monthly allowance to be transferred into a joint account, which you can draw on and not have to worry about taxes."

At his words and their undeniable meaning, Abby's breath caught halfway up her throat and lodged there.

Painfully.

Cash carried on, "If it isn't enough, you'll come to me and we'll discuss it. You won't get overdrawn and you won't get into financial trouble."

Something painful shot through her belly at what this statement revealed he knew, but he kept right on talking.

"I'll fix up your house so it's safe and habitable. Then we'll rent it, the payments will go into your current account, which you won't touch. Ever."

"Cash," Abby forced out on a whisper.

He ignored her. "You'll move in with me, properly, after my aunt and uncle's party. If you want to work, you'll work, but I'd rather you not as I travel often and I'd prefer you were with me. This will be your choice. Any salary you bring in also goes into your current account and you won't touch that either."

"Stop talking," Abby begged.

Cash didn't listen. "You'll stay with me for as long as what we have remains good. When it doesn't work for one or the other of us, we'll move on. I'll supplement whatever you've accrued so that you can live safe and comfortably no matter what might befall you until the day you fucking die."

Abby was back to not being able to breathe.

"Is that understood?" Cash asked.

She shook her head.

Cash's brows drew together as his face darkened.

Abby bravely ignored that and asked softly, "Cash, don't you get it? This is over."

"It's not fucking over," he clipped.

Abby, finally losing control of her emotions, cried in desperation, "It's over!"

Then he said aloud what Abby had been battling for weeks and the words lacerated the tattered remains of her heart.

"It's the best you've ever had, Abby. It's better than what you had with Ben. You know it. I know it. Stop lying to yourself and stop hiding from me. It's not only not over, you don't even fucking *want* it to be over."

Abby's head exploded, white lights flashing in front of her eyes, rage tearing through her system, she shrieked, "How *dare* you Cash Fraser! How...*fucking*...dare you!"

And then, crazed, she fought him, striking out blindly with her fists, kicking with her legs.

It took him a while to contain her, so frenzied was her battle, but he caught her wrists, controlling her angry pummelling. She kept at him, testing his strength, bucking and kicking, not attempting to get away but wanting to hurt him as much as she hurt.

Which was a lot.

Too much.

Too much not to let some of it go.

Then something occurred to her, registering on her brain as she watched the muscles in his arms move and flex. She felt the heat of him, the strength of him, the weight of the thigh he threw over hers, pinning her legs. She heard his breathing. She smelled his scent.

He was alive. He was real. He was solid.

And her anger turned to something else, a new kind of desperation as she pushed at his hands at her wrists in a different way, her neck twisting, her mouth finding his jaw, her tongue tasting him. Her lips moved up his jaw and found his already opened and her tongue darted in.

He released her hands and his arms moved around her, pulling her tight to him. She pushed off on her foot, rolling him to his back. Crawling on top of him, she used her mouth and hands on him—*every-where*—gently setting his hands away any time he tried to touch her.

This was all about Cash. Alive Cash. Breathing Cash. Warm Cash.

Just *Cash*.

Only when she finally straddled him, wrapping her fingers around him and guiding him inside, did she allow him to touch her. He knifed to sitting, one of his arms around her, his fingers twisting in her hair, pulling her head back, arching her neck.

She moved on top of him urgently, his mouth at her neck, her chest, and it didn't take long before she exploded, feeling him take over her strokes with his hands lifting and pressing on her hips, his insistent rhythm prolonging her third orgasm of the morning until he slammed her down one last time and joined her.

She'd barely caught her breath when his fingers thrust into her hair at her scalp and he tilted her face towards his.

His mouth on hers, he declared harshly, "It's not fucking over."

The battle was lost.

Even Abby wasn't stupid enough not to know that.

Therefore, she nodded her head.

"Say it," he demanded.

Abby closed her eyes tight and his hand fisted in her hair.

"Abby, fucking *say it*," he repeated.

Her eyes opened slowly and she whispered, "It's not over."

All of a sudden she was flying through the air only to land on her back with Cash covering her.

His mouth came to hers again and his voice was rougher, deeper, throatier when he informed her, "Darling, you just made me a promise. And you better fucking believe that I'm holding you to it."

Before she could respond, he kissed her, hard, deep, long and wet.

And when he was done, again before she could get a word in, before she could even catch her breath, he stated, "I'm taking you out to dinner tonight. Somewhere nice. Be ready at seven."

She stared at him, unable to speak.

"Abby, did you hear me?" he asked.

She nodded.

His eyes travelled over her face and she watched, captivated, as they grew warm and the hardness in his expression went soft.

His hand came to the side of her face and his thumb slid along her cheekbone.

"I know you're terrified," he murmured gently. "But I promise you aren't going to lose me until one of us is ready to be lost."

She hated it that he knew her thoughts, no matter how she strived to keep them hidden.

Tears filled her eyes and she sucked in her lips before she whispered, "You can't make that promise, Cash."

His mouth touched hers, his eyes open, and he said, "I just did."

He moved away, pulled her properly into the bed, covering her with the sheet.

She watched, mind again blank, as he dressed and came back to her.

He didn't say a word as he slid the hair off her neck, leaned in and kissed her there.

But instead of leaving, like he normally did, his fingers curled around her neck, his eyes caught hers and held them.

He looked at her, silent, for what seemed like years but was only moments before his fingers gave a gentle squeeze.

He turned out the light and then he was gone.

18

THE WARRIORS ASSEMBLE

Abby parked on the street across from her house.

She couldn't park in her drive, there were three white vans parked there.

And she couldn't park in front of her house, a skip containing a distressing amount of debris was sitting there.

As she got out of her car, a man walked out her front door carrying a toilet. She watched as he went straight to the skip and hefted it over the side.

She winced when she heard the toilet crash into the skip.

"All right?" he called, and her eyes went from her toilet, which she hadn't realised until that moment held sentimental value, to the man.

"All right," she called back.

Before she could witness more, she hightailed it to Mrs. Truman's.

Mrs. Truman had the door open before Abby's foot hit the first step on her stoop.

"Bang bang, *crash*," Mrs. Truman snapped irately as Abby ascended the steps. "All day yesterday, all day today. Those workmen are *loud*. My dogs are in a state!" She stepped out of the way for Abby to precede her into the entry, all three dogs moving around Abby's calves calling for attention. Mrs. Truman continued as she slammed the door, "I want a word with Fraser. You give me his phone number the minute you take off your coat."

Abby considered the emotional turmoil Cash put her through that morning (she was blaming him as it was far easier on her peace of mind than to blame herself or the unthinkable, *give in* to her current dilemma). Once she handed her coat to the older woman, Abby very unkindly pulled her mobile out and gave Mrs. Truman the number.

"Hang on, hang on," Mrs. Truman chanted, her arm up, hand waving in the air. "Let me get my phone."

She led Abby and the three dogs (who appeared to be happy and excited, not in a "state") down her hall into the sitting room where Fenella and Cassandra were both seated. Fenella was biting into an enormous scone filled with clotted cream and jam. Cassandra was holding a saucer in one hand and daintily sipping from a delicate china teacup in the other.

Abby greeted them both with a wave and all three dogs jumped up on the sofa beside Fenella and her scone.

At Mrs. Truman's orders, Abby was there to have tea with Fenella and Cassandra in order to devise a strategy to defeat a ghost.

Bearing in mind that Abby's move from being Cash's pretend girlfriend to his real girlfriend (or possible mistress, depending how you looked at it, and Abby was trying not to look at it *at all*) was approximately nine hours old, it was likely not good that she was already withholding something from him.

Trust was important in a relationship.

Then again, Cash would probably, first, flip out that she was going to sit down with his cousin, a witch/clairvoyant, and Mrs. Truman and decide a plan of action to conquer a ghost.

Then he'd have her committed.

So Abby thought it her best option to enter the part of her life's journey that included Cash by, essentially, lying to him.

She was, she found, totally okay with that.

"Abigail, I'm ready, give me his number," Mrs. Truman demanded as Abby seated herself in an armchair next to Cassandra and across from Fenella.

Mrs. Truman was standing with hand on hip, other hand curled around a phone, thumb at the ready.

Perhaps at this juncture calling Cash wasn't such a good idea.

"Maybe you can call him *after* we have our chat," Abby suggested.

"But I'm angry *now*. I might cool off after I eat a scone. I baked those scones myself and I bake the best scones of anyone I know," she bragged with not a shred of humility. "If I eat a scone, I might want to take a nap instead of have my word with Fraser."

Abby came up with a better idea. Not only was it her turn, it would mean Cash's torture would last a whole lot longer (and he couldn't hang up).

Therefore she suggested, "We'll have you to dinner."

"When?" Mrs. Truman snapped.

"Tomorrow?" Abby asked.

Mrs. Truman immediately dropped the phone into its receiver, accepting Abby's invitation by announcing, "I don't eat celery." She sat down beside Fenella and reached for the teapot. "Or peppers. They give me wind."

Abby heard Cassandra chuckle and Fenella raised her eyebrows, her lips pressing together in an effort not to laugh.

Mrs. Truman poured Abby a cup of tea and splashed a dash of milk in it while going on, "And if you make beef, I won't eat it unless it's well done. I'm English. We cook our beef through. That's the way we've always done it. That's the way we'll always do it. No one does tradition like the English."

"I bet the Italians would have something to say about that," Cassandra put in.

"Pah!" Mrs. Truman retorted.

"And the Spanish," Fenella added timidly.

"And practically everyone else, but the Americans," Cassandra finished with a cheerful wink in Abby's direction and Abby decided instantly she liked her.

Mrs. Truman handed Abby her tea. "Are we here to talk tradition or are we here to talk ghosts?" Once she'd divested herself of Abby's tea, she turned to Fenella and pointed at her. "You! Start!"

Fenella's eyes moved to Abby and she began, "Well—" but Mrs. Truman cut her off.

"And don't be all mealy-mouthed about it. Spit it out!"

As ordered, Fenella rushed on.

Eyes on Abby, she asked, "You didn't slip when you were in the bathroom, did you?"

Abby blinked in surprise and then looked at Mrs. Truman. "Did you tell her?"

"No. I. Did. Not," Mrs. Truman stated clearly. "Abigail Butler, how many strangers do I ask in for tea?"

Abby didn't have time to respond, Mrs. Truman went on talking.

"I heard her banging on your door and I went out to see what all the racket was about. She told me who she was and I decided to ask her over and pump her for information. *She* told *me* about Vivianna Wainwright and how she thought you'd been injured by a ghost. *I* told *her* I knew all about it and we were going to figure out a plan to defeat the ghost and she said she wanted to be involved."

Abby's surprised eyes went to Fenella. "Are you sure?"

"Well, no," Fenella replied hesitantly then swallowed. "Vivianna's scary and she's mean. She never hurt any of us, not us girls, but she doesn't like Alistair and she's always doing stuff to him. And the servants. I don't want to be on her bad side."

"Then maybe you shouldn't be involved," Cassandra said gently, and Fenella's eyes moved to her.

"I also don't want her around anymore." Fenella looked at Abby. "I don't want her to hurt anyone else, and especially not someone like you."

"Like me?" Abby asked, confused.

"Like you," Fenella answered.

"What does that mean, like me?" Abby pushed when Fenella's answer didn't contain any further information.

"The love of Cash's life!" Fenella announced way-too-loudly, almost in a screech.

Abby felt her heart stutter to a stop.

"I'm not the love of Cash's life," she whispered.

"You are," Fenella returned.

"Honestly, Fenella, I'm not. We're—" Abby began.

"You are," Fenella interrupted. "Even if it wasn't obvious to everyone around, she knows. She *knows.* Vivianna knows exactly who Penmort's master loves best and dearest. True love. Complete, devoted and unconditional. Only those loves does she kill."

Abby's eyes skipped around the room to Mrs. Truman then to Cassandra and back to rest on Fenella.

They all were watching her.

"Fenella, honestly, Cash and I are—"

"In love," Fenella finished.

"No, we aren't," Abby insisted, her voice getting stronger.

"Okay, well, I haven't known Cash all that long but I do know some stuff. First, I know he never brought a woman to Penmort and he's had loads. Loads and loads and *loads,*" Fenella stated.

"We get it, loads. Move on," Mrs. Truman demanded, circling her hand.

"Second, every time he comes, he acts like the minute he enters he wants to leave. He doesn't like Suzanne and he *hates* Alistair. The only one he really likes is Mummy. When you were there, it was different. He was different. I've never seen him that way with anyone. None of us had. Mummy, Honor and I were in a lather about it for *days!*" Fenella went on.

"I still don't—" Abby started to protest, even though everything Fenella was saying was *freaking her out,* but Fenella talked over her.

"And everyone knows Vivianna's spell. She not only cast a spell over her immortal soul so she'd forever haunt Penmort, she also cast a spell so she would know, without doubt, the one true love of its master, for eternity, so she could make every ancestor pay for her spurned love. Only the true loves were put to death. The other ones, well, I reckon she just annoyed them." Fenella's eyes went to Cassandra and she informed her as an aside, "She can be annoying too, not just scary."

Abby felt the need to point out the obvious, "Cash isn't even Penmort's master."

At that, Fenella made a weird, squeaky noise in the back of her throat.

"What?" Cassandra asked, leaning forward.

Fenella's gaze darted around the room not landing on any of them, and finally, eyes on her knees, she said softly, "Everyone knows Cash should own that house. Everyone knows he was the true heir. Everyone knows Anthony Beaumaris loved Myra Fraser. He just didn't marry her because she was a loon."

Abby bit her lip in order not to laugh, or yell, at Fenella describing Cash's mother as "a loon."

"That doesn't change the fact that he doesn't own the house," Mrs. Truman put in and Fenella looked at her.

"That's true. But he *should*," Fenella replied. "The line has never gone from brother to brother. It's always gone from father to son. *Always.*"

"He still doesn't own Penmort," Cassandra pressed.

"But he *should*," Fenella returned firmly. "And Anthony died while making provisions to the castle's covenant that would transfer title to his son, even if born out of wedlock."

Cassandra's eyebrows went up and she murmured, "That's interesting."

"It is," Fenella murmured back. "Especially when you know that Anthony died in a car accident."

Abby's breath caught at this news and she stared at Cash's cousin.

"A car accident?" Abby whispered.

Fenella nodded. "Something was wrong with the brakes."

"That's terrible," Mrs. Truman remarked.

Fenella pulled in a breath. "When I say something was wrong with the brakes, I mean something *weird* was wrong with the brakes. The police reckoned they'd been tampered with but they could never prove anything."

"Oh my Lord," Abby breathed.

"*Very* interesting," Cassandra muttered while sitting back.

Mrs. Truman's gaze snapped to Cassandra. "Why? Outside of the fact that Fraser's father was likely murdered, of course."

Cassandra took a sip of tea and put the cup back in her saucer. "It's interesting because, if that's so, Cash Fraser is, rightly, Penmort's master. And Vivianna likely knows that or senses it. Which means Vivianna's actions last week weren't simply meant to be a warning or simple malice. It means Abby is genuinely in the line of fire."

"Listen to me people," Abby cut in with frustration (and maybe a hint of fear). "I'm not Cash's true love. Okay? Seriously. Not. His. True. Love. Therefore, I don't fit the profile of the victims."

Everyone stared at her.

Finally, Mrs. Truman spoke, "He does seem rather fond of you."

Cassandra's eyes locked on her. "For a bloke who doesn't feel strongly for you, he seemed pretty outrageously pissed off on your behalf the other night."

Fenella added on a mini-shriek, "I think it's love. Mummy does too!"

Abby threw a hand up and rolled her eyes to the ceiling, muttering a defeated, "Bloody hell."

Mrs. Truman made a "humph" sound before commanding, "Let's move on. Cassandra, what have you got?"

Cassandra leaned forward and put her cup and saucer on the table, sat back and stated, "Not much that's good."

"Explain," Mrs. Truman demanded.

Cassandra drew in a breath and looked at Abby. "As a mortal, you can't fight a ghost. They've got paranormal powers, you don't. Most ghosts just hang out and haunt. Some ghosts, the not-so-good variety, cause havoc. Others, like Vivianna, who was a witch and a pretty good one as far as I can tell, can be pretty powerful."

"This is not sounding good," Abby mumbled.

"If you want to defeat a ghost you have four options," Cassandra continued.

"And those are?" Abby asked.

"The first, you find its mortal remains and burn them," Cassandra replied.

"I've seen that on TV," Abby told her, and she had. That show with two hot brothers, one sensitive, one wise-cracking, both running around fighting demons, burning bones and shooting spirits with shotguns loaded with salt.

That show was *great*!

Cassandra nodded. "It's true."

"Well, it's gross to dig up a grave and burn bones, but let's do that," Abby suggested brightly.

"Can't," Mrs. Truman put in.

"Why not?" Abby queried and Mrs. Truman looked at Fenella.

"I've done a little research over the years, seeing as I've lived with Vivianna for-what-feels-like-ever," Fenella told them. "I found out the townspeople didn't really like her much. They were into all that hocus pocus stuff back then and knew about the burning-the-bones-thing so, after she threw herself off the castle, they gathered together the pieces and burned her remains."

Abby did a little shiver at the thought of gathering up Vivianna's "pieces" then she inquired, "Then how can she still be around?"

"Either they didn't salt it first, doesn't work if you don't salt it," Cassandra explained. "Or, if they did, which they likely did, because everyone knows you salt the body before burning it, then Vivianna probably knew she'd have to get around that. So, she left some earthy remains somewhere."

"Okay then," Abby said slowly. "We'll find her remains and burn them."

"In a week?" Mrs. Truman demanded then finished on a firm, "Impossible."

Abby stared at Mrs. Truman thinking she was unfortunately right.

"Okay, what's choice number two?" Abby asked on a sigh.

"Choice number two was what we were doing at your house Saturday night," Cassandra answered. "A mortal can't fight a ghost, but a ghost can fight a ghost. We were seeing if there were any of your relatives hanging around who could help out. Normally you can't leave the place you haunt. And that place has to be either where you died, where you lived, or somewhere you spent a lot of time. But I know a spell that can untether a ghost. Not for long, but for long enough for your relative either to take down Vivianna, or provide you with protection while you're at the castle."

"I'm guessing that didn't work," Abby remarked.

Cassandra shook her head. "Nope. Fortunately for them, and you under normal circumstances, all your relatives have gone on to the next plane. Under these circumstances, it's rather *unfortunate*."

"What's choice three?" Abby asked.

"Choice three is that you take a potion, which would make you able to fight a ghost. It would give you keener senses so you'd see her, even if she wasn't making herself visible. If done right, the potion would mean you could sense she was coming, giving you a warning. If done *really* right, the potion would allow you to combat her, physically or at least ethereally," Cassandra explained.

Abby thought that sounded great. "Let's do that."

Cassandra shook her head and Abby's shoulders fell.

"The potion needs three weeks to ferment. A month to work well. About six months to work well enough to fight back. It isn't often you need to fight a ghost. I didn't have any in my larder. I made a batch after Mrs. Truman called and explained what was going on but it won't be ready in time," Cassandra told Abby.

"What happens if I take it early?" Abby queried.

"You get sick. Very sick. Stomach cramps, nausea, vomiting, fever, delirium, cold sweats. You name it, you'll get it. It only lasts a few days, a week at most, but you'll look like death and not only will you *want* to die, those around you who don't know you took the potion, like your boyfriend and, say, doctors, will *think* you are. Dying that is," Cassandra said.

"Well, that's out," Abby muttered.

Cassandra leaned toward Abby, her eyes going soft, and said gently, "I've sent out feelers to see if any other witches have a usable potion, Abby. I know it doesn't sound good but maybe we'll catch some luck."

Abby gave her a small smile before asking, "What's option four?"

"Option four is your cat," Cassandra told her.

Abby blinked. "Zee?"

Cassandra nodded. "Not all felines have the ability, but your cat does."

"What ability?" Fenella asked.

Cassandra looked at Fenella. "Ghosts don't like cats on the whole. But cats like Abby's they'll avoid like the plague. Cats like Abby's can do what Abby could do if we had a usable potion. See the ghost, even when hidden, sense it before it comes, and fight it."

"Fight it?" Abby prompted.

Cassandra leaned forward and nabbed a scone and a knife. "Fight it, yes. But not destroy it. Fend it off. Say, if Vivianna was stalking you or even attacking you, your cat could do her damage. Weaken her. Make Vivianna disappear until her strength returns."

"*Let's do that!*" Fenella screeched.

Cassandra's eyes went back to Fenella as she cut open her scone and started to slather it with cream. "Two problems with that."

"Bloody hell," Abby muttered and thought, *Great, two* more *problems.*

"One," Cassandra continued. "When Vivianna came back, she'd be angry. *Very* angry. Abby would be gone, but your family would be in targeting range."

"That's not good," Mrs. Truman commented under her breath.

"Two, I said Abby's cat could fight it, I didn't say her cat would win," Cassandra noted. "And Vivianna can't die. But Zee can."

"That's out," Abby stated instantly.

Everyone went silent.

Then Fenella cried, "So what are we going to do?"

"I need a scone," Abby muttered, leaning forward and seizing her own scone.

"I've got some amulets, some powders, some potions. All for protection. Some of it pretty potent stuff. I'll give Abby everything I've got and show her how to use it," Cassandra answered Fenella.

"And then what?" Mrs. Truman asked.

Cassandra sat back with her fully-loaded scone and responded, "Then we hope." She took a big bite and chewed.

Suddenly Mrs. Truman's back went ramrod straight and she looked from right to left.

Then she said, "That better be Jennifer."

"What better be Jennifer?" Fenella asked.

The doorbell rang and Cassandra, Fenella and Abby stared at each other in astonishment. They hadn't heard a thing that would herald a visitor.

Then again, nosy Mrs. Truman undoubtedly had super-powered ears.

"Is Jenny coming over? I thought she was out with her pensioners on a field trip," Abby asked, going for a double dip of clotted cream. Since she'd likely be dead in a week's time, she might as well go to her grave with clogged arteries and cellulite.

"Yes," Mrs. Truman answered while getting up and bustling toward the door. "She's got a lead. She was checking it out. She must have news."

With that Mrs. Truman was gone.

Abby spooned jam on her scone and glanced from Cassandra to Fenella. "It's nice of you both to do this."

Fenella just smiled and waved her hand in front of her face.

"I'm not nice," Cassandra said. "I'm getting paid thirty quid an hour for this gig."

Abby's hand froze and the jam slipped from her spoon back into the pot. "What?"

Cassandra's eyes went from the jam to Abby. "Thirty quid an hour."

"But," Abby began then looked back to her scone and jam, clearing her throat. "I didn't...that is to say, I'm happy to pay you, I just didn't—"

"I work for Mrs. Truman. She's paying me," Cassandra informed her, and Abby's mouth dropped open.

"Really?" she breathed.

"Sure," Cassandra replied.

"I'll have to pay her back," Abby muttered while squishing the top of the scone on her jammy, creamy bottom.

"I wouldn't try that," Fenella warned.

Abby looked at her. "You wouldn't?"

Fenella shook her head. "I mentioned I wanted to contribute, seeing as Vivianna is a family problem, really. Mrs. Truman was a tad..." Fenella hesitated then leaned forward and whispered dramatically, "*Upset.*"

Abby could very well imagine Mrs. Truman's "tad upset" being described more aptly by an American as "having a conniption."

She decided not to mention it to the older woman. She also decided to bake her some cookies. And, maybe, buy her a knickknack.

Or two.

"This will not do," Mrs. Truman declared, walking back into the room, followed by Jenny.

And Jenny was followed by a man the like of which Abby had never seen.

Well, she had.

In a movie.

And blowing on a bagpipe.

But not in someone's living room during afternoon tea.

He was wearing full Scottish gear, kilt, hose, ghillie brogues, garter flashes, knife in the hose, belt, sporran—the whole enchilada.

He came directly to Abby, arm out, his shock of white hair wild, his face red either from cold or it was that way normally, his crooked, slightly demented smile wide and his huge body lumbering ungainly across the room.

"Wee lass, am I happy to meet ye," he declared. Abby put her hand in his and he pumped her arm so hard, her whole body shook. Jam splodged out of the scone in her other hand and splatted on her knee. "Uh. Sorry," he mumbled, letting go of her hand, his eyes on the jam.

"That's okay," Abby murmured, dropping her scone on a plate and grabbing a napkin to wipe up the spill.

"Praise be!" he cried. Abby jumped, looked up at him and he shouted, "A fine beauty and a sweet lass. Nothing better for our native son."

"Oh my," Fenella whispered, eyes wide and staring at the Scot.

"Were none too happy, we Scots, when Cash Fraser found himself an American. But one as fine as you, lassie, we couldn't be unhappy for long," he told her and then gave her an exaggerated wink.

"This is preposterous," Mrs. Truman announced, arms crossed on her chest, narrowed eyes on the Scotsman.

"Mrs. Truman, give him a chance," Jenny mumbled. "We need all the help we can get."

"I'll give him a chance," Mrs. Truman returned. "A chance to turn around and walk out my front door."

"What's this I'm hearing?" the Scotsman bellowed.

"Maybe you should tell us who you are," Cassandra suggested, peering at him closely.

"Excellent idea," the Scotsman declared and put his hands to his hips, planting his legs wide. "I'm Angus McPherson," he told them as if that said it all, which it did *not*.

"You are not," Mrs. Truman informed him irritably, and he blinked.

"I'm not?" he asked.

"No one is *really* named 'Angus McPherson,'" she stated.

He shook his head and then recovered.

"Well, I am," he retorted.

"Are not," Mrs. Truman shot back.

"*Am too!*" he roared on a forward lean.

"All right!" Abby cut in loudly, standing and facing Angus. "Why don't you," she stopped and turned to Jenny, "or maybe, Jenny, it should be you who tells us why Angus is here."

Angus didn't catch Abby's hint.

"I'll be hunting the ghost who wants to murder the true love of a Scotsman, that's why I'm here," Angus declared.

"Oh my," Fenella said again.

"Um..." Abby began, then was uncertain how to proceed so she went for the most obvious point, "I'm not his true love."

"Balderdash!" he shouted.

"I'm not," Abby insisted.

"I've seen the pictures, lass. That boy loves ye, make no mistake," Angus decreed, and Abby's eyes went to Jenny who made a slight grimace and shrugged.

"Scones!" Angus boomed. "Jam! Cream! The only three things the English could ever do right."

He pushed forward toward the plates of food while the women tensed for The Truman Detonation to End All Truman Detonations.

They didn't get it.

Instead, Mrs. Truman asked calmly, "Mr. McPherson, would you care to desist eating my food before you tell us how you're going to make Abigail safe?"

"Don't you worry, I got my ways," Angus replied, cutting open a scone.

"Why don't you share your...*ways?*" Mrs. Truman suggested

without it sounding even a bit like a suggestion but an awful lot like a demand.

"Can't," he returned, flipping open his scone. "Family secret."

"I'm afraid we're not ready to rely on, nor pay for I might add, any ridiculous and likely ineffectual family secrets," Mrs. Truman proclaimed.

Angus loaded cream on his scone. "Oh, I'll not be expecting payment, woman. I'm doing this for a fellow *Scot*," he boomed out the word "Scot" and all the women jumped, except Mrs. Truman.

Then Cassandra murmured, her eyes on Angus, her voice strangely filled with awe, "Oh my goddess, you're *The* McPherson."

Angus slopped an enormous spoonful of jam on his scone, but his head turned to look at Cassandra and his loud voice had gone quiet when he replied, "That I am, lass."

"I thought The McPhersons were a myth," Cassandra breathed, still staring wide eyed at Angus.

At her comment, Angus chuckled, "No, love, we're real."

"What's this?" Mrs. Truman demanded to know.

Cassandra continued staring at Angus. She sat back, glanced at Mrs. Truman then her eyes moved to Abby.

"You've got nothing to worry about," she informed Abby.

Abby looked at Angus, who had straightened and was consuming his scone, unabashedly getting cream and jam all over his mouth. She looked back at Cassandra.

"Really?" she asked, not convinced.

Cassandra nodded. "Really. The story goes that the McPhersons have been hunting ghosts successfully...*very* successfully...for generations."

"Twelve, to be exact," Angus put in, mouth full.

"Twelve generations?" Fenella whispered.

"Aye," Angus answered. "Proud. Stalwart. Strong. The McPhersons," he proclaimed these words like he'd said them a million times before. "Never saw a ghost I feared, and I've seen some nasty pieces of work, make *no* mistake. Started training when I was eight, never looked back."

All the women stared at him speechless until Mrs. Truman broke the silence.

"So what you're saying is, this *gentleman*," Mrs. Truman made the word "gentleman" sound like saying it caused physical pain, "knows what he's doing?"

"If the stories are true, which apparently they are," Cassandra said, "then yes."

"Been wanting a crack at Vivianna Wainwright since Anthony Beaumaris approached me the week before he died to ask me to have a go at her," Angus informed them, and all the women pulled in breath at this shocking revelation. "His brother wouldn't let me near the castle after he died, though." Angus finished in an undertone, "Something wrong with that one. Bad seed."

Abby's eyes moved to Fenella who luckily didn't appear to hear Angus's last.

"Fraser's father asked you to deal with Vivianna?" Mrs. Truman asked.

Angus shoved the last bite of scone in his mouth, nodding, chewing and wiping his mouth before he spoke again. "Didn't want his woman and son in the castle with Vivianna around. Anthony loved her, intended to marry her, knew Vivianna would take her out."

Abby stared at the Scotsman. "But I thought that Anthony didn't want to marry Myra. I thought—"

"Aye, he did, lass. Told me himself," Angus interrupted her. "He was an interesting character, Anthony. Not an easy man to like. But he knew what he wanted and he wasn't going to let anything stand in his way. Not her illness, not a ghost. He fully intended to take care of her and his boy." Angus shook his head and finished softly. "Shame he never got the chance."

Abby felt her heart squeeze and her eyes flew to Jenny.

"Cash doesn't know this. I'm certain he doesn't." Jenny was giving her a look that said, clearly, it was none of her business, but Abby's gaze swung back at Angus. "I don't know what to do with this."

"I'll tell him," Angus offered immediately.

"No!" Abby cried and put her hands to her mouth, feeling her pulse beat in her throat. Her mind flying in a million different directions, she dropped her hands and continued, "Cash doesn't know about Vivianna and I don't want him to know. Not yet." *Or ever*, Abby thought but didn't say out loud. "I don't want him to know about you. I mean, who you are, what you do. He'll think you're nuts. He'll think *I'm* nuts. If he hears this, he won't listen to anything you say. Maybe we can find a way for you two to meet that doesn't involve ghosts and ghost hunting and... whatever, and you can tell him."

And, if Abby was able to finagle a meeting between Cash and Angus, she might suggest Angus lose the kilt.

Angus shrugged. "However you want to do it, love. Some folks believe. Some folks need to see to believe. Some folks need their loved ones hurled off the top of a castle by a spirit-bitch-from-hell to believe." When Abby's mouth dropped open, her racing pulse stopped dead and her breath caught in her lungs, Angus leaned in and gave her a merry wink. "We'll see that last one doesn't happen to you."

Bloody hell, Abby thought.

❦ ❦ ❦

Abby stood at Cash's bathroom sink, eyes on the medicine cabinet and she stared at her bottles and tubes, which were intermingled with Cash's limited toiletry collection.

This vision stirred many feelings in her, too many, both good and bad.

Indeed, she had too many things on the whole to think about.

Not just feelings, *everything*.

She tried to prioritise them.

After about two seconds she realised this was impossible.

Instead, she decided not to think at all. She'd think about everything later. Tomorrow, or the next day, or after she was certain she wasn't going to be hurled off the top of a castle by a spirit-bitch-from-hell.

So she closed the medicine cabinet door and saw herself standing there, wearing another one of the nightgowns Cash gave her. This one was a dusty-pink satin with ultra-thin straps that went over her shoulders and criss-crossed to hold together the sides of a dipped-low back.

The hem fell to just above her knee and the satin hugged her body closely, but not uncomfortably, like it had been made for her.

She loved it. It was elegant and graceful and the satin felt like heaven against her skin.

Still, it wasn't the kind of thing you slept in. It was too delicate. She'd worry all night that she'd snap one of the straps or something.

But Cash had bought it for her obviously wanting her to wear it.

Since she was his...whatever...she didn't know if she could say no.

And she wasn't going to ask.

So she was wearing it.

She walked to the door, opened it and turned out the light.

Both lights were lit on either side of the bed. Cash was on top of the covers, legs out, ankles crossed, shoulders against the headboard, laptop on his thighs. He was wearing a pair of black, drawstring pyjama pants and his glasses.

He looked good.

His eyes came to her and he smiled.

That made him look even better.

Abby sighed and walked to her side of the bed.

She slid under the covers and her eyes caught on her hand cream that was sitting on her bedside table.

Her side of the bed. Her hand cream. Her bedside table. All in Cash's house.

Instead of thinking about how this made her feel, she reached for the hand cream and opened it.

Abby was on her side, her back to him and she heard Cash speak, "Darling, can I ask a favour?"

A favour?

Could he ask a favour?

Or, if he was giving her a monthly instalment on which to live, and didn't want her to work, was she essentially still working for him? Not as an escort, pretend girlfriend and glorified whore, but as his mistress, which could be considered a real girlfriend but was also kind of a glorified whore.

While she was struggling with this, Cash called, "Abby."

She rolled to her back but her head turned to look at him.

"Yes?"

"Did you hear me?" he asked.

She looked away and squirted the lotion in her hands while mumbling, "Sorry, miles away."

She put the cap back on, returned the tube to the nightstand and rubbed the lotion in her hands.

When she was done, Cash demanded softly, "Abby, come here."

She looked at him again and he lifted his arm out in invitation.

She accepted and scooted under the covers toward him. When he had her close, his arm bent and he skillfully tucked her into his side, her cheek on his ribcage, and his fingers cupped her shoulder.

"You with me?" he asked quietly.

She nodded and stared at the screen of his laptop, which showed a complicated, multi-coloured pie chart with lots of numbers, words and arrows pointing at wedges of the pie.

"Now, can I ask you to do something for me?" he inquired.

"Sure," she told him.

His fingers gave her a squeeze and Cash continued speaking gently. "Next time we go out to dinner, don't have a cream tea at Mrs. Truman's in the afternoon. You barely touched your dinner."

Abby continued to stare at the pie chart.

It was true. She'd barely touched her dinner.

And it wasn't just dinner. It was a *special* dinner.

A special *celebratory* dinner.

She hadn't known that when she got all dressed up. She hadn't known that when Cash had taken her to a beautiful, romantic inn in the country. She'd begun to realise it when she saw they had a booking and were led to a secluded table with the champagne already chilling in a stand at the table's side. She knew it for certain when they didn't order but were served a pre-ordered, delectable meal of lobster, shrimp and avocado salad followed by individual beef wellingtons and finished with decadent, rich, dark chocolate pots.

Cash didn't declare his undying love, give her a bouquet of the finest roses, nor did he hand her another velvet box containing expensive jewels.

Nevertheless, his point had been made.

Beautifully.

Unfortunately, that afternoon, Abby was suffering a mini-nervous breakdown after all that had befallen her. It was the kind of mini-nervous breakdown that every girl knew could be staved off by engaging in an eating frenzy. Therefore, she followed her first scone, which was more than enough, with another one.

During dinner, she'd also had her mind on a million things, starting with her grandmother's house being torn apart and ending on the possibility of her body flying apart when it landed at the bottom of Penmort tor.

Therefore, she had barely touched her delicious special celebratory meal.

"Sorry," she muttered and put her hand on Cash's stomach.

His fingers gave her shoulder another squeeze just as Abby felt Zee's kitty body land on the bed.

Her cat cautiously walked across the bed and stopped. Likely considering his options, he chose Abby's ankle and deposited himself half-on, half-off it.

He started purring loudly.

Abby relaxed into Cash's side and her hand slid from his stomach to wrap around his waist.

Cash's left hand moved across the touchpad and clicked the buttons while the fingers of his right hand started to stroke Abby's shoulder.

Abby watched the chart disappear and a spreadsheet with an insane amount of data, including words and numbers, came up. Cash scrolled through it so fast there was no way he could read it. Abby certainly couldn't. But he clicked it closed and then pulled open another one that had more columns, more rows, more words and big numbers.

He started to scroll through that at alarming speed and Abby called, "Cash?"

She meant to ask him about his work, particularly why he did so much of it.

But when he replied, "Yes?" for some reason she didn't ask.

Instead, she forged on to an even less comfortable subject. "Um, can I tell you something?"

His finger on the touchpad froze and he murmured, "Anything, darling."

She pushed up on a hand and turned to look at him. His eyes caught hers and his hand slid around to rest on the back of her neck.

"Promise you won't get mad?" she asked.

His fingers gave her a squeeze before he assured, "Promise."

She bit the side of her lip and watched as, behind his glasses, his eyes fell to her mouth and something changed in his face. She couldn't put her finger on it but it looked like humour mixed with warmth.

"I asked Mrs. Truman to dinner," she admitted, and his eyes moved directly back to hers.

"I'm sorry?" he asked.

"Tomorrow," she went on.

"Abby—" he started.

She pushed back and blurted, "I know I should have asked before making plans and I know Mrs. Truman can be a pill. But she was angry about the workmen making noise and demanding to phone you at the office. I had to do something!"

Abby was, of course, making it sound like she was protecting Cash, rather than deliberately throwing him under the bus which had been her earlier motivation, but she thought that was the best way to go.

"It's fine, Abby," Cash told her.

"Well, um...I'm not done."

Cash just looked at her, silent.

Abby went on, "Fenella was there and Mrs. Truman invited her along."

Cash's brows drew together.

Abby soldiered forth. "Then she invited Cassandra then Jenny."

Cash's eyes narrowed.

"Then Fenella called Nicola and she invited her."

Cash stared at her a moment before he closed his eyes and sighed.

"And Nicola asked Honor," Abby finished on a whisper.

Cash's eyes opened and pinned her to the spot.

She tried to put a positive spin on things. "Suzanne can't make it."

"Well thank God for that," Cash remarked dryly, and Abby bit her lip again.

"I'm sorry, Cash. It mushroomed out of control before I could—" Abby stopped talking when Cash's arm suddenly curled about her waist and he pulled her close so her torso was resting on his, their faces barely an inch apart.

"Stop saying you're sorry," he muttered.

"Okay," she breathed.

"It's fine," he told her.

"I'll do all the shopping," she babbled on, even though he said it was fine. "And cooking. And I'll try to get them to go home early so you can get work done, if you have things to do."

He blinked slowly, as if she'd somehow surprised him, and even though she thought this was strange, she kept right on going.

"Just, you know, find a way to take me aside and give me a warning when you get home, if you have things to see to, that is. I'll take care of it so you can get away. Promise."

He stared at her for a moment she could swear like she was some strange but wonderful, fantastical being.

Then he bent his neck and touched his mouth to hers.

Something about his kiss was different.

It was strange.

But it was also definitely wonderful.

Abby didn't get a chance to process it. He shifted her so she was back in position, cheek on his ribcage, and he went back to scrolling through spreadsheets, opening and closing charts and reading through documents at alarming speed.

Zee had moved away when Cash pulled her up, but he came back, walked up Abby's leg and jumped down into the space made by the crook of her hips. He curled in a tiny kitty circle and started purring.

Cash didn't say a word at the addition of Zee, he just kept clicking through documents.

Abby watched them fly by as she stroked her cat and Cash twirled a lock of her hair between his fingers.

Before she knew it, she was asleep.

19

TWO IMPORTANT THINGS
HAPPEN TO ABBY

Abby opened the front door to Cash's house to see Mrs. Truman standing on his stoop, Jenny, Nicola, Fenella, Honor and Cassandra all behind her.

"Parking is atrocious!" Mrs. Truman snapped by way of greeting then pushed in, grumbling, "We must have walked three miles to get here."

"We didn't walk three miles," Cassandra muttered with a grin in Abby's direction.

"Felt like it," Mrs. Truman groused, shrugging off her coat.

Abby ignored Mrs. Truman and welcomed the other ladies with a cheek to cheek touch, took their coats, hung them in the cupboard under the stairs and led them all to the garden level.

When they arrived downstairs, they were all looking around in wonder.

"We've never been to Cash's house. It's *gorgeous*," Fenella squealed, and Abby looked around.

She'd lit some candles. She'd also gone shopping in Bath that day. She bought a tall, large, cylindrical glass vase out of which sprouted fragrant white hyacinths that sat dead centre on the dining-room table. Another identical, but smaller vase held the same flowers and sat on the edge of the bar that separated the kitchen from the seating area. A third sat on the table between couch and armchairs, also stuffed full with hyacinths.

During her shopping efforts, Abby had purchased a handsome scarlet-red table runner, which ran the length of the dining table. Cash's sleek, classy, black crockery lay amongst his silver and glassware, the plates hiding the circular, quilted grey pads that Abby also bought. Scarlet napkins Abby picked up with the table runner were folded in rectangles and sat at a slant on each plate.

The aroma of roasting rosemary chicken filled the air and Nina Simone sang softly in the background.

Abby was pleased with Fenella's comment and further pleased that she was right. Cash's place *was* gorgeous. But now it didn't look just show-home gorgeous, it looked *home*-home gorgeous.

"What's that smell?" Mrs. Truman, sniffing the air disdainfully, demanded to know.

"Chicken," Abby answered.

"Chicken?" Mrs. Truman clipped. "I thought we were going to have beef."

"*You* talked about beef," Abby told her. "I never talked about beef."

Mrs. Truman shot her a glare and then mumbled, "I was expecting beef. All day, I've had a taste for beef. Now I get chicken."

Abby fought a smile and caught Nicola staring at Mrs. Truman in barely-hidden horror.

"Ignore her. She's crotchety," Abby told Nicola. "You'll get used to it."

Nicola's eyes came to Abby and she nodded, looking relieved at Abby's amused acceptance of the older woman.

But Mrs. Truman spoke.

"I'm not crotchety. I'm particular," Mrs. Truman informed Nicola. "I like things a certain way. Manners. Behaviour," her eyes came to Abby, "for instance, people keeping their promises."

"I didn't promise you beef," Abby asserted.

"You did," Mrs. Truman told her.

"Didn't," Abby shot back.

"I'm going to look at the rest of the house," Jenny cut in. "Abby, you want to show us around?"

Abby's eyes went to the clock.

Cash had said he'd be home by six thirty, but it was five past seven. It wasn't unusual that he was late.

What was unusual was that he hadn't called.

She shook her head at Jenny but invited, "You all have a look. I'll get everyone a drink."

"White wine," Mrs. Truman ordered sharply as she headed for the stairs, not even attempting to conceal her curiosity at viewing the rest of Cash's house. Then she finished, "Chilled."

"That sounds good to me," Nicola put in, following Mrs. Truman.

"Me too," Fenella added. She was right on her mother's heels.

"You know what I drink," Jenny told Abby and turned to the stairs.

"G&T," Cassandra requested, moving after the others.

"I'll just help Abby," Honor, to Abby's surprise, stated, and the women climbed the stairs.

"That's nice of you," Abby muttered, even though she was unsure.

She hadn't yet made her mind up about Honor.

Honor's eyes were on the stairs and after Cassandra's booted foot disappeared, she turned to Abby and said in a whisper, "Not really. I needed a chance to talk to you when Mummy wasn't around."

Abby went on guard and looked at Honor.

Her face seemed intent, though not unfriendly, but something about it made Abby mentally brace.

Still, Abby replied in a soft voice, "Okay. Can we talk while we make the drinks?"

Honor nodded and Abby asked her to see to Cassandra's gin and tonic, telling her where to find the liquor and glasses while Abby went to the fridge for the wine.

When she had the wine and was uncorking it, she turned to Honor. "What is it?"

Honor glanced to the side, her eyes catching Abby's. "Fenella told me what's going on."

Abby bit her lip, not sure this was a good thing.

Honor continued, "It's okay. I don't think you're crazy. I know

Vivianna exists. I know what she does. So does Suzanne. And, he's never mentioned it, but I know Alistair does too. The only person who hasn't seen her is Mummy."

Abby pulled the cork out of the bottle and asked, "Really? Why not?"

Honor shrugged. "Don't know. Always thought that was strange, but she never shows or makes a peep when Mummy's around. Anyway, she...Vivianna I mean...doesn't do harm to us girls. I think she even likes Suzanne."

Abby could understand that. Evil, Abby guessed, would know (and like) evil.

She didn't mention this philosophy to Honor for obvious reasons, and Honor kept talking.

"I get the feeling she hates Alistair. A lot. She's always doing things to annoy him when Mummy's not around. Moving his stuff. Tripping him up as he's walking through the house. Screaming when he's on the phone." Honor stopped and shivered, mumbling, "God, I hate it when she screams."

Abby's hand arrested while taking down a wineglass. "She screams?"

Honor nodded. "That's the worst. It isn't like a regular scream. It's low, eerie, sinister. Just hideous."

"That's awful," Abby whispered, thinking it bloody well *was*.

Who could live like that?

"Yes," Honor replied and her eyes went to the stairs before she moved to the refrigerator for ice. "We don't have much time and that isn't what I wanted to talk to you about."

"It isn't?" Abby inquired and Honor shook her head.

"I wanted to talk about Alistair," she told Abby, and dumped some ice into Cassandra's drink.

Abby's body went solid and she had to force herself to pour the wine while querying, "What about him?"

"He's dangerous."

Abby stopped pouring the wine, stared with stunned, frightened fascination at Honor and breathed, "What?"

Honor came close, took the bottle from Abby and began to fill the glasses, all the while talking swiftly. "He's not a good man. I don't like him. Neither does Fenella. We never did. When Daddy died Mummy…"

She stopped and Abby watched her force a swallow, betraying an intense emotion that made Abby's heart go out to her before she forged ahead.

"Things weren't good for Mummy. She was…" Honor halted again and finished with the wine, putting the bottle on the counter. "Let's just say, she had to marry Alistair. She didn't marry him because she loved him. She married him because she needed to find a way to take care of us and she had no choice."

"Oh, Honor," Abby whispered, feeling for Honor and definitely for Nicola.

But Honor shook her head again.

"It's okay. We've all gotten used to it. Even Mummy. The thing you have to know is, a long time ago, I found the diaries," Honor told her.

Abby's brows drew together in confusion "The diaries?"

"Yes, Lorna's diaries," Honor answered. "I found them in the library, years ago, and kept them hidden. I don't think anyone even knows they exist."

"Who's Lorna?" Abby asked.

"Anthony and Alistair's mother."

Abby just looked at her, not knowing what this meant, and Honor got closer, her eyes going to the stairs then back to Abby and she started speaking quickly again.

"See, Alistair isn't a Beaumaris. Lorna was raped."

At this news, Abby sucked in breath and put her hand to the counter to hold on but Honor continued.

"Some gardener did the deed and then took off. Very unpleasant. She never told her husband, I don't know why. She should have. Maybe, back then, they didn't talk about that kind of thing or he wouldn't have believed her. Doesn't matter, she didn't. Before the rape, she was happy, except for Vivianna. She was in line for the axe from Vivianna, I just know it. From what Lorna wrote, Vivianna was playing with her, getting ready to go in for the kill. He loved her, Richard Beaumaris did, you could tell from what she wrote. Except, after Alistair was born, Richard turned on her. He knew Alistair was not a Beaumaris, thought she'd cheated on him. His love died and Vivianna backed off when it did, but Lorna never said a word."

"Oh my God. That's horrible," Abby whispered, her heart hurting, thinking about Cash's grandmother living that sad life.

Honor nodded and gave Abby a look that said she definitely agreed but she kept talking hurriedly.

"According to the diaries, regardless of how he was conceived, Lorna loved Alistair. She loved both her boys. Anthony and Alistair never got on, though. Lorna thought it was as if Anthony could sense what made Alistair. Furthermore, Alistair was not a nice kid. She loved him but he did things that scared Lorna. Scared and confused her. Things, I think, she only told her diary."

"That's not good," Abby muttered.

"No, it isn't," Honor agreed. "And he hasn't changed. *Really* hasn't changed. So much so, I think he could, and probably did, meddle with the brakes on Anthony's car."

Abby felt her eyes grow wide and her fingers clenched the counter anew while she breathed, "No."

"Yes," Honor returned. "Alistair hated Anthony as much as Anthony hated Alistair. Fenella told me what Angus McPherson said and it all makes sense. He had motive. Hatred, of course. But Anthony was spending all his time in Scotland with Myra and then Cash came along. If Anthony was going to move to the castle with his family, it's likely he was going to kick Alistair out."

Abby nodded that this made sense and Honor went on.

"But, the thing you have to know is, this means Alistair doesn't own the castle. Cash does. True and legal. All Cash has to do is ask for a DNA test."

The importance of this news hit Abby like a physical force and she rocked back.

Honor either didn't notice it, or more likely was on a mission to get all of her story out before the others returned.

"I had a solicitor friend of mine look at it and the castle's covenant is precise. First, the castle never, but never, goes out of the hands of a blood Beaumaris, which Cash is and Alistair isn't. Second, it's passed down from father to son. Always father to son. If there is no son then to a daughter. *Only* to a brother if the castle's master dies without any heir. My friend looked up some records and Anthony was having the covenant scrutinised when he died in order to alter it so Cash could inherit. But, in the end, he didn't have to. Regardless of Cash's legitimacy, he was the next in line to inherit. Anthony knew that. Alistair knew it too. Cash was too young and Cash's mother too crazy and too poor to fight it. But my friend says it was all his, all the lands, all the money, all the investments, all the businesses, and especially Penmort. It's always been Cash's. Always. All this time," Honor finished.

Abby found she was breathing heavily, and they heard the others approaching so Honor leaned in, took hold of Abby's upper arm and her voice was soft but urgent.

"I've put the diaries in a safe deposit box but I've copied the pages about the rape and I have them with me. Before I leave, I'll put them somewhere and tell you where to find them. And I've written down the information on the box and will leave you the keys so you can take Cash there," Honor told her.

"Why?" Abby asked and her voice sounded strangled so she repeated it, "Why? Why are you telling me this? Why are you doing this? For Cash? *To* Alistair?"

Honor's face changed, pain, anger and heartache, likely for herself and even for her mother and sisters, all chased through it, but as feminine feet came down the stairs all she said was, "You love him, and because of that, I can trust you. And I know Cash is a good man. I also know Alistair is *not.*"

And her tone said eloquently that her words about her stepfather were *true.*

Abby had no time to deny her love for Cash or thank her or give her the hug she probably desperately needed as the others arrived.

Honor's hand dropped from her arm and Abby watched as the guard slid back over her expression.

"*Cash's whole house is gorgeous!*" Fenella shrieked.

"It's impersonal," Mrs. Truman announced. "This is the only room that's homey."

Nicola's eyes were on Abby, her face soft, and she said, "I think the house is lovely, but you're right. This room is definitely the most welcoming."

Abby watched as Nicola's hand reached out and her fingers touched a hyacinth on the bar. She smiled at Abby, indicating she knew exactly why the rest of the house was cold and this room was warm.

Abby, still reeling from her conversation with Honor, gave Nicola a weak smile and quickly looked away.

As Honor started handing out drinks, Abby stiffly started to make Jenny's Manhattan, her mind awhirl with an all-new set of earth-shattering worries.

"You okay?" Jenny whispered, and Abby, not having noticed her friend had gotten close, jumped.

"No," Abby whispered back and then continued, "We'll talk later."

Jenny opened her mouth to speak but Abby's mobile, lying on the counter, started ringing.

"I'll finish this," Jenny said, taking the cocktail shaker from Abby, and Abby moved across the kitchen and grabbed her mobile.

The display said UNKNOWN CALLER and Abby was disappointed it wasn't Cash. She was beginning to get worried.

She took the call and put the phone to her ear.

"Hello?"

"Is this Abigail Butler?" an efficient female voice asked.

"Yes," Abby replied, ready to launch into her kind, but firm and very short "no thank you" speech that she delivered to all telephone marketers.

Then the female voice spoke and what she said opened a hole under Abby, through which she fell, plummeting uncontrollably toward the painfully blazing molten core at the centre of the earth.

"This is Emma at Mr. Fraser's offices. There's been a car accident and Mr. Fraser's at hospital."

"What?" Abby breathed, clutching the phone to her ear so tightly, pain shot through her fingers and it was a small miracle the phone didn't fuse to her ear.

"A car accident. Mr. Fraser's at hospital," Emma repeated.

"What hospital?" Abby asked sharply, her voice overloud, cracking through the air like a gunshot and the hum of conversation in the room silenced.

"Royal United," Emma answered, then went on speaking but Abby didn't listen.

She disconnected abruptly, dropped her mobile on the counter and shot to the oven, turning it off. She didn't look at anyone as she ran to her purse and grabbed it.

"Cash has been in a car accident. He's at the hospital. I've got to go," she announced, hearing the gasps and murmurings of surprise.

But she kept going, mind blank, her body's functions performed through an acute but focused panic.

She moved swiftly, taking the stairs two at a time. In the distance, she heard her mobile ring again but she didn't go back for it.

She was in the foyer, her coat in the crook of her arm, when she was swung back with a firm hand on her arm.

It was Jenny.

"Abby—" Jenny began.

Abby yanked her arm free. "I've got to go."

"*Abigail!*" Mrs. Truman barked.

Abby swung to the older woman and screamed, "*I've got to go!*"

Mrs. Truman wasn't trying to detain her and she wasn't wasting any time. She had her purse and was putting on her coat as she started to issue orders.

To Jenny she said, "You drive. Abigail's car is right outside. I'm coming with you. I know where Royal United is."

She shoved through Jenny and Abby and pulled open the door, looking back.

"Nicola, blow out the candles and make sure the house is safe. We'll meet you there."

Then she leaned forward, grabbed Abby's hand and tugged her gently out the door to the car.

Abby gave Jenny the keys, threw her coat through the door and got in the back seat of her car, buckling up. Mrs. Truman sat up front with Jenny. She listened as Mrs. Truman softly gave directions and Jenny drove safely, efficiently, but very quickly.

Abby sat in the back, her body feeling strangely numb considering she was breathing heavily, but her mind was flashing from thought to thought.

Or, more accurately, image to image, sound to sound and feeling to feeling.

She saw Cash sitting at the table in the pub the first time she laid eyes him, so handsome he took her breath away at the same time he scared her so much, she almost turned around and left.

She heard Cash's deep, rich laughter that first time in his car after he met Mrs. Truman.

She heard his beautiful voice on the phone telling her he was thinking about their first full-on kiss.

She felt his warm, strong hand on her neck.

She saw his eyes when he'd warned her she'd made a promise he was going to make her keep.

She saw him casually tossing her shoes across the room.

She felt the strange, moving, tender touch of his lips last night.

She heard his voice telling her they had all the time in the world.

Her hands came up and curled around the back of Jenny's seat and she pleaded urgently, "Jenny, go faster."

Jenny didn't take her eyes from the road as she muttered softly, "I'll get you there, honey."

Mrs. Truman twisted toward Abby and her face, usually composed, sometimes angry, other times grouchy, was now filled with unhidden concern.

"Abigail, breathe," Mrs. Truman ordered gently.

Abby's eyes shifted to the older woman, her breath coming in short pants. "I am."

Mrs. Truman shook her head. "Deep breaths, dear." When Abby didn't obey, Mrs. Truman repeated, "Deeply, Abby. Breathe deeply."

Abby nodded and took in a deep shuddering breath. Mrs. Truman watched her as she took in another one then another. Only when Abby's breathing became controlled did Mrs. Truman turn back to the road and continue with her directions.

What felt like a year later, Jenny turned into the A&E entrance of Royal United Hospital and Abby released her seatbelt in preparation for exiting the car.

When she straightened from the belt, out the front window she saw Cash standing with a man outside the doors to A&E.

Standing. Eyes open. Body intact. There was no blood. There were no cuts. No gaping wounds. No bandages. No slings. No limbs in casts. No crutches.

Just tall, handsome, beautiful, breathing Cash.

Abby threw open the door the minute Jenny came to a halt. She shot out of the car and ran on her high-heeled shoes like she'd been told she had only one second to reach him, to get her hands on him or he'd disappear forever.

The man he was with saw her, his face registered surprise and Cash's glance followed his. Abby watched Cash's brows draw together as he saw her.

He started approaching but stopped because Abby didn't slow. He only had a moment to brace before she hit him, full body, full velocity, full weight. On impact, his arms came around her and he went back on a foot.

"Abby, what on—?" he started, but Abby shoved her face in his neck and wrapped her arms so tightly around him she felt her muscles strain with the effort to hold on.

She felt Cash's arms tighten as his voice murmured in her ear, "Darling, what's happened?"

Abby didn't get a chance to respond, not that she would have. Her mind was blank and she had no faculties left to her but the ability to hold on tight.

"What's the meaning of this?" Mrs. Truman demanded from somewhere behind Abby.

"I was hoping you could tell me." Abby heard Cash reply.

"She got a call. She was told you were in a car accident and at the hospital," Jenny informed Cash, and at her words Cash's body went still but his arms constricted.

She heard him mutter a terse, "*Fuck,*" before he hesitated and she actually felt him forcing his body to relax before he called, "Abby."

Abby didn't move.

One of his arms still tight around her waist, the other hand came into her hair as he urged, "Darling, look at me."

Abby still didn't move.

He gave her hair a gentle tug. "Abby."

Her head came back, she looked at him and the minute her eyes locked on his, hers filled with tears.

He saw it, his face went soft and he muttered, "Darling."

"You're all right," she whispered, her voice sounding husky and choked but filled with blissful relief.

"I'm fine," he murmured, his hand going from her hair to stroke her spine. "I wasn't in an accident. Moira was."

"Moira? Who's Moira?" Mrs. Truman wanted to know, but Cash didn't answer, his eyes were on Abby.

"Moira?" Abby asked.

"Yes, darling," Cash told her.

Abby blinked, reality beginning to intrude, the black nightmare slowly edging away.

However, not enough for Abby to move even a centimetre away from Cash's hard, warm, living body.

"Is she okay?" Abby queried.

"Banged up but they're releasing her. We'd both just left the office. I was behind her when it happened. I stayed while we waited for the ambulance and then came to the hospital to wait until Glyn got here." He shifted their bodies so she could see the man he'd been standing with. "This is her fiancé, Glyn."

Abby's eyes moved to the man, shorter than Cash by several inches, he was fair, blue-eyed and he looked a mixture of worried and stunned. The former for Moira, the latter, likely at Abby's behaviour.

Reality crashed in and Abby's arms loosened their hold but Cash's didn't.

He held her close as Abby said to Glyn, "I'm so sorry. I thought it was Cash." She took in a shaky breath and repeated, "I'm so sorry."

"That's okay," Glyn said and his eyes moved to Cash. "I'd better get back to Moira. Thank you for staying."

"Not a problem," Cash returned, and Glyn nodded, his gaze swung around the assemblage and then he turned back to the A&E and walked in.

"Cash Fraser," Mrs. Truman's curt voice came at them, and Cash let one arm drop as he turned both Abby and himself to face the older woman when she continued, "Would you care to explain how this could happen?"

Abby took one look at Mrs. Truman and knew that in all her bad moods, this one was the worst. She looked outraged.

"Mrs. Truman—" Abby started, knowing exactly how it happened.

She'd panicked and overreacted, she hadn't let Emma tell her the whole story before she freaked out and took off.

She was so stupid. Stupid, stupid, *stupid*.

Cash's voice talked over hers. "I don't know, but I'm sure as fuck going to find out."

He was reaching in the inside pocket of his suit jacket and Abby's fingers curled around his wrist.

"It was me," she whispered when his hand stilled and his head tilted down to look at her. "It was me. I think Emma was going to explain, but I heard 'car accident' and you at the hospital and I—"

"That still doesn't explain why Fraser didn't call himself," Mrs. Truman snapped.

"I did. Four times. Her mobile was going directly to voicemail," Cash returned.

Abby knew why this happened. She'd been on and off the phone with Jenny and Fenella several times, giving them the complicated directions through Bath to Cash's house.

Cash went on, "I had to follow the ambulance to the hospital so I called my office and told them to phone Abby and explain that I'd be late." His eyes came back to Abby's and a muscle was working in his jaw. "Obviously, they didn't perform that simple task very well."

"Please don't be angry at anyone. It was me. I—" Abby started.

"Abby, there's a big fucking difference between 'Mr. Fraser will be late due to his PA having a car accident' and 'There's been an accident and Mr. Fraser is in hospital,'" Cash replied, his voice holding a sharp edge of anger.

"Cash, really—" Abby started to protest, but Cash cut her off.

"Abby, a minute ago you were staring at me with tears in your eyes and I could feel your heart beating through my fucking clothes," he clipped, the sharp edge of anger became blunt and heavy. "I don't employ staff to terrify my girlfriend. I employ them to be professional and know how to fucking communicate."

"Cash!" Abby cried, worried she'd gotten the unknown Emma into serious hot water, but he ignored her and looked at Jenny.

"I'll take Abby home," he informed Jenny, and Abby's eyes moved from being narrowed in annoyance at Cash to Jenny.

Abby saw her friend was staring at her. Jenny's face was pale, her eyes were knowing and her lips were pulled in between her teeth. This last was probably to stop herself from speaking, as in asking Abby what in *the heck* was going on in her screwy, messed-up head.

"Oh thank God, you're safe!" Nicola called, rushing forward with Fenella on her heels, Honor and Cassandra striding up quickly behind them.

"Jesus," Cash muttered.

Mrs. Truman turned toward them and waved both hands in the air.

"It was a mistake. Someone named Moira was in a car accident. Cash was being a good employer. All's well," she announced, then turned back to Cash, silently conveying it was his fault if her next words were true, "Except, maybe, the chicken."

"I'm so sorry. It's all my fault. I—" Abby started but stopped when Cash's arm gave her a none-too-gentle squeeze that stole her breath and her ability to speak.

"Oh, my dear, not at all. We're just glad Cash is all right," Nicola said, smiling kindly back and forth between Abby and Cash, both her face *and* body showing visible signs of relief.

"Now I *really* need a G&T," Cassandra muttered to Honor and Honor grinned, straight-out, no guard up, not only at Cassandra but also at Cash and Abby.

"I hope dinner isn't ruined!" Fenella fretted somewhat loudly.

"We'll throw together an omelette or something if it is," Nicola suggested, turning everyone around by ordering in the kind of voice only a mother could pull off, "Everyone, back to the car."

They all moved away but not until after Abby showed Jenny the key to Cash's house on her key ring (all the while avoiding her searching eyes) and Mrs. Truman gave Cash one last glare.

As Abby's BMW disappeared from sight, Abby turned to Cash and looked up at him.

"I feel like an idiot," she told him, because she did.

"Don't," he commanded, voice steely.

His hands coming to her neck, he brought her forward several inches, his head bending so his forehead rested on hers. She could see his black eyes, intense with some feeling she couldn't read but whatever it was made her heart skip several beats.

"Don't," he repeated, this time softly, his fingers flexing at her neck.

Abby was trying to avoid the look in his eyes and how it was making her feel but he was so close, she couldn't escape it.

"I hope Moira's going to be all right," she whispered.

"She will," Cash replied.

Abby's eyes moved to the side away from his but something happened to her.

It was like she no longer had control over her actions, like something deep in her that she didn't know was there surfaced and took command.

Her eyes closed and she heard her voice say so quietly there was nearly no sound, "I'm glad it wasn't you."

She felt his mouth on hers and before giving her a soft kiss, he said there, "I know, darling."

Her body, still not under her control, moved into him, closer, closer, until her head went under his chin, her hips connected with his, her hands curled into the lapels of his suit jacket, her cheek rested on his chest and his arms slid around her waist.

In her ear, she could hear his heart beat, and against the skin of her cheek she could feel it, and all she could smell was the scent of him.

She let go of her breath, and also against her control, she felt, for the first time in six years, at peace.

20

TWO IMPORTANT THINGS
HAPPEN TO CASH

Cash sat in the dark of his study on the ground floor.

He'd swivelled his chair to face the moonlight streaming in through the windows.

His eyes were on the shadowy, bare branches of the trees he could see in his garden.

His mind was on Abby, asleep upstairs in his bed, as well as on her foolish best friend who he was trying to find one good reason not to murder.

He didn't want to murder her because she was foolish. He wanted to shake her for that.

No, he wanted to murder her because she'd pointed out something to Cash that evening that he'd not considered.

And something he couldn't ignore.

After its dramatic start, the evening had progressed relatively well. The food had not been ruined and Abby recovered from her upset to be a gracious and amusing hostess. This was aided by Nicola and even, to Cash's surprise, a far more relaxed, friendly and interesting Fenella and Honor. Mrs. Truman maintained her normal surly but hilarious behaviour, and Cassandra was an unusual but amusing dinner guest.

Jenny, however, was quiet most of the evening, her face thoughtful, her eyes, Cash found, were nearly always watching Abby, Cash or the both of them together.

When Abby made tactful excuses for Cash to go to his study to work, he'd done so, gratefully, leaving the women to their conversation, which had taken an alarming turn to some preposterous-sounding American television show about two "hot" brothers who hunted ghosts.

He was not in his study for long when there was a soft knock on the door.

He hoped it was Abby.

Why he hoped this, he didn't know. So they could have a moment alone to talk about their dinner guests or to share a bit of quiet. Or, better yet, so he could put his hands on her, touch his mouth to hers, show her nonverbally how much it meant to him that she'd come rushing to the hospital in a panic at the thought he might be hurt.

However, it wasn't Abby.

It was Jenny.

At his call, she put her head around the door and asked, "Can I have a quiet word?"

At this unforeseen turn of events, he went on guard but nodded.

Jenny came in, sat across from his desk and had her quiet word.

Or, more specifically, she had several of them.

And as she spoke, Cash's hands itched to cup her shoulders and give her a good shake.

For, he found, she had overheard a conversation he had with James at a party some time ago, a conversation Cash remembered perfectly. She had not heard all of it, thankfully, but she'd heard enough of it for *her*—Jenny—to get the spectacularly asinine idea to pimp out her best friend.

Therefore she knew about Cash and Abby's initial arrangement because she'd been the person who'd orchestrated it.

He also discovered Abby's final secret, the reason why Abby sold her body and not her family's possessions.

Jenny informed him about the enormity of loss Abby had endured the past six years (something he already knew). She also described Abby's inability to cope with this as each blow landed one after the other (something he also had figured out). Further, she told him about the debt in which Abby had unexpectedly found herself (again, he'd already discovered this fact).

Finally, she explained how Abby had centred her attention on her house as the sole, remaining entity that represented her grandmother, mother, father, and lastly, and most especially, Jenny stressed, Abby's dead husband, the dear, funny, caring, attentive, beloved, faultless Ben.

Then Jenny told Cash he had to back off, that Abby was clearly becoming confused. She explained to him, carefully, that whatever his agenda was, it was lost on Abby. Whereas he had some final purpose from which he'd move on without Abby, Abby was getting muddled, and cautiously Jenny shared that she feared Abby's heart was getting involved.

Therefore, Jenny told him, he had to have a talk with Abby to get her back on track or preferably wind up their agreement and let Abby get back to her "real" life. And, so Abby wouldn't feel any harm from this, Jenny was perfectly willing to settle any debt that Abby might owe Cash or provide, through Cash, any further payment he might owe Abby.

Cash had been silent throughout her speech, and when Jenny stopped talking, she swallowed and stared at him, obviously waiting for his answer.

"Are you finished?" Cash asked, his voice cool and controlled, his thoughts lethal.

"I think so," Jenny answered.

"Obviously, Abby hasn't had time to speak with you," Cash told her.

Jenny's expression turned confused. "Speak with me about what?"

"If she hasn't spoken with you, then it's not my place to explain," Cash returned.

Jenny squared her shoulders. "If it's about Abby, then you should tell me. Sometimes she gets—"

Cash cut her off by saying sharply, "Stop."

Jenny's mouth snapped shut and her eyes got wide. This was likely because Cash was angry and he'd been hiding it, but he had decided it was time to let it show. She'd said enough, he wasn't going to sit and listen to her belittle her best friend even if it was with the "best intentions."

He didn't know what he looked like but from her expression she read his rather severe displeasure.

He spoke again, his voice deceptively quiet but clearly unhappy. "I hope you've realised your mistake at encouraging your vulnerable friend to embark on such a..." Cash paused, searching for an appropriate word. He found it, "Questionable venture."

"I—" she started, but Cash cut her off.

"Luckily for you, Abby isn't good at being a cold-hearted prostitute." He watched Jenny blanch and carried on, "From practically the minute I met her, I knew she wasn't what she said she was. I investigated her, discovered the truth and we've moved on from that. I'll let Abby explain what that means when she's ready."

"But—" Jenny started, but Cash talked over her.

"As for backing off, that's not going to happen. Patience and understanding don't work with Abby. Backing off means Abby retreating and I'm not going to allow her to do that."

Jenny leaned forward and put her hand on his desk. "You don't understand. She's—"

But Cash ruthlessly persevered.

"I do understand. I know she's lost her parents, her grandmother and her husband. I know how. I know when. I know she hasn't recovered, not from any of it and especially from Ben. I know she's terrified of living her life and letting anyone in for fear of losing someone else. Even if I didn't know it, the events of this evening would have demonstrated that fact rather forcefully."

Jenny closed her eyes and he saw her knuckles get white as she clutched the edge of his desk.

He went on, "Now I'll explain something *you* don't understand." He watched her eyes open and his gaze locked on hers. "You don't know me and I don't appreciate you making assumptions about me or my behaviour or my intent, especially in regards to Abby. I know you're her friend but it's none of your fucking business until Abby makes it so. Do you get my meaning?"

She sat back and he saw her teeth clench before she hissed, "Now you're making assumptions about me."

"I'm not the one who sat there and calmly described my efforts to pimp out my best friend," he returned.

"I didn't pimp her out!" Jenny snapped.

"No?" Cash replied.

She was shifting in her chair, not with discomfort but with anger. "You've known her, what? Two weeks? You've no idea what she's gone through, what she was going through. Completely no idea."

"No, Jenny. I have every idea," Cash responded evenly.

"You can't. I've known her for decades. I lived through all of this with her!"

"It wasn't you she threw her arms around tonight," Cash retorted.

"No, Cash," she snapped. "It was me who stood behind her when she sat by her mother's bed, her head on her mother's hand, when Mom Deux took her last breath. It was me Ben called when Abby lost it when her dad died. It was me Abby called after the police left when they gave Abby the news that Ben had been crushed to death in his own fucking car. It was me who had to phone Abby when her grandmother died. And it'll be *me* who picks up the pieces after *you're* through with her."

Cash sat back and took in a breath through his nose, trying to find patience then he said, "All right, Jenny, then you've earned the right to know that now, it's me who's restoring her treasured family home. It's me who's going to sort her latest financial disaster. And, for the foreseeable future, it'll be my house you come to if you want to see your friend. Further, it'll be me who gives Abby the life she deserves and it'll be me who makes certain she carries on with that life even if I'm not in it. To make certain I'm clear, there will be no pieces to pick up. I'll take care of her while she's in my life and I'll be certain she's taken care of when she's no longer in it."

Her eyes narrowed. "I haven't gotten through to you at all, have I?"

"No. What's gotten through is you're intent on enabling the fear that's keeping Abby from living her life," Cash answered.

"Right," she stood and glared down at him. "And I should encourage her to fall head over heels for some guy who'd pay for sex and who calmly sits there and tells me he's going to keep doing it, but in a *nicer* way, of course."

Rage shot through him at her words, but with some effort Cash remained seated and held her angry gaze. "Actually, what I'm telling you is that you shouldn't stand in my way."

"Is that a threat?" she snapped.

"No," Cash replied truthfully and it wasn't.

Cash didn't believe in threats. He felt strongly that you never threatened anything you had no intention of doing.

The truth was, if Jenny stood in his way with Abby, best friend or not, he'd show no remorse in getting what he wanted.

Or in this case, keeping what he had.

Jenny stared at him, her chest rising and falling quickly with her breathing.

Cash stared back coolly, but he was still very angry.

Finally she clipped, "Fine." Then she walked to the door but turned to him and declared, "I'd prefer Abby didn't know we had this little chat."

"I'll not lie to Abby," he told her, watched as she pulled her lips between her teeth and relented, "However, I also won't tell her unless she asks."

She nodded jerkily and put her hand on the doorknob and something Cash couldn't control or explain made him ask, "Why don't you want her to be happy?"

Jenny turned back to him, her face the picture of stunned, hurt surprise, and she whispered, "Of course I want her to be happy."

Cash's voice gentled when he assured her, "Jenny, I can make her happy."

Jenny's expression melted to one of thoughtful concern.

"Yes, Cash. You already are."

Cash felt her words hit him like strangely pleasant, velvet-gloved blows, but she went on.

"But for how long? You want to give her the life she deserves? That isn't a life filled with cashmere robes and diamond bracelets. That's a life filled with happiness. If you take a part of her life, she might be missing out on someone who doesn't start his relationship with her talking about when he'll no longer be in it. And that also means, however long you two last, somewhere along the line she has to start again."

Her voice pitched lower as her verbal blows became far less pleasant. In fact, they felt like jabbing knifepoints piercing his skin.

"She's had to start again enough, Cash. Don't you think?"

With that, she opened the door and was gone.

And Cash stared at the door long after she'd gone, knowing and hating the knowledge that she was right.

Some time later, another knock came at the door and he tensed. But this time it was Abby telling him their guests were leaving.

He'd walked to the front door with her to bid their guests goodnight. Jenny did well, giving him a cheek touch and a squeeze of the arm, indicating to those who might be watching that all was well between Abby's best friend and her boyfriend.

He closed and locked the door, and by the time he turned around, Abby had wandered down the hall. He followed her and found her in the spotless kitchen, getting a glass.

He stood at the end of the counter watching her fill the glass with water then she walked to him and grabbed her purse that was sitting on the counter by his hip.

"Abby," he called, not certain what he meant to say, just knowing something needed to be said.

But she was rooting through her purse.

"Mm?" she mumbled, pulling a small, thin, gold case out of her bag and opening it.

"Did you have a good night?" he asked softly and watched with rising unease as she selected four identical pills from the case, flipped the case shut and dropped it into her bag.

"Yes," she answered distractedly and picked up her water.

"What's that?" he inquired as her fingers closed around the pills.

"Ibuprofen," she replied and started to lift her hand to her mouth.

But his own shot out and caught hers firmly at the wrist.

Her eyes flew to his and her brows drew together. "Cash."

"The usual dose of ibuprofen is two tablets," he told her.

"I know, but—"

His thumb moved along her palm, forcing her fist open. "Then take two."

She was looking at him quizzically. "Two isn't enough."

He placed his other hand under both of theirs, turned her wrist and the tablets fell out of her now-opened palm into his own. He took two tablets and gave them to her, his fingers closing around the other two.

She accepted them but her gaze was still on his. "Cash, I'm telling you, two isn't enough. Three isn't enough. Only four will work."

His eyes moved over her face and he saw she looked slightly pale and had a not-very-Abby-like pinched look to her mouth.

"Do you have a headache?" he asked.

"No," she answered.

"What's the matter?" he pressed when she gave no further explanation.

"I'd rather not say."

"Do you often take double the recommended dose of medication?" he pushed.

"No, I don't often take medication. Cash, I don't get it. What's the big deal?"

Cash sighed before saying, "Abby, if you tell me what's the matter, I can call Tim and ask him what you should do about it."

Her eyes went wide. "You're not calling Tim about this!"

"What is it?"

"I'd rather not say."

His hand came to her neck and he put pressure there while saying warningly, "Abby."

"I've got cramps, all right?" Her eyes rolled to the ceiling and she breathed, "Geez."

Even with his mind filled alternately with the vision of a panic-stricken Abby somehow gracefully flying toward him in high heels outside an A&E and the disquieting conversation he'd had with her best friend, Cash still couldn't stop himself from roaring with laughter.

While laughing, he used his hand to guide her close until he felt her hips against his. When he was done, he looked down at her and she was scowling at him.

"Cramps aren't funny," she informed him irritably.

His hand moved from her neck, down her back to circle her waist.

"I'm sorry, darling. Are you in a lot of pain?"

"Yes," she snapped.

He gave her a squeeze. "Does it happen every month?"

"No," she replied shortly. "Every other month. Apparently I have a testy ovary. Now can we stop talking about this?"

He smiled while he told her, "It's perfectly natural."

"Yes, I am aware of that, Cash Fraser," she retorted. "I still would rather not talk to my new boyfriend about period cramps. Jenny, I could talk to. But I don't converse with Pete, my handyman, who was also my grandmother's handyman, who I've known since I can remember, about period cramps. Okay?" Cash kept smiling at her, and she heaved an enormous sigh before asking, "Can I have my tablets please?"

He lifted his hand and dropped the two tablets into her opened palm. Keeping his arm around her, he watched her take them deciding tonight was not the night to talk about their future, a future which had limits. Limits that Abby had to understand before she embarked on any future with him.

They'd talk about it tomorrow.

Or, Cash thought, after his aunt and uncle's anniversary.

Or, he thought (understanding his own selfishness, but with Abby pressed close, not caring), even later.

She put her glass on the counter and relaxed into him.

"That'll work?" Cash asked softly.

"In about half an hour, yes," she replied.

"I'll let you get to sleep and finish up in the study," Cash told her.

A look crossed her face that he could swear was disappointment before she nodded.

His hand not around her lifted to her jaw, his thumb sliding along her soft cheek. "I'll be up soon."

"Okay," she whispered.

She tipped her head back and he knew she expected a kiss. Not just expected one but wanted one. And not a demonstration of passion, but rather one of affection.

His eyes roamed her face, memorising the beauty of it in anticipation of tenderness, before he bent his neck and touched his mouth to hers.

"Go to sleep," he muttered against her lips.

"Don't be long," she whispered back and gave his waist a squeeze with her hands before she pulled away and walked up the stairs.

He wandered the room, turning off the lights and extinguishing candles when, at the last lamp, he stopped and looked around.

His arrival that evening had not been conducive to him paying much attention to anything but Abby. Dinner was more Abby, her delicious meal as well as a throng of women in his dining room.

So he hadn't noticed until now how Abby's simple touches had transformed the room from what had always been only living space to what was now lived-in space.

He pulled in a slow breath and on the exhale he muttered, "Fuck," before he turned out the last lamp and walked up the stairs to his study.

Now it was much later and it had taken him some time to regain concentration on his work. He'd finished that, switched off his laptop, the lamps, turned his chair to the window and sat brooding in his darkened study like a character out of a Brontë novel.

On that thought, he pushed out of his chair and walked upstairs to his bedroom, seeing Abby's motionless form under the bedclothes. Cash could tell, even in the dark, she'd curled around his pillow.

He prepared for bed, pulled back the covers and slid in. Careful not to disturb her, he tugged at his pillow. As she was asleep, and he always had her in sleep, she gave up the pillow in favour of him, her limbs curving around him as she pressed close. He put his pillow behind his head and settled back.

"Cash?" she whispered, her voice sexy and husky.

"Yes, love, go back to sleep."

Abby had not lied when she'd told him she liked her sleep. Therefore, he was surprised when she got up on her elbow and pulled her hair out of her face.

"Is it late?" she asked.

"Close to midnight," he replied.

"Are you tired?"

No. He wasn't tired. He was in bed with Abby and her voice was just-woken-up-throaty. However, she'd also started her period and was uncomfortable even talking about it, therefore he had a feeling she'd not be thrilled with the idea of having sex while on it.

Instead of answering her question, he said, "I have a meeting first thing in the morning."

"We have to talk."

His body went still but she didn't notice it. She pressed into him, reaching across the bed, groping for a moment before she found the lamp switch and muted light filled the room.

He watched as she blinked adorably, her eyes adjusting to the light, then they focused on him.

She further surprised him by keeping her position. Her torso on his, her forearm came to rest on his chest, holding herself elevated but still close.

Her face was drowsy but the look in her eyes was serious.

Cash mentally braced.

With Abby, it could be anything. She could say something that would lead to a heated row. She could suffer an emotional breakdown. She could do something outrageous to make him laugh. Or she could put her mouth on him and make him come.

He had to be prepared.

However nothing he could do would prepare him for what came next.

"Something's happened," she told him.

"What?" he asked.

She looked away and bit her lip, then sighed and looked back to him. "I don't even know where to begin."

His hands stole around her hips. "Darling, just start at the beginning. Whatever it is, it'll be all right."

After he said that, she did something that so surprised him, his entire body reacted to it, tensing along his length as her hand came up to rest on his cheek.

And with a soft voice, her eyes on his, she said, "I met this man yesterday at Mrs. Truman's. I wasn't going to say anything about him until the time was right. But then Honor talked to me tonight."

The tension in Cash's body increased and she felt it, her thumb moved to his temple and circled there soothingly.

"Cash," she whispered. "Penmort is yours."

His body froze solid.

"I'm sorry?" he growled.

"Honor told me," she said.

He felt his eyes narrow. "Honor told you what? Exactly."

She licked her lips and took in a breath, "She told me she found your grandmother, Lorna's, diaries."

Cash's eyes stayed narrow but now in confusion. "Keep talking."

Abby nodded and went on, "She says she thinks no one knows about them. She's read them. Cash..." She hesitated, then in a soft explosion, she burst out, "*God*! I don't know how to tell you this."

Losing patience, Cash rolled her to her back, positioned his body on his elbow and loomed over her. "Just say it."

She stared at him a moment before she said swiftly, "Your grandmother was raped."

Cash's body jerked and instantly both her hands came up to frame his face.

"Cash, look at me, please, honey, look at me." When the shock from her announcement receded, Cash's eyes focused on Abby's face. She was staring at him with a look that was immensely gentle, and she whispered, "Alistair was the product of that rape."

Cash blinked slowly.

Abby kept talking.

"Honor says all you need to do is ask for a DNA test and Penmort is yours. She says she's had a friend examine Penmort's covenant and the castle can't be held outside of the bloodline. Alistair isn't of the line. Honor says the castle, and everything, is yours." One of her hands moved away from his face and she went up on one elbow, getting closer as her other hand drifted down to his shoulder. "Honey, the castle has always been yours."

His eyes never left her concerned face as sensations tore through him, some of them exultant, some of them toxic.

When his father had died, Penmort and its holdings were vast. They had to be for anyone to maintain such a huge property. There was land.

There were lettings in the local town, both commercial and residential. There were investments. His father owned the controlling share of several lucrative businesses and kept a domineering hand in all of them earning a reputation as a clever but ruthless mogul.

At the time, it had been worth multiple millions, translated into today's money, it would have been billions.

Alistair had dwindled that down to nothing. Almost as if he was doing it intentionally, he pulled out of good investments and threw money at bad ones. He sold the controlling shares, the properties, the lands and he lived high. Travelled widely. Spent freely. Until there was nothing coming in and thousands going out, monthly.

"That fucking *bastard*," Cash exploded and pushed away. Hurling the covers wide, he knifed out of bed and looked for something to throw.

Instead, his eyes fell on Abby, who'd sat up in the bed and was watching him.

She was wearing an espresso-brown silk nightgown edged in delicate ecru lace.

A nightgown he'd bought for her. A nightgown that cost more than many people spent on clothes in a year. A nightgown the likes of which he'd worked since he was twelve years old, scratching his way up from nothing, so he could afford.

And still he was working fourteen hour days so he wouldn't blink at such a purchase.

"*Fuck!*" Cash roared, his arm shot out, his fist closed around the lamp and he yanked it out of the wall. The light going dead, he threw it across the room.

He heard its glass base shatter against the wall then he heard Abby shoot out of bed.

Cash was pacing, the whole time Abby at his side, her hands on him. She tried to get in his way but he either abruptly turned and headed the other way or walked around her.

"Cash, please, stop. Look at me," she begged.

"We had nothing. My grandfather worked driving a fucking taxi. And we still had nothing," Cash growled, his hand had shot through his hair, his fingers closing around the back of his neck and he kept them there as he paced. "Then he died. Mum couldn't hold down a job for more than a few months. Eventually no one would hire her, and we *really* had fucking nothing."

Abby planted herself in front of him and threw her arms around him, crushing her body against his and she held on, finally effectively halting him.

"Please, honey, stop walking," she pleaded. "You might cut yourself. Let me clean up the lamp."

At her words, something inside him imploded.

He pulled viciously out of her arms but bent low, put one arm behind her knees and one at her waist. He lifted her and carried her to the bed. Tossing her on it, he came down on top of her.

"You're not going to clean up the lamp, Abby," he clipped. "You're never going to clean anything again. Aileen's going to clean up the fucking lamp. That's what I fucking pay her for. That's why I fucking work so goddamned hard."

Her hands were on him, stroking his back slowly, soothingly, and she whispered, "Okay, Cash."

Cash felt Abby's hands moving on him, her soft body under his, the silk of her nightgown against his skin and he sucked in breath.

On his exhale, he shared, "My father left the money, the holdings, everything, to my mother, but Alistair took her to court. It was years, battle after battle, appeal after appeal. And he got it back."

Abby's hands stopped moving and her arms slid around his back to hold on tight.

"I looked through her papers," Cash told her. "She had a case. A strong one. She was sick, drove her attorneys up the wall, and then she ran out of money and they jumped ship."

"Oh, Cash," she breathed softly.

He dropped his forehead to Abby's and muttered, "I can't fucking wait to see his face when I kick his ass out."

Abby's body went still under his, she hesitated then suggested quietly, "Maybe you should wait until after the anniversary celebration. I think Nicola's looking forward to that."

Cash replied instantly, "Oh, I'll wait." Something occurred to him, he pulled slightly away and asked, "Why did Honor tell you this?"

He heard her hair slide along the covers as he saw the shadowy outline of her head shake in front of him. "I think..." she started, paused and went on warily, "I'm not sure, but I don't think Alistair was very..." She hesitated again then finished, "*Nice* to them. *Any* of them."

Cash caught her meaning.

Alistair not being "nice" included Nicola.

In a low voice that came directly from his gut, he knew because he felt it, Cash promised, "He's going to pay."

Abby's arms flexed around him and she warned, "Be careful, Cash. He scares me."

Belatedly, Cash realised his weight was likely too much for her and he rolled to his side, taking her with him.

His arms moved around her and he pulled her close. Her arms stayed tight and she tucked her face in his neck.

"Don't worry, darling. I won't let him hurt you, or anyone, not again."

Her head tilted back and she replied, her voice showing her surprise, "Cash, I'm not worried about *me*."

His chin dipped down and he looked at her face in the shadows and he repeated, "I said I won't let him hurt anyone."

She pushed her body into his as she pressed him verbally, "Even you?"

It struck him, uncommonly slowly, that Abby was worried about him. And this knowledge sheared the edge off his anger.

His hand slid up her back, sifted into her hair and he tucked her face back into his neck.

"Even me," he murmured.

She nuzzled closer and whispered, "I'm sorry about all this."

"Stop saying you're sorry," Cash demanded.

She nestled even closer and continued softly, "Well, I am. About you, your mom. Nicola and the girls. And your grandmother. What she must have gone through."

Absently, Cash's fingers caught a lock of her hair and started winding it around his fingers.

"Don't think about it," Cash gave her the advice he was going to use himself.

"Okay," she mumbled, "I'll try."

He held her until everything about her enveloped him, her scent, her feel, her touch, her warmth, the sound of her breathing. After he felt the peace only Abby could bring him, he pulled her right in the bed, yanked the covers over them, and settled her into his side.

When he felt her head go heavy on his shoulder, her arm slackening around his stomach, he called, "Abby."

"Yes, honey?" she mumbled sleepily.

His arm around her waist got tight and his fingers at her hip gripped her briefly.

"Thank you for telling me," he muttered.

She gave him a squeeze and pressed deeper into his side.

"You're welcome."

He waited until her breathing evened, her body relaxed and he took her slumbering weight.

Only then did he allow himself to sleep.

THE BATTLE BEGINS

Abby drove her car along the winding roads toward Penmort, concentrating closely because she didn't really know where she was going, and also because she was scared half out of her mind.

She had no idea how she'd let Angus talk her into this.

Yes, she did.

Tomorrow night Cash and she were going to the castle and spending the weekend there, staying Friday through Sunday. A "family" celebratory dinner was to be held Friday night. The extravaganza was Saturday night. And they were to leave Sunday after a brunch of family and close friends.

And if she didn't meet Angus tonight she might not make it to Sunday.

Angus called Jenny's phone that morning when Jenny and she were on their way to pick up her great-grandmother's gown. Abby had taken it to the cleaners on Monday to have it cleaned and pressed. Jenny and she were headed there to pick it up as well as do other shopping for the weekend when Angus called.

Jenny, Abby noted, was acting weird.

She was far more quiet than normal, especially when Abby explained all that had happened with Cash that week.

Jenny, who Abby expected to freak out, simply turned to her and said, "That's nice. He's a good man, Abby, and I think he wants to make you happy."

She sounded like she didn't entirely believe her own words even though she wanted to. Furthermore, she shared no advice, guidance, concerns, warnings or even giggles, smiles or lewd questions about how Cash looked naked.

Definitely weird.

Abby had gone on to share her new life philosophy, something to which she was certain Jenny would have a reaction.

She'd come up with it lying in Cash's bed last night, waiting for the cramps to go away and allowing herself the time, finally, to think of everything that had befallen her and what she was going to do about it.

When she got the call that Cash had an accident (she thought), she was definitely reacting, or more to the point, overreacting because of what had happened with Ben. But she hadn't been reliving losing Ben. She'd been upset because she couldn't fathom the thought of losing Cash.

Which was something she couldn't ignore even if she wanted to.

But he'd said himself that they weren't going to lose one another until one of them wanted to be lost.

Which meant he knew one day he would move on.

Abby didn't like this idea. It hurt even to contemplate it.

But she lay in his bed asking herself how she would behave if someone had told her that her time would be short with Ben.

In order to avoid the pain, would she have turned away, left him behind and not spent her years of love and laughter with him?

Never.

What she would have done was packed much more love and laughter in those years. She would have treasured every moment, even the bad ones, for the precious memories they would become.

So she had a monumental shift in thinking.

For she knew upon feeling the immense relief that Cash was alive and well that she cared about him. And she had to admit, finally, that what she and Cash had was good.

No, it wasn't good, it was great.

No, it wasn't even great, it was *magical*.

She couldn't kid herself anymore and she didn't even want to.

But this time, she'd been given a boon. She already knew their time together would be short. That meant she could prepare. And that was exactly what she was going to do.

She was going to pack as much into her time with Cash as she could fit. And she was going to savour it while she had it.

She was going to stop living her life in fear.

She was just going to live.

Abby thought Jenny would be thrilled to hear this, though she didn't tell Jenny that Cash had intimated the end at the same time he was initiating the beginning.

Instead, Jenny got a strange look on her face and gave Abby a hug.

Abby leaned back in her friend's arms and asked, "Are you okay?"

Jenny pulled her lips between her teeth and bit them.

When she released them, she nodded and said, "Just happy for you."

She didn't look happy nor did she look okay, but Abby had let it go.

When Jenny was ready to share what was troubling her, Jenny would share. That had always been the way no matter how much Abby wheedled her.

So she let Jenny have her space.

That's when Angus had called.

Jenny handed Abby the phone and Angus told her he'd been at the castle and "on the job" for the last two nights, but the "ghosty she-bitch," a.k.a. Vivianna, wasn't showing.

"She's a clever girl, but not more clever than A McPherson!" he'd decreed grandly.

Then, without further ado, he told Abby his scary plan. A plan which consisted of Abby going to the castle and offering herself up as bait to a murderous, vindictive ghost.

Angus had already spoken with Fenella and Cassandra and everything was in place. Alistair and Nicola were out for the evening, as was Suzanne, none of them to return until late.

Honor and Fenella would have Abby over to dinner and Abby would draw out Vivianna so Angus could take her down. However,

Cassandra would give Abby some protection and Angus would give her some coaching before Abby went in.

Though, Angus assured her, Abby had nothing to fear. Angus would always be a "hairsbreadth" away.

There were a variety of things Abby didn't like about this plan.

First, she didn't want to be bait. Vivianna was a spirit-bitch-from-hell and Abby didn't want to be anywhere near her until she *had* to be near her.

Second, she didn't want to be bait (Abby thought that was worth pointing out twice).

Third, dinner with Honor and Fenella to draw out a ghost meant that she'd have to tell Cash she had other plans, plans that didn't include him, and she didn't figure he'd like that much.

That morning before he left for work when he, as usual, slid her hair off her neck, she felt it and she woke. Her eyes opened when his lips touched her skin.

She looked at his shadowy form and he murmured, "I'm leaving, darling."

She'd muttered back, "Hang on," and with sleepy energy she'd flipped her legs around his body and jumped out of bed. He rose with her and she grabbed his hand, led him to the guest bedroom and flicked on the lights.

"Abby—" he started, but Abby was mumbling sleepily to herself.

"I should have come in and got it last night but I..." She stopped by the bed and he halted beside her, looking puzzled and somewhat impatient. She let go of his hand, reached under the pillow and pulled out an envelope. "Honor said she'd leave it here and she did," Abby finished.

Cash's eyes went from hers to the envelope and Abby explained about the copied diary pages and the safety deposit box.

Abby had not had time to process their emotional evening or any of the profound secrets Cash had let slip during his tirade. Secrets about his surprising history of being poor (something about which she had no idea; she thought, especially with his manner, that he'd been born to money, *lots* of it). Secrets about his father leaving his mother and him a fortune that had been taken away (something which neither Angus nor Honor, nor Fenella, mentioned, and she wondered if they knew).

Secrets about the reason he worked so very hard (something which made her heart hurt).

That morning, he seemed none the worse for wear, his usual charismatic self. But a deadly light shone in his dark eyes when she explained what the envelope contained.

When she was done, his arm went around her waist. He hauled her into his body and his mouth came down on hers in an intense, thorough, mind-numbing kiss.

When he was done, her knees were weak and she sagged into his body.

After she'd recovered, she lifted the envelope and slapped it on his chest. This was done in an effort to be cute and try to control her heated body caused by the ferocious triumph she felt in his kiss *and* her concerns about what that might mean for his safety.

"Be smart with this, Mr. Fraser. Don't make me regret giving it to you," she teased mock-severely, and he smiled but his smile didn't reach his eyes.

His eyes were still deadly serious.

His fingers closed around the envelope and he tucked it into his inside jacket pocket.

Then his hand went into her hair and he asked, his burr so rough it vibrated against her skin, "Fancy living in a castle?"

A shiver slid through her at his question, right before it hit her he was Penmort's master, true and legal.

Her eyes moved over his handsome face and she realised it suited him.

Instead of answering his question, Abby snuggled closer and admitted, "That night we were there, Alistair stood by the fireplace and I thought he seemed out of place." Her fingers curled into his lapel, she went up on tiptoe and tilted her head back as she got closer to his face. "You wouldn't seem out of place. As crazy as this sounds, a castle suits you, Conner Fraser."

At her words, his fist tightened in her hair, his mouth crushed down on hers and if she thought the first kiss was filled with ferocious triumph it was nothing to this one.

He'd lifted his head nary an inch when he was done and asked, "How long does your period last?"

"Not long," she'd breathed, still recovering from the kiss and having some difficulty in this endeavour.

"How long?" he pushed.

"A couple of days," she answered.

He grinned against her mouth and muttered, "I won't make it."

She couldn't help it. Abby laughed, straight-out, nothing hidden, nothing buried, nothing held back, both hands clutching his shoulders and her body shaking with hilarity.

When she'd controlled her mirth she saw he was looking at her with a partially startled expression, the rest held a warmth so intense it was breathtaking.

His hand went out of her hair and both arms wrapped tight around her as he shoved his face in her neck and he said something enormously strange.

"I've got you."

"Pardon?" she asked.

His head came up, his mouth touched hers, and he murmured, "Nothing." He scanned her face and his fingers came up, trailing her hairline, tucking the fall of hair behind her ear. "Go back to bed, darling. I'll see you tonight."

After another touch of his lips against hers, he was gone.

When she'd called him that afternoon to tell him she had dinner plans with Honor and Fenella, she'd given him the excuse she and Jenny cooked up as to why he wasn't invited.

Although Cash seemed not to have any reservations about discussing Abby's menstrual cycle, she and Jenny were betting on the fact he wouldn't feel the same about his cousin.

So, Abby had told him Fenella was having "female problems."

This surprisingly worked.

Cash, sounding distracted, said only, "All right, love. Call me when you leave the castle so I'll know when to expect you safely home."

He didn't seem curious to know why Abby all of a sudden would be Fenella's Female Problems Confidante, and he didn't seem angry she wouldn't be home for dinner.

So now there she was on her way to the castle and perhaps her catastrophic end, and she was thinking she didn't want the last thing she said to Cash to be a lie.

Therefore, when she pulled into the pub where she was meeting Angus and Cassandra to get instructions before going to the castle, she yanked out her phone and dialled Cash.

He answered on the second ring.

"Everything all right?" he asked as greeting.

"Yes. Why?" Abby queried in return.

"Shouldn't you be on your way to Penmort?"

"I am. I pulled over to call you." There she was, lying again (kind of).

"You pulled over to call me," he repeated.

"Yes," she replied.

Silence.

"Cash?" she called.

"Yes?" he answered.

"You were silent," she told him. "I thought maybe we were disconnected."

"I'm here," he said.

More silence.

"Cash!" she snapped into the silence.

"Abby," he returned.

"You were silent again," she informed him and heard his chuckle, so she asked, "What's funny?"

"Darling, *you* called *me*."

She felt like an idiot. "Oh. Right."

"Did you have something to say?" he inquired.

She bit the side of her lip before she admitted, "Not really."

This time she heard his roar of laughter.

When he'd stopped laughing, he asked, "Were you biting your lip?"

"Pardon?"

"Biting your lip," he repeated.

"Yes. Why?" she answered.

"No reason," he said, the warmth of his voice coming at her in delicious waves over the phone. "Listen, love, I'm in a meeting."

Abby felt the blood drain from her face and definitely knew she was an idiot.

"You are?" she breathed.

"Yes, I have to go."

"I'm an idiot," she muttered.

"You're exquisite," he returned softly, and Abby felt her world pitch crazily as she listened to him say, "I'll see you later tonight."

Then he disconnected.

The minute he did a sharp rap came on the window and she jumped.

She turned to the side and saw Angus's red-cheeked face peering in at her.

"Lassie! No time for love banter, we've got things *to do*," he boomed before he stepped back and opened her door.

Abby unbuckled her seatbelt and got out to see Cassandra approaching and Angus again in full Scottish gear.

She looked at Angus and asked with disbelief, "You hunt ghosts in a kilt?"

"I always wear a kilt," he informed her.

"Why?"

"I'm Scottish!" he bellowed.

"Oh...kay," she said slowly, not wanting to get him wound up.

He had serious business to attend to that night, he needed to stay focused.

Cassandra got close, gave Abby a cheek touch, stepped back and Angus began talking.

"Wee Honor and Fenella have been smart," Angus said. "They've been well away from the castle anytime they talk or call someone about the ghosty she-bitch. Vivianna can be anywhere, hear anything and you won't see her. You go into the castle, you don't talk about her or why you're there. Everything's normal. Aye?"

"Aye," Abby repeated, and he grinned.

Cassandra came forward and held something out to Abby. Abby took it and saw it was a glass amulet surrounded with ornate silver fili-gree and filled with powder and what looked like flower petals, this suspended from a thin, leather thong.

"Wear that," Cassandra instructed. "Protection. It should keep her from you. But if it doesn't and Angus doesn't get to you in time and you're in danger, take it off and throw it to the ground. Smash it with your heel. You'll see a purple mist form. The mist should shroud you enough to get away."

Angus butted in, "And you *run* away. She attacks, and I'm not there within seconds, she gets through the protection charm, you smash it and you *go*."

Abby gulped, then she nodded.

Cassandra continued, "You head out of the castle and off the grounds. She can't leave the grounds. Go into town. Keep your mobile in your back pocket at all times. You call me or Angus when you hit town and we'll come and get you. Don't go anywhere near the castle unless one of us has come to get you."

"What about Honor and Fenella?" Abby asked.

Cassandra shook her head but Angus spoke. "They'll be safe. Me and this wee lassie," he jerked a thumb at Cassandra, "been doing some research about our spirit-bitch-from-hell. She made one mistake."

Finally, Abby thought with some relief, *Vivianna made a mistake.*

Cassandra took up the thread. "She empowered herself with the ability to murder. Ghosts, most of the time, can't harm people in a physical way. They can make noise. They can often move things, but only after a good deal of practice. This is mostly done to be annoying or frightening, but sometimes they'll move something so it will be in someone's way, trip them up, say to fall down the stairs."

Cassandra paused and when Abby nodded, she continued.

"They can also appear and drive people towards danger or scare them to death. But Vivianna can actually touch the mortal flesh of her victims. She's been able to do so since the beginning. That's rare."

"But only those she intends to kill," Angus cut in. "Only those who she's given herself the power to kill. Only the true loves of a Penmort master. Which means Honor and Fenella are safe."

Abby knew she'd made this point before but she felt it was still pertinent. "I don't mean to sound like a broken record but seriously, honest to goodness, I'm not Cash's true love."

Cassandra and Angus looked at each other then back at Abby.

"If you aren't, then you have nothing to worry about," Cassandra said.

"Well, that's a relief," Abby smiled.

"But if you weren't, she'd no' have been able to touch you, lass," Angus put in gently.

Abby stared at him and asked, "What?"

"Thought she'd already harmed you? Shoved you in the back?" Angus asked.

"Yes, but—" Abby started.

Angus cut her off by saying, "True love."

Abby blinked.

Then something started to bud in the region of her heart, something that felt a lot like hope.

"I still don't think—" Regardless of the hope in her heart, she continued to resist but Cassandra interrupted this time.

"Okay, we get it. You both are in the throes of a new relationship and you're worried it's getting too heavy too fast, so you're in denial. You've got to move past that, mate. Whether he loves you, he doesn't love you, whatever, it's been established you're a target and you're vulnerable. Let's move on."

"He loves her," Angus muttered under his breath.

"Let's move on," Cassandra said firmly.

"I'm saying he loves her," Angus repeated, louder this time.

"Let's move on!" Cassandra snapped, now firm and loud.

Angus's hands came up. "All right, all right. Don't get your knickers in a twist."

Cassandra looked at Abby. "We have another piece of somewhat good news."

Abby didn't like the "somewhat" part but she'd take any good news attached to Vivianna.

"What's that?"

"She plays with her victims," Angus stated.

Abby felt her stomach drop and whispered, "Pardon?"

"Plays with her victims," Angus reiterated. "She doesn't go in for the kill right away. She messes with 'em, sometimes for years. At the very least until they provide Penmort with an heir."

"Oh my *God*," Abby breathed.

"This is good news," Cassandra informed her, and Abby turned to the witch.

"How can this be good news?" she cried. "I don't want her *playing* with me!"

"A broken arm is a lot better than dead," Angus commented logically.

"Easy for you to say!" Abby exploded. "I've got an evening gown to wear Saturday night and the cuts on my arms she gave me last time are still pink!"

Angus stared at her like she might have a screw loose, but Cassandra got close.

"What we're saying," she started quietly, "is tonight's not your night to die. Even if this doesn't work, you should leave the castle breathing."

Abby turned wild eyes to Cassandra but she kept talking.

"Just keep your head, Abby. Angus knows what he's doing. So do I. If Angus doesn't take her down, the only thing Vivianna might learn tonight is that she's got a worthy adversary. But we'll outsmart her." Her hand came up and gave Abby's upper arm a squeeze before she said, "I promise."

Abby felt slightly mollified by her promise, but not much.

"Now, get to the castle," Cassandra finished.

"Keep a clear head. Eyes open. Stay vigilant. Anything that doesn't feel right, you reckon it isn't and you move," Angus coached her. "You feel any cold draughts, a chill, she's close." Angus came near too and both Cassandra and he crowded her, but Abby didn't move. Angus went on gently, "Remember, lass, wherever you are, I'll be watching."

Abby nodded. She gave them a shaky smile and got in her car. She put the amulet around her neck, tucking it into her sweater so it couldn't be seen.

She looked to the side and saw them both standing where she left them, close together.

She gave them an idiotic thumbs up, started her car and headed to her doom.

❦ ❦ ❦

It was after a glass of wine, after dinner, Abby, Fenella and Honor were sitting in the drawing room and they were drinking coffee.

Nothing had happened, except they'd had a pleasant night (when they weren't all looking around thinking something was going to happen, that was).

"Do you need to go to the loo?" Fenella asked on a prompt, her voice overly loud and squeakily high.

"No, she doesn't have to go to the loo," Honor snapped.

"I thought maybe she needed to use the loo," Fenella repeated, bugging her eyes out at Honor as if Honor hadn't already caught on that Fenella was quickly losing endurance for the wait for Vivianna to show.

"She doesn't need to use the loo," Honor repeated right back, also bugging out her eyes and if she could use the throat-slit gesture to shut her sister up without Vivianna seeing, she would.

Not that clever, ghosty she-bitch Vivianna hadn't already cottoned on to their game.

Abby took in a breath.

She had an idea, it was a scary idea, but Fenella was right, something had to give.

So she shared, "I thought maybe you girls could give me a tour of the castle."

"I'd *love* that!" Fenella shrieked.

"*Great* idea," Honor cried, jumping up from her chair.

Fenella got up as well and clapped her hands together, appearing like she was genuinely looking forward to this. "There's so much to see. Where to start?"

Honor leaned into Abby and confided, "She loves this old heap."

"It isn't an old heap. It's beautiful," Fenella shot back then squealed, "The armoury! Let's start in the armoury!"

Considering the circumstances, Abby would have picked a room that didn't hold ancient weapons, but she followed Fenella anyway.

And Fenella was right. It wasn't an old heap.

It was beautiful.

And it was perfect—absolutely perfect—for Cash.

If she could build something that represented his strength, his energy, his beauty, it would have been Penmort.

The armoury was filled with ancient weapons, and even more ancient flying pendants, which dripped in veritable rags from their poles, they were so old and *way* cool. There was a billiards room with an enormous billiards table. There were the inner and outer halls with their colossal fireplaces that led to the huge dining room with a gleaming table that sat twenty. There was the grand stair hall with intricately carved balustrades and a grand piano at the foot. There was also a study with an ornate carved desk that was so huge two people could sleep on it without touching.

On the second floor were bedrooms, many of them having their own sitting rooms, dressing rooms and bathrooms. The second floor also held the morning room, and the leather gallery filled with portraits of Beaumarises past. Lastly, the second floor also held a beautiful, cosy sewing room which was situated in a turret.

Fenella told Abby the third floor held the now unused servants quarters, nursery and school room. She explained as well that the rooms below the ground floor were also mostly no longer utilised but had been, in olden times, for the running of the house, including the kitchens, housekeeper's and butler's offices and quarters, a coal room, laundry rooms, things like that.

Fenella said on the first floor they'd missed the conservatory and library. As these were Fenella's favourite places, they were to be their final destination.

They had made it to the long, handsome, wood-panelled gallery, filled with portraits of ancestors (and, Abby noted with some surprise and a vague sense of alarm, that all the women were blonde and all the men looked quite a bit like Cash).

Except, of course, Alistair's portrait, which was the largest of any and the most pompous.

Something about it, its size and the prominence of place, turned Abby's stomach.

"I know," Honor whispered beside her, obviously reading her thoughts. "Makes you sick, doesn't it?"

Abby didn't speak, but she nodded.

Honor turned dancing eyes to Abby. "I wonder what Cash will do with *that* when he moves in?" she asked, motioning to the portrait with her head.

"I hope he burns it," Abby murmured, and Honor took her arm in both hands, leaned into her and gave her arm a squeeze.

Then she muttered, "I'll bring the marshmallows," and Abby couldn't help it. It was such a divinely evil comment, she laughed.

"This is my favourite," Fenella called, and Honor and Abby moved toward Fenella who was standing off the main gallery in a big bay window where there were two, smaller portraits.

Abby walked up to Fenella's side and saw she was gazing at a man who looked shockingly just like Cash.

It wasn't an old portrait. By his clothes you could see that it was recent, not from this decade or the last, but not hundreds of years ago either. And it wasn't like any of the other formal poses of the other pictures.

This man was a man on the move, a man with energy, a man with a healthy appetite for life. So healthy, he seized it by its throat and consumed it.

How the artist captured it, Abby had no idea. He was striding across a field, Penmort resting grandly atop its tor in the distance. He had two dogs at his heels, beautiful German Shepherds. He was in outdoor clothing, tweed blazer with patches at the arms, boots over his trousers, mud up the heels and ankles. He had broad shoulders, an athletic build and you could tell he had a wide, strong gait, made easy for him by having long legs. He held a shotgun, cocked open and lying over his forearm, the gun butt tucked into his side.

The picture was in profile, but the man was looking over his shoulder as if someone had called him, or perhaps he was calling his dogs. Therefore, the artist had been able to capture him full face.

And he was heart-stoppingly handsome.

On closer inspection, he didn't look just like Cash. There were subtle differences. His forehead was broader, for one. He wore his hair shorter, for another. The planes and angles of his face were harder and sharper, but no less attractive.

But the similarity was uncanny.

"Who is that?" Abby asked.

"Anthony Beaumaris," Fenella answered, and Abby's body jerked at the realisation she was gazing upon Cash's father.

"My God," she breathed, and she felt her chest constrict at the knowledge that this man, this compelling, dynamic, striking man had had his life cut short.

Something made her lift her hand as if to touch the portrait, as if touching it would mean she'd touch him. But when her finger was just centimetres away, the scream began.

And it was just as Honor described it. It was low, it was eerie, and it was *sinister*.

Abby's blood ran cold.

Her hand dropped.

She turned wide eyes to Fenella and breathed, "What is that?" even though she knew what it was.

Exactly what it was.

"Go," Fenella whispered in a barely there voice.

Abby blinked at her. "Pardon?"

But Fenella was looking over Abby's shoulder, her face pale, her eyes frightened, and she shrieked, *"Go now!"*

Abby whirled then froze when she saw Vivianna in the gallery, floating, the tattered edges of her dress whipping around her viciously as if they were in a frenzy, as if they could do harm. Her mouth was opened, emitting a scream that filled the very air.

Her face was bloodthirsty.

Her eyes were on Abby.

"Go!" Fenella screamed, and Abby went.

She hadn't been stupid. This time she wore jeans and flats with rubber soles, good for gripping and easy to run in.

And Abby ran. She ran for dear life.

She skirted Vivianna and made it out the door, to the hall and was flying down the stairs, her breath coming in terrified pants, when Vivianna formed in front of her.

Right in front of her.

Abby, to her shock, ran into her like she was a solid, physical thing.

And to her further stunned surprise, a burst of purple sparks shot out between them, coming from the place where the amulet rested against Abby's chest.

Both Abby and Vivianna flew backward. Abby, landing painfully on her hands, Vivianna, arms wheeling and out of control, descended away from Abby, going nearly all the way down the flight of stairs.

Vivianna halted her descent. She bent her head and looked at what appeared to be a burn mark on her dress where Abby's amulet had hit her.

Her head shot up and her eyes narrowed on Abby. She opened her mouth and let out another blood-chilling scream.

Then she shot forward, straight toward Abby. But Abby scrambled back up the steps, crawling on all fours like a crab.

Even though Abby moved, and fast, Vivianna was nearly on top of her when the spirit was jerked back at the waist, her scream abruptly halting.

"That's it, she-bitch! The McPherson has come to play!" Angus bellowed from a dozen steps away. His hand held a strange whip, the end of it was curled around Vivianna's waist. He was reeling her in and Vivianna was struggling against the bounds.

"Go lassie, I got her," Angus called.

"Abby! This way!" Fenella shouted from the top of the stairs, and Abby turned, crawling up the stairs on all fours again, stumbling in a terrified frenzy, sometimes using her knees and sometimes her feet.

She got to the top of the stairs and they heard a grunt. Honor was there too, and Abby, Fenella and Honor looked over the balustrade and down the stairs to see Angus falling, his kilt awhirl, Vivianna drifting after him.

"Angus!" Abby screamed, not thinking and running toward the fallen Scotsman.

When she turned on the landing, she saw Angus was at the bottom, on his side, his head came up and he boomed, "No, lassie! Go the other way!"

But Abby kept moving toward him and Vivianna came at her again. They collided, the purple sparks flew and Vivianna reeled back. Apparently aided by the velocity Abby was going, this time Vivianna went far further, sailing down the stairs, past Angus, into and through the inner hall, right *through* a wall.

Abby, however, had been ready for it and when they collided, she shoved her foot into the stairwell to keep herself steady and threw herself forward. She descended the rest of the stairs and crouched by Angus.

"Are you hurt?" she asked as she heard Fenella and Honor come rumbling down the stairs behind her.

"Get her outta here!" Angus roared.

"Are you hurt?" Abby shouted.

"Let's go. Go, go, go, go, *go!*" Honor yelled, pulling Abby up.

But Vivianna had melted back through the wall and was nearly upon them.

Abby's hand went to the leather around her neck. She yanked the necklace over her head, threw it to the ground and stomped on it with her heel.

A purple mist immediately blew up, enveloping them. Abby bent low, her hands grasping Angus under his arm. She tugged up with superhuman effort, got him to his feet and the four of them ran awkwardly through the inner hall, into the outer hall, out the entrance lobby and into the night. The whole time they ran, the purple mist followed them.

And they kept running, Abby dragging Angus, until they'd gone out the gate at the side of the castle, down the steep hill, through the castle's outer wall, down a winding path into town and past several storefronts. Once they hit town, the mist evaporated.

There, Angus pulled Abby to a halt and stopped, bent over, hand to his side, and wheezed.

"Are you okay?" Abby asked, crouching low and looking up at him.

"Lassie," he rasped, took in a deep breath then panted, "When I say go..." He took in another breath and gasped, "You better bloody well *go!*"

They heard running steps and Cassandra approached, stopping on a skid.

Abby stood up and Cassandra's eyes fell on her, dropping immediately to her sweater.

"What happened?" she asked.

"She attacked," Fenella told Cassandra.

Cassandra looked at Angus. "Did you get her?"

"No I didn't *get* her," Angus snapped, straightening. "The she-bitch bested me," he looked mortified for a moment then bellowed, "She bested A McPherson!"

"Be quiet," Honor hissed. "We're in town."

Abby turned to Cassandra and announced, slowly, clearly and loudly, "Your...amulet...*rocked*!"

Cassandra leaned back, put her hands on her hips and smiled. "Did the trick, eh?"

"It *rocked*!" Abby repeated, incapable of further speech.

"I'm good with a charm," Cassandra informed her.

"Well, you better make sure we all have some," Angus announced. "Vivianna knows she's met her match. She might have been surprised Abby had magic tonight, but she'll no' make that mistake again."

Abby looked at Fenella and Honor, her shoulders drooping, and she muttered, "Great."

"Don't worry. I have some other tricks up my sleeve," Cassandra said so confidently, Abby actually believed her.

To her surprise, Angus grinned at Abby, "Lucky for you, lass, now *I* know what *I'm* up against. And The McPherson's got more tricks than a spirit-bitch-from-hell, believe you me."

Fenella got close and put her arm around Abby's waist. "Well, that sounds good. Doesn't it?" she asked.

Abby, who would vastly prefer not to be battling a ghost—and that night she'd learned *exactly* what that meant and it petrified her—had to admit Fenella was right.

❧ ❧ ❧

It didn't occur to Abby, until she quietly closed and locked Cash's front door, that she'd forgotten to phone him when she left the castle.

This wasn't surprising, considering she was *freaked out* when she'd left the castle. And this freak out meant she had to concentrate on her driving, and therefore she hadn't thought to call Cash. Instead, her thoughts had centred on getting home in one piece.

It wouldn't do to survive Vivianna only to die in a tragic car accident.

Although it was late, the castle more than an hour's drive away, she wasn't surprised to see no light shining from upstairs, but a light coming from the back hall.

This indicated Cash was downstairs, likely working, maybe drinking a whisky, maybe getting concerned (or more likely angry) waiting for her call.

She took off her coat and soundlessly hooked it on the banister with her purse and she headed downstairs.

Her shoes were quiet, the rubber soles making no noise.

This was how she could get through the house and down the stairs without Cash hearing.

Or, more to the point, this was how she could get through the house and down the stairs without Cash *and* Suzanne hearing.

For Suzanne was there.

Abby knew this because, four steps from the bottom, she turned her head and she saw them in the kitchen.

She saw them in the kitchen embracing.

More than embracing.

One of Suzanne's arms was locked around Cash's neck, her other hand in his hair, her body was pressed to his. His hands were gripping her waist just above her hips. Her lips were on his, his were on hers, and both of their mouths were open.

Abby felt her heart clench as her stomach lurched and neither of these felt good.

In any way.

So, unfortunately, when she spoke, her voice held a fierce tremor that betrayed her emotion when she asked what was supposed to come out coolly, "Am I interrupting something?"

ABBY TELLS CASH

At the sound of her voice, Cash threw Suzanne away from him and Abby watched as she flew several steps back.

Her hands going behind her, she collided with the counter.

Her eyes went to Abby and her expression could only be described as smug.

Then Abby heard Cash ask bitingly, "Where the fuck have you been?"

Abby's gaze shot to Cash and he was standing, turned to her, hands on hips, staring at Abby, looking angry.

Angry.

At Abby!

Cash was *angry* at *Abby*.

Abby's mouth dropped open.

Her eyes slid back to Suzanne whose smugness had hit the stratosphere.

Mindlessly, Abby turned and ran up the steps taking them two at a time.

She got to the upstairs banister and had her purse in her hands before strong fingers closed around her upper arm in a vicelike grip and she was yanked backwards.

Her eyes flew to Cash's.

"Let me go!" she shouted, tugging at her arm in his grasp.

"What the fuck are you doing?" he asked, eyes narrowed on her purse, fingers not letting her go.

She stopped struggling and yelled, "I'm leaving!"

"The hell you are," he snapped, wrenched her purse out of her hands and threw it into the lounge.

Abby watched it sail then land on the floor.

She looked back at Cash and screamed, "Would you stop throwing my stuff!"

He ignored her demand and used her arm to pull her close. "You should have been home an hour ago. Or, it would seem, you should have fucking *phoned* an hour ago to say you'd be home now."

Abby saw Suzanne join them at the top of the stairs. She was pulling on her coat, flipping her hair over the collar and looking happy as a clam.

Abby's eyes moved back to Cash and she drawled with saccharine sweetness, "I'm *so* sorry I didn't give you plenty of heads up to get rid of your kissin' cousin before I got home."

She watched Cash's head jerk, his brows shot together and then his lip curled in disgust.

"You think I'm fucking around on you?" he asked, deep voice filled with incredulity. "With *Suzanne*?" and he uttered her name like it tasted foul.

Abby looked back at Suzanne and she'd lost her smug, happy look.

Abby's eyes clashed with Cash's again when she accused, "I just saw you kissing her."

"No, you just saw *her* kissing *me*," Cash shot back instantly.

"I'll leave you to it," Suzanne cut in, moving toward the door, and Cash turned, taking Abby with him, his hand still on her arm.

"I'll deal with you later," Cash clipped to Suzanne.

"I'll look forward to that," came Suzanne's sultry purr.

Cash's body went solid and the air in the room, already thick, became suffocating.

"Don't mistake me, Suzanne." Cash's voice was a low, menacing warning, and Abby watched as Suzanne paled.

Recovering swiftly, she offered, "I'll let myself out."

"You do that," Cash stated then, dismissing Suzanne completely, he turned back to Abby and started, "As for you—"

At that, with a vicious tug, Abby yanked her arm free and vaguely heard the door close behind Suzanne. She was too deep in a tizzy at all she'd experienced that night at the castle, and what she'd just seen, to proceed with caution.

She stomped around Cash and into the lounge, muttering angrily, "I cannot *believe* after all I went through tonight..." She bent down to pick up her purse and looked up at Cash who had followed her. "For *you*," she snapped, rising. "Only to come home to see you groping Suzanne."

"Abby, I'll repeat, I was *not* groping Suzanne," Cash returned.

"Whatever!" Abby shouted, beside herself, experiencing a layering of freak outs that she couldn't quite overcome. "How would you feel if you came home and saw me in the arms of another man?"

Cash's eyes narrowed and his hands went to his hips. "I wouldn't fucking like it, but I would also give you the chance to fucking explain."

"Right," Abby snorted with disbelief. "You'd *freak*."

And he *would*.

"I would. Then I'd give you the chance to fucking explain," he fired back.

Abby shook her head and walked to him with the intent to walk right by him and get her coat. "I'm not talking about this. I'm going home."

Cash's fingers curled around her upper arm firmly, effectively halting her, and when she looked up at him, he stated, "You *are* home."

"*My* home," she snapped back.

"Yes, darling," he returned calmly. "*Your* home." Then he jerked her purse out of her hand again and threw it on a chair, making his point.

She looked at her purse and something came over her, something she couldn't control.

She had an excuse, of course.

Her whole life, within weeks, had been turned on its head. And that included living with an impossibly rich, incredibly handsome, very famous International Hot Guy.

And that also included going head to head with a *ghost*.

So, Abby thought, it was really only a matter of time before she lost her mind completely.

Which was exactly what she did.

In slow motion, her eyes moved from their perusal of her bag to Cash.

Then she shrieked, "*Stop throwing my stuff!*"

Cash pulled her close and his arm started to slide around her as he said, "Abby, you need to calm down."

"Calm?" she asked. "*Calm!*" she screeched. "*You* be calm!" She yanked out of his arms and took two steps back. He came for her but she lifted her hand, pointed a finger at him and he stopped. "You be calm in the face of what I've seen, *and* done, and then *seen* tonight. A ghost, Cash. I came face to face with a fucking *ghost!*"

Distractedly she noticed his whole body jerked as if he'd been punched in the stomach, but she just kept right on ranting.

"And let me tell you ghosts are *scary!*" she shouted and started pacing. "They scream and you...would not...*believe* how *awful* it sounds. They melt through walls. They melt *back* through walls. They *float*. And they *attack!*"

She stopped ranting and glared at him.

Quietly, looking like he was fighting the urge to check her temperature, he said, "Abby, there are no such things as ghosts."

"I would have said the same thing a few weeks ago, but believe me, there *are* ghosts. They're *mean* and they're *nasty* and this one particularly," Abby returned as if she had any authority on ghosts (although she felt, at that moment, she *did*).

"Maybe I should get you a drink," he suggested.

"I don't want a drink," she retorted.

"Then maybe I should call Tim," he replied softly.

"You are *not* going to call *Tim!*" Abby shouted.

He took a step toward her, saying, "Abby, you have to calm down."

"Have you heard of Vivianna Wainwright?" Abby asked suddenly, and Cash halted and watched her a moment.

"I see. Fenella has been—" he murmured.

Abby cut him off. "No, Cash. Fenella has been nothing."

"Darling—" he started again and Abby interrupted again.

"I didn't slip in the bathroom," she announced and watched as his body went still. "Your hand doesn't slam through a mirror when you slip. It slams through a mirror when you're *shoved*."

Cash stared at her a moment before saying softly, "Darling, you've been going through a lot lately."

"Yes," Abby agreed on a toss of her hair. "I have, including becoming the target of a ghost."

"Abby—"

"Cash, listen to me!" she yelled. "I'm not crazy. I know what I saw. I know what I *felt*. I was standing at the sink, looking in the mirror and there she was behind me. She came at me, shoved me between the shoulders and I slammed forward. My hand going up to shield my fall, it went through the mirror. Only then did I slip and hit my head on the basin. And tonight, it was *worse*."

His gaze was locked on hers, his jaw clamped and she saw a muscle working in his cheek.

Then his eyes moved over her face and down to her sweater where they stopped and narrowed.

"What happened to your jumper?" he asked, and Abby looked down to see there was a burn mark on her sweater, just like the one on Vivianna's dress, where Cassandra's amulet had sparked.

She hadn't noticed it until now.

"Cassandra's protection amulet," Abby explained. "It kind of... exploded when Vivianna and I clashed."

Cash's eyes jerked to hers and he repeated, "Cassandra's protection amulet."

"Yes."

She watched as something dawned on him and his mouth tightened as his eyes went to the ceiling.

Finally he muttered, "I don't fucking believe this shit."

"Believe it," Abby returned.

He looked at her again. "Abby, no matter what these people are telling you, I promise you, there are no such things as ghosts."

"There are," Abby retorted.

"No, there aren't."

"You felt it yourself," she told him.

"I felt what?" he asked.

"The minute we walked into the castle, the entry swayed. You were there. You said you felt it!"

"That wasn't a ghost," he said.

"Then what was it?" Abby queried.

His face now held a hint of soft concern. "I don't know, darling, but it wasn't a fucking ghost."

Abby stared at him, had an idea and asked, "Did you pick up the diaries?"

At her swift change of subject, Cash's head cocked to the side. "Diaries?"

"Your grandmother's diaries," Abby prompted.

He watched her a moment and said, "Emma went to get them today."

Immediately Abby inquired, "Do you have them here at the house?"

"They're in the study," he answered, and Abby was on the move.

Walking around him, she went to his study, flipped on the light and saw his briefcase open on his desk. A stack of several, slim, elegant, leather-bound books sat beside it.

Abby walked up to the desk, grabbed the first one off the stack and started sifting through it, randomly picking pages and skimming. She found nothing so she threw that diary down and picked up the next, doing the same.

"Abby, what the fuck?" Cash muttered, but then Abby saw it.

She immediately started reading.

"My favourite brooch is missing. The one Richard gave me. I can't find it anywhere and Richard is asking where it is. I know she took it. She knows how much I love it. It's just the kind of thing she'd do. Especially since Richard is getting annoyed that I haven't been wearing it. I was searching for it on my hands and knees beside the bed when I heard Vivianna laugh."

Abby looked at Cash and saw his eyes were on the diary and his jaw was again clenched, but he didn't say anything so Abby persevered.

Using her thumb against the edges, Abby flipped pages ahead skimming quickly. She found another passage and started reading.

"I'm frightened. She's watching all the time. Everywhere I turn, if

I'm alone, she's there. Hovering. And anytime Richard is out of the house, she screams. And screams and screams and screams. We've lost three servants this week alone. They can't bear it. I don't know how long I can bear it either. I keep telling Richard about Vivianna but he just won't listen. He thinks I'm being silly. He finds me amusing. He tells me it's a legend, a myth, that I shouldn't believe the servants' gossip and let them make me anxious. I can't get him to understand that she's real. It's getting worse, it feels different now. I think she means to harm me."

Abby's eyes went to Cash's face again and Cash remarked, "My grandmother Lorna died of a stroke when I was seven years old. She wasn't murdered by a ghost."

"She stopped being a target," Abby told him.

"And why is that?" Cash asked.

Abby stared at him, not wanting to get into the "love of their lives" business, not again and definitely not with Cash.

Therefore, she said, "She just did."

Cash looked into her eyes and stated quietly, "Darling, do you have any idea how preposterous this sounds? Vivianna Wainwright is a ghost story handed down generation to generation. She isn't real."

Abby stared at him all of a sudden wondering why she'd told him. Of course he wouldn't believe her. If she was him, she wouldn't believe her either. It *did* sound preposterous, even though it was true.

Abby closed the diary and set it on his desk. She looked to the side to avoid his eyes and lifted her hand to pull her hair off her face. Bunching it at the back of her head for a moment, she decided to give up and maybe lie and say she got a little crazy when she was on her period. Men bought that kind of excuse all the time.

She sighed, looked back at him, dropped her hand and he watched it fall as she said, "You're right, I—"

But Cash interrupted her. "What's happened to your hand?"

Abby's chin dipped. She lifted her hands, palms up, and studied them. They were dirty, smudged with black and there were angry red scrapes along the heels of her palms. She hadn't noticed it before, considering her Layering of Freak Outs, but she knew how it happened.

She'd fallen hard on the stairs, landed on her hands, then she'd used them to crawl back up.

Her head lifted.

"Cash—" she began, but his eyes were doing a sweep of her body and landed on her legs.

He went on. "And your knees."

Abby looked down at her legs and saw her jeans from knees to ankles were covered in dust, likely gathered from scrambling up the stairs.

She tilted her head to look at him and went back to deciding to tell him the truth.

Therefore, she whispered, "I was running away from her. She formed in front of me and we collided on the stairs. I fell back on my hands. Then she attacked and I was scrambling on my hands and feet back up the stairs—"

"Stop," he demanded and Abby stopped.

He kept staring at her legs then his eyes moved to her sweater and he took a step forward, getting close. His hand came up and he touched the dark purple-black burn mark on her sweater.

His hand dropped, but his fingers wrapped around her wrists, and he lifted her hands, palms up, between them. He looked down at them and his thumbs slid gently along the angry red marks and smudges.

"Fucking hell, it's true," he muttered, and relief shot through her that he believed her.

"Yes," she replied softly.

His fingers closed around her hands, pressing them together and he pulled them against his chest, also pulling Abby closer.

His eyes locked on hers and he ordered, "Tell me everything."

Abby drew a breath in through her nose and bit the side of her lip.

Then she told him everything.

Vivianna and the bathroom. Telling Jenny and Mrs. Truman. Fenella, Cassandra and the séance. Angus, the kilt-wearing Scottish ghost hunter. Details about Vivianna's spell, her abilities and her targeting Abby. Abby going to Penmort to be bait. Vivianna forming in the gallery, then attacking. The amulet that *rocked*. The mad dash to town surrounded by the protective purple mist.

Everything.

Everything except the true love part, that was.

When she was finished, she realised Cash got stuck on an earlier point when he said in a dangerous voice with equally dangerous eyes, "You went to Penmort to be bait?"

"I had to draw her out," Abby explained.

"You had to draw her out," Cash repeated, but he was looking like he was only just stopping himself from shaking some sense into her.

"Yes," Abby said.

"Why?" he asked.

"Pardon?" Abby asked in return.

"Why did you have to draw her out?" Cash inquired.

Abby looked at him, confused. "So Angus could take her down, of course."

"What does this have to do with you?" he pressed.

Abby was even more confused.

"It doesn't have to do with me. It has to do with you."

She watched Cash's face change, but she misinterpreted it as puzzlement and carried on.

"At first, Jenny and Mrs. Truman and I started this whole thing because I knew I'd have to go to the castle during the anniversary celebration. I couldn't *not* go. I mean, obviously, for whatever reason, you wanted me there so I had to go. Since I didn't want to, you know, *die* while I was there, I had to do something."

Cash kept staring at her with that strange look on his face so Abby persevered.

"Then I got to know Fenella and she's really nice. She's a bit strange, but she's nice. And she's lived with Vivianna her whole life, and Vivianna scares her. So then I was kind of doing it for Fenella as well. Then I got to know Honor so I'm doing it for her too. And now I know Penmort's yours so...well, as you can see, *something* has to be done. And I'm kind of the only person who can do it. With Angus and Cassandra, of course."

Cash kept staring at her with his hands holding hers against his chest, the heat of his body close.

Abby thought maybe he wasn't taking it all in. It was, she knew, a lot to wrap your head around.

She continued, "Anyway, it's all good. Angus got a good look at her tonight so he knows what he's up against, and Cassandra says she's got more stuff she can throw at her. So next time, it'll go better."

Cash's hands tightened on hers before he asked, "Next time?"

"Yes," Abby said. "Probably tomorrow night."

Cash moved forward very slightly but enough to bring him closer to Abby.

"Abby, there isn't going to be a next time. You aren't going back there."

Abby blinked and reminded him, "Yes I am. We're spending the weekend there."

"No. *We're* not. Our weekend plans have changed. I'm going to the party Saturday night only. You're staying home."

Abby felt her eyes grow wide and she said, "But we have to go. Nicola is expecting us and something has to be done about Vivianna."

"We're not going," Cash replied firmly.

"We *have* to go," Abby returned.

One of Cash's hands released hers, the other curled around her palm and he turned, pulling her from the room saying, "We're not discussing this."

He flicked off the light switch and kept walking to the stairs and down to the garden level while Abby babbled, "You can't be serious. We have to discuss it. You don't understand. Angus and Cassandra know what they're doing. I'm not kidding. They *seriously* know what they're doing. You should have seen them. Things didn't go great tonight but no one got hurt."

Cash let her go at the bottom of the stairs and walked to the light switch, flipping off the dimmer lights that illuminated the kitchen area.

Then his eyes came to Abby. "We're not discussing it. You aren't going."

Abby watched as he walked back across the room to the light by the couch that was lit. She saw his laptop open and some papers spread on the coffee table, a tumbler with a finger of whisky still in it sat next to his work.

Abby's voice gentled when she went on, "Cash, I'll be safe, honestly. They won't let anything happen to me."

He'd bent to the lamp but straightened and his eyes pinned her to the spot.

"You aren't going," he stated.

"Do you intend to live there?" Abby asked softly and watched Cash's entire body freeze.

Then he started, "Abby—"

"Do you?" she pushed.

He didn't answer, but she watched his jaw get tight.

"Do you want me with you?" she whispered, heart in her throat, stomach clenched, and she stopped breathing.

Their eyes held for a moment and Abby began to feel lightheaded with lack of oxygen.

Finally he bit off tersely, "Yes."

Abby went on softly, "Honey, I'm not safe there unless something is done. And, for whatever reason, I'm the only one who can force her out. It has to be me who does it and we both know it has to be done."

His eyes were so hot on her she could actually feel them scorching into her. His jaw was tight and they stared at each other for long moments.

Then he bent at the waist and she thought he was going to turn off the lamp, but his fingers curled around the phone, yanking it out of the charger.

He walked to her and held out the phone.

"Call them, all of them," he demanded. "Every person who's involved in this fiasco. I want them at my office tomorrow at noon."

"What?" Abby asked. "Why?"

"Do it," Cash returned.

Abby's eyes slid to the digital clock on the microwave then back to Cash. "It's nearly midnight."

His hand came out. Fingers wrapping around her wrist, he lifted it and put the phone in her palm.

"Call them. Now."

"I don't know their numbers," Abby said, watched his brows draw together and hurried on. "I mean, I haven't memorised them. They're in my mobile, in my purse, upstairs."

He lifted his hand and curled it around her neck. "I'll get your purse."

He gave her a squeeze, walked up the stairs and got her purse. He came back, scrawled his office address, phone number and directions on a piece of paper and gave it to her.

Then he stood next to Abby while she called everyone, including a seriously cranky, woken-up Mrs. Truman.

When she was done, he took the phone from her, put it back in its charger, turned off the lamp, grabbed her hand and guided her upstairs.

When they were in his bedroom, Cash turned on the lamp at her side of the bed. Zee, curled sleeping at the foot of the bed, lifted his head and blinked in annoyance. Then Cash's hands went to the buttons of his shirt.

Abby stood there watching him and asked, "Can we talk about Suzanne now?"

Cash pulled the shirt off his shoulders and tossed it on the armchair while saying, "No. She's already had more of my time tonight than she deserves."

"I'd kind of like an explanation," Abby requested quietly.

His eyes went to Abby's as he sat on the armchair and yanked off his shoes, and to her surprise, without any further coaxing, Cash explained.

"She showed up about fifteen minutes before you. She said she was in Bath having dinner with friends. They'd taken off but her car wasn't starting. Her mobile had lost its charge and she needed to call AA. I didn't believe her but I couldn't leave her out in the cold either. I let her come in. She made her call and she spent ten minutes being supremely annoying. Then she came on strong, as she always does. We heard you come in. She knew it had to be you, I was distracted by your arrival, she moved in for the kill and she kissed me. That's it."

Abby couldn't believe her ears.

Who behaved like that?

"What's the matter with her?" Abby whispered.

"She's a bitch," Cash replied dismissively, standing again, his hands going to the waistband of his trousers.

"I don't know anyone who acts like that," Abby muttered, her head tilted down to watch her feet as she flipped off her shoes.

"Darling, come here." She heard Cash call.

Her head came up. She saw his face had grown warm and immediately she walked to him.

His arms circled her when she got close.

"Are you okay?" he asked.

"About Suzanne?" she queried in return.

"I don't give a fuck about Suzanne. What I don't like is you scrambling around on a staircase pursued by a ghost," he told her.

Abby wrinkled her nose and admitted, "It wasn't fun."

His eyes had moved to her nose then his lips went there and he kissed her.

Abby held her breath at this tender action, but before she could process its sweetness, his head came up and he murmured, "Let's get you to bed."

With that, his hands were on the hem of her sweater. He pulled it up, her arms lifted, he yanked it off and threw it to the side.

Shortly after, they went to bed.

❧ 23 ❧

STRATEGIC PLANNING

Abby woke when Cash's body moved into hers. She drowsily noted she was in a strange position, curled into a ball against Cash, the top of her head pressed into his side. His arm was extended and curved around her spine.

He moved her, sliding her up the bed. Her body uncurled to accommodate his and he rolled mostly on top of her.

His face went into her neck and he murmured in a sleepy burr, "Are you awake?"

"Yes," she whispered.

His mouth moved from behind her ear to her jaw and he asked, "Are you still on your period?"

Abby answered, "Probably," and she heard the disappointment in her voice.

His lips hit hers and brushed there softly before he said, "Go back to sleep."

He started to move away but her arms went around him, stopping his retreat.

Her mind was groggily registering that they didn't have all the time in the world, so there was no time to waste.

She pressed up and pushed off on a foot, rolling him to his back, positioning herself on top of him, her mouth going to his neck and she tasted him there.

She felt his hands at her bottom and he said, "Abby."

"Quiet," she whispered.

His hands trailed up her back as her lips moved on his neck.

"You don't have to do this, darling," he told her, his voice low and rough.

Her head came up and she looked at him in the dark.

On a soft smile, she replied, "I know."

Then she bent her head and used her hands and mouth on him, *everywhere* on him, wherever she wanted, however she liked, and she took her time.

And he let her.

And he enjoyed it.

A lot.

After she was finished with him, he kissed her with residual passion mixed with sweet gratitude and left the bed.

Abby curled around his pillow and her last thought before falling back to sleep was, *That was brilliant.*

❧ ❧ ❧

"Do you want to tell me what's bothering you?" Kieran Kane was standing in his kitchen with his wife who was wiping down the counters like she was preparing to perform surgery on them.

Jenny glanced at him. "Nothing's the matter."

He grinned. "Right."

She stopped wiping, straightened to look at him and repeated, "Nothing's the matter."

Kieran ignored this out-and-out lie and asked, "Is it Abby?"

She put a hand to her hip. "And why would you think it was Abby?"

"Partly because you got a phone call at midnight from her communicating Lord Fraser's demands that you appear in his offices today. And partly because it's always Abby."

Jenny threw the sponge in the sink and snapped, "It's not always Abby."

At her answer, Kieran felt the usual gut clench when the topic came up, and he asked gently, "Is it our appointment at the fertility clinic on Monday?"

He watched her face pale, but she said, "No."

He put his coffee cup down and got close, sliding his hands around her waist. His face chased hers as her eyes moved anywhere but to him until she finally gave in on a sigh and looked at him.

"Whatever happens, happens, pumpkin," Kieran murmured. "I'm happy to adopt and I'm happy for it just to be the two of us for the rest of our lives. You know that."

Jenny sighed again. "I know it."

He touched his forehead to hers. "Don't let it worry you."

Her eyes slid away and she whispered, "You always talked about wanting a son to go out and—"

His mouth hit hers effectively silencing her, a trick he'd learned years ago and one he utilised more than occasionally.

When he lifted his head, he said, "I want you. All the rest is just icing. You know that too."

Jenny's lips tipped up at the ends and she replied quietly, "I know it."

"Stop worrying," Kieran demanded.

"Okay," Jenny lied.

Kieran grinned then muttered, "Liar."

Before the glittering spark in her eye could be translated verbally, he kissed her, far deeper this time.

Then he went to work.

❧ ❧ ❧

Kieran was barely out the door when Jenny's mobile rang.

She was glad of it. Anything to keep her mind off the appointment Monday, even if it had to do with Abby, her new boyfriend (who Jenny didn't know whether to love or hate) and the ghost that wanted Abby dead.

Regardless of what Kieran said, Jenny wanted a baby and she wanted to give him a son. She wouldn't plunge into a suicidal depression if she couldn't, but she would still be devastated. They'd been trying to get pregnant for ages (and working hard at it), so she didn't think the news would be good.

She was not looking forward to Monday in any way.

So she resolutely set these thoughts aside and grabbed her mobile.

The display said CASSANDRA CALLING.

Jenny took the call and put the phone to her ear.

"Hey, girl," she said by way of greeting, as usual hiding her dark thoughts of moments before.

"Hey, mate," Cassandra replied. "Listen, can you talk?"

Jenny thought Cassandra had called for a gossip session and asked, "Is this about our summons to Cash's offices today?"

"No," Cassandra answered. "Though, gotta admit I was surprised. And pleased. It'll help, him being in the know." She hesitated and went on with a smile in her voice, "And I wouldn't mind seeing where he works, see if it's like in the movie."

"I'm noticing not a lot about Cash is like that movie," Jenny replied and heard Cassandra chuckle.

"Yeah, that actor, whatever his name is, was fit, but I don't think I've ever met anyone who can suck the entire life force out of the room like Cash can. He's a powerhouse. I can see why they wanted to make a movie about him. But there's no *way* you could capture something like that on film," Cassandra noted.

Jenny didn't want to talk about what a powerhouse Cash was because she thought it sucked that practically everything about him seemed wonderful, but he was, if their secret conversation was anything to go by, *not*.

Jenny changed the subject. "Why'd you call?"

Cassandra took a moment before answering, "Are you sitting down?"

Jenny felt her heart lurch and lied, "Yes."

"Okay, mate, take a breath," Cassandra advised, and Jenny did as she was told then heard Cassandra say, "My friends in Virginia, they made contact."

Jenny knew what she was saying. In desperation, she, Mrs. Truman and Cassandra had come up with the idea days ago.

Jenny stumbled to a chair at the kitchen table and sat.

"Ben?" she whispered.

"Yes," Cassandra answered.

Jenny closed her eyes and felt tears prickling the backs of them at the very thought of what this might mean when she asked, "He didn't go to, um...the other plane?"

"He did. They used the entire coven to pull him out," Cassandra told her.

Jenny's eyes opened but only to blink in shocked surprise. "You can do that?"

"In life and death circumstances and if the coven is powerful, yes."

"My God," Jenny breathed.

Cassandra carried on, "They're un-tethering him. He'll be at the castle Saturday night."

"My God," Jenny repeated.

"Are you okay?" Cassandra asked.

"No," Jenny told her in all honesty. "You're telling me the ghost of my good friend is going to fight the ghost who wants to kill my best friend. A ghost who happens to be under the mistaken impression that Cash Fraser is in love with my good friend ghost's wife." Jenny wasn't making much sense but didn't care.

Ben was going to be at the castle.

With Abby.

And Cash!

"Widow," Cassandra said softly, taking Jenny out of her thoughts.

"What?" Jenny asked.

"Widow. Abby's his widow, no longer his wife," Cassandra replied.

"She'll always be Ben's wife," Jenny retorted.

"She stopped being his wife a long time ago, Jenny," Cassandra returned gently.

Jenny shook her head sharply, not about to fight this point, not wanting even to *think* about this point, so she said, "Whatever. Ben has got to know, your coven friends have got to tell him that Abby can't see him. She'll freak."

"He'll do what he has to do," Cassandra said.

"Cassandra, you don't know how it is. Abby can't see him. She'll *freak*," Jenny repeated.

"He'll do what he has to do or she'll *die*," Cassandra noted firmly.

Jenny hated to admit it, but she had a point.

Jenny thought it was time to move on to the next subject. "Are we carpooling to Cash's offices?"

"I'll drive," Cassandra offered.

"All right then, see you soon," Jenny said, and they rang off.

Jenny put her phone on the table.

"Well, one thing's certain," she told her mobile. "I'm not worried about the fertility clinic anymore."

Jenny's phone had no response.

❧ ❧ ❧

Abby walked into Cash's offices and saw him immediately.

He was behind a glass wall in a conference room with at least a dozen other people. He was sitting at the head of the table wearing one of his impeccably tailored suits, this one black with a shirt of deep grey and a fantastic black tie with a grey and red pattern on it. He had a heavy, expensive-looking black pen with gold accents in his fingers. He was upending it, the pen sliding through his fingers, only for him to catch it at the tip and upend it again.

Someone was standing at the foot of the table speaking to the group and there were charts projected on the wall behind him. Cash's attention was focused on the speaker, but Abby had only taken a few steps into the reception area when his head turned and his black eyes hit her.

She'd been in a clothing crisis all morning not knowing what to wear to this meeting, especially since it was at Cash's office.

It was one thing when she was getting paid to be his girlfriend and going out to dinner at restaurants surrounded by people they didn't know. It was another to *be* his girlfriend and go to his office where all his staff could see (and judge) her.

She'd decided professional class was her best bet. But even when she was working she rarely wore traditional suits. Instead, she dressed, as Ben used to say, like Princess Diana with attitude (but without the hats).

That day she chose one of her old work suits. A soft fawn colour with a fitted skirt, the hem brushed her knees and it had slits up each side. One of the reasons she bought the suit was that the jacket fit like it was made for her, had a nipped-in waist and a succession of smart, intricate pleats falling from her waist at the back.

She wore this with a shiny cream satin blouse that she always unbuttoned just one button below professional, as she did today.

She'd put on her mocha suede high-heeled boots, matching wide belt and you could see a hint of flesh-coloured fishnet stockings covering her knees between the top of the boots and the hem of the skirt.

She wore her pearl earrings and choker her parents gave her for her wedding, and her gold watch. She had blown her hair dry sleek, left it long and did her makeup in her "Edgy Professional" look. Lastly, she'd worn her mother's taupe coat, but had taken it off on the way up in the elevator and now it was over her forearm, her mocha, patent-leather clutch shoved under her arm.

She held her breath as Cash's eyes did a sweep of her, finally coming to rest on her face.

Then she watched him smile a slow, lazy, gorgeous smile and she felt that smile shoot straight from her heart, through her belly, right between her legs.

At that point Abby heard, "Can I help you?"

Tearing her gaze with some difficulty from Cash's smile, Abby turned her head to the young, attractive, very professionally dressed woman seated behind the reception desk. She moved toward her.

"I'm Abigail Butler. I'm here—" Abby started, but the girl shot out of her seat.

"Abby. Right," she said, rounding her desk. "Cash said you were coming." Her head tilted to the conference room and she continued, "As you can see, he's in a meeting but he'll be out in a minute." She motioned toward a hallway, walking ahead, obviously expecting Abby to follow (which she did) and went on, "I'll take you to his office. Can I get you a coffee? We have an espresso machine. I can make you a latte or cappuccino."

"Just a regular coffee, white and strong, if you don't mind," Abby replied as the woman turned to a door, opened it and led Abby in.

Abby took two steps in and halted.

It was an enormous corner office with a stunning view of Bath afforded from all of its many windows. The desk was huge, messy, covered in papers, file folders, some open, some stacked, two phones (who needed *two* phones?) and Cash's laptop.

Outside the messy desk, the rest of the office was immaculate. Just as she'd noticed in the reception area and hall, the décor was a successful mixture of traditional and modern. Wood-panelled walls, heavy, elegant furniture but with modern art, fixtures and fittings.

His office not only held his desk but two large, black leather chairs facing it. There was a stylish but comfortable-looking couch with a low table in front of it against one wall as well as a smaller conference table that accommodated six to the other side. One entire wall was taken up with a built-in unit with illuminated shelves, one containing glasses, a wider one containing decanters of liquor, still others containing interesting bronze sculptures, and there was even a counter with a sink as well as several spaces covered with doors and all the doors had locks.

"White coffee. Strong," the woman said. "Be right back." And Abby turned to see her rushing out.

"Wait," Abby called.

The woman stopped and looked back at Abby.

Abby smiled. "I didn't get your name."

The woman blinked at her then said, "Emma."

At this news, Abby winced and muttered, "Oh dear," and watched Emma blink again as Abby moved to her. "I think I might need to apologise."

Emma was looking at her as if a spaceship was hovering outside Cash's windows and Abby had just stepped off of it.

"Sorry?" Emma asked.

"The other day, when Moira got in an accident, you called and I didn't let you finish. I think Cash got a little—" Abby explained, and Emma cut her off.

"It's okay," she said quickly.

But shutters had come down over her eyes telling Abby that she did, indeed, get into trouble and it was anything but okay.

Therefore, Abby blurted, "My husband was killed in a car accident." She watched Emma give a start and Abby continued, "Four years ago. I overreacted when you called. Panicked really. I tried to explain that to Cash that I hadn't let you finish but he was a bit, um..." How could she explain it? She tried to be tactful. "*Put out* that I was in that state."

Emma regarded her for a moment then Abby watched as her gaze unshuttered and her eyes went soft. "I get it now and that's understandable."

"Still, I'm sorry," Abby pressed, and Emma smiled at her.

"That's okay." She nodded, meaning it this time. Then she turned saying, "I'll just get your coffee."

Emma left and Abby threw her coat and bag on Cash's couch. She went to the windows and looked at Bath.

Cash had asked her to arrive half an hour earlier than the others. He hadn't explained why and she hadn't asked. Now, clothing crisis averted, the Emma apology over, she had time to wonder why.

As she contemplated this, Abby had no idea what was going on outside Cash's door.

She had no idea that Cash Fraser had many women come to his office. However, they were there briefly, so briefly they waited in the reception area and they were rarely offered coffee.

She also had no idea that Cash had not taken a single one of them on a business trip.

She also had no idea that his expense report for Germany had been gossiped about at length by a motor mouth in the finance department. Fuelled as well by the pictures in the papers, interest about Cash and Abby was running rampant.

Therefore, she had no idea that the traffic in the hall outside Cash's open office door while she stood pondering his desire to have her there early was far heavier than normal.

Emma brought her coffee, chit chatted with Abby for a few minutes, and then explained she had to get to her desk.

She had to do this because Emma knew that Cash would not be

pleased if she chit chatted with his glamorous new girlfriend in his office instead of doing the work he paid her to do. She also did this because she could not *wait* to call motor mouth Jade in the finance department and tell her that this one was actually *nice*.

Abby had taken a few sips of coffee and had come to no conclusions why Cash would want her there early when Cash walked in.

His eyes never leaving her, he went straight to his desk, tossed a file and his pen on it and both skidded several inches across the mess before coming to a stop.

Abby watched this and her gaze went back to Cash. "You're fond of throwing things, aren't you?"

He didn't answer but she watched him grin as he came to the side of the desk and rested a thigh against it, crossing his arms on his chest.

She walked to him, putting her coffee cup on a coaster she could just see from under some papers.

She motioned to his desk and remarked, "I'm surprised. You aren't very organised."

"Moira has a dislocated shoulder and a broken wrist," he replied, and as she was now within reaching distance, his hands came to her waist and he pulled her closer, his arms circling her. "I made her stay home until Monday."

Abby's head tilted to the side. "Made her?"

"She wanted to come back to work yesterday."

Abby was surprised at this news. Moira had only just had her accident.

She lifted her hands and rested them on his chest, leaning into his strong body and tilting her head back farther to look up at him.

"She's a workaholic, like you," Abby guessed.

"She gets off on the hunt, like me," Cash returned.

A weird thrill shot through her at his words.

"The hunt?" Abby asked, not quite able to hide her curiosity and his head dipped down so he could touch his mouth to hers.

"I'll tell you about my work sometime," he offered.

She was surprised at this. She had asked him once about his work, and he'd told her it was confidential.

She wasn't certain but she had the feeling that his offer signified something huge.

Instead of making a big deal of it, Abby teased, "If you tell me, will you have to kill me?"

"God, I hope not," he replied on a grin.

His arms tightened, bringing her even closer and he kissed her, hard, wet and open-mouthed.

When he was done, Abby's fingers had curled into his lapels to hold herself upright and Cash did something new. He slid his nose along the side of hers and the tenderness she felt from this was playing havoc with her heart.

She swallowed and asked, "Why did you want me to come early?"

His head moved away and she saw he was still grinning but this one was wicked.

He answered without delay, "I wanted to make out with you before they arrived."

His intent, and the honesty with which he shared it, made her laugh. Throwing her head back, her hands slid up his chest to rest around his neck, the tips of the fingers of one hand going into his thick hair.

When she stopped laughing, her eyes caught movement, she looked around his arm and saw the door was open and someone was walking past.

She looked back at Cash, pulled slightly away and suggested, "If you want to make out with me, maybe we should close the door."

"No."

At his answer, Abby's lips parted in surprise.

"No?" she repeated.

His arms got even tighter and his face dipped close to hers again.

"No," he said again. "I employ thirty-five staff and they're all curious about you. Too curious. I make this statement, they'll have something to talk about for a couple of days and they'll get back to work."

"Oh," Abby said, somehow both weirded out and disappointed by his answer.

He gave her a little squeeze and went on, and even though she knew it was stupid, stupid, *stupid*, what he said next made that budding hope she experienced in her heart the night before start to take root and bloom.

"Twenty-five years ago, if you told me I'd be standing in an office like this and it would be mine, I wouldn't have believed you." She held her breath at his sharing of this secret, and his face got closer, his voice got deeper, rougher and far, far sexier when he continued, "And if you told me I'd be holding a woman like you in my arms, I'd have told you you were mad. So, darling, I'm going to show you off any chance I get. If you don't like that, tough. You're going to have to get over it."

Yes, even though it was stupid, that hope was definitely beginning to bloom.

"Cash—" she whispered, then didn't know what to say.

So she decided to *show* him how his words made her feel. She got up on tiptoe, pressing his head down with her fingers in his hair and *she* kissed *him*, hard, wet and open-mouthed.

His hand slid up her back, his fingers sifted into her hair at her nape and his head slanted, deepening an already deep kiss. This made Abby's knees give out and his arm crushed her to him as she felt her body electrify from his kiss.

Some time later from far away (but she wished it was farther, *much* farther) she heard a tap at the door then, when Cash didn't stop kissing Abby, a polite cough.

Cash's head came up and he looked over his shoulder, his voice a mild growl when he said, "Yes?"

"The others are here," Emma told him, standing uncomfortably at the door.

"We'll be right there," Cash replied, and Abby, peering around Cash's body, saw Emma disappear instantly.

Cash's arms moved from around her but both his hands came up to curl on her neck.

"After this weekend, as soon as I can arrange it, we're going on holiday," he informed her, his brogue still a soft, effective rumble that slid across her skin.

"We are?" Abby asked, sounding dazed because she was.

It had been a *great* kiss.

"We are," he returned. "No phones, no receptionists, no nosy neighbours, no aggravating cousins, no ghosts, just us."

"Okay," Abby agreed, and she felt Cash's fingers flex at her neck before he smiled.

He let her go but caught her hand and gently pulled her to the door, asking blandly, "How annoyed is this meeting going to make me?"

Abby thought about Mrs. Truman.

Then she thought there was a very good possibility (in fact, it was a certainty) that Angus would be attired in full Scottish regalia.

"Um, on a scale of one to ten?" Abby inquired, and Cash stopped at the door and looked down at her. She bit the side of her lip then mumbled, "Fifteen."

At that, he threw his head back and laughed. She felt his rich laughter go straight from her stomach, this time up, to rest close to her heart before he tugged at her hand, leading her out the door and down the hall.

And she didn't know Cash's laughter in his office was not unheard of, but it was also not commonplace. So that, as well as their passionate embrace, as well as what was to come, was going to be the talk of the office for the rest of the month.

They walked, hand in hand, down the hall and Cash stopped them when they hit reception.

Abby took one look at her motley crew and mentally groaned.

Jenny, luckily, looked like Jenny, wearing the black trousers that did great things for her behind, high-heeled black boots and a black turtleneck.

Honor was also dressed like a normal person.

Fenella, however, was wearing a pink monstrosity that was fifty years too old for her and looked like it was created to be worn to attend a tea party at a retirement home.

Mrs. Truman was wearing English Old Lady, from the tip of her felt hat with a sharp feather sticking out of it, through her boxy tweed suit, to the toes of her rubber-sole shoes.

Angus was, as Abby feared, in full kilt.

But it was Cassandra that had gone OTT looking like the rock 'n' roll gypsy from hell. She had a scarf wrapped tightly around her head, its fringed ends mingling with her long dark hair. She had three, thin, rock 'n' roll scarves around her neck and yet *another* fringed scarf wrapped around her hips over her jeans. As an unnecessary finishing touch, she was wearing enough jewellery in her ears, around her neck, at her wrists and on her fingers to set off the metal detectors in the Pentagon thousands of miles away.

"Fucking hell," Cash muttered under his breath, and Abby looked up to see he was not amused.

"I need tea," Mrs. Truman announced loudly.

Abby suppressed a hysterical giggle, but just barely.

Cash walked forward, taking Abby with him, and his eyes went to Emma. "Is lunch set up?"

"Yes, Cash. Everything's ready in the conference room," Emma answered, her surprised eyes on the assemblage.

Cash led the way to the door of the conference room. As Abby walked beside him she noticed there were an awful lot of people standing around pretending to be in conversations, but surreptitiously watching what was happening in the reception area.

That's when she started to freak out that all Cash's employees were going to think she was a bad influence on him.

She stood beside Cash as her posse trooped into the conference room, greeting Cash and Abby as they passed. All except Angus who shook Cash's hand so hard, Abby's body also shook as Cash was still holding her hand.

"Angus McPherson," he declared when he was done shaking Cash's hand. Then he puffed out his chest and boomed, "Proud to be working for ye, Cash Fraser!"

Cash stared at Angus a moment before he tilted his head down to look at Abby, brows raised, and she scrunched her nose at him.

Luckily, Angus didn't take offense to Cash's non-greeting and headed into the conference room.

Abby started to follow but Cash halted her with a tug on her hand. She looked up at him in time to see his face disappear by her ear.

"Somehow, I think you owe me for this," he murmured there.

Somehow, she thought he was right.

His head came back and when she caught his eyes, she winced and shrugged which, fortunately, made him grin.

When Cash and Abby entered and Cash closed the door, Abby noted they were all partaking of the buffet like they'd just come off a month-long forced fast.

When they had their plates piled high, they sat around the conference table. Cash was at the head with no food, Abby to his right and she'd decided to take her cues from him and also not load up a plate (even though the buffet looked really good, Cash didn't do things in half-measures that was certain).

Cash didn't waste any time and once everyone was settled he immediately asked, "Who's in charge?"

"I am," both Angus and Cassandra said at the same time.

"That would be *me*," Mrs. Truman said over both of them.

Cash's body stayed facing forward, just his head turned to Abby and his brows went up.

"Um," Abby started, looked amongst the faces, trying to decide who would take the least offense. Then she tried to be diplomatic, "Let's say Angus as he's had more experience with this type of thing."

Mrs. Truman let out an affronted "humph," Cassandra sat back smiling and Angus leaned forward happily.

Cash put both elbows on the table, linked his fingers, rested his chin on them and looked at Angus.

"Tell me your plan," he ordered.

Angus glanced at Cassandra, then said, "We're thinking the showdown will be Saturday night."

There was silence as Cash waited for Angus to say more.

Angus said no more.

Cash closed his eyes, pulled breath in through his nose, and when he opened his eyes again, they were aimed at Abby.

Abby pressed her lips together.

Cash's attention went back to Angus and he suggested with barely restrained patience, "Perhaps you'd like to fill in the blanks."

Angus shoved an entire chicken goujon in his mouth and shifted in his seat excitedly while he chewed.

Not done chewing, he stated, "See, we're thinking tonight, we'll give her a chance to get settled in. Not Abby. Vivianna. Make her think we're not going to try anything. We'll wait for Saturday night to draw her out."

"And how is Abby going to stay safe from this evening through to tomorrow?" Cash asked.

Cassandra leaned forward. "That's where you come in."

Cash looked at Cassandra but didn't speak.

It was Honor who spoke next and she informed them, "I didn't just find Lorna's diaries." Cash's eyes shifted to her and she continued, "Two of the other victims had journals in the library too. I've had those for years as well."

Cassandra picked up there. "Angus, Honor and I have been studying the journals and researching the past murders. What we found is that Vivianna doesn't appear, nor is she active, when the master of the house is with the victim. Therefore, if you stay close to her side, Abby should be safe."

"And what if we get separated?" Cash inquired.

"You make sure she's with Mummy," Fenella put in.

"Nicola?" Cash asked.

"Vivianna doesn't do anything when Mummy's around," Fenella told Cash.

"Do you know that for certain?" Cash queried, and when Fenella looked blank, Cash turned to Cassandra. "And are you certain she won't be active when I'm with Abby?"

"Not one hundred percent certain, no," Angus cut in, picked up a salmon and cream cheese sandwich quarter, shoved the whole thing in his mouth and went on while chewing, "Pretty certain, though."

Cash's head cocked sharply to the side before he told Angus, "Pretty certain isn't good enough."

"Abby will have protection," Cassandra noted. "I'll give it to her, and Fenella, Honor and I'll take care of your rooms."

"Take care of our rooms?" Cash asked.

"Protection spell," Cassandra replied. "Some special pixie dust sprinkled here and there, a few incantations." When Cash's jaw got tight, Cassandra's voice dipped low. "I know how it sounds, but I promise you, I also know what I'm doing."

"She does, Cash," Abby whispered when Cash looked far from convinced, but Cash didn't take his eyes from Cassandra.

"She'll be safe in your rooms," Cassandra asserted. "Even if something happens, she gets outside the castle walls, or to your rooms, she'll be safe."

Cash's head turned to Abby and he muttered, "I'm supposed to trust this?"

To that Abby replied softly, "I do."

Abby watched a muscle jump in Cash's cheek and she knew he didn't like any of what he was hearing but he looked back at the table and forged ahead. "Let's talk about Saturday night."

"We have it all figured out," Angus told him. "Fenella and Honor are going to get Nicola to talk Suzanne into taking Abby up to one of the parapets. Fenella tells us that Vivianna likes Suzanne, she's less likely to suspect her of setting a trap, so once she gets—"

Cash cut in by saying, "No."

Angus blinked, then repeated, "No?"

Abby looked at Cash and saw he was no longer being patient, he was now angry.

"No," Cash retorted. "Abby's not going anywhere near the parapets. Not with Suzanne."

"Suzanne wouldn't hurt Abby," Fenella squeaked, and Cash's head turned to her.

"She also wouldn't help her," Cash returned.

"He has a point," Honor muttered, and Fenella turned wide eyes to her sister.

"Moving on!" Mrs. Truman commanded. "What's Plan B?"

"She likes the conservatory. Maybe Abby can pretend to wander—" Fenella started.

"No," Cash stated again.

"Not the conservatory either?" Jenny asked.

"Too many windows," Cash answered and looked at Angus. "I don't want Abby near any windows or stairs. She uses only the bathroom in our room. And she's definitely not stepping foot on the fucking roof."

Oh Lord, Abby thought, *Cash is using the F-word.*

Softly, in hopes of calming him, Abby murmured, "Cash."

But at the same time, Jenny mumbled, "Maybe we can arrange the showdown in a silk tent in the Sahara."

Cash's gaze sliced to Jenny. Jenny caught his scorching glare and bit her lips.

Then Cash announced to the table at large, "This morning, I did some research as well. Five women, not including Vivianna Wainwright, have died at Penmort. Two fell from the roof, one fell down the stairs and two fell through a window." He paused and skewered Angus with a look. "I'll repeat, no roof, no windows, no stairs. Now, what else have you got?"

Everyone looked at everyone else.

Finally Angus spoke. "The gallery."

"The gallery is on the second floor," Cash reminded him. "That's a flight of stairs."

"Yes, but Vivianna likes that room and Abby can stay away from the stairs and the windows," Angus replied. "The gallery is huge. We'll have plenty of room to move in there."

Cash took a moment to consider this then he jerked his head in a nod. "The gallery."

Mrs. Truman spoke up. "You can't be anywhere near."

Cash looked at her. "I get that," he said then continued, "But I'll not be far."

"You can't be anywhere near," Mrs. Truman repeated.

"I'll not be far," Cash repeated in turn.

"Cash," Cassandra put in. "She may not appear before the master but that doesn't mean she can't see him. You can't hide from her."

"Abby's not going up alone," Cash returned.

"No, she isn't. Me and Cassandra will be there," Angus said.

"If she can see me, she can see you," Cash retorted, and Angus shook his head.

"She can't see me, lad, not unless I want her to," Angus replied softly.

"And how does that work?" Cash asked, his voice dripping with disbelief.

"Glamour," Cassandra answered. Cash turned to her and raised his brows in question so Cassandra went on, "The McPhersons have a cloaking glamour. It's magic, handed down for generations and hard to explain. Just trust me, it works."

With visible effort, Cash allowed this to pass, then he asked Cassandra, "And where will you be?"

"I'll be close," Cassandra told him.

"You'll be *very* close," Cash told her, and Cassandra nodded. Cash turned to Angus. "How will you get her?"

"Can't say. Family secret," Angus replied.

Cash looked at him a moment before he said with soft menace, "I'm sure everyone in this room will take your secret to their grave."

And Abby was sure too. The way he said it, anyone in that room would be stupid not to.

Cash went on, "Now, tell us, how are you going to get her?"

Angus looked at Cassandra then Jenny then Mrs. Truman, and Abby noted that they all shifted uncomfortably in their seats.

Finally, Angus's eyes went to Cash and he spoke, "Witch's trap."

Cash waited for more.

Angus didn't give it to him so Cash demanded, "Explain."

Angus glanced at Cassandra and back to Cash. "I'll set a witch's trap in the gallery. To be trapped, she has to form, which Abby will get her to do. Then I'll drive her to the trap. She won't see it, she won't feel it, but once she's in the circle, she won't be able to get out of it."

Cassandra took over. "Once she's inside the trap, I'll be there. Angus and I'll fold her up and take her to a coven in Cornwall for a vanishing ritual."

"Fold her up?" Cash inquired.

"Yes," Cassandra answered. "Literally. I'll fold her up using magic and insert her into a case that Angus's family has been using for centuries. The case is protected and no matter how strong she is, she won't be able to get out. Transport will be safe, but I'll go with Angus to make the delivery just in case. The coven in Cornwall is powerful and they've been alerted. They're ready. They'll perform the vanishing ritual the minute Vivianna is delivered to them."

"And that's it?" Cash asked.

"That's it," Angus replied.

"She'll be gone?" Cash pressed.

"Straight to hell," Cassandra stated.

"You're certain?" Cash pushed.

Cassandra and Angus both nodded.

Mrs. Truman butted in and her eyes were on Abby. "Honor and Fenella have finagled invitations to the party Saturday night for Jenny and me. We'll be there too."

Abby saw Cash's body get tight, so hurriedly she suggested, "Perhaps you should leave this to the experts."

It was Jenny who spoke next. "We're not going to be there to help."

Mrs. Truman finished for Jenny by declaring, "Moral support."

"This doesn't get better," Cash muttered.

Mrs. Truman's eyes narrowed on Cash and she snapped, "Cash Fraser, Abigail is not going to face this peril without what's left of her family at her side."

Abby felt a jolt shoot through her belly at Mrs. Truman's words and then her eyes moved to Jenny.

She had no idea when Mrs. Truman became family but since she'd known her for as long as she could remember, and since Jenny had been in her life for more than half of it, she realised Mrs. Truman wasn't wrong.

Therefore, her gaze going from Jenny to Mrs. Truman, Abby whispered with feeling, "Thanks guys."

"Pah!" Mrs. Truman exploded and Abby waited for more but there wasn't any.

Abby smiled at Jenny. Jenny's eyes moved to Cash and Abby thought she looked weirdly pensive. Then she looked again at Abby, the strange look left her face, and she smiled back.

"Are we done?" Honor asked.

"We're done," Angus boomed, and Abby looked at Cash to see if he agreed.

"Good, I'm getting seconds," Honor announced, and Abby watched Cash sit back in his seat. He crossed one arm on his chest but brought the fist of his other hand to his mouth. "Abby, can I make you a plate?" Honor called.

"Yes, please," Abby called back, but her eyes didn't leave Cash when she told him quietly, "It's going to be okay."

Cash was contemplating the top of the conference table, but at her words, only his eyes moved to hers and he regarded her from under his brows.

Even after all that, clearly unconvinced, Cash growled in his rough burr, "It better fucking be."

And Abby thought, *bloody hell*.

24

ABBY HELPS CASH CELEBRATE

Abby stood by their big four-poster curtained bed at Penmort, rubbing lotion into her hands and thanking her lucky stars that she was still alive and breathing.

They'd arrived at the castle sometime after seven for the family celebration that went off (almost) without a hitch. No earthquakes. No eerie screams. No ghosty she-bitch hauntings. No running for your life through the castle.

Nothing.

Apparently Angus and Cassandra's guess had been correct. Throughout the evening an on-edge Cash had glued himself to Abby's side and Vivianna didn't show. There wasn't even a cold draught, much less a murderous spirit appearing over the dining table wreaking havoc while they ate their pudding.

In fact, once Abby, Fenella and Honor stopped glancing at each other with expectant doom, and later a very tense Cash relaxed (somewhat), it was only Nicola and Suzanne who made the evening uncomfortable.

Nicola, because she was unusually quiet in a way that made Abby concerned.

Suzanne, because she was not unusually being a screaming bitch in a way that made an obviously edgy Cash furious.

And he had absolutely no problem letting that fact be known.

He did this by actually calling her a "lying, fucking bitch" right at the table.

At his words, Abby and everyone had been shocked speechless, even though Abby and (likely) everyone thought she deserved it.

Suzanne had, of course, been unrelentingly bitchy throughout the meal, not only to her sisters, but also to her mother and even, although subtly (she was a bitch but not a bitch with a death wish), to Abby.

And knowing his patience was wearing thin, in what Abby thought could only be desperation to press a reaction, any reaction, from Cash, Suzanne had cattily alluded to the fact that she'd serviced him in bed.

No joke, *serviced him in bed*!

She didn't come right out and say it, but her inference wasn't lost on a soul at the table. It earned horrified gasps from Fenella and Honor, Alistair rolled his eyes wearily to the ceiling and Nicola jerked out of her quiet reverie to turn a sharp gaze on her daughter.

But before anyone could say a word, his voice low with fury, Cash growled, "You lying, fucking *bitch*."

Once she'd pulled herself out of her speechless shock, Abby murmured a soothing, "Cash."

Cash ignored Abby, his body rigidly controlled, he scowled at Suzanne in a way that made Abby grateful a table lay between them.

But Suzanne glared right back.

Everyone held their breath.

Suzanne broke the staring contest, turned to her mother and demanded, "Are you going to let him speak to me that way?"

"Yes," Nicola said calmly, and not only Suzanne's but also Abby's, Honor's and Fenella's eyes grew round at her single word.

"*What?*" Suzanne snapped.

"You've been prodding the sleeping lion all night, Suzanne," Nicola replied softly, demonstrating uncanny mother's observational abilities and she went on, "You wanted a response, you got one. You woke the lion, dear. Don't turn to me to pull you to safety."

Fortunately this served to piss off Suzanne enough for her to jump up, throw her napkin on the table and storm out of the room.

After Suzanne disappeared, Nicola's eyes slid to Cash and she apologised for her daughter. A muscle jumped in Cash's cheek, but he jerked his chin in acceptance of her apology.

Fenella quickly filled the conversational void with chatter, and Abby, sitting next to Cash, curled her fingers on his thigh and gave him a reassuring squeeze.

Cash's gaze came to her, still angry but also, she noted, somewhat astonished.

The look faded as did his anger and his fingers curled around hers on his thigh. He gave them a squeeze then left them there, holding her hand under the table.

Without Suzanne there, and with Cash's hand in hers, the rest of the evening had been kind of fun (if you didn't count Alistair being totally fake and Nicola being practically silent, that was).

Now Abby stood by their bed in their room.

Nicola had given them a lush corner turret room. It had a heavy, ornate wardrobe, chest and bureau and was decorated in a mixture of olive and emerald greens and dove grey, a bizarre colour combination, which somehow worked. And in its circular turret it had two inviting, overstuffed chairs sharing an ottoman and a small table.

Abby was wearing her cashmere robe and her favourite of the nightgowns Cash had given her. This one black silk, ankle length with daring, sexy slits on either side from the hem to her lower hip. The cut was simple, the back low and the gown fit her at bodice, midriff and hips fit like a second skin.

Abby was distractedly rubbing lotion in her hands and thinking that, even if Cash didn't seem in the best mood (which was an understatement), she had more to tell him. More he needed to know.

She should have told him before, but she figured him coming to terms with his ancestral legacy being haunted by an evil spirit who wanted to murder his new girlfriend was enough to handle.

In the meantime they'd been kind of busy.

But, Abby decided, it was time.

Even though she didn't like it, she had to do it.

For Cash.

She heard the door to the bathroom open. She had her back turned to it and saw the light hit the room before Cash pulled the cord and it was extinguished.

She didn't turn, but she felt him come close. His hands went to her waist, slid around to her belly and put pressure there, pulling her back into his warm, hard, strong body.

His mouth came to her ear where he asked in his rough burr, "You doing okay?"

At the concern in his voice, Abby felt her heart leap, her belly melt and she turned her head. His came up and she caught his eyes as her hands went to his at her belly.

She didn't answer him, instead she inquired, "Can we talk?"

Something she couldn't catch flashed across his face before he murmured, "Of course."

She took one of his hands in hers, curled it away from her body and tugged on it, leading him to a chair in the turret. He was wearing navy-blue pyjama bottoms and a dark-grey flannel robe open at the front so she could see most of his chest and the tight muscle across his abdomen.

She ignored the view (and the fact that Cash looked good in a robe), pressed him into the chair and, unresisting, he sat. She then lifted one of his arms and settled in his lap, curling close.

For a brief moment she felt his body tense under hers as she settled, almost as if he was surprised.

Then he relaxed, one of his arms curved around her waist, the other one came to rest across her lap, his fingers flexing into her hip.

His eyes caught hers. "What is it?"

Abby pulled in breath.

Releasing it, quickly and as gently as she could, she told him what Fenella, Angus and Honor said. *Everything* they said. About his father, about his father's intentions toward his mother and him, and lastly about Alistair (maybe) killing his father.

When she was close to finished, she lifted a hand to rest on the side of his face and leaned into him, her voice dropping to a whisper.

"I'm so sorry, honey. I know this is a lot to process and I should have told you before. But I didn't know how and—"

He cut her off with words as well as his fingers tightening their grip on her hip and his arm giving a squeeze. "Stop saying you're sorry."

She blinked at him. "But, I just told you there's a possibility that your uncle murdered your father. *Anyone* would be sorry about that."

"I know Alistair murdered my father," Cash shared bluntly, and Abby gasped at this news. But he talked over her gasp. "I know my father intended to move my mother and me to Penmort." Abby stared at him and Cash gave her another squeeze, his voice dipping low. "I know everything, Abby."

"You do?" she breathed.

"Yes," he said shortly. "I do."

"How...when..." she stammered. "How?"

Cash shifted. Twisting her so her back was against the arm of the chair, he pulled her body farther across his lap, her legs were hanging over the other arm and his torso was partially resting on hers. It was a far more comfortable and intimate position and Abby's brain registered just how much she liked it when he continued.

"When my father died, the police suspected Alistair but couldn't pin anything on him. Even though the trail was cold, there was enough to explore so I took up the threads of their investigations. I discovered the man who tampered with the brakes of my father's car got nicked for another job. He told his cellmate what he'd done. With a little persuasion, his cellmate told me."

Abby felt her heart start to beat faster.

"You should go to the police," she encouraged.

Cash shook his head. "The person who Alistair paid to do it is now dead. Died in prison. Diabetes. His cellmate is still alive but it's hearsay. There's no point."

Abby put her hands to his neck and asked, "If you know, then how can you be here? How can you sit at his table? How can you—?"

Cash interrupted her. "It's *my* table, Abby."

"You know that *now*," she returned. "But you just found out Alistair isn't a Beaumaris."

"It's been my table for two months," Cash replied, and Abby's breath stuck in her throat. "Alistair is in debt up to his teeth. I bought the notes. If he paid the loans he's taken against the castle, which he doesn't, he'd be paying *me*."

Abby felt her eyes grow round and Cash got closer.

"That's why you're here, darling. I've been playing with him for a year, making him think I might be interested in one of his stepdaughters in order to keep his attention off the fact I was stealing his house from under his nose. This weekend you're here to rub his face in one failure, his not securing a Beaumaris to marry one of his stepdaughters, while I rub his nose in the ultimate failure for any Beaumaris, true or not, by informing him he needs to pack his bags and get...the fuck...out."

Abby stared at him and whispered, "You've owned it all along?"

Cash nodded and carried on, "I took it and then *you* gave me proof that it was mine in the first place. Either way, he's out."

Abby was stunned. She was also worried.

"But, what about Nicola?" she asked.

Cash muttered dryly, "She can stay."

"Fenella? Honor?" Abby pressed.

His head descended and his mouth touched her collarbone. "I'm beginning to like them. You bring out the best in people. They can stay too," he replied generously. Abby opened her mouth again, but Cash beat her to it when his head came up and he stated flatly, "Suzanne goes."

Abby stared at him a moment then her voice went soft. "So all this time, you knew your dad wanted to marry your mom?"

He shook his head, his jaw went hard as did his eyes, and he muttered, "*That* was news."

"Did you know he wanted you to inherit?" Abby asked.

"I knew he was scrutinising the covenant. I guessed why," Cash replied.

"You need to talk to Angus," Abby told him.

"I'll talk to Angus, after you're safe," Cash agreed. "All of this will happen after we know you're safe."

"Cash—" Abby started to argue, thinking it was priority one that Alistair get his due.

"Abby," he broke in. "After you're safe."

Abby didn't let it go. "You can't wait! He killed your father, Cash. You've been working on this for—"

He cut her off. "After you're safe."

"Cash!" she snapped, and his face came close to hers.

"After...you're...*fucking*...safe," he enunciated clearly, slowly and more than a little inflexibly.

All right then, after she was safe it was.

All of a sudden, all he said, what he'd done, dawned on her.

And she felt something odd steal over her, odd and thrilling.

She was, she realised, proud of him.

It wasn't her place to be proud, but she couldn't help it.

She was.

And, she thought, the man who held her in his lap, in a turret, in his ancestral home, a home he'd been born to but denied and then cheated, but he'd won it all the same—that man, Abby concluded, should celebrate.

And she knew exactly how he should do it.

Even though it scared the daylights out of her (for a variety of reasons), since she was living on limited time, she didn't waste any of it.

Abruptly she asked, "Will you do something for me?"

His eyes moved over her face and she knew he was trying to read her mind.

Clearly failing, cautiously he replied, "That depends."

She smiled.

When she did, his eyes dropped to her mouth, but she pushed him back, slid off his lap, grabbed his hand and pulled him up from the chair. Then she tugged him to the door, which she threw open and stepped out of the room.

With a sharp yank at her hand he hauled her back and she looked up at him.

"You're not leaving this room," he told her.

She smiled up at him. "I'll be safe. I'm with you."

She started to move forward again but Cash stayed planted.

She pulled at his arm. He still didn't move.

She stopped, turned and softly uttered two words, "Cash, please."

He looked to the side, pressing his lips together. Then his body came unstuck and he walked down the dark hall with her, down the stairs, his hand in hers, his body close.

She led him to the study and closed the door behind them.

She took his hand again, moved with him through the shadows to the huge desk which had been there for maybe hundreds of years. A desk his father used, his grandfather used, and so on.

A desk that Alistair used.

Abby walked Cash around the desk and pushed back the chair. She stopped Cash in front of her, dropped his hand and leaned back against the desk.

"Abby, what in fucking hell—?" Cash, she could tell, was losing patience.

Abby interrupted. "Alistair uses this desk."

"And?" Cash asked irritably.

Her hands went to his waist inside his robe and she pulled him closer. She got up on tiptoe and leaned into him as his hands came to her hips.

"Abby—" he started.

She put her lips to his jaw and murmured, "I'm done with my period."

She felt him grow still.

Her hands slid up his sides, around, then up his back as she pressed against him.

His head tipped down as hers tilted back and she put her mouth to his.

Using every smidgeon of courage she had, her heart beating madly, she whispered, "Cash, I want you to fuck me on *your* desk."

Cash's body went solid.

For a moment.

But Abby didn't have to ask twice.

His mouth captured hers in a bruising kiss and her robe was off her shoulders in a flash, pooling on the floor at her feet.

All the while kissing her, Cash leaned forward and Abby arched back. He did something and she heard objects hit the floor, but she didn't pay much attention. She was busy trying to pull his robe down his occupied arms at the same time kissing him back.

When he was done clearing the desk, she tugged his robe off. He yanked her nightgown up then her underwear down, and before she'd finished her gasp and stepped out of them, his hands were at her bottom, lifting her and planting her on the desk.

From that point on it went wild. It was rough, hard, wet, completely out of either of their control and every second was absolutely *glorious*.

Not long later, her back was on the desk and her behind at its edge. Her knees were cocked, her legs pressed high against his sides. One of her arms was wrapped around Cash's back like she was never going to let go, the other hand in his hair, holding his mouth to hers.

She felt the delicious tightening, she knew what it was, she knew it was coming, and best of all, she knew it was going to be *good*.

Cash was driving deep. His mouth disengaged from hers and his hand fisted in her hair, yanking her head back with a tender savagery that made her neck arch.

Cash's lips went to her ear and he growled, "The best thing I've done in my whole fucking life is walk into that pub."

Abby felt her heart squeeze and her breath catch, but it was too late. She was too far gone. She couldn't respond. All she could do was breathe his name.

He drove in deeper and demanded, "I want it."

She did everything she could to hold back and wait for him.

"Cash," she whispered.

He ground his hips into hers, way deep, beyond delicious, and his fist in her hair pulled her head back further as he ordered, "Give it to me, Abby. I want it."

Seeing as it was one of the only things she could give to Cash Fraser, Fabulously Rich and Famous International Hot Guy, and seeing as she wanted him to have everything he wanted, she gave it to him.

❧ ❧ ❧

After Cash finished and pulled away, he slid her underwear up her legs himself. After he'd done that, he gently slipped her off the desk to her feet. Holding her close to his body, he replaced her robe then let her go for a moment so he could replace his.

He sat in the desk chair taking her with him, settling her in his lap with her body curled into his, bent legs against his chest, cheek on his shoulder, head tucked under his jaw. Once he had her cocooned against him, he circled her entire body with his arms.

Neither of them spoke. Both of them were still catching their breath. Even after their breathing evened, they stayed silent.

Abby was thinking about what he said before she came. She had no clue what he was thinking.

Then he told her.

"I'm going to fuck you in every room in this house."

Her head tilted back to look at him.

"Tonight?" she whispered in disbelief.

His chin dipped down, she could see the flash of white where his mouth was indicating he was smiling.

His lips touched hers before he replied, "Darling, as much as I love it that you'd think I'd be up to such a staggering feat, I'll take my time."

She immediately felt like an idiot. Of course he wasn't going to do it in one night. In fact, at that moment, there were five other people in the house (not to mention a latent ghost). They couldn't even *get* to every room of the house.

Feeling embarrassed, she tucked her head under his chin. When she did, his arms tightened and immediately she felt the embarrassment slide away.

They were again silent.

Eventually he called, "Abby."

"Mm," she replied.

"Thank you for telling me everything you told me tonight."

It was her turn for her arms to steal around him and give him a squeeze.

"I should have said something earlier."

"It wasn't easy to say," he replied.

"Still," she muttered.

His arms gave her a mild shake before he commanded, "Darling, look at me." Abby tilted her head back again to peer at him in the dark. When he continued, his voice was soft and rough and very effective. "It wasn't easy to find the right time and it wasn't easy to find the right words. You did both. Thank you."

She stared at his shadowed but still handsome face and whispered, "You're welcome."

His face tipped until their foreheads were touching and he slid his nose alongside hers.

When he did, Abby closed her eyes and committed every nuance of that moment to memory.

"Unless you have any other bright ideas, maybe we should go to bed," he murmured.

She opened her eyes, bit her lip, and thought about it a second, finally informing him, "Nope. No other bright ideas."

He laughed softly, lifted her up as he stood and put her on her feet.

Then he took her to bed.

When she was pressed into his side in their big curtained bed, in a big imposing castle (*his* big imposing castle), close to dreamland and feeling that peace spread through her that only Cash had been able to give her for many a year, she heard him speak.

"I meant what I said."

"Pardon?" she mumbled.

"When you were about to come. What I said. I meant it."

She felt her body go tight as all thoughts of sleep fled.

Then she felt her belly get warm.

Quietly, she shared, "The first time I saw you, I almost ran away."

Surprisingly he responded, "I know."

Abby forced her body to relax and after she succeeded in that monumental task, she snuggled closer.

Moments slid by.

Finally, taking her heart in her hands and hoping with everything she was that Cash would know what to do with it, she whispered, "I'm glad I didn't."

His arm around her waist tensed and he replied, "I am too."

Yes, he knew what to do with it.

Abby smiled against his shoulder, cuddled the last smidgeon closer and fell asleep.

25

LOSING ABBY

Cash was in the library, his eyes swiftly scanning the books.

If Honor had found clues to Vivianna Wainwright in the library, Cash thought there might be something she'd missed. Something that might give him insight into how to defeat a fucking ghost. Something that might help him to feel a little less fucking useless.

Cash Fraser's thoughts were sprinkled liberally with the F-word such was his mood.

He'd left Abby at the breakfast table with Nicola, Fenella and Honor.

He didn't want to but once the conversation turned to catering and flowers, Abby saw his impatience and urged him to go.

He refused.

Abby enlisted Nicola and Nicola urged him to go.

He wanted to refuse but he didn't.

Cash felt there was something wrong with Nicola. She had a fragility about her that was atypical.

However, Cash didn't have time to worry about Nicola when his thoughts were centred on Abby and what was to happen that night.

He'd left Abby only after pulling her to him and engaging in a lips-to-ear whispered conversation that, to any who observed it, would look like lover's talk.

Instead it was Cash telling Abby if she left Nicola's fucking side he'd not be responsible for his actions.

After biting her lip (this time, Cash could swear, it was to hide a smile, although he had no fucking clue what there was to smile about) Abby agreed.

Only then did Cash leave.

He spied an unusual book, thin and old, pulled it from its shelf and leafed through it, finding it was a (bad) epic poem about the Civil War.

He replaced the book and his mind went back to Abby.

He had, he realised, been wrong. He'd thought he had her that first weekend they were together.

He hadn't had her then.

He knew this because he had her now.

All of her.

The all of her he saw that she gave her husband in their wedding photo.

And the feeling of having all of Abby was something Cash had not anticipated.

He should have. She'd given him clues. Hell, she'd given him clues from the first day they'd met.

He, of course, thought she was a professional escort. So when she'd wiped the gloss from his lips at the pub and leaned into him in an affectionate way when he put on her cape on their first date, he thought it was a show.

It wasn't.

It was just Abby.

The night she'd thought he was in an accident, her guard came crashing down.

Quickly after, she invited him in, laughing in abandon with her face turned up to his. Calling him for no reason (and then hilariously expecting him to carry the conversation). Squeezing his thigh comfortingly when he was angry. Curling in his lap to be close when she had to share hard facts but in a gentle way. Leading him to the study and asking him to fuck her on the desk.

That was Abby.

All of Abby.

All for him.

On this thought, for some unknown reason, Cash's mood turned darker and he wondered if Benjamin Butler had any time to think before he'd died. To think about his wife. To think about leaving such an exquisite creature behind. To think about how fucking lucky he'd been and how abhorrent it was that their time was cut short.

Cash hoped he had not.

His mind occupied with Abby's dead husband, suddenly Cash felt a warm draught against his ankles.

He looked down and saw nothing.

He looked to the door. It was, as he left it, open.

He looked to the window. It was, as he'd entered, closed.

The draught ascended the length of his body, curling around.

Cash took a step back and it disappeared.

"Fucking hell," he muttered, thinking the situation with Abby, the castle and the ghost was screwing with his head.

On that thought, the draught came back, circling his wrist in an odd way, almost but also strangely not, putting pressure there as if to lift his hand.

He took another step away.

"Here he is!" Cash heard Fenella screech, and the draught disappeared.

He turned to the door to see her entering, yanking her mother behind her, Abby following, Honor coming up the rear.

Abby's sentries.

Cash stared at them.

Then he repeated, "Fucking hell."

"Well, I knew he couldn't have gone far," Abby stated, rushing forward.

The minute her back was to the others, she gave him a comical, wide-eyed look which Cash couldn't quite interpret and at which Cash was in no mood to laugh.

"I'm still not certain why we *all* had to go in search of Cash. Abby could have found him on her own," Nicola noted, her words explaining Abby's look.

Abby had made it to Cash's side and her fingers curled around his biceps as she leaned into his body and looked back at Nicola.

"I could have got lost," she bald-faced lied.

"Yes, it's a big castle." Honor drawled, her eyes on Cash.

She looked like she didn't know whether to laugh or scream, and Cash felt her pain.

"And I'm blonde," Abby went on. "I think it's a scientific fact that blondes are a bit scatty."

At her words, Cash started leaning towards laughter and looked down at Abby. "I'm not certain that's science."

"Really?" she asked. "I thought there were some studies done about it."

"I don't think so," Cash replied.

"Well, there should be," she mumbled, giving him another look. This one he could read quite clearly and it said *shut up*. Then she turned a bright smile to Nicola and declared overly cheerfully, "Well, I found him now! All's well!"

Cash's mood disappeared and he burst into laughter.

His arm went around her waist to pull her closer. When it did, her hands detached from his biceps, one arm slid around his back and she looked up at him right before his head descended and, still laughing, he kissed her. It was swift, it was light, but it was definitely a kiss.

When he lifted his head, he saw she was smiling up at him dazzlingly as if his laughter was a gift from the gods, better than any diamond bracelet, any cashmere robe.

The smile still on her lips, her thumb came to his mouth and she swiped at her ever-present lip gloss the kiss had transferred to his lips. As she did so, Cash felt the room around them melt and all he saw was her exquisite face, her smile, her glow.

And he knew, regardless of all that was happening, ghosts, brothers murdering brothers and sons exacting retribution, Abby was happy.

And Cash had made her that way.

In that instant Cash saw that not only had her guard come crashing down, the pain she couldn't quite hide that lurked in the back of her eyes from the minute he'd sat across from her at the pub had disappeared.

He'd taken it away.

"Jesus," he muttered, powerful sensations he didn't completely understand shooting through him like spears and he watched her face turn confused.

"What?" she asked.

"Jesus," he repeated.

Abby turned into him. "Cash, are you okay?"

As if his actions weren't under his control, his hand went to her jaw tilting her face up further. His mouth came down on hers and he gave her a kiss that was not swift, it was not light, and it could have quite possibly been the physical definition of *a kiss*.

"Oh my." Cash vaguely heard Fenella whisper from far away.

"Maybe we should leave them alone," Nicola murmured from just as far.

"The bloke who played Cash in the movie didn't kiss *that* good," Honor noted blandly.

Regardless of their onlookers and the conversation they were holding, Cash's focus was entirely on Abby. He kept kissing her as if they were the only ones in the room, and she kissed him back the same way.

"Honor, shush," Nicola snapped quietly. "Let's go."

"We can't go. Abby's going to town with me," Fenella said, and on that, with disappointment at the brevity of their kiss (and the fact they had an audience who wouldn't shut the fuck up and get the hell out) Cash's head came up. Instead of pulling away, he slid his nose alongside Abby's.

"I said, *let's go*." Cash heard that Nicola's voice was now getting sharper, if not louder.

"Are you okay?" Abby repeated in a whisper, her eyes on his.

"Yes," Cash replied, his voice vibrating low. "I'm very okay."

And this was true.

Regardless of their current circumstances, he'd never felt so fucking okay in his life.

Abby's brows drew together and her mouth twitched in a way that it looked like she wasn't sure whether to smile or to frown.

"Abby, are we going to town?" Fenella called, and Cash's hand flexed where it still held Abby's jaw. Not in a demonstration of affection, instead in a reflexive action denoting his restrained desire to wring Fenella's neck.

"Um..." Abby muttered, her mouth deciding it wanted to smile, which it did. "We were coming to tell you that we're going to town. We need your car."

That got Cash's full attention.

"My car?" he asked as he dropped his hand from her jaw.

"Yes, your car," Abby answered.

"Town is a two-minute walk away," Cash told her.

"I know," Abby replied.

"Why do you need my car?" Cash inquired.

Her smile turned mischievous. "Because I want to drive it."

Cash burst out laughing and both his arms went around her, pulling her into his body.

"Does that mean we're going to town?" Fenella semi-yelled, like they were three rooms down, not fifteen feet away.

Once he'd sobered, Cash looked at his cousin. "You're going to town."

Abby's body melted into his and her head tipped back further to smile at him.

"You're going to have to walk me down to the car," she whispered.

"I know," he whispered back.

"*Now* can I get to the business of preparing for one hundred guests to descend tonight? Or do you girls want me to go into town with you, just in case Abby gets lost?" Nicola asked, but for the first time since they arrived last night, she looked cheerful, if not her normal cheerful.

"You go, Mummy. We'll be fine," Fenella assured Nicola as Cash started to lead Abby to the door.

"I'm glad to hear that since you've lived two minutes from town since you were ten years old," Nicola mumbled as she headed busily out the door, casting a smile back at Abby and Cash before she disappeared.

Honor gave them a small wave and followed her mother. Cash walked Abby and Fenella to his and Abby's room to get his keys.

However, when his fingers closed around the keys on the bureau, the warm draught he'd forgotten with the arrival of Abby and her entourage came back. It was stronger this time, almost insistent, and it felt like it was trying to prevent him from picking up the ring.

It disappeared again when his fingers closed around the keys and Cash's hand moved away from the bureau.

He shook off the bizarre feeling thinking it was just the castle. The place was centuries old, it likely had hot and cold draughts everywhere.

He escorted Abby and Fenella down to the old stables. The stables were now a five car garage where Alistair and his family kept their (far too expensive for Alistair's circumstances) cars and where Cash had parked the Maserati last night.

Fenella folded her body into the passenger seat and Cash stood in the driver's open door with Abby.

She tipped her head back to look up at him and he could see the excitement on her face at the prospect of driving his car.

"Thanks for letting me drive your car," she murmured.

He put his hand to her neck and teased, "I'm thinking maybe I should have asked you if you were a good driver before giving you my keys."

She grinned and leaned into him before she replied, "I'm not only a good driver, I'm a *granny* driver."

Cash smiled at her amusing description of her driving style and squeezed her neck before asking, "Do you know how to drive a stick?"

Her grin turned playful as she exclaimed, "Of course! I'm half-American, you know."

"That's why I'm asking," he retorted.

She shook her head, her soft hair sliding on his hand, her face telling him she wasn't going to stoop to a response.

Cash went on, "Call me when you're heading back. I'll meet you at the gate."

She nodded, got up on her toes, hand to his stomach, and touched her mouth to his.

He felt her touch, the warmth of her body and the excitement in her eyes all with a heady intensity that was not unusual with Abby, however it was, in that moment, significantly more profound.

When her mouth moved away, her eyes caught his and her soft, tender look told him she'd felt the same.

Any vestiges of Cash's earlier dark mood melted away.

With effort (for he vastly preferred spending the morning in other pursuits with Abby, say, sexually christening another room in the castle), he dropped his hand.

She got in.

He slammed the door and returned her wave, nodded to Fenella, left the garage and headed up the steep hill to the gate.

As he climbed, he heard his car start and he turned to watch her roar out of the garage, *not* like a granny driver, but instead like an Indy car driver.

Then he stood watching as the car turned on a screech of tires into the long, steep, winding lane that led through the wood to the main road that skirted the town.

And he continued to watch, body now frozen, as she raced down the lane, nearly missing the hairpin turn at the bottom, two tires in the turf at the side of the lane.

He still watched from his high vantage point as she negotiated the lane, brake lights blazing the entire way.

Even so, it seemed she was picking up speed as the high performance sports car hurtled down the hill and she was clearly just keeping it on the road.

A feeling of foreboding swept over him and before his mind made the conscious decision to do so, he started running. He didn't keep to the lane but took the more direct path, sprinting through the trees on the hill at the side of the castle, his eyes on the car as he went.

It, with Abby *in* it, was accelerating and visibly out of control.

He dodged trees as he ran, watching as she jumped the curb and drove through the turf, brake lights glowing but not slowing, straight toward the high, thick, stone wall that surrounded Penmort estate.

He made it to the bottom of the hill just as the car slammed into the wall with an ugly, loud crash of crunching, twisting metal.

At the sight and sound of Abby in his car slamming into a wall, Cash didn't slow even as his mind erased and a blind panic filled him.

He was tearing across the field toward the smoking car when his blank mind saturated.

Memories collided in his brain, overlapping each other, one crowding the other out as Cash ran.

Abby, tall, exquisite, arresting, wearing winter white standing in the door at the pub.

Abby telling him he looked good in glasses.

Abby's eyes on him, soft and reverential, after she woke from her nap.

The fresh, sweet taste of Abby when he kissed her after she'd sipped at her bizarre cocktail.

In bed, Abby and her cat snuggling into him and falling asleep while he worked.

Abby excitedly babbling about how much she loved cashmere.

Abby, looking classic and elegant, standing in his arms in his office.

The strange, poignant sleeping positions Abby would assume, always close, always in the protective curve of his arm.

He reached the car and saw the demolished bonnet folded into itself and the airbags inflated before both seats of the car.

Cash didn't give a thought to his car, only to one of its occupants.

He yanked open the driver's door to see Abby was shoved back behind the airbag. Her head turned to him, eyes wide but blinking, face pale.

She was breathing, moving, there was no blood in sight, no bones protruding, and relief ripped through him.

She whispered, "Fenella."

Cash pushed his arm between Abby and the airbag. "You first, love. Then I'll take care of Fenella."

He found the release on the seatbelt as she murmured, "It was stuck in go."

Cash put one arm under her knees, the other behind her back and cautiously slid her out of her seat, doing a quick body scan as he did so.

What he didn't do was reply.

"Cash," she called softly as he straightened, Abby cradled in his arms, and started striding away from the wreckage. His eyes went to hers and she went on, "The car was stuck in go."

"Quiet, darling," Cash muttered.

"I couldn't get it to stop," she whispered.

He knew that.

He knew it.

And he knew why.

But he couldn't think of that now.

He had to focus on Abby. If he didn't focus on Abby, he would do something he would regret. Something that would take him away from her for he'd be in prison. Prison would mean that he would really lose Abby instead of just experiencing the gut-twisting, soul-destroying thought of losing her while watching her slam into a wall in his car.

"Quiet, Abby," he repeated gently. "We'll talk later." He stopped close to a tree and set her on her feet but didn't release his hold on her. "Can you stand?"

She tipped her head to look at him and pulled her hair away from her face with a visibly trembling hand, but she nodded.

Cash left her and jogged back to the car. Fenella was carefully alighting and he put an arm about her waist. She looked up at him, speechless for once, wearing the same wide-eyed, pale expression as Abby. He supported her weight and walked her back to Abby.

When they arrived at Abby's side, Fenella spoke. "What just happened?"

Abby's eyes went to Cash and she replied, "I don't know."

But by the look on her face, he knew that she did.

At that moment Suzanne, in her sporty Mercedes two-seater, turned from the main road into the lane. Her eyes were on the wrecked car and she slowed to a halt.

"Wait here," Cash ordered and jogged to Suzanne.

She was out of the car before he arrived.

"My God, Cash, what happened?" she breathed, eyes on the wreckage then they turned to him and did a sweep of his body. "Are you okay?"

Cash didn't answer, instead he asked, "Do you have your mobile?"

She was staring at him and her eyes moved to Abby and Fenella.

"Suzanne," Cash's voice was low with impatience, "mobile."

Her head gave a jerk and she looked back at Cash mumbling, "Of course."

She leaned into the car, got her bag and pulled out her mobile, handing it to Cash.

Cash was touching numbers when he demanded, "Go back to the house, get Honor's Land Rover, come back and pick up Abby and Fenella."

He finished dialling, pressed go and put the mobile to his ear as she started, "But—"

"Do it!" Cash snapped, and he heard his call to the police connect as Suzanne hustled back into her car and took off up the lane.

Cash walked back to Abby and Fenella as he reported the wreck. The minute he arrived at Abby's side, he slid his arm around her shoulders and curled her front to front. Both her arms wrapped around his waist and she pressed her cheek to his chest as he kept talking.

After he made his report, he disconnected and looked down at Abby.

"The police are coming. Suzanne is getting Honor's car so she can take you back to the castle."

Abby nodded mutely and Cash carried on.

"Glue yourself to Nicola's side," he ordered.

She pressed deeper into him and nodded again.

He continued, "I'll bring the police to you." His eyes turned to Fenella. "Nicola needs to do something, you get Abby off the castle grounds immediately."

Fenella replied instantly, "Yes, Cash."

He heard cars approaching and turned to see Suzanne's Mercedes and Nicola's Audi headed their way. Honor and Nicola were both in the Audi.

Cash walked Abby and Fenella toward the cars and watched all the women alight.

"What on earth?" Nicola whispered as they arrived, her eyes on the wrecked Maserati.

Honor's face was ashen and her eyes were on Fenella. Then they moved to Cash and he watched a spark of anger flare before she subdued it.

"There was an accident," Cash announced unnecessarily. "Take Fenella and Abby back to the castle. I'll wait for the police."

"Is everyone okay?" Nicola asked, her eyes doing a scan first of her daughter then of Abby.

"We're fine, Mummy," Fenella assured her mother, linking her arm through Abby's, gently disengaging her from Cash and moving them both toward the Audi. "Let's get back. I *seriously* need a cup of tea."

Fenella, Cash was surprised to see, took charge and got the women in the car and Honor drove the Audi very slowly back up the lane.

Suzanne stayed behind, her eyes on Cash.

He pulled his gaze from the Audi and spared Suzanne a glance before engaging her phone.

"Cash—" she began.

"Not now, Suzanne," Cash returned, entering James's number into the mobile as he spoke.

She, as usual, pushed it.

"Cash, you should know. Alistair—"

His eyes cut to her and in a voice vibrating with barely controlled rage, Cash repeated, "Not now."

She watched him a moment and he heard James answer.

He walked away from her.

She got in her car and drove to the castle as Cash gave James his orders.

❧ ❧ ❧

Nicola, her three daughters, Abby and Cash were in the drawing room. Alistair had left early that morning to do errands unknown and had not yet arrived back home.

Everyone except Cash was sipping tea as Abby then Fenella told their stories to the police.

There were a good deal of knowing looks exchanged between the sisters, even Suzanne, and Abby.

Nicola ignored the knowing looks and held her body rigid as if the slightest movement might shatter it.

Cash also held his body rigid, but in an effort to control his impulse to hunt down Alistair Charles Beaumaris and split his skull open against the nearest hard surface.

The police were making preparations to leave when Alistair surged through the door.

The room, already fraught, went wired.

Abby was seated on the sofa, Cash standing by her side. The moment Alistair entered, her hand shot out, her fingers closed around his and squeezed.

Tight.

Cash's body stayed taut for a moment then released and he squeezed back.

Alistair looked, Cash noted with repugnance, excited.

His eyes swept the room and fell on Cash. The excitement melted and for a moment Alistair looked startled before he hid it.

"What happened?" Alistair asked, walking further into the room. "When I drove up, I saw your car wrecked, there's police crawling all over it. What's going on?"

"Abby had an accident," Nicola said, her voice soft, her eyes on Alistair and they were intense. She stood and continued, "Fenella was in the car with her."

Cash watched as Alistair blanched, then his gaze moved to Fenella. "Are you all right?"

"Fine," Fenella replied, but her tone was sharp.

Alistair looked to Abby. "Abby, how are you?"

"Alive," Abby answered, her voice cold, her eyes shooting icicles at his uncle across the expanse.

Alistair's gaze skittered across the room, avoiding everyone else's and coming to rest on the police. "Well thank goodness everyone's all right."

"Yes," Nicola declared firmly. "Thank goodness."

The police, who had paused in their exit, began to move again, one of the men saying, "We have everything we need. We'll call if—"

Suzanne interrupted him. "Excuse me."

They stopped and turned to her as she went on, something shifting on her face, looking at first calculating then moving swiftly to demure.

Cash braced.

Suzanne kept talking. "I'm sorry, I mean, this is probably nothing. A freak coincidence but..."

She trailed off, playing what Cash knew was a game, as did Abby. Abby scooted closer to him on the couch and her hand tightened in his as they waited for Suzanne to speak.

"What is it?" one of the police asked.

"Well, it's only that, Cash here..." She motioned to Cash with a flick of her wrist and Abby's hand flexed spasmodically in his. "See, his father died in a car wreck," Suzanne finished, what sounded inanely.

Both policemen shifted awkwardly on their feet, their eyes going to Cash.

"I'm sorry, sir," one of the police mumbled.

"No," Suzanne went on to announce. "You don't understand. Foul play was suspected."

Cash felt Abby's body jerk through his hand and his own eyes riveted on Suzanne.

"It was?" the policeman asked.

"Yes, indeed it was," Suzanne answered blithely. "They never pinned it on anyone but, you know, it does seem an odd coincidence that Cash's father *might* have been murdered and here we are, decades later, and Cash's expensive, high performance, Italian sports car, which was, I assume, running smoothly last night during its trek from Somerset to Devon, this morning, with no warning, strangely both accelerates on its own *and* its brakes go out, *both at the same time*." Suzanne licked her lips, sat back in her chair, and finished. "I mean, don't you think that's utterly *bizarre*?"

Alistair cut in and all eyes moved to him as he declared, "Nothing was ever proved."

"I know nothing was ever proved, Alistair," Suzanne shot back. "That doesn't change the fact that foul play was suspected. The police, you'll no doubt agree, should have all the facts." Her eyes moved to the police. "It was a long time ago, but I'm sure there's still a case file somewhere."

Alistair moved further into the room, his eyes narrowing on Suzanne.

"Nothing was ever proved," he insisted.

"You said that already," Suzanne returned mildly.

Alistair's gaze flicked to Cash then to the police. "There's no reason to dredge that up again just because of an accident. We're planning a celebration tonight and it will only serve to distress my family, my nephew—"

"It does seem weird," Fenella piped up, interrupting Alistair.

"Very peculiar," Honor added.

Cash saw Nicola's mouth twitch in a way that looked like she was trying to control a smile before she turned her face away.

"You see," Suzanne smoothly carried on. "Anthony Beaumaris was a rich and powerful man. Now his son is. It could be someone has it out for him and his family. We could all be in danger."

"That's ridiculous," Alistair spat.

Nicola turned to her husband. "I don't know if it's ridiculous considering Abby and Fenella were in that car. If someone's after Cash, they couldn't know Abby would drive his car. It was the first time Abby ever touched the steering wheel. And it could have been any one of us sitting beside her. If someone intends Cash harm, what happened this morning proves that we could all be in danger."

"You're not in danger," Alistair retorted.

"I was today," Fenella reminded him, and Alistair's narrowed eyes shot to her.

Then Alistair turned to the police declaring, "This is rubbish."

"It doesn't sound like rubbish to me," Honor commented. "How often does this happen? I mean, this kind of thing doesn't happen to most people even once, but now it's happened to Cash *twice*? That's just plain weird."

"We'll look into it," one of the police muttered, obviously desiring not to be caught in the middle of a family squabble, and they again turned to leave.

"I think that's a good idea," Suzanne encouraged, standing and giving them a charming smile as she moved their way. Cash watched her eyes warming to an inviting, suggestive allure that Cash was used to having directed at him. She touched one of the police on his arm and murmured, "I'll just walk you to your car."

Watching her walk the police out, Cash reconsidered allowing Suzanne to stay at the castle.

And definitely Honor and Fenella could stay.

Abby's hand released his as she rose and looked at Nicola.

"I'm so sorry. Every time I'm here it seems I'm having some kind of acci—" she started.

Cash watched, surprised, as Nicola's eyes sliced to Abby and her voice was unusually forceful when she interrupted, "Don't you apologise. You have *nothing* to apologise for. Not one thing."

At the fierceness in her tone everyone in the room went still except Cash. He moved to Abby's side and slid an arm around her waist.

Abby and Nicola stared at each other and finally Nicola blinked and turned away.

"Right!" she exclaimed shrugging off her mood. "I've a million and one things to do. Honor, go rescue those policemen from Suzanne, I need her. Fenella, you take a rest and when you feel up to it, find me. Abby, you and Cash try to salvage your afternoon." Her gaze turned to Alistair. "And you..." she paused giving him an unreadable look, "do whatever it is you do."

Then she hurried from the room.

Honor glanced at Cash and Abby before she followed her mother.

Cash put pressure on Abby's waist and started to lead her from the room, but he was intercepted by Alistair putting a hand to his arm.

"Cash," he started. "Son, you don't believe—"

Cash's eyes had gone to his arm when Alistair touched him but they cut to his uncle as Cash pulled his arm away.

"Don't ever," Cash's voice was lethal, "call me 'son.'"

Cash saw red started creeping up his uncle's neck as Alistair took a step back and Cash continued moving, guiding Abby to their room.

Once they arrived, he shut the door and Abby stormed deep into the room.

Then she started pacing.

She also started ranting, however she did this quietly.

"I do *not* believe," she hissed, "that Alistair tried to *kill* you."

"Abby—" Cash started, but she talked over him.

"On the day of his anniversary! Valentine's Day!" she snapped.

"Nicola has been planning this for nine months! Nine!" she clipped, lifting both hands up to Cash to show him nine fingers. "And he attempts the murder of *my* boyfriend," she thumped her chest for emphasis, "on Nicola's special day!"

Cash bit back a smile at her words and tried again, "Darling, calm —" but she kept going.

"He tried to kill you on Valentine's Day," she repeated. "And nearly killed his *stepdaughter*!"

Cash leaned his shoulders against the door and crossed his arms on his chest deciding to let her get it out. She needed to vent so they could move on with the weekend and she could keep her wits about her. She was going to need them.

He watched her pace and rant, her arms waving around. He thought, regardless of their murderous circumstances (now *both* Cash and Abby were on different firing lines), she looked quite adorable in her muted fury.

And while he watched her something suddenly occurred to him. Something he hadn't considered before. Something vital that freed a lock deep inside him that he didn't know was secured.

Throughout their short relationship, she'd reminded him of his mother. Not in good ways, but in bad. Her mood swings, erratic behaviour and the depth of her pain, which he could not fathom, nor did he think he could do anything about.

He thought about Abby manically packing her bag, taking too many pills to kill unknown pain, raving about a ghost.

He was used to this bizarre and alarming behaviour from his mother. He was used to a life of hour to hour, even sometimes minute to minute, not knowing where her crazed mind would take her, dragging Cash along with her.

And he'd accepted it from Abby, but held himself aloof, protecting himself with an exit plan.

But Abby wasn't mentally ill.

Abby was simply spirited. She also had been in the final throes of escaping a deep grief that had her imprisoned in its grip for four years.

She was now over that grief. She had let her guard down and given herself to him.

Not only that, she was putting herself in danger for no other reason but to make his legacy safe. It had nothing to do with her, but she was doing it anyway.

Risking her life.

For Cash.

When his thoughts came back to the room, the edge he'd carried all his life had faded away. The peace he felt with Abby settled around him like a warm, nurturing shroud.

And at that moment, Cash Fraser vowed he was going to keep that peace and the only person in his life who'd ever given it to him.

Not for a while.

Forever.

Abby completely missed his life-altering resolution and was still seething.

"It took everything I had not to walk right across the room and *kick him in the shin*."

He grinned at the visual she created, uncrossed his arms and walked to her as she stood, no longer pacing but planted and solid and glaring at him.

He stopped close and slid his arms around her. "Are you done?"

"No," she snapped.

He waited. She was silent.

Then she took in a deep breath and said, "Okay, maybe I'm done."

Cash burst out laughing and while doing so he felt her body relax. She leaned into him and wrapped her arms around him.

He looked down at her to see she'd tipped her head back to watch him laugh. The anger had gone out of her face. The awe he'd seen only once had replaced it.

"I love it when you laugh," she whispered.

That shroud drew closer, grew warmer and his arms tightened around her.

He didn't comment on her words, instead he asked, "Are you okay?"

"You mean after crashing your fabulously expensive sports car into a wall?" she queried in return.

He felt his mouth twitch. "Yes, after that."

"Pretty much," she replied. "Though now, if we have to make a quick getaway, we have no wheels."

"A rental will be delivered within the hour," Cash told her.

She looked surprised for a minute before she smiled and relaxed further into him.

"Are *you* okay?" she asked.

"No, but I will be," he answered.

Her arms gave him a squeeze and her head tipped to the side. "What do you think Suzanne is up to?"

"No idea," Cash replied.

Though he did have an idea. However he was willing to ride it out and see where it took them.

"Surprising ally," Abby whispered.

Cash bent his head and put his mouth to the skin below her ear, not wanting to talk about Suzanne, not wanting to talk *at all*, and murmured, "Indeed."

As his tongue touched her neck, Cash felt her body tremble against his and immediately he started walking her backward toward the bed.

She didn't resist and her hands slid up his back, but she commented softly, "You seem weird today."

Cash's mouth glided to her jaw then across her cheek to her lips.

"Not weird," he said against her mouth.

"I—" she started, but her legs hit the bed and Cash kept moving, forcing her body to fall back, his going with her, his mouth taking hers in a kiss before he landed on top of her on the bed.

One of her hands sliding in his hair, she kissed him back.

They would talk later, Cash thought, before his mind cleared of everything but Abby, her perfume, her soft body under his, her hands on him.

Right then, Cash was intent on salvaging the afternoon.

26

NICOLA

Abby stood at the mirror over the bureau spritzing perfume at her ears and wrists.

Cash had showered first while she dozed in bed and he dressed while she was taking a long, relaxing bath. When she was towelling off, he'd called through the door that James was there and he had to go talk to him. He didn't explain why James was there and he'd been gone before Abby had a chance to ask.

That afternoon Cash had left their room once, to go get them some food for a light lunch. After making love and eating, they'd spent hours in bed, cuddling and whispering to each other about what could be causing Nicola's strange mood, what was behind Suzanne's even stranger behaviour and both their surprise at Fenella's demonstrated fortitude.

Well, Abby did most of the whispering. Cash spent his time holding her, running his hands over her skin and gliding his lips along her shoulder, her neck, her jaw, her collarbone (and other places besides).

He would, however, often mutter things like, "Mm," or "I've no idea," or "Let's just see how it plays out, shall we?"

Other than that, he seemed pretty happy to let Abby talk her way through things using him as a mostly silent sounding board.

Abby noted that Cash was completely at ease with all the nefarious goings-on.

Abby was not.

Regardless of spending the afternoon in bed with Cash and her relaxing bath, Abby was wired.

Although Cash appeared laidback about the attempt on his life, he was that morning more intense with Abby than ever.

Cash, Abby thought, was always a bit intense but this was different.

Not in a bad way. In a good one.

A *really* good one.

One that made that blooming hope in her heart start to blossom out of control even though she knew it was stupid, stupid, *stupid* to let that feeling flourish.

That afternoon she felt his intensity of the morning somehow settled even though it didn't diminish. It was as if he'd come to some conclusion.

Although Abby wanted to know what that conclusion was, she didn't ask him to share, scared of what it could mean.

Hope and his actions were pressing her to think it would be good.

Reason and her indisputably bad luck made her think it would be bad.

The time was nigh for what would have been the end of their arrangement. She was to pretend to be his girlfriend for the three weeks prior to the weekend at the castle then continue for one week after.

Then it would be over.

And, Abby thought, maybe now that he was close to getting what he'd worked so hard for, it was time for him to move on to his life as master of the castle, a life without Abby.

The rational part of her brain reminded her that Cash had asked her to move in to the castle with him.

The much stronger irrational part of her brain reminded her that her luck sucked and she'd learned the hard way that all good things came to an end usually heartbreakingly sooner than she expected.

On that thought she picked up the diamond bracelet Cash gave her and struggled with the complicated clasp for a moment before securing it.

She stared at her reflection in the mirror.

Her great-grandmother's gown was a bold red satin with a long flowing skirt. The bodice came up in a soft, inverted V at the base of her throat where there was an opening through which a wide band of satin was fed. This band held up the bodice at her chest and went over her exposed shoulders, crossing between her shoulder blades and holding the dress in place at her sides. The rest of the back was open with a drape at the small. The hem of the skirt swept the floor with a decorous hint of a train.

Abby wore a pair of red pumps with satin-covered, pencil-thin, four-inch heels, pointed toes covered entirely with bugle beads and complicated, thin, beaded ankle straps.

She'd dried her hair with curlers in to give it volume, parted it at the side and swept the sections back softly in a twisted, loose knot at the nape of her neck.

Regardless that the satin fit smooth and snug to her skin, she'd somehow managed (magic?) successfully to hide Cassandra's protection amulet that hung from a thin silver chain to rest between her breasts under the dress.

She'd done her makeup in the only one word style she had, though it was emphasised when she spoke it aloud, the look was "*Drama!*"

The only other adornment she wore was Cash's bracelet and a pair of her mother's ruby studs in her ears, the rubies surrounded by small diamonds.

She thought, assessing herself, she didn't look half bad.

"Please, God," she mumbled to the mirror. "Don't let me die in great-granny's dress."

After her muttered prayer, the door opened and Cash walked in.

Abby turned to look at him and her breath caught in her chest.

He was wearing a black tuxedo, clearly expensive, with an immaculate cut that made it obvious it was tailored just for him. His crisp, white shirt had a series of pin-tucks at the chest, there was a flash of gold at his cuffs, but other than that it was simple and, on Cash, alarmingly masculine.

Abby felt her knees go weak and she had to put her hand to the bureau to hold herself upright.

She caught the hungry look in his eyes as they swept the length of her and her fingers clutched the edge of the bureau as her weak knees were joined with a full-body tremor.

She had the distinct feeling he liked the dress.

Deciding something must be said before she spontaneously combusted under his hot gaze, she muttered, "You look nice."

His eyes, resting in the region of her belly, cut to hers, and he replied, "You don't."

Abby felt her body jolt at his words, thinking she'd misinterpreted his look, and whispered, "I don't?"

He started walking toward her slowly, his eyes holding hers captive.

"No." His voice was low and rough. "The word 'nice' describes a lot of things. What it does not describe is you in that fucking dress."

Abby stood solid as he stopped close in front of her and his hand came up. The tips of his fingers slid down the satin at her side from the curve of her breast to her waist where his hand flattened and his fingers curled, pressing forcefully into her flesh, searing her there like a brand.

It was safe to say she wasn't wrong in her first conclusion about how Cash felt about her dress.

"Cash—" she breathed, but he talked over her.

"After this is done, we have to talk," he announced.

At the serious look on his face, Abby's worry came crashing back.

She swallowed her fear before querying, "About what?"

Cash didn't hesitate with his reply. "About you. About me. About our future."

Her heart hammering, the fear taking control, her voice was higher when she inquired, "What about it?"

His fingers at her waist pulled her closer and his head dipped further to look down at her. "Not now. Later. Now we need to focus on getting through the night."

Abby stared at him, holding back the fear (just barely) and requested, "Maybe you can give me a hint."

His hand slid around her back, it encountered skin and stilled for a brief moment then pressed in, moving her to him.

His face dipped closer. "Things have changed."

"What things?" Abby asked.

"Everything," Cash replied firmly yet mysteriously.

Abby had no idea what that meant, but before she could ask, he touched his lips to hers.

When his head came up, he muttered, "Now, darling, you need to focus on tonight."

"Okay," she agreed, but even as she did, she didn't.

There was no way in hell she'd be able to focus on taking down a ghosty she-bitch when Cash's life was also in danger and her future with Cash was in question.

On that thought, her brain reminded her of her pledge to live the time she had with Cash to the fullest.

So their upcoming, scary-as-heck talk might mean the end.

Now they were still in the middle.

Not to mention, she might end the night flung out a window.

Obviously there was no time like the present.

Therefore she decided to carry on like there was going to be no end. Or, if there was, however that might come, she was intent to give him something which he could use to remember her even after she was gone.

She lifted her hand to rest on his cheek and whispered, "I have something for you."

She saw a flash in his eyes but before she could read it or lose her courage, she pulled away and walked to the bedside table.

She opened the drawer and retrieved a small, black velvet box tied in a black satin ribbon.

She came back to him, held the box in the palm of her hand between them and caught his eyes.

"Happy Valentine's Day," she murmured.

His gaze held hers for a moment then dropped to the box. She saw a muscle leap in his jaw, a reaction that usually indicated he was angry. She bit her lip in concern but his hand came up, he took the box from her, pulled at the bow and tossed the loosened ribbon on the bureau before he flipped open the box with his thumb.

Inside was a pair of cufflinks Abby purchased while out shopping with Jenny the day Angus called. They were gold, set with oval onyx. Seeing them, she thought they were smart, handsome, elegant and *very* Cash, therefore she felt at the time he had to have them.

Now, spying the cufflinks in his cuffs, also gold, probably more expensive than her gift, she thought they were kind of lame.

How many men needed *two* pairs of gold cufflinks?

Hurriedly she told him, "I didn't think when I got them. I just liked them. Of course you already have a pair." His eyes went from the cufflinks to hers, their black depths were blazing but she couldn't quite read why, so she blathered on. "You don't have to wear them. If you don't like them, I can take them back and find something else. A tie pin or—"

She stopped talking when he caught her in his arms, jerking her forward almost violently. She crashed into his body and his arms held her tight as he buried his face in her neck.

"I like them," he said into her neck, and Abby lifted her hands to his upper arms and held on.

"You do?" she whispered.

He didn't take his face from her neck but his arms tightened to the point he was squeezing the air out of her.

"Yes," he replied. "I fucking well do."

Okay, he was saying the F-word and she didn't know if that was good or bad.

However she had a priority concern.

"Cash," she wheezed. "I can't breathe."

He let her go instantly, took a step back and immediately exchanged his cufflinks for hers.

Abby watched this, and no matter how stupid she knew it was, her careening thoughts shifted back to hope.

After he'd completed his task, without looking at her he went to his briefcase that was sitting beside one of the armchairs in the turret. He put the briefcase in the seat of the chair, bent to open it and came back to her, carrying his own small black velvet box, this one tied with an ivory satin bow.

He again got close and leaned in. His fingers curling around her wrist, he lifted her hand palm up and deposited the box in it.

The whole while he did this, Abby stared up at him.

He let her wrist go and put a hand to her neck.

"I hesitate to give you a gift after the last time," he murmured, his voice low but teasing. "However, it *is* Valentine's Day."

She pulled herself out of her trance and looked down at the box. She lifted her other hand and yanked at the bow. She did as he'd done and tossed the ribbon to the bureau before opening it.

In it was a pair of extraordinary diamond chandelier earrings. A not-small-by-any-stretch-of-the-imagination diamond at the base led down to a complicated fall of diamonds set in platinum.

She stared at the earrings, frozen in shock not only at their beauty but at their obvious cost.

She didn't know what to do and had no clue what to say.

She lifted her eyes to his and stupidly whispered the first thought that came to her mind, "You one-upped my present."

At her words, he threw back his head and burst out laughing, his arms snaking around her to pull her again tightly to him.

She absorbed his laughter into her body and held on to his waist.

He pulled back slightly and touched a finger to her ear before saying softly, "As charming as those are, darling, I want you to wear my diamonds."

"Cash," Abby replied, her fingers curling around the box still in her hand even as they went straight to her ears to take out the rubies. "You'd have to pay me *not* to wear your diamonds."

He chuckled at her words and held her loosely as she switched her jewellery and then leaned into him to peer around and check herself in the mirror.

"They're exquisite," she breathed.

Cash's arms flexed around her and she straightened to look up at him.

"Yes," he murmured, his eyes on her face. "Exquisite."

Abby felt her body melt into his as her arms wrapped around his waist.

"I want to kiss you," she told him. "But it'll mess up my lip gloss."

As his head descended, he muttered, "Fuck your lip gloss."

In the end, not only did she have to repair her lip gloss, they had a post-gift-exchange, Valentine's Day make-out session that might have been so long and intense, Abby thought it should be entered into a record book.

Needless to say they were late descending the stairs to join the party.

❧ ❧ ❧

"Jennifer, don't get drunk," Mrs. Truman snapped at Jenny.

"I'm *not* getting drunk," Jenny snapped back.

"Pumpkin, you're getting drunk," Kieran put in on a smile.

Jenny shot a glare at her husband and then tipped back her champagne glass, draining it down her throat.

Abby pressed her lips together and her gaze locked with Cash's. He was standing at her side holding a glass of champagne, looking cultured and amused and almost criminally attractive.

Abby tore her eyes away from Cash and studied her friends.

Jenny was wearing a fantastic champagne-coloured strapless silk dress with princess seams, built-in boning and a mermaid-tail skirt. There was a tiny chiffon ruffle along the bodice. Her hair was swept back in an elaborate updo and she looked amazing.

Kieran wore a well-cut dinner jacket and was more than his usual handsome.

Mrs. Truman looked like The Queen times about five thousand. She was wearing a boxy grey gown. From enormous shoulder pads to hips and down the long sleeves, the gown was elaborately sequined and beaded. The silvery-grey chiffon skirt was gathered effusively at the bottom of the sequins at her hips, floating down to her stout-heeled, square-toed, dove-grey satin granny pumps.

Three hours ago, when she and Cash finally drifted down to join the already-started proceedings, they were all there, drinking champagne, eating from the trays of hors d'ouevres that were being passed around and mingling with the guests.

The minute Abby's eyes hit Mrs. Truman, she thought the only thing missing was a priceless tiara extracted for the festivities from the Tower of London and a dozen bodyguards.

A waiter passed and Jenny expertly nabbed another glass of champagne like she'd attended champagne-glass-bearing-waitered-trayed-gala-affairs every weekend since birth.

Abby looked at Mrs. Truman and caught the woman's eye roll as Trevor, Alistair and Nicola's practically silent servant got close and said something in Cash's ear.

Trevor then melted away and Cash's hand came to her waist as his mouth went to her ear.

"James is at the door. I have to speak with him," he murmured.

Abby turned her face to his. "Why is James here?"

Cash touched his nose to hers and whispered, "I'll explain later."

He pulled away and looked at Kieran.

"If Nicola leaves this room, you get Abby to safety. Our room upstairs is closest," Cash ordered. Kieran nodded and Cash looked back at Abby, his voice gentling when he finished. "I won't be a moment, darling."

With that, Abby watched him saunter away, his long legs carrying him across the room swiftly, his gait powerful, his strides wide, and everyone he passed glanced at him with unconcealed admiration.

Abby sighed.

"Girlfriend, we need to talk," Jenny muttered in Abby's ear and Abby looked down at her friend.

Jenny was staring at her, eyes serious, the set of her face determined.

"What? Why?" Abby asked as Jenny took her hand, made their excuses to Mrs. Truman and Kieran at which both of whom scowled but, Abby thought, both for different reasons. Kieran, Abby suspected, because he knew what Jenny was going to say. Mrs. Truman, Abby guessed, because she did *not*.

Jenny led Abby to a large window that faced the tor at the side of the castle. It was quiet, secluded and felt somehow removed from the busy hall.

Once there she turned Abby so that Abby faced her and Jenny's back was to the room.

"It's not a good time but it'll never be a good time and it's looking like the sooner the better," Jenny started ominously, and Abby blinked at her.

"What's not a good time?" Abby inquired.

"I've been thinking about this since it happened, wondering if I should say something, thinking I shouldn't but I can't help but think I should," Jenny stated, and Abby looked down at her friend, confused at her words and the tone of her voice which shook with emotion.

"Since what happened?" Abby asked.

"Since Cash and I had our little chat," Jenny answered.

Abby stared at her friend, stunned.

Her voice was breathy when she inquired, "Cash and you had a chat?"

Jenny nodded and went on, "That night all the girls came to dinner, he and I talked. It wasn't pleasant." Abby sucked in breath at this news as Jenny carried on, "I can see it." She hesitated and switched from nodding to shaking her head. "You, I can see you...I can see it happening."

Concerned, Abby moved closer to her friend, a woman who rarely couldn't find the words to express herself.

"Jenny, you aren't making any sense," she said softly.

"You've fallen in love with him," Jenny blurted, and Abby felt her eyes round.

"With who?" she asked idiotically.

"With Cash!" Jenny replied on a muted cry, then looked over her shoulder to see if anyone had heard to find that only Mrs. Truman had her eagle eyes on them. Jenny turned back. "You've fallen in love with Cash."

Abby felt her heart start beating faster, but she went into denial. "Jenny, I've known him three weeks."

"The night Ben brought you home from your first date you phoned me, woke me up and told me you were going to marry him. A year and a half later I was your maid of honour," Jenny reminded her.

This was true.

It was also true that the minute she laid eyes on Cash in that pub, she'd had a feeling that she'd only felt once in her life. It was the same feeling she had when Ben's eyes caught hers when she was standing at a coffee bar ordering her latte and Ben was standing at the end of it waiting for his.

Except with Cash that feeling was infinitely stronger.

Abby felt like someone threw a bag of bricks at her and it landed heavily against her belly.

"Jenny—" she started.

"Get out," Jenny talked over Abby, her eyes reading Abby's thoughts, her voice now urgent. "Get out now." She came closer and her fingers curled around Abby's. "Abby, honey, it kills me to tell you this, but he doesn't feel the same way."

Abby felt her body jerk as if she'd been struck at the same time the room started spinning.

She heard Jenny's voice come at her from far away asking if she was okay. Abby blinked several times and with a good deal of effort, she focused on Jenny.

"How do you know?" she whispered.

Jenny got even closer and whispered back, "He all but told me, Abby. He cares about you, that's obvious. He wants you to be happy, he even told me that. But he isn't in this for the long run, he told me that too."

Abby felt that bloom in her heart start to wither. "He mentioned something, but—"

Jenny gave her fingers a squeeze, cutting off her words. "Then you've got to get out now, before it's too late."

Even though the hope she'd been feeling started to fade away, Abby still whispered, "I can't."

"You *have* to Abby." Jenny's other hand grabbed Abby's and she held their hands tightly together between them. "He's a...I don't know. He's a *force of nature*," she said. "You're going to...hell, you're already caught in his magnetic field. When he cuts you loose, you're not going to want to be let go, but you won't have any choice. Abby..." she shook their hands between them, "it'll destroy you. You know it'll destroy you." She paused and her voice went low before she finished, "Again."

Abby closed her eyes and looked away.

She could try to fool herself that his behaviour meant they were developing something deeper.

What she couldn't do was ignore the fact that Cash told her best friend (of all people) that their relationship was finite.

He would never do that.

Unless it was.

Even though she knew she was living on borrowed time, she'd been unconsciously holding on to that hope in her heart, wanting more, wishing the magic was real.

Instead of yet another path that led to heart-wrenching despair.

But Abby knew better than that. She'd been taught that lesson time and again.

And every time Jenny had picked up the pieces.

She squeezed her eyes tight and clenched her teeth tighter as the pain of the dying dream of years filled with anguish ending in a life filled with magic seared through her soul.

She opened her eyes and looked at her friend's concerned face.

"He told me earlier tonight we had to talk about our future," she confided, her voice aching, her throat burning. "He's very astute. I'm guessing he's cottoned on to how I feel and wants to remind me where we stand."

"Abby—" Jenny started, but Abby kept talking as she squeezed their hands.

"Don't worry Jenny," she whispered. "Please, don't worry." Then she said out loud what she knew she had to do to guard her heart before, as Jenny surmised correctly, it was too late. "After tonight, it's over."

The word "over" came out in a croak as tears clawed their way up her throat, and Jenny let go of their hands and got even closer.

Her friend put her cheek to Abby's and in her ear she murmured, "I'm sorry, Abby, so sorry. I started this and now here you are. I'm so sorry."

"It's not your fault," Abby replied, gulping back tears, succeeding, in an extreme effort of will, at fighting them back before a single one was shed.

Jenny leaned back and her fingers curled around Abby's upper arm. "It is, but we won't argue that." Her hand tightened and she looked deep into Abby's eyes. "You'll get through this, girlfriend. You always do. I don't know anyone on this planet who's stronger than you."

At that Abby laughed, but there was not even a hint of humour in it.

Before more could be said, Mrs. Truman descended on their *tête-à-tête*.

"What are you two whispering about?" she demanded to know.

Jenny turned to Mrs. Truman but caught Abby's hand. "Nothing."

Mrs. Truman eyed Jenny, then she looked at Abby assessingly. "It doesn't look like nothing to me."

"It's nothing," Abby lied.

"Well," she said on an angry-to-be-left-out humph. "You two were so absorbed, you haven't noticed that something's happening."

Abby and Jenny looked into the room to see people were coming from all corners of the house, squeezing into the large space, making it small.

As she looked, Abby saw Cash arrive. His eyes scanned the room and for the first time in her life Abby wished both that she wasn't so tall and that she wasn't wearing a pair of elegant, expensive high-heeled shoes when Cash's eyes easily found her.

She watched as his powerful body wended its way through the crush toward them, and he arrived at the same time as Kieran.

Jenny dropped her hand as Cash got close, his arm moving along her waist, his chin dipped, and she saw his brows draw together as he examined her face.

"What's wrong?" he asked.

Abby swallowed, then lied, forcing her voice to sound cheerful, "Nothing."

His eyes shifted to Jenny for a mere moment and came back to her. They narrowed, his fingers dug into her waist, and he started, "Abby—" but people were tinkling their champagne glasses and Abby tore her gaze from him to glance over the crowd.

They were all looking in one direction and she could see Nicola and Alistair standing in front of the fireplace, a small pocket of space in front of them.

Honor, Fenella and Suzanne were at the edge of the crowd closest to Nicola and Alistair.

As Alistair lifted his hand for silence, conversation in the room died away.

"Thank you, thank you," Alistair's voice boomed pompously from his position as lord of the manor.

The smile on his face, even at Abby's distance, not only looked false, it did not reach his eyes.

He went on, "We, Nicola and I, thank you for coming. We thank you for being here to celebrate this, our special anniversary."

"Hear, hear," someone shouted, and Alistair bowed his head in a farcical attempt at noble.

Abby turned her attention to Nicola who didn't look thankful in the slightest. She looked pale, she looked tense and she looked weirdly expectant.

Alistair continued, lifting his glass, "Now, everyone, I hope you've charged your glasses so you can join us in toasting twenty-five years of—"

"One second," Nicola's voice cut in. It was pleasant as usual, however it was also raised and it carried across the expanse.

Alistair hesitated and looked down at his wife who did not meet his eyes.

"I would also like to thank you for coming," Nicola declared. "For it is, indeed, a special day."

There was shifting of feet and smiles, but something about the way Nicola looked, her tone, put Abby on edge.

Nicola kept talking.

"I've been married to this man at my side for twenty-five years," she announced unnecessarily. "Twenty-five extraordinarily *unhappy* years."

There were some chuckles and murmurs as many thought Nicola had flubbed her speech.

Abby, however, did not. Nor, she could tell by the way he tensed at her side, his arm curling her closer, did Cash.

"There wasn't abuse, not overtly," Nicola went on. Abby felt Cash's body jolt and the chuckling and murmurs stopped immediately as the room grew silent. "Mostly neglect. And, on occasion, cruelty. Not only to myself, but to my daughters."

"Oh dear," Mrs. Truman muttered as the feeling in the room turned uneasy.

Alistair's face, magnanimous a moment ago, had soured, indicating without words the veracity of Nicola's awful speech.

His hand came up to curl around her arm and he muttered, "Dearest—"

She yanked her arm free and gave him a cold look.

"I'm not, nor have I ever been your *dearest*," she informed him and looked back to the crowd. "I asked you all here tonight not so you could celebrate twenty-five years of a very, *very* bad marriage. But instead so I could publicly apologise to my daughters for being weak and not protecting them the way I should. For desiring for them a life without want and sacrificing a home filled with love in order to do it. And now what I ask of you is to lift your glasses in a toast. Not to the continuation of that bad marriage, but to the end of it." She turned back to Alistair and finished, "Because, *dearest*, tomorrow morning, my daughters and I are moving out. I want a divorce."

There were shocked gasps, excited murmurs and a good deal of uncomfortably shifting feet.

Except Mrs. Truman, who was chuckling.

She turned back to Abby and Cash and muttered loudly and with authority, (even though she had none), "Met him and was in his presence for about two seconds. Didn't like the look of him. Just desserts, I say."

Jenny's gaze shot to Abby's, and even with their heartbreaking conversation of moments before, they both emitted short, shocked but entirely unamused giggles.

Their giggles stuck in their throats and their eyes flew back to the fireplace when they heard Alistair's voice vibrating with fury demand, "How dare you!"

Nicola ignored him and lifted her glass, shouting, "A toast! To the end of the bad and heralding the beginning of the good!"

But she didn't get her glass to her lips.

Alistair's fingers closed around her wrist and he jerked her hand down, the champagne spilling all over Nicola's throat, chest and down the front of her elegant, black, strapless, bias-cut gown.

There were more stunned gasps but Cash didn't gasp. The instant Alistair's fingers curled around Nicola's wrist, he moved, pushing forward through the crowd toward the couple on display.

"You *bitch*! How *dare* you humiliate me in front of my friends?" Alistair demanded, getting in another jerk, causing the rest of the champagne to splash against Nicola's chest and also in her face, triggering another now-horrified murmur to race through the crowd.

Fenella got close to the couple.

Her body rigid, she demanded loudly, "Unhand Mummy!"

Alistair's eyes sliced to Fenella and he barked, "*This is none of your goddamned business!*"

It was then Cash arrived at the scene. He moved between Fenella and Alistair, positioning himself in front of the three sisters, his back to the crowd.

Even so, his deep voice carried when he ordered, "Take your hand off her."

Like a demented schoolboy who was abusing a toy, Alistair gave Nicola, who was now fighting his grip on her wrist, another hefty wrench and her entire body shook with it. So much she nearly came off her feet.

All three sisters pressed in behind Cash, but at Alistair's action, Cash's deadly voice cut through the room. "Take your hand off her," he repeated. "*Now.*"

Alistair, clearly mad in the face of Cash's warning, enraged tone, narrowed his frightening eyes at Cash. "Who do you think you are? This is *my* wife and *my* house. I'll do what I damn well please and I won't let the bastard son of a Scottish bitch-in-heat stand there telling me what to do!"

Abby felt as if all the air in the room was sucked away as, with a vicious tug, Nicola tore free of Alistair. She stepped aside and Abby watched in disbelief as Alistair, robbed of one victim, turned his eyes to another and he took a swing at Cash.

At this juncture two things happened at once.

One, Cash easily caught his uncle's fist in his hand, twisted his arm, twirling Alistair so his back was to Cash, and then he jerked Alistair's arm up forcing him to emit an ugly grunt of pain.

Two, Vivianna Wainwright materialised in the air above Alistair, her dress and hair drifting and snapping about her. Her eyes, cruel and filled with venomous hate, were on Alistair.

As the room went entirely still, Vivianna opened her mouth and screamed.

❧ 27 ❧

SHOWDOWN, PART ONE

Vivianna's scream filled the room and with it mingled other terrified noises, muted shrieks and urgent voices.

Then, moving as one, the crowd shifted, panicked, toward the door.

Except Abby, Jenny, Mrs. Truman and Kieran who all stood frozen staring at the scene in front of them.

And Nicola, Fenella, Suzanne and Honor who were gazing wide-eyed up at Vivianna.

And finally Alistair and Cash, both immobile, heads tipped back, Alistair's mouth agape, Cash's jaw set.

Vivianna moved.

She trailed the length of the mantel, her phantom arm out, melting through the vases and figurines it displayed. Some of them rocked, several fell crashing to the floor.

She picked up speed, whipping through the room in a ghostly frenzy, causing screams from the edges of the crowd who had not yet acquired escape. She shot through the light fixture hanging from the ceiling rose in the room's centre. The fixture swayed alarmingly, the crystals jingled, dust drifting down.

After that, she darted forward, toward Cash.

Abby strangled back a scream and barely checked an urge to dash forward as Cash released his restraining hold on his uncle. He bent into him, covering his uncle's body protectively as Vivianna descended and made a pass. Abby was so terrified she didn't process the fact that she saw Vivianna's trailing skirts drifting *over* Cash's body, like they were real, not *through* it, like they were ethereal.

Vivianna's speed sent her through the fireplace and she disappeared.

Cash came up quickly, bringing Alistair with him. He whirled, sending Alistair flying several feet, but he didn't watch his uncle move.

His eyes immediately turned to Kieran.

"Get the women out of here," he ordered.

"But Abby has to stay. She has to go up to the gallery." Only Mrs. Truman would argue with a Cash Fraser who looked ready—no, more to the point he looked like he *wanted* to tear someone limb- from limb.

"Kieran, get them the fuck out of here," Cash repeated, his glance going back to the fireplace, his addition of the F-word boding bad tidings.

"Abby has to stay!" Mrs. Truman shouted.

Cash's torso twisted and he shouted back, "She's on the ground floor! She's not fucking climbing steps when that thing is loose."

Kieran was on the move, hustling Abby and Jenny toward the door. They moved with him quickly as Fenella and Honor guided a stunned Nicola in their direction.

Suzanne didn't move. "I'll stay with—"

Cash cut her off with one word, "Go."

She looked at him. "Cash, I can help."

He leaned into her and roared, "*Move!*"

At that, as anyone would, Suzanne moved.

They were closing in on the exit when Vivianna reappeared, forming in front of them rapidly, her spiteful eyes on Alistair. They swung to Abby and her gaze was so poisonous the entire assemblage skidded to a halt upon viewing its venom.

Without hesitation she zoomed toward Abby. Fenella let out a choked scream and before Abby could take even one step back, Vivianna swept low to the floor, her body swirling around Abby's ankles and then up.

Abby stood frozen, not because she wanted to, but because she was stuck, and even though she told her legs to move, for some supernatural reason, they didn't.

Before terror could fill her, all of a sudden an arm hooked at her waist. She was jerked back and then half-dragged, half-walked backward. Cash's arm was about her, his body tight against hers.

Vivianna stopped her swirl and hovered, eyes narrowed on Cash and Abby.

Or more accurately, Cash's arm held protectively around Abby's body.

She opened her mouth and screamed, the sound far louder and far, far, *far* more terrifying.

"Stop it! Stop it! Stop it!" Fenella shrieked, hands to her ears. Then she pointed one finger at Vivianna, who had turned to her, and Fenella screeched, *"Why don't you leave them alone?* Why can't you just *go away?"*

Vivianna's scream stilled and she aimed a twisted smile at Fenella before she darted toward her. Abby saw Fenella's body brace, but Vivianna sifted right through her and then she turned, curling around the room.

Cash took the opportunity and moved. Half-carrying, half-dragging Abby, he sprinted toward the door but Vivianna zipped in front of them and they collided with her.

Abby and Cash flew backward like they'd hit a wall, bright white and red sparks bursting from Abby's chest as they did so.

Vivianna reeled back as well but caught herself, ready this time for Abby's protection, and made a mad dash back toward Abby and Cash. His arm curved tighter around her, his upper body leaned into hers, forcing her forward and to the side, preparing to shield her from impact.

But before he'd accomplished his task, in front of them the body of a straight, tall, immensely handsome, see-through man appeared.

When it did, Vivianna's face became startled and she tried to halt her progress but she slammed into him and his arms immediately went about her, imprisoning her in his grasp.

Abby—half bent, Cash's chest pressing heavily into her back, her head turned to the action—stared in stunned disbelief at the ghost of

Anthony Beaumaris, Cash's father, standing before them, subduing a struggling Vivianna.

He turned, his eyes on Cash, and his mouth formed one word, a word heard shimmering through the air rather than emitting from his lips.

"Gallery."

Then he and Vivianna disappeared.

Before Abby could even begin to process this, Cash yanked her up and, with a hand at her wrist, whirled her around. His fingers still around her wrist, he pulled her arm out and bent double. He released her wrist, his shoulder went into her belly and she was being lifted. Once he had her in place, he began running, her torso hanging over his back, her legs down his chest.

He sprinted past everyone through the hall. Even though she couldn't see where they were going, when she saw they'd passed the stairs, she knew he was heading to the front door.

"Cash, we have to go to the gallery," Abby cried urgently, but her voice was halting as she rocked on his shoulder.

"No fucking way," Cash growled back, stopping after he descended the stone steps of the entry to heave open the door, but Abby started struggling, writhing on his shoulder.

"Cash, your father said take me to the gallery," she shouted.

He'd taken two steps outside when he lost control of her squirming body. She slid for a second out of control down his arm before he caught her. His arm under her shoulder blades, the other rounding her thighs, he put her safely to her feet.

He grabbed her hand and started to move.

Abby planted her feet, but her shoes skidded across the stone as he pulled.

He stopped, spinning around to look at her, and clipped, "Abby!"

"Cash, no," she cut him off as the others came dashing out of the house to surround them. "We have to go to the gallery."

Cash ignored their audience and bit out, "We're not going to the fucking gallery."

"We have to finish this tonight!" Abby yelled desperately.

Why she cared anymore about the end of Vivianna, knowing she and Cash were through, was a mystery to her.

No, she had to admit, it wasn't.

Jenny was right.

Abby was in love with Cash. She was in love with him and Penmort was his legacy. He wanted it and she wanted it for him. All of it. With none of it controlled by a ghosty she-bitch.

She didn't have the chance to sort through the sad fact she was, indeed, in love with Cash Fraser, International Hot Guy, in love with him enough to risk her life, because he tugged briskly at her arm.

Abby stayed determinedly fixed.

"We'll find another way," he declared when she didn't move.

"There is no other way," she shot back.

He leaned into her and repeated on a shout, "We'll find another fucking way!"

A different Scottish voice, this one disembodied, came from behind Cash. "Take her to the gallery."

Cash turned and he, Abby and their entourage stared into the vacant dark.

"Angus?" Honor called softly.

"Take her to the gallery." Angus's voice, closer and softer now, although he still didn't appear, encouraged again. "Don't worry, laddie, I've got your back."

Cash stared in the direction of the voice, lips thin, jaw clenched and Abby held her breath.

Finally Cash growled, "Something happens to her—"

Angus's voice cut him off. "I've got your back. More importantly, I've got hers."

Cash closed his eyes and sucked breath into his nose. Then his eyes opened and they sliced to Abby. She watched a muscle leap in his cheek before he moved toward her.

"Let's fucking do this," he muttered. Hand still in Abby's, he led her back through the door. But once they were inside, he stopped and looked back at Kieran. "Get them safe, off the castle grounds."

"We'll go with you," Nicola, clearly having recovered from her shock and morphing straight into Mom Mode, offered.

"No," Cash replied shortly, and turned back.

But he was thwarted again.

"Well, I'm going," Mrs. Truman proclaimed.

Cash came around again and he and Abby watched as the older woman stomped toward them on her granny pumps.

"You're not coming with us," Cash stated firmly.

"I am," Mrs. Truman retorted, halting and glaring up at Cash.

"No, you are not," Cash returned.

She planted her hands on her hips and snapped, "Yes, I am, Cash Fraser. You can't tell me what to do. I don't care how tall you are!"

Abby felt then quelled the crazed desire to laugh out loud.

"I'm coming too," Jenny put in, coming to stand by Mrs. Truman.

"And me," Fenella moved forward as well.

"Me too," Honor joined the group.

"I am too," Suzanne announced, not joining the group but striding confidently forward.

She rounded Cash and Abby and went straight to and up the stairs.

"Fucking hell," Cash muttered and his eyes moved to his uncle. "Can you do one thing for your wife and get her to safety?"

But alas, at Cash's query, Alistair Beaumaris proved he was the Jerk to End All Jerks.

"You'll not be in my house, doing whatever it is you're going to do, without me in it," Alistair announced and stomped forward too, skirting a now even angrier Cash and heading toward the stairs.

Nicola gracefully linked arms with Kieran as if they were about to embark on a moonlit stroll, not battle a she-bitch-from-hell, and moved forward. "Well, it looks like we're all going."

"Jesus," Kieran mumbled, pained eyes on Cash, and everyone shoved in the door, moving around Cash and Abby and climbing the stairs.

Cash looked down at Abby and remarked dryly, "You're racking up quite a debt, darling, because I think, somehow, you owe me for this too."

Abby bit her lip and shrugged. But this time Cash did not laugh, chuckle, smile or even grin. He glared at her so ferociously she gulped at his scorching look and then he led her toward the stairs.

However behind them a disembodied male chortle could be heard and Abby knew Cash definitely heard it.

She knew this because his hand squeezed hers painfully tight and he muttered, "You definitely fucking owe me."

Abby didn't have time to worry about Cash's dire statement.

She had stairs to climb.

She held her breath through the first set of stairs then she let it go on the landing only to hold it again on the second.

It wasn't until they hit the gallery that she allowed herself to relax.

Not *relax* relax, as in, putting your feet up with a book and a nice big glass of pinot noir at the end of a trying day. But just *kind of* relax, as in making it up a stairwell made dangerous by a phantom yet the real battle still yawned ahead of you.

The gallery was ablaze with lights and everyone was there when they entered.

"Maybe I should go get some champagne," Honor offered.

"Nobody fucking leaves this room," Cash returned immediately, dropping Abby's hand and cutting a scowl throughout the group.

Honor's brows went up and her eyes slid to Abby.

Abby gave her a grimace of solidarity but shrewdly decided against speaking.

"Well I, for one, think this is *very* interesting," Suzanne remarked from across the room.

She was standing, arms crossed under her breasts, the cleavage bared by her fuchsia gown that had a daring V, which went nearly to her navel, became all the more pronounced with her stance. She had a foot out and a hip jutted and her eyes were aimed at Alistair.

"Suzanne, please," Nicola begged. "Now is not a good time."

"Of course you're right, Mum," Suzanne agreed. "Though, I will say, I *do* hope Anthony Beaumaris hangs around after Vivianna is gone. I would just *love* to hear what *he* has to say."

"Shut your goddamned mouth," Alistair snapped.

"Make me," she snapped back, and Alistair made as if to move but Cash's voice cracked through the room like a whiplash.

"You take one step closer to her, Alistair, I'll throw you out the fucking window myself."

Alistair's body froze, but his hate-filled eyes shot to Cash.

"I should never have invited you to this house," he clipped.

"No, you shouldn't have," Cash concurred and Abby's tense body went solid when he spoke his next words. "I'll not make the same mistake."

"I wouldn't step foot in your home even if you paid me," Alistair returned.

"You did five minutes ago," Cash retorted.

Abby's breath caught and the air in the room went still as everyone's attention riveted on Cash.

Alistair's face paled, his lips parted in shock, but he quickly recovered and slid into bluster. "What are you on about?"

"I'm on about the lien I have on Penmort," Cash informed him. "The one I purchased two months ago from a very grateful bank who hadn't been receiving payments for six months. Nor, I expect, did they want to foreclose and be saddled with a castle they would likely never be able to unload. I don't share that reluctance. I'm foreclosing *now*."

"I *knew* this would be interesting," Suzanne commented happily.

At the same time Fenella muttered, "Oh my."

And at the same time Honor let out an amused chuckle.

Alistair ignored their onlookers. He only had eyes for Cash.

"You can't be serious," he breathed.

"Deadly," Cash shot back.

Alistair's hands fisted at his sides as his face grew red and he declared, "I'll pay you."

"You don't have the money to pay me," Cash reminded him.

Alistair leaned forward. "Then I'll start selling. The Wedgewood collection alone—"

Cash's body went visibly tight before he clipped out, "You sell one piece of my legacy, I'll see you in court, day in and day out, until the only thing you have left is the clothes on your *fucking* back."

Abby, already close to Cash, got closer and her fingers curled around his.

His hand gave hers a light squeeze right before Alistair grinned and scoffed, "*Your* legacy? That's damned funny. Penmort has never been held outside the legitimate line."

"That isn't exactly true," Honor put in airily, and everyone looked to her as she continued, talking like she was a history teacher and they were her class. "In 1697, Edward Beaumaris, never married, died without a legitimate heir. However, being somewhat of a rake, he had five illegitimate children, three boys and two girls. The first born boy, Randall, assumed the Beaumaris name and took over as master of the castle."

"Edward Beaumaris obviously didn't have a brother," Alistair retorted.

"Actually, he had four," Honor returned, a font of ready knowledge about the Beaumaris family.

Clearly, Abby thought, over the last twenty-five years Honor had spent a good deal of time in the library.

Nicola let out a soft laugh.

Alistair's gaze cut to her and his voice was hideous when he hissed, "Shut your bloody mouth."

At that, Cash dropped Abby's hand and in three long strides he was in Alistair's space.

Alistair, taken unawares, belatedly shuffled back, but Cash kept advancing until he had his uncle pinned against the wall.

Once there, Cash leaned threateningly closer but didn't touch the older man.

"Your days of malice toward the Fitzhugh women are over, starting now. I hear you've even looked at one of them funny, tomorrow or twenty years in the future, I swear to Christ you'll wish you were never fucking born. Do you get my meaning?"

"Back off," Alistair demanded, but his voice held a betraying tremor.

Cash didn't move.

Instead he repeated, "I asked, do you get my meaning?"

"Frankly, I'll be thrilled if I never see them again," Alistair snapped, his voice and words ugly.

"I'm sure they feel the same," Cash replied, stepped back and moved away from Alistair, his eyes going to Nicola. "You and your daughters are free to stay at Penmort for as long as you wish."

"You're not taking Penmort!" Alistair shouted, and Cash stopped on his way back to Abby and turned to his uncle.

"I am," Cash announced. "Tomorrow, I've got six people coming to the castle to do an inventory. You've got a week to find other accommodation, gather together your clothes and other personal belongings, none of which will have any attachment to the history of this building, and you're getting the fuck out."

Abby wanted to clap her hands, jump up and down and shout, "Hurrah!" but Alistair wasn't finished.

"I pay on the notes, you've got no—"

"You fight me, I'll drag your ass into court and demand a DNA test," Cash returned, and Alistair's mottled face became confused.

"A DNA test?" he asked.

Cash, for some reason, didn't utter an immediate retort.

Abby watched as his jaw grew tight and he stared at his uncle a moment before he replied, "You don't want to continue this conversation with an audience."

Alistair, proving once again he wasn't exactly the sharpest tack in the box, queried snidely, "Are you insinuating I'm not a Beaumaris?"

"Trust me, Alistair, you want to back down," Cash advised.

"How bloody *dare* you make that accusation! Of all the bloody cheek, *you*," he jeered, "claiming *I'm* not a blood Beaumaris."

"Look around you," Cash stated, indicating the portraits with a jerk of his head, all the pictures of the past masters of the castle sharing a strong resemblance with Cash. His voice had grown quiet when he continued, "Now look at me. What do you see?"

Alistair didn't take his eyes off Cash. "I see a bloody upstart is what I see."

"Back down," Cash warned.

Alistair wasn't smart enough to catch Cash's hint. "Do what you will. I'll see you in court."

Cash shrugged and turned back around, moving toward Abby again while saying, "So be it."

Alistair's gaze swept the room and he snapped, "I don't believe this. In my own home—"

"It isn't your home, Alistair. After Richard Beaumaris died, it stopped being your home," Honor told him, and Alistair's eyes shot to her, but he was smart enough, after his last crack to Nicola and Cash's reaction, to clamp his mouth shut. Honor carried on, "Cash is being nice. I don't know why, he's got no reason to be, but he is. I, however, don't feel like being nice after you manhandled my mother in front of an audience."

Cash had made it to Abby and his arm curved around her shoulders, curling her front to his side even as his eyes were on Honor.

Softly, he murmured, "Honor, don't."

But Honor kept going and announced flatly, "Your mother was raped by a gardener. You're the product of that rape."

As if struck, Alistair reeled back several paces at her words.

Nicola whispered, "Oh my God."

Suzanne watched Alistair, a startled look on her face. But it shifted quickly and triumphantly to a satisfied smirk.

Honor was relentless. "She wrote all about it in her diaries. I found them and Cash has them now. They're evidence enough, but if you push him and he demands a DNA test, the whole world will know you for what you are."

"I kind of hope he does," Mrs. Truman muttered loudly to Kieran, and Abby pressed her lips together to stop from smiling.

Instead she turned to the older woman and whispered, "Mrs. Truman, please."

Mrs. Truman widened her eyes in faux innocence and asked, "What? Everyone can see he's not a very nice man." Then she declared as a finale, "Comeuppance."

Abby heard Jenny's half-amused, half-embarrassed giggle and opened her mouth to speak but Alistair got there before her.

"I fail to see," he started quietly, "what's funny about my mother being raped."

"Nothing," Mrs. Truman returned tartly. "I'm sure everyone in this room agrees it's very sad about your poor mother. Tragic. What's more tragic is that you carried on your father's legacy of cruelty rather than fighting whatever wicked impulse you have that makes you behave the way you behave, and instead, being a good husband and father to a widowed family as it is *abundantly* clear you have not been."

She leaned forward at the hips and declared, "You reap, good man, what you sow."

"That'll be enough, Mrs. Truman," Cash murmured firmly.

Mrs. Truman looked at Kieran and announced, "I was done anyway."

Finally everyone fell silent. Abby watched as Alistair visibly battled with his new knowledge, and she almost, but not quite, felt sorry for him.

Cash's fingers squeezed her shoulder. Her eyes moved from Alistair and her head tilted back to look at Cash.

"Are you okay?" he asked softly.

"Yes," she lied. "Are you?"

He ignored her question, his fingers tensed again at her shoulder, and, his voice still soft, he warned, "Don't lie to me Abby."

She sighed and replied, "Okay, well, I *was* just attacked again by a ghosty she-bitch, so of course I'm a little—"

Cash cut her off. "That's not what I'm talking about."

Abby blinked at him, confused. "What are you talking about?"

"I'm talking about walking into the hall earlier and seeing you looking like your whole world had come to an end."

Abby felt her heart start racing and she kicked herself for being, yet again, so very, *annoyingly* transparent.

She searched her brain for a plausible story.

Luckily she didn't have to search far.

"Cash, someone made an attempt on your life today but I got in the way. Tonight we're at war with a ghost. You've just thrown your uncle out of his home. This is all going to wear on me."

He pushed in at the same time his arm tightened around her shoulders bringing her even closer.

When they were front to front, his hand lifted to her neck and he accused quietly, "You're lying again."

"I am not."

"You are."

"Am not!"

"When I came back to the hall, you weren't where I left you. You were standing with Jenny in an out-of-the-way place. The kind of place you'd engage in a private conversation," Cash informed her, and Abby wished he wasn't so damned clever because at times it was pretty annoying. "What did she say?" he pressed.

"We were getting ready for the toast," Abby lied again.

Cash's mouth grew tight before he demanded, "Stop lying."

"Cash."

"Abby."

They held a brief staring contest before Abby looked away and muttered, "I'm not talking about this now."

Cash's arm gave her a shake, and as he intended her gaze went back to his.

His hand at her neck moved to cup her jaw. "I hope to God whatever she told you, you're smart enough to come to me before you jump to any ridiculous conclusions."

"Cash—" Abby began, but he cut her off.

His brogue was rough and dangerous when he finished. "Because, darling, if you don't and you go off half-cocked, it's going to piss me right...the fuck...off."

All right then.

Abby scratched a chat with Cash on her mental to-do list.

After she helped take down a centuries-old spirit from beyond the grave, that was.

She decided to give up. "Can we just focus on the matter at hand?"

"We can, after you promise you'll be in bed with me at the night's end," Cash returned, and Abby's body gave a small jerk.

"Of course," she whispered, and watched as the intensity faded from his eyes before she went on, "If I'm not in a hospital bed wearing a full body cast, that is." And she watched as the intensity shot right back.

"This isn't funny," he clipped.

"I wasn't joking," she replied.

His eyes rolled to the ceiling, his hand dropped from her jaw, and he muttered, "Fucking hell."

Abby got up on tiptoes, put her hand on his shoulder, his gaze came back to her and she advised softly, "You really shouldn't say the F-word so much."

"Darling," he retorted. "*You* really should learn not to be cute when I'm annoyed."

She dropped back on her heels saying, "I'll make a note of that."

His other arm slid around her. "I think that's smart."

"Um, sorry to interrupt your, um, whatever." Cash and Abby's heads turned to see Fenella at their side. "But, Abby, don't you think you should do something?"

Cash released his firm hold on her. Not entirely but enough for her to move a modest distance away but his arm along her shoulders kept her at his side.

"Pardon?" she asked Fenella.

"You know, *something*," she urged. "To upset Vivianna."

Cash tensed and Abby queried, "Like what?"

"I don't know," Fenella answered. "Last time, you nearly touched Anthony Beaumaris's portrait. I don't think she wanted you to do that. Maybe—"

"Snog Cash." Suzanne all of a sudden was there.

Abby's eyes moved to Suzanne and she breathed, "*What?*"

Suzanne looked at Cash then to Abby and repeated, "Snog Cash."

When they just stared at her Suzanne went on.

"Listen, she thinks of the Beaumaris heirs as hers and she thinks, in some twisted way, she's looking after them. Even so she doesn't appear before them unless they're in harm's way, which isn't often." Her gaze went back to Cash and she commented, "You're a healthy lot, don't put up with much either, never did."

"How do you know this?" Honor asked.

Abby hadn't noticed her getting close but she saw now that Honor was studying her sister, unable to hide her curiosity.

Suzanne looked at Honor and shrugged. "She talks to me."

"Talks to you?" Fenella squeaked.

"Yes," Suzanne answered. "Ever since I was eight years old. We'd moved in, we were here a few months, Alistair said something nasty, it was the first time he did. I remember it like yesterday. I was crying in my room. She came and talked to me."

Abby, Cash, Fenella and Honor were all staring at her.

Finally Honor spoke. "You think you might have wanted to

mention this to us? You know, sometime in the last *twenty-five years*," she ended on a near shout.

"At first I thought you all would think I was crazy," Suzanne returned, blithely ignoring her sister's raised voice. "Then, even when I knew you saw her too, I kept it to myself."

"Why?" Fenella asked.

Something shifted across her face, something that looked like pain, before she hid it.

"I just did," she answered and her eyes went back to Abby. "She's exposed herself now in front of Cash so I'd guess she won't hesitate to do it again. She probably knows you've set a trap. She also probably figures she'll win. She always has. You aren't the first one to try to get rid of her, you know."

Abby didn't know but didn't say anything as Suzanne kept talking.

"I don't know what Anthony is up to, but if she's given him the slip, to draw her out you'll have to make a claim to what she considers hers."

"She's been holding my hand or in my arms all night," Cash reminded her.

"Obviously, that isn't enough." She grinned wickedly. But it wasn't her usual unpleasant wickedness. This grin was actually kind of endearing, and Abby thought distractedly she should do it more often. "You'll have to go for the gusto."

"It's my understanding she can be anywhere, hear anything," Cash replied. "She's probably listening to you right now."

Suzanne shook her head. "No. Over the years I've learned to sense her. She's not here."

"So how is she going to know Abby's kissing me?" Cash inquired.

"You, if you're in this house, she's tuned into. Completely," Suzanne replied softly, her words freaking Abby out, but not as much as her next words would do. "Not what you're saying, not what you're doing, what you're *feeling*."

"Oh my," Fenella breathed.

Before her mind kicked in, Abby turned to Cash in embarrassed horror and muttered, "Oh my Lord, Cash, if that's true, we shouldn't have had sex on the desk in the study. She probably *watched* or at least she *felt*. *Bloody hell*, I hadn't thought of that."

Slowly, Cash's head turned to the side, his chin dipped down, his eyes locked with Abby's and for the first time since he left to talk to James, his mouth formed a delicious grin.

"Oh my," Fenella breathed again.

"You had sex on Alistair's desk!" Honor hooted loudly, and everyone in the room turned to look at them as Abby felt the heat come up in her cheeks and she mentally kicked herself for being stupid, stupid, *stupid*. "That's *hilarious*!" Honor shouted.

Abby ducked her head, praying for a miracle (or a little, teensy bit of Angus's mojo) that would make her a real invisible woman.

When this unsurprisingly didn't happen, she turned into Cash's body and buried her face in his chest begging, "Please, kill me."

Cash's arms went around her as Abby heard Mrs. Truman yell, "Abigail Butler, what did I tell you about hanky panky? And on a desk! My goodness, your *grandmother* is probably *spinning* in her *grave*."

Abby tilted her head back, looked up at Cash, and whispered, "Are you going to kill me? If you are, now's a good time."

His face descended, his captivating grin firmly in place and against her lips, he murmured, "No, darling, I'm not going to kill you."

"Damn," she whispered right before his mouth took hers in a kiss.

It wasn't a brush-on-the-lips kiss.

It was an open-mouths, tongues-engaged, knees-weakening, stomachs-dipping, bodies-melting *kiss*. Abby leaned into Cash, his head slanted, deepening the kiss, and she felt his arms tighten around her as her hands slid up his arms, along his shoulders, one gliding up his neck and into his hair.

She absorbed his low groan, a delectable tremor shuddering through her moments before they heard the spine-chilling scream.

28

SHOWDOWN PART TWO

Cash's mouth broke from Abby's, both their heads jerked to the side and they saw Vivianna only feet away and hovering before she shot forward.

Abby's body tensed for flight but they had no time, Vivianna was almost upon them.

Cash's arm came up to fend Vivianna off, something Abby knew wouldn't work because, well, she was a ghost.

Then it did.

Worked that was.

Vivianna slammed into Cash's upturned hand as if her body was corporeal. The scream stilled and she flew back.

Abby heard gasps around her but all she could do was stare.

"What on—?" she breathed, but she heard a whisper in her ear.

"Draw her to the circle," Angus ordered, and belatedly Abby's brain kicked in.

She pulled out of Cash's arm and took a step back. His eyes sliced to her, she gave him a short jerk of the head and watched his jaw grow tight.

She started edging toward the corner of the gallery where she knew the circle had been drawn, according to Cassandra not only magical but also invisible.

Unfortunately the room was huge and the circle was far away, a distance to Abby at that time that felt like a million miles.

Regardless Abby kept creeping and saw that Vivianna's eyes were on Cash, not filled with malice, but instead with pain and longing.

This was a problem considering she wasn't paying a lick of attention to Abby.

Normally that would be a good thing.

At that moment it was not.

Abby kept backing toward the corner, giving Vivianna's floating form a wide berth and trying to be obvious but not *too* obvious.

Cash, eyes on Vivianna, started to move slowly toward Abby.

Vivianna's head, just as slowly, turned to Abby.

When Vivianna's malice-filled eyes hit her, Abby's mind disengaged, fear shot through her and she stopped moving.

"Abby, come here," Cash commanded, lifting his hand to her.

Abby's gaze darted between Cash and Vivianna, and she whispered, "Cash."

"Darling, you'll be all right. Come here," Cash said softly, still advancing and Abby started backing up again.

Abby had no idea what he was on about because the only way she'd be all right was to get the damned ghost in the circle. He knew that. Hell, practically everyone in the room knew that.

"Cash, I have to—"

"Come here."

"Cash—"

Then it happened.

Vivianna twirled toward Abby and advanced at the same time Cash bolted forward.

Abby started running to the circle. She chanced a glance over her shoulder to see if Vivianna was following and saw the spirit collide with Cash. Cash's arm went around her waist and he hurled her bodily *toward* Abby then tore in their direction.

Abby stopped and ducked, Vivianna sailing over her as Cash caught Abby at the hips, whirled and threw Abby back from whence she came.

She reeled and would have landed right on her ass if Kieran hadn't caught her in his arms.

Cash wasted no time and shot forward in Vivianna's direction.

Abby watched in shock as Cash caught Vivianna's skirts in a fist and pulled her down into his arms. Subduing her wild struggles quickly, he carried her kicking and punching to where the circle was supposed to be. Once there, he let go and jogged out toward Abby, Vivianna zooming after him so fast she was nearly a blur.

When it looked like Vivianna would make it to Cash, Abby heard Fenella scream right before Vivianna slammed against an invisible barrier.

Bright sparks of white lights like sparkler dust exploded up and down, in and out, in a wide circle, so thick and riotous you could barely see through them.

Vivianna flew back into the circle.

Cash made it to Abby's side, and with an arm hooked around her waist, he pulled her out of Kieran's arms and against his body.

Vivianna came tearing toward them again.

And she again slammed into the circle, more blazing lights burst and she sailed back.

They watched, everyone inching slightly nearer to the circle as she did this again.

And again.

And again.

Then she stopped, suspended in the air in the middle of the circle.

Eyes on Cash, then on Abby, she opened her mouth and screamed.

This scream was different, still eerie but filled with frustration.

"That's it, wee ghosty. Scream all you want. We've got you now," Angus's voice came from a now-visible body. He was standing at the edge of the circle, in full kilt, hands on hips, grinning like the lunatic he was at Vivianna.

Vivianna stopped screaming and glared at Angus.

"Angus!" They heard shouted and everyone turned to see Cassandra at the door. She was in top to toe, full-on, rock 'n' roll gypsy gear, wearing enough silver and scarves to outfit a five-member rock band. She had a big, battered, brown leather case with her. She put it on the floor and gave it a hefty shove with the bottom of her booted foot.

It went sailing across the room and Angus, also with his foot, stopped it.

Angus's head turned to Vivianna. "You're going on a road trip, lass."

Vivianna's eyes went from the case to Angus, her body still hovering.

Instead of looking worried, however, she crossed her arms as if this all was a mild annoyance.

Abby had the feeling this was not a good sign.

Cassandra came to stand beside Angus. She now had what looked like a long, gnarled, stout twig in her hand, about a foot long, maybe longer. She was pointing it at Vivianna and muttering under her breath. Abby couldn't catch all that she was saying, but she could tell that it rhymed.

"Who's she?" Nicola breathed from the other side of Kieran.

"A witch," Jenny answered.

With effort Nicola took in this new utterly inconceivable nugget of information and then asked, "What's she doing?"

"Folding her up," Honor, at her mother's side, replied.

At that, a stream of bright-pink glitter dust poured forth from Cassandra's wand, and Nicola, eyes huge and trained on the wand, wisely decided to stop asking questions.

They watched as Vivianna did indeed look like she was folding in on herself from the bottom up.

Feet, skirts, knees and up.

Thighs, hips, waist and up.

Regardless of what would seem dire circumstances for the ghosty she-bitch, she kept her eyes on Angus, her arms crossed on her chest.

Her face, Abby saw with a queer curl of fear starting in her belly, now looked bored.

"Something's wrong," Abby whispered, but Cash saw it too.

"Angus." Cash's voice cut through Cassandra's muttering.

"Not long now, lad," Angus replied, still grinning.

Cash pushed Abby behind him and demanded, "Angus, look at her."

Peering around his body, Abby watched Vivianna's arms uncross and lift toward the ceiling as her ribcage was folded up.

Then Abby watched as Vivianna's eyes moved toward Cash and Abby.

She grinned.

Cash tensed.

Abby took several steps back and Cash shouted, "Angus!"

Before anyone could move Vivianna's arms shot straight down. She hurtled herself toward the ceiling, her body coming out of the fold as she did. A firework of every colour purple you could imagine, from the palest lilac to the brightest violet to the deepest aubergine, detonated, bursting forth, filling the space and bouncing (thankfully harmlessly) off everyone standing at the circle.

Then the circle itself exploded yet again in a burst of white.

Abby heard cries and shouts, but all she saw was Cash whirling.

The instant his eyes hit Abby, he barked, *"Run!"*

Abby, heart in her throat, ran and this time she didn't look back.

But six feet from the door she was lifted clean off her feet.

Not by Cash.

Instead by Vivianna.

All of a sudden Abby found herself floating close to the ceiling, Vivianna's bitch-from-hell arm locked around her waist and Abby was hanging in mid-air like a ragdoll.

Fenella, again, screamed.

Abby struggled.

Vivianna shot toward the door.

Suzanne, luckily, got there before her and slammed it closed, whirling and throwing her back against it, arms wide.

Vivianna halted. Abby's body still moving forward, she let out a whoosh of air and Vivianna turned and shot toward the hall, taking Abby with her.

Fenella was running to the double doors that led to the hall and Abby saw Angus again with his whip. His arm came up and out sharply, the whip whistling through the air. Abby's body jerked reflexively as the whip came toward her but its end passed straight through Abby and curled around Vivianna.

Vivianna knew it was coming, she made another turn against the direction of the whip's tip and it fell useless to the floor.

Abby kept struggling as Vivianna moved them in another direction, always away from Cash but, Abby noted with no small amount of alarm, toward a window. Abby saw (intermittently) that Cash had his eyes on them and was circling slowly, his face like thunder, body both taut but strangely loose, looking like a big cat waiting for its opportunity, ready to strike.

They stopped on another jarring halt, this time something strong and vital had wrapped around Abby's ankle preventing their progress.

Abby looked down to see Jenny had a hold of her. Vivianna tugged at Abby's body, Abby shoved at Vivianna's arm and Jenny held on tight, lifting her other hand to hold on too, her feet slipping across the floorboards in her effort to hold on.

Mrs. Truman dashed behind Jenny and wrapped her arms around Jenny's waist.

"Let go of Abigail!" Mrs. Truman shrieked, angry, affronted eyes on Vivianna as if she could not *believe* this phantom would have the audacity to put her vile ghost hands on Mrs. Truman's precious Abigail Butler.

Mrs. Truman was leaning all of her weight back, holding on to Jenny for all she was worth, but Abby felt Jenny's hands slipping.

"Don't let go, Jenny!" Abby shouted desperately just as Jenny lost her grip and both she and Mrs. Truman flew backwards, arms windmilling.

Vivianna only managed to move inches away when Kieran was there, his fingers closing around the ankle Jenny let go and Abby felt another set of fingers on her other ankle. Her head turned and she saw Nicola had a hold of her there.

"Angus." Cash's voice was close. It was a low, angry growl but Abby couldn't see him.

"Hang on," Angus replied.

"Hang on!" Nicola cried, putting all her weight into holding Abby safe. "What do you mean 'hang on?' Abby's suspended in mid-air! Do something!"

"We're resurrecting the circle," Cassandra called calmly.

"The circle is out. We're moving to Plan B," Cash declared.

"We don't have a Plan B!" Jenny yelled, running back toward Abby, jumping up and grabbing on to Abby's hand.

"Plan B is getting the fuck out of here," Cash announced.

"I'm good with that," Abby noted quickly. "Plan B sounds good to me. Let's do Plan B, like, *now*," Abby ended on a screech just as Honor arrived, made a leap and grabbed Abby's other hand.

Abby heard Cassandra say, "Let him in, Fenella."

"But, Abby doesn't want—" Fenella replied.

"Let him in!" Cassandra returned impatiently.

Abby heard a door open and all of a sudden Vivianna's body shook. It felt to Abby like Vivianna was fighting something even as she was holding on to Abby. As this happened, Abby heard the unmistakable noise of a feline's low growl. Abby kept shoving against Vivianna's arm, but twisted to see that Vivianna was trying to push off Abby's cat, Zee, who was attached to Vivianna, growling, hissing, spitting and scratching.

Abby's stomach did a nosedive.

"Who brought my cat?" Abby shouted, glaring down at her friends.

"We did. Mrs. Truman and me," Jenny answered.

Vivianna jerked this way and that, still keeping firm hold on Abby's waist and all of Abby's limbs were pulled to the breaking point.

"I thought I said no Zee!" Abby snapped.

"We figured we could use all the help we could get!" Jenny snapped back. "And it looks like we weren't wrong!"

Abby thought, somewhat hysterically, even though she wanted to, she really couldn't argue with that.

Vivianna's struggles were fierce and Abby's body was wrenched painfully with Vivianna's fight against Abby's cat as everyone kept hold on her limbs.

"Hold her steady," Angus encouraged from somewhere behind Abby.

"*You* hold her steady! This ghosty she-bitch is *strong* and she's *freaking out*!" Jenny cried as Vivianna gave a mighty tug at Abby's waist and all of Abby's friends went skidding several inches along the floor boards.

"Angus, goddamn it!" Cash shouted from somewhere close but also somewhere Abby could not see.

She didn't have time to look as she was still shoving against Vivianna's arm and praying she nor Zee would be torn limb from limb.

Abby, however, didn't have to see Cash. She knew by the tone of his voice that his patience was depleted and she knew *exactly* how he felt.

Suddenly Angus shouted, "*Now!*"

Abby saw something golden and glistening fall around them. It settled at Abby's waist then passed through, as if it was a mirage. Vivianna was yanked back viciously, Zee leapt away and at the same time all Abby's protectors jerked her forward.

Vivianna's arm came loose from Abby's waist and Abby was falling.

She twisted automatically, not wanting to fall flat on her face. But before she hit the ground, strong arms wrapped around her, one at her back, one at her thighs.

Abby looked up to see Cash had hold of her and he didn't waste any time. He started sprinting, Abby in his arms, toward the door.

Abby saw Suzanne open it for them. Then she looked back, watching Angus struggling wildly with what looked like a golden rope which was lassoed around a mad-as-hell Vivianna's waist.

She saw no more. They were out of the room and heading down the hall.

Halfway down the hall Cash stopped and put her on her feet. He grabbed her hand and started running again, dragging her on her high heels toward the stairs.

Abby noted absently that Zee was right there with them.

They rounded the stairs and both of them (as well as Zee) came skidding to a halt.

There was a ghost on the stairs.

And it was not the ghost of Cash's father.

Abby took one look at him and her chest expanded painfully at the same time her heart stopped beating.

Then, heart restarted, hammering in her chest, she whispered, "Ben?"

Ben's ghostly eyes took in Abby for a moment, roaming lovingly over her face and down her body.

They moved to Cash.

The minute her dead husband's eyes hit her lover, Abby's heart stopped beating again.

"Take her to the north parapet," Ben told Cash, his beautiful, deep, sweetly familiar voice disembodied and hanging weirdly in the air.

"I'm not taking her to the parapet," Cash ground out and Abby looked up at him.

His face was pale and tight, his eyes scorching and locked on Ben. One look at him and Abby knew that Cash knew to whom he was speaking.

"Trust me. Take her to the parapet," Ben repeated, and Cash ignored him, making to move forward.

Ben's gaze swung to Abby.

"Honey," his beloved voice whispered the casual endearment, Cash's body stilled and Abby felt her mouth fill with saliva as her eyes pricked with tears. Ben continued gently, "Get him to take you to the parapet."

Abby's head shook jerkily both with fear and the all-consuming desire *not* to be seeing her dead husband's ghost, not now, not *ever*, and Ben went on.

"Please, Abby, trust me. We don't have much time."

He looked behind him, down the stairs, then back at Cash and Abby.

In an instant, he shimmered to nothing.

Immediately Cash pulled on Abby's arm and moved forward saying, "Let's go."

Abby pulled back. Cash stopped two steps down and looked up at her, his hand still clasping hers.

"Darling, let's go," he demanded softly.

"Take me to the parapet," Abby whispered.

Cash shook his head, but his voice was still quiet when he replied, "No fucking way."

"Cash."

"Abby, no fucking way."

"Cash," Abby said. "Ben would never hurt me. They have something planned. You have to take me to the parapet."

"Abby, I'm certain you've already noticed that none of their plans are working. I'm not taking you to the parapet."

She tightened her hand in his and walked down one step all the while looking into his eyes. "Please Cash. You can trust Ben, I promise. Take me to the parapet. Let's finish this." She stopped, noted he looked unyielding, so she begged, "Please."

"You were flying through the air," Cash returned.

"I know that."

"She's not sending you over the fucking parapet."

"No, she's not. You won't let her," Abby told him and finished on a whisper, "Neither will Ben."

"Goddamn it, Abby," he gritted through his teeth, and she felt a thrill of renewed fear mingled with elation because she knew he was relenting.

She didn't think she wanted him to at the same time she was glad that he was.

"We don't have much time," Abby urged on a tug of his hand, like she knew what she was talking about, which she did *not*.

He sucked air in through his nose, looked to the side then his eyes came back and locked on hers.

He walked up the steps.

Abby let out the breath she didn't know she was holding.

Swiftly Cash guided her, hand still gripping hers, to the parapet. Zee raced along with them.

The whole time Abby did everything she could not to think about Ben on the staircase and what that meant.

Had he not gone on to the next plane like the rest of her family?

Had he been hanging about their house for the last four years, watching her mope around for three of them, then alone with the new owners for the last one?

How did he get to the castle?

Did Cassandra do this?

Did Jenny and Mrs. Truman know about this?

What did Cash think of seeing Ben?

What did Ben think of seeing Cash?

(Clearly, Abby failed at not thinking about Ben.)

They walked quickly up flight after flight of stone stairs, each one edging the side of the square parapet until Cash pushed up a wooden door in the ceiling. Zee darted forward and Cash led her through. When he had Abby on the roof, the cold air biting into her skin and through the thin satin of her dress, he shut the door.

"Cash," Abby whispered.

Cash's eyes sliced to her.

"Later," he returned sharply.

"We have to—" Abby started.

Cash cut her off. "We have to keep you alive. That's the primary focus. We'll deal with the rest of it later."

Abby started to move closer, saying, "Cash—"

He opened his mouth to interrupt when they heard his name, his real name, Conner, said in a musical voice that shimmered through the air around them.

Cash and Abby turned toward the side of the parapet that faced the tor.

Yet another ghost was hovering there only a few inches off the ground. This one was a woman, older, pretty, dainty. She reminded Abby of Nicola but she had several years on her and a sadness about her that hadn't yet fully blossomed in Nicola, and hopefully with tonight's events, never would.

"Gran?" Cash asked, his voice sounding stunned.

"Conner," she replied on a charming smile that wiped all sadness from her expression.

"Holy crap. You're Lorna." Abby thought these words were in her head, but when Lorna's eyes came to her she realised she'd breathed them out loud.

"And you're Abby." Her smile deepened and her gaze moved back to her grandson. "The Beaumaris men always had good taste."

"Wow," Abby whispered, delighted at the compliment even in their highly unusual, very scary circumstances.

"Gran, what's happening?" Cash clearly wasn't feeling into family reunions of the spirit world. He had an objective, he was focused on that objective and even his grandmother's phantasmic return from the grave wasn't going to divert him from that objective.

Before Lorna could answer, they heard Mrs. Truman shriek from far away, "What are you doing up there!"

Abby moved to the edge but only caught a glimpse of Mrs. Truman, Jenny, Kieran and the rest of them standing in the courtyard outside, everyone illuminated by the blazing lights that customarily lit the castle. Abby saw all of them were looking up at the tower before Cash yanked Abby away.

"Don't go near the edge," he warned, his voice sounding a wee bit irritable.

"Cash Fraser!" Mrs. Truman shouted. "You get Abigail off that parapet *this instant*!"

"Who's that?" Lorna asked, and Abby jumped when she saw Cash's ghostly grandmother floating at her side close to the edge looking down at the assemblage.

"Who's *that*?" Mrs. Truman screeched, obviously catching sight of Lorna.

"That's my friend," Abby told Lorna, then shouted as loud as she could, "It's okay Mrs. Truman! Everything's under control! This is Cash's grandma!" Lorna turned amused eyes to Abby and Abby continued in a normal voice, "Um, sorry for shouting."

Cash's arm still around her ribcage, grew tighter. She didn't know if this was amusement or something else. She reckoned it was something else so she decided not to look at him. She was already freaked out enough.

"That's quite all right," Lorna said on another sweet smile.

"Well!" Mrs. Truman shrieked. "She should know better! Cash's Nan! You get Abigail and Cash off that parapet! Right now!" When no one immediately acquiesced to her demand, she finished on a bellow, "Don't make me come up there!"

Cash let Abby go, leaned over the edge and yelled, "Kieran, I don't care if you have to stake her to the turf, do *not* let her come up here."

"You got it, gov," Kieran shouted back.

At Kieran's response, Abby glanced at Cash and saw his eyes roll to the heavens.

"And who's that?" Lorna asked, peering over the edge again.

"Kieran, my best friend's husband," Abby replied. "My best friend is the redhead. Her name is Jenny."

"Her gown is lovely," Lorna commented, narrowing her eyes to look closer.

"I'll tell her you said that," Abby promised on a smile.

Lorna looked at Abby. "Your gown is lovely too."

Abby put her hands out at her sides, tilted her chin down, her eyes skimming her dress, then she glanced back at Lorna. "It's my great-grandmother's."

"It's extraordinary," Lorna remarked.

"If I can interrupt your little chat," Cash bit out, and Abby and Lorna looked at him as he continued, "Perhaps, Gran, you can tell us what the fuck is going on?"

That's when they heard another ghostly voice say, "Conner, don't speak to your grandmother that way."

They all turned to see Cash's father not hovering but standing on the roof like he had real feet even though he was see-through.

"Holy crap," Abby breathed again, eyes staring at Anthony Beaumaris. "You just told Cash what to do."

Anthony looked at Abby and replied, "He's my son."

Abby kept staring.

Her night so bizarre, her mouth somewhere along the line became disconnected from her brain, so she blathered on, "I know but still, he's a big guy and he's scary. I'd *never* tell him what to do."

Anthony gave her a look that stated, quite clearly, even in its super-natural weirdness, that he thought maybe she was a little touched.

His gaze moved to his son. "Bodes well for your future, son."

"As pleased as I am to see you both," Cash clipped, sounding anything but pleased, shrugging off his dinner jacket and settling its voluminous warmth on Abby's shoulders before he continued, "On the top of a tower in the freezing, fucking cold at midnight when Abby doesn't have a coat and her life hangs in the balance, I'd prefer it if someone would tell me what in *the fuck* is going on," Cash clipped.

Abby leaned toward Lorna and muttered, "He has a short fuse."

Lorna's disembodied voice muttered back, "They all do, dear."

Abby decided to explain Cash's behaviour. "He says the F-word a lot when he's angry." Lorna looked at her. "And other times besides," Abby finished, feeling the need to be truthful (it *was* Cash's grandma).

At that, Cash lost what little patience he had left and snapped, "We're going."

"You're not going," Anthony returned.

"We're going," Cash shot back.

"You *can't* go," Lorna put in.

"Why the hell not?" Cash retorted.

"You have to save Abby and you're the only one who can do it."

They all turned at the new voice drifting through the air.

Ben's voice.

Abby saw he stood in the opposite corner, also see-through, his phantom feet on the roof's floor. Zee was sitting by Ben's feet, his tail sweeping casually from side to side as if he stood beside his dead master a thousand times.

"Ben," Abby whispered, her heart leaping into her throat making her voice sound suffocated.

"Not now, Abby," Ben returned tersely, his eyes on the door in the floor and at that moment, it flew open.

Abby jumped. Cash positioned himself in front of her and took two steps back, guiding Abby to the middle of the tower, his hands behind him, fingers curled into Abby's sides.

Angus emerged from the door, grunting and straining, pulling the golden rope.

He came fully into view and kept tugging. Vivianna came after him, still fighting frantically against the rope at her waist. Cassandra was last through, her wand pointed at Vivianna, a pale, slim thread of gossamer gold coming from the wand and hitting Vivianna in the back. Its purpose, Abby suspected, aiding in binding the ghost.

"Jesus," Cash murmured.

"We got her, laddie," Angus proclaimed stoutly.

"Jesus," Cash repeated.

Abby wasn't paying attention.

She was watching Ben, Anthony and Lorna position themselves in a circle around Angus, Cassandra and Vivianna. Zee had started prowling the edges of the roof, his yellow cat eyes turned to the restrained ghost.

"Not gon' get away now, are you, beastie?" Angus taunted.

Abby examined Vivianna who had stopped fighting against the rope and her head was whipping this way and that, taking in her fellow phantoms, Cash and Zee.

It dawned on Abby that the spectre actually looked scared.

"If you'd paid attention this morning, son, not only would Abby not have wrecked your car, but I would have guided you to Vivianna's Book of Shadows," Anthony noted mysteriously, his words causing Cash's body to grow still, his eyes never leaving Vivianna.

"It's hidden behind a secret panel in one of the bookshelves of the library," Lorna put in.

She, too, didn't take her eyes from Vivianna and stayed close to the bound ghost.

"Vivianna's invincible...almost," Anthony noted. "Only her Book of Shadows holds the secret to her demise."

"And that would be?" Cash, his eyes also locked on Vivianna, asked.

"Her death has to be re-enacted," Ben answered.

Cash replied instantly, "She committed suicide."

Cash and Abby were moving round in a slow half-circle watching as Angus and Cassandra positioned Vivianna to the edge of the tower closest to the tor. Once there the three other ghosts and Zee moved in.

"She didn't commit suicide," Lorna said quietly.

"She didn't?" Abby whispered.

"She poisoned her ex-lover's wife. Killed her." Anthony picked up the story. "In order to commence her plan to rain terror on Penmort throughout eternity, she drew him up here and confessed to the crime. In a rage, he threw her over the side," Anthony told them, and Abby gasped.

Abby gasped again as Angus whipped the lasso over Vivianna's head freeing her, and Cassandra dropped her wand, the gossamer thread disappearing.

They both stepped away.

"Cash!" Abby cried, even as she felt and saw Cash's body get tense.

But Vivianna was going nowhere. She was pinned to the spot, hovering several feet off the ground with Ben, Anthony and Lorna's hands extended to her. Somehow, though Abby had no clue how, they were imprisoning her.

"You're safe, love." Anthony's voice was gentle and it reminded her exactly of Cash's (except, of course, with an English accent rather than a Scottish one) as it slid through the air all around her. Anthony went on, "There's a reason Vivianna didn't appear before any of the masters of this castle."

"Because they can touch her," Abby guessed.

"Yes, dear," Lorna affirmed. "They can touch her. She's only vulnerable to a master of Penmort."

"You have to push her over the side," Ben informed Cash, and Abby's hands came up to clutch Cash's waist.

Ben's eyes dropped to her hands and she pulled them quickly away.

Then Abby heard, "She doesn't love you."

Abby's head shot up and she stared at Vivianna. The spirit's eyes were pained and afraid and they were staring beseechingly at Cash.

"She'll never love you." Vivianna's voice, strangely pleasant and warm, filled the air. Even so, Abby felt a cold chill slide across her skin that had nothing to do with the frosty night. "She'll always love him." Her head moved to motion to Ben, and Abby felt her chest grow tight.

"Push her," Ben urged.

"*I* love you. I've *always* loved you," Vivianna told Cash, and Abby bit her lip, feeling her body tremble, knowing this reaction, too, had nothing to do with the bitter night. "I'll always love you."

"Damn it, man, *push her!*" Ben demanded, eyes on Abby.

Cash took a step forward and Vivianna quailed.

"You deserve better!" she cried desperately, and Cash stopped.

Abby's eyes slid to Cash's face. She saw he was listening. He didn't like what he was hearing, and worst of all, it was penetrating.

Abby felt her pulse start beating wildly in her throat and blood started rushing to her ears because of course this would penetrate. Cash knew how she felt about Ben. He'd thrown it in her face during their first colossal fight.

He just didn't know how she felt *now*.

Vivianna carried on, "You deserve someone who loves you. Who'll take care of you. Who wants no one but you. Who *longs* for no one but *you!*"

"Shut it, ghosty," Angus growled, but Vivianna ignored him.

"Her heart belongs to another man. It always will. She'll never feel that way for you, my love, my dearest heart. *Never!*" Vivianna wailed.

Abby could take no more, putting her hands over her ears and stomping her foot, she shouted, "Stop it!"

Vivianna's eyes moved to Abby and she spat, "You'll never be good enough for him!"

Abby took her hands from her ears, planted them on her hips, stepped clear of Cash and leaned forward shouting, "I know! That doesn't mean I don't love him!"

The air and all of the beings on the roof went deathly still.

Abby, beside herself and definitely not in control of her own actions (most specifically her mouth), turned to Cash.

"I love you, all right?"

She was still shouting, not the least bit romantically, not that it mattered. She was in the iron jaws of the freak out to end all freak outs, and she didn't notice Cash's body jolt at her words but instead jabbered on.

"I know it sounds stupid. We've only known each other a short time and blah, blah, blah." Abby circled her hand in the air like an idiot and kept rattling away. "Doesn't matter, I know what I feel. I knew it with Ben the minute I saw him. I knew it with you." Abby turned to Vivianna. "So, *you* can go straight to hell, okay? You don't know what you're talking about. You're just mean and nasty and a poor loser! Haunting a castle for centuries and killing people because your boyfriend broke up with you. Who does that?"

"Abby," Cash called, interrupting Abby's rant and her eyes cut to him.

"What?" she snapped.

"Come here, darling," he demanded quietly.

"I don't want to. I'm freaking out. All right? And I'm cold. And I need a drink. Tequila. STAT." She turned back to Vivianna and threatened, "And if one, single bugle bead on these shoes is missing after tonight's fiasco I'm holding *you* responsible," she finished while jabbing her finger in Vivianna's direction.

"Abby," Cash called again, and Abby's eyes sliced back to him.

"*What?*" she shrieked.

"I said, come here."

Abby rolled her eyes heavenward, sighed heavily and stomped the two feet to Cash.

His hand came up and his fingers curled around her neck as his chin tipped down to look at her.

"You're in love with me?" he asked softly.

"Yes, like, no duh," she retorted sharply, then she called as if he was a block away, "Hello! Cash! I totally freaked out when I thought you were in an accident." Abby turned her head to Anthony. "Your son is very clever, but it would seem he can be a bit—"

She didn't finish. Cash's fingers tightened at her neck and jerked her forward, making her body slam into his.

She tilted her head back and her breath caught at the intensity in his eyes right before his nose touched hers.

"You love me," he stated in that low, deep, rough voice, which was one of the many things she loved most about him.

Abby realised what she was about at the same time she realised that in all her many years of stupid, stupid, *stupid* behaviour, this was, by far and away, the stupidest.

Still, she couldn't stop herself from whispering, "Yes."

Close up, Abby watched Cash's eyes smile and her heart leapt at the sight.

"Well, this is going to make eternity interesting," Ben remarked drolly from his place at Vivianna's side.

Cash's head came up and Abby's turned to the side.

She wasn't sure but she thought she could actually *feel* her heart breaking.

And it hurt.

A lot.

"Ben," she murmured.

"Abby," Ben replied, his mouth twitching.

"I'm sorry," Abby whispered.

"Honey, why? Because you're alive and happy?" Ben asked, and Cash's hand dropped from Abby's neck as Abby turned fully to face Ben, but she felt Cash's other arm slide around her waist and he pulled her gently into his side.

"Um," Abby answered Ben hesitantly. "Yes?"

Ben laughed.

No joke.

He laughed out loud like she was hilarious, his laughter curling through the air around them.

When he stopped, his gaze was on Cash and he informed him, "She's a little nutty."

"I've noticed that," Cash murmured.

"It's cute," Ben went on.

Cash's fingers at her waist flexed as he said, "I've noticed that too."

Abby looked between Cash and Ben, her heart had stopped breaking but her blood pressure had started rising before she demanded to know, "What's going on?"

"I know what's *no'* going on," Angus cut in impatiently. "And that's the fact that no ghosty she-bitch is being hurtled over the side of the tower straight to the depths of hell. That's what's *no'* going on."

"Yes, Conner, do you think we can get on with this? Abby's cold," Anthony added.

"And, I hate to bring this up, but Cassandra told us we don't have much time," Lorna noted.

Abby looked at Cassandra and muttered in a threatening tone, "You have a bit of explaining to do."

Cassandra shrugged. Then she grinned.

Abby decided she'd deal with Cassandra later and looked to Cash.

Cash was looking at Vivianna.

At that moment it occurred to Abby that, even though she was a ghost, and a murderess six times over, not to mention not very nice, it still couldn't be fun to be the person who had to send her plunging to the depths of hell.

Abby looked at Vivianna and asked, "Do you think you can play nice? You know, not murder anyone else and maybe not scare people?"

Vivianna's eyes narrowed, her face twisted with hatred, and she hissed, "I'll see your broken body at the bottom of the tor before I—"

She didn't finish.

Without hesitation Cash strode forward, put a hand to her chest and thrust her over the side.

Abby's blood ran cold as Vivianna's chilling scream split the air.

Abby ran after Cash, put one of her hands to his back, one to his stomach and plastered her front to his side.

Then she, Cash, his father and grandmother, Abby's dead husband, her ghost hunter, her clairvoyant witch and her cat peered over the edge and watched as Vivianna's body plummeted down—her skirts billowing, her hair wafting, her arms reeling—until they could see no more through the dark.

Mere moments later the scream died and a burst of violet and lilac sparks shot straight up the tor, the side of the castle, and they all stepped back to watch them fly into the air over the parapet.

Abby stared up as the sparks glimmered then faded away.

Cash's arm curled around her body, holding her close to his warmth.

She felt weird, thinking she should be happy that Vivianna was gone. But instead she was somehow sad.

"Well, that's done then," Cassandra mumbled.

They heard scuffling then Mrs. Truman shoved through the door in the floor, Kieran on her heels, hand reaching toward Mrs. Truman as if to detain her, Jenny right behind Kieran.

Once she gained the roof, Mrs. Truman whirled on them, planted her hands on her hips, her breath coming in huffs, her eyes cutting amongst the humans and ghosts and she shouted, "What's the meaning of this!"

But Abby's eyes were on Kieran and Jenny, both of whom were also on the roof and both were staring at Ben.

"My God," Kieran breathed.

Abby, nor Ben, had any chance to explain.

Cassandra moved forward and said urgently, "We don't have much time. We have to get them back home."

Before anything could be said, Lorna moved in front of Cash and Abby. Her eyes were on her grandson.

"You'll be happy?" she asked, her voice quiet but fervent, her face intent.

Abby looked up at Cash and saw his jaw clenched.

"Yes, Gran," he replied.

Lorna smiled and looked at Abby.

"You remind me of..." she murmured, hesitated and the sad look came back into her face. "Well, *me*...a long time ago."

Abby's heart went out to her and she asked, "Is 'home' a happy place for you?"

Lorna nodded. "Yes, my dear. Very happy." Her face went soft and the sadness again disappeared. "Now it will be even happier."

Her eyes moved back to Cash, roamed his face fondly then they turned to Cassandra and she nodded.

Cassandra lifted her wand, muttered some rhyming words, ended it with "so mote it be" and a spark of bright silver light shot from her wand and hit Lorna.

Lorna's gaze turned to Cash, she smiled, her entire body started glimmering and she faded away.

Abby's arm slid around Cash's waist and she held on tight.

Without delay, Anthony moved in front of them.

"You've taken care of Alistair?" he queried, eyes on Cash.

Cash nodded and Anthony nodded in return.

Quietly Anthony stated, "She's different, you know. Where she is now."

Abby felt Cash's body grow rigid at her side and she knew Anthony was talking about Cash's mother.

"Healthy?" Cash asked.

Anthony nodded again. "And happy."

Abby swallowed the tears crawling up her throat and pressed deeper into Cash.

"I don't want you taking the Beaumaris name," Anthony announced. "I want you to usher in the era of the Frasers. Your grandfather deserves that, as does your mother."

Cash jerked his head in agreement and Anthony looked at Abby for a moment before training his eyes back on his son.

"This one's going to be a handful," he declared, and Abby didn't know what to make of that.

She heard amusement in his voice when Cash replied, "I've already figured that out."

Anthony grinned and Abby caught her breath.

His grin melted the forbidding, somewhat scary look of his face and morphed him into an almost exact heart-stoppingly handsome replica of his son.

Anthony's eyes went back to Abby and he noted roguishly, "The Beaumaris men have always had good taste."

"I've heard that before," Abby muttered.

He threw back his head and laughed the same, rich, deep, beautiful laugh as Cash.

When he was done, he turned to Cassandra and gave her a sharp nod.

She lifted her wand and spoke again, the silver beam shot from her wand and hit Anthony.

His eyes went to Cash, his body glimmering and then fading away.

Before he was gone, Abby saw his mouth move, his body disappeared but the words shimmered in the air around them.

"I'm proud of you, son."

Abby tried hard not to emit the hiccoughing sound of her sob, but she didn't quite achieve this feat. Cash turned to her, both his arms moving around her and he kissed her forehead.

Ben appeared before them and Cash pulled slightly—but only *very* slightly—away.

Abby held her breath but let it go to say, "Ben."

"He's freaking tall," Ben commented, eyes shifting to Cash.

"Oh, Ben," Abby whispered, torn asunder, wanting to laugh and wanting to scream and lastly, but most especially, wanting to cry.

She also wanted to touch him, having lived for that opportunity for four years. But oddly, even as she wanted it with a desperation that was the definition of longing, at the same time she did not want it, but instead wanted to move on.

"And kind of bossy," Ben continued, breaking into her confused thoughts.

"He is that," Abby murmured, and Ben grinned.

Cash showed no reaction at all.

Ben's eyes came to Abby and he told her gently, "You gotta let yourself be happy, honey."

"I—" she started, but he shook his head, lifted his hand as if to touch her and Cash tensed.

Ben's hand dropped away, not because of Cash but because Ben *couldn't* touch her, and Abby saw the frustration slide through his expression before he hid it.

Then his face assumed the look she'd seen a million times. It was the look he got when he was being serious and trying to cut through her stupid, stupid, *stupid* stupidity.

"You gotta let yourself be happy." His voice was fierce and demanding and it was at that moment that Abby realised she'd forgotten Ben could be pretty bossy too.

"Ben—" Abby started again only to be interrupted again.

"I don't want to hear it, beautiful. This can't go on, the way you've been."

"But I—" Abby began *again* only to be interrupted *again*.

"I don't want to hear it," he leaned in. "Let yourself be happy."

Abby stared at him.

"Promise me, Abby," Ben insisted.

As his gaze held hers, Abby felt the tears burning in her eyes.

Finally she whispered, "I promise."

He watched her a moment then pulled back. He turned to Kieran and Jenny who were both standing in each other's arms.

Jenny was silently crying.

Kieran's face was white and his throat was moving convulsively.

Ben lifted his hand to them. A sob broke from Jenny and Kieran's arms tightened around her.

Ben looked at Cassandra and nodded.

Cassandra lifted her wand and started speaking and Abby felt sudden, fierce anguish rip through her.

She pulled from Cash's arms and got as close as she could to Ben's glimmering form. She lifted her hands as if she could press them against his fading chest and tilted her head back.

"I love you," she choked, tears clogging her throat.

Ben's hand came toward her face but it was melting away as his voice floated through the air, "I know, baby. I love you too."

And then...

He was gone.

A whimper of sorrow slid from Abby's throat and she was turned into Cash's arms. She wrapped her own arms around him and buried her face in his chest, the sobs tearing through her, her body trembling uncontrollably. Cash's arm at her back tightened, his fingers digging into her side, his other hand slid up, fingers curled warmly around the back of her neck and through this, Abby sobbed.

Suddenly, fear sliced through her. She pulled back and her eyes cut to Cassandra.

"Tell me he went to a better place!" she demanded loudly.

Cassandra's face was gentle when she replied, "He went to a better place, mate. I promise you, he went to a better place."

Abby stared at her a moment, assessing her honesty then she turned away and pressed her forehead to Cash's chest and took a deep breath to control her tears.

Suddenly another emotion, this one anger, took hold of her.

Her head tipped back and she shouted at Cash, "I *hate* Vivianna! She's a *bitch*!"

Cash's hand moved from the back of her neck, his arm coming around so his fingers could curl at her neck at the side.

"She's gone, darling."

"Good!" Abby snapped. "She's pissed me off. All this drama! For what? Seriously! What a bitch!"

Cash stared at her a moment with the look on his face that he got when he was openly wondering about Abby's sanity when Jenny called out knowledgeably, "Don't worry, Cash. Anger is good. You only have to worry when Abby gets quiet. If she's blabbing and pissed, all's well."

Abby twisted to look at her friend and demanded, "Shut up, Jenny."

"I'm just saying—" Jenny started.

"Shut *up*!" Abby shot back.

"All righty then," Jenny mumbled, and Kieran's mouth twitched.

"People!" Mrs. Truman cut in sharply. She was peering over the side of the parapet. "We've got company."

Everyone moved to the edge and looked down to see the flashing lights of police cars. Something was happening with four policemen, the Fitzhugh women, Alistair and a man who Abby could swear, even from that distance, was Cash's friend James.

"What on—?" she breathed, but Cash was on the move.

He grabbed her hand and she and Cash led the way. Everyone clattered down the stairs from the turret (this made dangerous by Zee darting between Abby's legs on more than one occasion) down the hall, descending more stairs and then swiftly out the front door.

Abby hustled to match Cash's long strides as he guided them across the courtyard to the police.

"What's happening?" he asked when they'd stopped, and Abby noted that Alistair's face was red and he'd been in mid-bluster when they arrived.

"We've had a reported disturbance," a policeman answered Cash's question.

"What sort of disturbance?" Mrs. Truman demanded to know as if the last hour of disturbance upon disturbance hadn't happened.

"We've got thirty-seven people at the station claiming they've seen a ghost and an extra seventeen people reported the same via the phone," another policeman responded.

"A ghost!" Mrs. Truman shouted, then lied through her teeth, "Codswallop."

Jenny giggled.

Abby turned wide eyes to Cash.

But Cash wasn't listening. He was looking at James.

His eyes moved to the policemen, who looked like they were both talking to—and positioning themselves to detain—Alistair.

"And why are you here?" Cash asked the second set of policemen.

One of the policemen's eyes flicked to Cash but went back to Alistair as he answered, "I'm sorry to tell you this, sir, but we have a man being questioned at the station. He's alleging that he was paid by your uncle to tamper with your car. We need to take Mr. Beaumaris in for an interview."

"He did it," Mrs. Truman announced baldly, and both the police positioned around Alistair looked at her.

"How do you know that?" one of them asked.

"I'm seventy years old," Mrs. Truman explained on a humph as if his question was beyond ridiculous and beneath her notice but she was forced to reply, if only to demonstrate good manners. "At my age, you learn to read people. Just look at him." She gestured to Alistair as if that was all it took to try and fry him.

"I didn't attempt to kill my nephew," Alistair lied.

"You did and there's proof," James cut in. Everyone looked at him and he carried on, "Mick Johnstone recorded your conversation." Alistair's face blanched and James's eyes moved to the policemen. "He records all of his conversations for insurance and future extortion. Ask him about the tapes."

"And you came across this information how?" one of the policemen queried.

James shrugged. "He told his girlfriend then cheated on her. She kicked him out but he owed her money and never paid. She was willing to talk and she did."

"Did you offer her money to talk?" a policeman inquired, and James shook his head.

"No, she was happy to talk." His eyes moved to an Alistair who no longer looked pompous but was having difficulty hiding his fear. "She's pretty annoyed."

"You men," Suzanne remarked. "I hope you've learned from tonight's events that it's best never to cross a woman."

"Amen to that," Honor muttered.

One of the policemen approached Alistair saying, "You need to come with us."

"I will not leave my home!" Alistair declared, pulling his arrogance around him like a shield and stepping back.

The other policeman moved forward. "You come willing, or we'll be forced to arrest you and you'll come in cuffs. Your choice."

Alistair stared, the police braced and everyone watched.

Tense moments slid by.

Finally Alistair's shoulders straightened and his chin tilted back.

"I'll want to call my solicitors immediately," he demanded.

The policemen moved forward, one of them took Alistair's arm.

"Of course," he muttered.

Abby waited and watched Cash's uncle, hoping he'd turn, say something to Cash, maybe apologise for being such a jerk, or say something to Nicola, again something like apologising for being a jerk.

But he didn't look back as the police led him away.

James glanced at Cash then followed the police.

Everyone stood silent as the police car drove Alistair Beaumaris from Penmort Castle hopefully, Abby thought, for the final time.

"Well, it appears all's well at Penmort," one of the other set of policemen commented.

To which Suzanne muttered, eyes still at the gate where they last saw Alistair, "You can say that again."

Again everyone stood quiet and watchful as the second set of police took their leave.

Abby's mind was so blank, all thoughts forced out likely in an effort at self-preservation so she could keep her sanity, that when Nicola spoke she jumped.

"Honor, my dearest, I think *now* we could all use some champagne."

29

CASH CLAIMS PENMORT, HIS NEW FAMILY AND ABBY

Cash woke early, Abby's warm, soft body a dead weight heavy against his side. Her arm was draped across his midsection, her thigh thrown over his.

Last night, after they made their way through an alarming amount of champagne, or more accurately, the women and Angus had, Kieran and Cash stayed sober because someone had to just in case party guests, the police or any supernatural beings returned, Cash had led a drunken, giggling Abby to their room.

He'd taken off her extraordinary dress, slid her black nightgown on her body and guided her to bed.

She'd curled into him and fallen asleep as if she hadn't a care in the world. However this was likely because it was less falling asleep and more passing out.

As he did every morning, Cash gave himself a moment to experience the intensely pleasant peaceful feeling of Abby in bed at his side before he carefully moved away, trying not to disturb her.

The minute she lost purchase on his body, her arms snagged his pillow and she curled around it. There was something moving about her doing that every morning when Cash left her side, but he didn't give himself time to dwell.

Cash nabbed his dressing gown, shrugged it on, tightened the belt and walked from the room, soundlessly closing the door behind him.

He went directly to the kitchens where a woman named Jane, who he knew did the cooking for the castle, was sitting on a stool, reading the paper and sipping coffee.

The minute she saw Cash, she jerked straight and jumped from the stool.

"Mr. Fraser," she murmured. "You're an early bird. No one is ever up this early. It's always just me." She blathered on nervously, "I come in early to get myself sorted and because I like the castle when it's quiet. It never feels peaceful, except in the mornings."

Jane would, Cash hoped, find things different from this day forward.

"I'm always up this early," Cash informed her of a fact that she would need to know as she was now in his employ. He didn't, however, share that with her but instead requested, "Can you prepare breakfast for myself and Ms. Butler, please?"

"Of course, what would you like?" she replied.

Cash considered the question and smiled to himself when he could say with authority what Abby's preferences were for breakfast. "Coffee, strong, and something light. Croissants and fruit." She nodded and Cash continued, "Give it some time, half an hour or more, and if you would, please deliver it to our room."

She nodded again and busied herself with her task. Cash watched her a moment then looked about the vast kitchens, rooms used to prepare food for his line for centuries.

Now *his* kitchens.

Cash smiled again and walked out of the room.

Slowly he allowed himself time to move through his home.

He strolled through the armoury, the billiard room, library, conservatory, drawing room, inner and outer halls, dining room, but stopped in the study.

The tips of his fingers glided across the desk, another smile forming on his lips before he turned and looked out the still-dark windows of pre-dawn at the back of the desk, his brain knowing there were acres of wood and pastureland surrounding the castle beyond the tor. Land, luckily, that Alistair had not yet sold. Land, now, that Cash owned, as had his father before him and his father before him and so on.

He left the study, climbed the steps and walked to the gallery.

His mind did not wander to the events of the night before. Instead, he walked to the light switch, flipped it on and strode directly to Alistair's portrait.

His hands went to the frame and he lifted it. Pulling it off its mount, he turned its face away and set it on the floor against the wall.

Once done with this task, Cash turned to the alcove where his father's portrait hung. He took hold of it and moved it to the gallery proper. He hooked it on the mount that had held Alistair's portrait and straightened it, stepping back to make certain it was positioned properly.

Even though it was half the size of Alistair's pretentious painting, it looked far more like it belonged where it was.

Studying his father's image, Cash again did not let his mind wander to the night before. As with most everything else that happened last night, he'd process it with Abby when the time was right.

Instead he felt something settle in him, as if the small task of switching paintings was a far more grand and important feat than wresting his legacy out of the hands of a man who'd abuse his family and commit fratricide.

Cash considered this feeling and realised what he felt was justice.

He walked through the room, turned out the lights and headed to his and Abby's room.

As he moved through the house, Cash saw a glow coming from the sewing room. The door was open and he stopped in it to see Nicola, her face free of makeup, the heels of her feet up on the edge of a plush armchair, hair loose around her shoulders, arms wrapped around her calves, body enveloped in a soft throw, eyes staring unseeing out the dark window.

She looked, Cash thought, twenty years younger.

Her expression in profile was not sad nor was it troubled.

It was hopeful.

"Nicola," Cash murmured.

He watched her jump and her eyes flew to him.

"Cash," she whispered, but she didn't move.

Cash walked in. "You're up early."

She smiled up at him as he came within a few feet of her chair. Still she didn't move.

"I haven't slept," she told him.

"I'm sorry," Cash said.

"I'm not," she replied.

Seeing she was going to remain in her casual pose instead of assuming the role of courteous hostess per usual, Cash moved away from her. Her demonstration of casualness and familiarity, Cash noted incidentally, was something he enjoyed.

He sat on the arm of the chair opposite her.

"A great deal happened last night," he remarked, watching her closely for signs of post-traumatic stress.

Her hand came out from under the throw and she waved it in front of her.

"That," she stated. "Fenella, Suzanne and Honor filled me in last night." She grinned at him in a way she'd never done before. Her grin was filled with her usual friendliness, but now also had an easy openness which was something else Cash decided he liked.

It was then the sharp realisation hit him as to just how guarded she'd been, likely due to necessity, when Alistair had been around.

"Last night," Cash said, his voice had grown deeper, "what I said about you and the girls staying here, I meant it."

Her hand disappeared under the throw and he saw her pulling it tighter.

"I know, dear," she mumbled, her eyes moving back to the window. "But we couldn't."

"You can," Cash asserted, and her gaze came back to him.

"You're very kind, but we couldn't." When Cash opened his mouth to speak, she shook her head. "I don't know where we're going, but we can't stay here with you."

"Why not?" Cash asked, and he watched her expression turn confused.

"I...well..." She hesitated then continued, "You and Abby will want some time to—"

Cash cut her off. "Yes, we will."

The confusion left her face, she nodded and her lips tipped up at the ends. "So, we'll go."

"No," Cash returned. "You'll all stay at my home in Bath for a few months. Then you and the girls, if they haven't moved on, will come home."

"Cash—" she started.

"Nicola, I'm not arguing about this."

"We can't," she said more forcefully, her heels coming off the edge of the chair and she leaned toward him.

"Of course you can," Cash retorted firmly. "You're family."

At his words, Nicola pulled in a sharp breath and her eyes widened in what looked a good deal like wonder.

Cash decided to take that as the end of the discussion and stood, declaring, "It's decided."

Nicola stood with him, clutching the throw to her shoulders.

When he made a move to the door, her hand came out from under the throw and Cash stopped.

"Since Robbie," she started, her voice cracked, and she stopped.

Cash waited, knowing Robert Fitzhugh was her first husband. A man who died young after a valiant, but ugly and ultimately unsuccessful battle with cancer.

Cash watched Nicola swallow, take in a deep breath, and then she said in a stronger voice, "After Robbie, I messed up. I kidded myself for years. But since he died, well, since he died, we haven't had a real family."

"You do now," Cash returned and he saw tears fill her eyes.

He also saw the hope come back and some joy, but there was also sadness.

It was the sadness that cut through him like a razor.

"You miss him still," Cash noted gently, and he saw pain cross her face.

"Every day," she whispered.

That was precisely, after watching Abby with Ben last night, what Cash didn't want to hear.

Clearly, with her next words, Nicola read Cash's face as well.

"She will too," Nicola said softly, her eyes tender on Cash even as her words scored his soul. "But since she now has you, it'll be like she misses her parents. People she loves, but who're now lost. She'll never stop loving him, but she's a sweet girl with a lot of love to give and a lot of life in front of her." Nicola moved forward, her hand caught Cash's and squeezed. "Cash, my dearest, she'll always love him. But that doesn't mean she doesn't have plenty of love to give to you."

For some reason unknown to him, Cash confided, "I don't like to share."

Nicola laughed softly while giving his hand another squeeze before dropping it.

"Well, *that* doesn't surprise me," she commented then said sagely, "However, I figure you'll decide you can, even if you don't like it."

He hated to admit it, but he knew she was not wrong.

He grinned down at her as he lifted his hand to her face, his thumb sliding across her still smooth cheek. It was a gesture twenty-four hours ago he would never have made and likely she would not have accepted.

Now, however, she turned her face into his hand and smiled.

Witnessing her unguarded beauty, Cash thought not for the first time that his uncle was the greatest of fools.

He dropped his hand and muttered, "Do you want me to go down and order you some coffee?"

She shook her head. "I'll do it in a minute."

Cash nodded and moved away, glancing back at the door to see her resume her seat. She pulled her feet back up on its edge, a position he instinctively knew she'd taken thousands of times in the past and she would have the opportunity to assume thousands more times in the future.

Yes, he thought, *justice*.

He continued down the hall and was passing Suzanne's door when it was yanked open. Cash's hand was caught and he was pulled roughly into the room.

Cash's body froze. It turned. He gritted his teeth and his eyes sliced to Suzanne.

She'd closed the door and was standing in front of it wearing nothing but a short, revealing peach nightgown edged with beige lace and a matching short dressing gown, which was hanging open widely, leaving very little to the imagination.

He was disappointed her brief demonstration of humanity last night didn't last long. He also had every intention of removing her bodily from the door if he had to.

"Suzanne, move out of my way," he demanded.

"Five minutes, Cash," she requested softly, and his eyes drilled into hers.

He saw with vague surprise there was no malice or spitefulness nor any deviousness. Her blue eyes were open, warm and entreating, and he thought she'd never looked prettier.

"Five minutes," she repeated on a whispered plea.

Cash planted his feet and crossed his arms on his chest.

"Five minutes," he agreed on an unhappy growl.

She opened her mouth then closed it. She opened it again then closed it.

She looked away and lifted her hand, fingers sifting through her hair at her forehead, pulling it away from her face in an uncertain and even endearing way that reminded him of Abby.

Her eyes came back to his. "This isn't easy for me to say."

"Whatever it is you have four minutes and thirty seconds to say it."

She grabbed the edges of her dressing gown and wrapped them tightly around her body.

She sucked in her lips and then spoke so quickly it was as if she didn't get it all out as fast as she could, she would lose the ability to speak for the rest of her life.

"When I was a kid, I thought Vivianna was my friend. She liked me. She talked to me. She was always there when Alistair was mean to me. She always made me feel better." Her arms wrapped tighter around her body as she kept going. "She'd tell me stories about the Beaumaris men, their beauty, their virility, their honour, pride, stubbornness, confidence, arrogance. Cash, she had hundreds of stories about the masters of this castle, hundreds of *romantic* stories about generation after generation of men she loved."

Cash misread her meaning and stated, "Vivianna is gone, Suzanne."

"I know and I won't miss her," Suzanne replied swiftly. "What I'm saying is a little girl who lost her father finds herself in a big, creepy castle with a stepdad who's a git. To a girl like that, those stories were…" She hesitated and continued on a whisper, "Those stories meant the world to me."

Cash remained silent and Suzanne carried on in a voice so soft he almost couldn't hear her.

"Then you came to visit."

The realisation of what she was saying was so profound Cash's body jerked with it.

His tone was gentle when he murmured, "Suzanne."

She cut him off. "I've been in love with you since I was nine years old."

Cash sighed.

This he did not need.

"It's okay," Suzanne said hurriedly. "All this, all I've done these past months wasn't because I loved you. Well, not entirely, or at least not the way you'd think."

"Suzanne—" Cash started again, but she was back to speaking swiftly.

"It was because Vivianna told me about Alistair. It was because she knew you were the real master of this castle, that she knew he'd murdered Anthony and she knew he'd try to murder you. I behaved the way I behaved to you, and then Abby, to drive you away."

Cash's body froze at learning this knowledge, but Suzanne didn't notice and she carried on.

"I wanted to make it so unpleasant for you that you'd give up whatever it was you were doing all of a sudden reconciled with Alistair."

She started to take a step closer to Cash, thought better of it and stopped, but kept talking.

"She was in the room, Cash. Vivianna was, when Abby walked in that first time. You weren't there, she wasn't allowing herself to be seen, but I felt it the minute Abby walked in. I saw Abby, I felt Vivianna's wrath and I knew, I absolutely *knew* Vivianna meant her harm. Before dinner I did what I could both to make you angry and Abby uncomfortable enough to go, but you didn't. After dinner I got out of there the first chance I could, went to my room and acted out a crying rage which was when she normally would visit me. I hoped she'd come to me instead of doing anything to Abby." She paused, took in a breath, and went on, "She didn't come. She hurt Abby instead."

Cash watched as Suzanne closed her eyes and then opened them.

They focused on Cash and he saw the pain there before she whispered, "I know you don't like me and I know the reason you don't like me is because of the way I behaved. But I had to do something, didn't I?"

Her tone was so uncertain, so un-Suzanne, Cash didn't know what to make of her. He'd known the woman in front of him for a year (twenty-four of them if you counted when he'd visited in his teens) but he'd never met her.

"You should have said something," Cash told her brusquely.

She shook her head and looked away.

"Right," she muttered and turned to him again talking now in a high, sarcastic voice. "Um, Cash, you know, your uncle killed your dad and I'm guessing you're next. Oh, and by the way, I know that because a ghost told me and she's a nasty piece of work who wants to do harm to your girlfriend." She paused before asking irritably, "Is that what I should have said?"

"Suzanne—" Cash began, but her expression changed to one with which he was far more familiar.

She moved toward him but not to him. She began to walk right by him, muttering, "I knew I shouldn't have bothered."

But Cash's hand came up and grasped her arm, stopping her.

She looked up at him, eyes narrowed and cruel, and he warned, "Don't go back to the bitch, Suzanne."

"The bitch works for me, Cash," she spat. "Trust me, I know. I've had twenty-five years of perfecting her."

His voice gentled and he watched her head jerk as her face paled when he said, "I'm sorry about that." Cash let her go but got closer. Tipping his chin down to look at her, he finished, "But you don't need her anymore. Let her go."

He could tell she was holding on to the bitch, but only barely when she replied sharply, "It's not that easy."

"No," Cash agreed. "Probably not. But the woman who helped

Abby and me last night, and the one I saw a few minutes ago, is someone I'd like to get to know. The one standing in front of me right now is one I never want to see again."

She stared and he watched her force a painful swallow.

She didn't speak.

So Cash did.

"Thank you for trying to protect me," he said quietly and with feeling.

Her mouth dropped open then she snapped it shut before she stammered, "I...um, you're welcome."

"You're a bright woman, Suzanne," he muttered. "You'll find your way."

She stared up at him, silent.

He decided their conversation was finished and moved toward the door.

He halted and turned back when she called his name.

She had her dressing gown wrapped tight around her again and Cash thought she looked very young and very scared.

But even so, she had the courage to say, "I'm glad you're safe."

He nodded and moved to open the door but he turned back when she kept talking.

"And I hope you'll be happy." She hesitated then said, "With Abby. I like her. She's a bit mad, but she's tough and very sweet."

She ended on a whisper and Cash watched as pink stained her cheeks when he smiled at her, something he wasn't certain he'd ever done.

Without another word he exited her room, closing the door softly. He moved down the hall hoping that he could make it to his and Abby's rooms without Fenella, Honor, Jenny, Kieran, Cassandra, Angus or, God forbid, Mrs. Truman (all of whom spent the night) waylaying him.

He didn't succeed.

As he was passing the third door from his, it opened.

Cash stopped and turned to see Cassandra standing in the doorway. Her long, dark hair was down and tousled from sleep. She wore a pair of drawstring, flannel shorts and a tight camisole likely borrowed from

Honor as Cassandra was far too curvy to fit in anything Fenella or Suzanne owned.

She leaned a shoulder against the doorframe, crossed her arms on her chest and rested her heel against the side of her opposite ankle.

"I'm sorry, Cash, but we did what we had to do," she said quietly.

He knew to what she was referring, bringing back his grandmother, his father, and mostly, Ben.

Cash crossed his own arms on his chest.

"You knew the circle wasn't going to work," he remarked.

She nodded. "Both Angus and I had our doubts. Vivianna was strong and she was smart. She'd know about the circle and she'd know how to defeat it."

"You had it planned all along," Cash said, and watched her nod again.

"We tried the circle because we didn't want to use Ben if we didn't have to. But we knew we'd need to be prepared to throw everything at her. Abby didn't want her cat involved, but we brought Zee along too, just in case. Angus came up with the spell and I activated it, pulling back the veil and recruiting the trinity. One Vivianna had wronged, your grandmother. A past master, your father. And a protector of the innocent, Ben. All of them together, as well as Zee, who's a powerful little thing, worked. They sucked her power, kept her visible so she couldn't dematerialise and their presence rooted her so she couldn't move."

It was Cash's turn to nod, and Cassandra continued.

"You should know there was another way. A potion Abby could take to fight her. We could have waited six months and gone after her."

Cash's body got tight and he declared, "I wouldn't have allowed that."

She grinned and replied, "I figured that." Her voice dropped low. "Furthermore, as much as Abby was prepared to do it, I reckon Vivianna would have made mincemeat of her. When Angus found out I'd even mentioned the potion to Abby, he went off on one. Of course, we didn't know at the time that you had any power over her."

This surprised Cash. Angus had not seemed hesitant to put Abby in the line of fire. Apparently he was only happy to do so if he had Abby's back and felt in control of the situation, something he would not be if Abby had been in the position of going head to head with Vivianna.

Cassandra kept talking, again in her low quiet voice, her eyes had grown intense as they studied Cash's face.

"You should also know, when we made contact with your father, he wanted to come early. He wanted to spend time with you in the castle." Her arms came uncrossed, she took a step forward, put her hand on Cash's biceps and informed him, "It was a grave risk, Cash. The longer he was away from the other plane, the less likely it was we could return him there. If we didn't get him back in time, he'd be stuck here for eternity. Says a lot about him, that he'd take that risk and why he took it. Also says a lot about how he feels about you."

Cash clenched his teeth against the feelings this statement sent surging through him, not wishing to share them with Cassandra, who he liked well enough but not enough to engage in an intensely private moment.

Instead, he felt an overwhelmingly strong desire to get to Abby.

Cassandra took pity and finished, dropping her hand from his arm. "As for Vivianna never appearing in front of Nicola, we don't know why. Lorna nor Anthony understood it either. I suppose that will just have to remain a mystery."

Cash nodded again as she took a step back.

His voice was deeper than normal when he said, "Thank you."

She awarded him with a bright smile, suggesting she'd enjoyed every minute of her endeavours because in the end, they'd been successful. "My pleasure."

Then she took another step back and closed the door.

Cash turned to his room. When he made it safely to the end of the corridor Jane, the cook, was bustling down the hall balancing a silver tray.

"I'll get that," Cash said, divesting her of the tray and he put his other hand to the knob. "Mrs. Fitzhugh is in the sewing room. She'll be needing coffee."

Jane blinked at him and asked, "Which Ms. Fitzhugh?" When Cash didn't immediately reply, she hurried on, "I only ask because Suzanne is kind of funny about her coffee."

"Nicola," Cash replied, and watched her eyes go round. Deciding she'd likely hear it soon enough, he might as well tell her. "Jane, I've foreclosed on the house. Ms. Butler and I'll be moving in imminently. Mr. Beaumaris won't be back. The Fitzhugh women, however, will be staying."

She stared at him, mouth open, stunned speechless.

Then she made a noise in the back of her throat that sounded like strangled laughter. At the sound, her eyes bugged out in horror and she choked back her mirth.

"Sorry, sorry, erm, sorry, sir. I'm just shocked," she stuttered, but although her nerves weren't gone, her eyes were bright and cheerful.

She was, Cash knew, lying.

She wasn't shocked. She was happy. She disliked Alistair. She also probably liked Nicola.

Cash wasn't surprised and he smiled. "It's all right, Jane. He was an ass."

She was now staring at his mouth and he watched *her* cheeks get pink.

"Jane," he called and she snapped out of it with a jerk. "Coffee," he reminded her. "For Nicola."

"Right, right," she muttered, moving away, lifting her arms and waving her hands at the side of her head. "I'm on it."

"One more thing," Cash halted her. Jane turned and Cash finished, "I'm not 'Mr. Fraser' nor am I 'sir.' You call me Cash."

She gawked at him, eyes wide, face aflame, before she nodded, her mouth forming a smile and she began her retreat.

He watched her move down the hall. Then he opened the door and entered.

Abby lay motionless under the covers.

The black circle of Zee lay ensconced at the back of her bent knees.

Cash moved across the dark room, placed the tray on the table between the two armchairs in the turret and turned on the standing lamp there. Soft light filled the space.

He walked to the bed and bent at Zee, his fingers sifting through the cat's silky soft fur. Zee lifted his head with a sleepy mew.

"You get gourmet wet cat food for the rest of your life," Cash muttered to the feline, and as if Zee understood, he let out a stronger but still sleepy mew and stretched his neck to press into Cash's fingers, which were scratching behind his ears.

With a final stroke for Zee, Cash moved away to sit in the curve of Abby's lap afforded by her position curled around his pillow. He looked at the bedside clock and noticed it was nearly seven.

Obviously, he'd slept in.

His eyes moved back to Abby and he pulled her hair off her neck then rested his hand there.

"Darling," he called, but she didn't move.

He gave her neck a gentle squeeze and repeated his endearment.

She shifted slightly, her eyes opened and only they moved to him. She kept her face nuzzled in the pillow.

He thought, somewhat distractedly, that she looked rather adorable.

"Please tell me you aren't going to work," she grumbled sleepily.

"I'm not going to work."

She closed her eyes. "Good, come back to bed."

He would, he knew, be delighted to do that.

Later.

However they had to talk first.

"Abby, we have to talk."

Her eyes opened immediately, but this time her head turned.

"About what?" she asked, her voice sexy and husky, but there was an edge of alertness to it.

"Get up, love, this is an awake and functioning talk," he told her.

"I don't want an awake and functioning talk," she returned. "I want to sleep and be awake and functioning on Thursday." She closed her eyes, again muttering, "Maybe Friday."

His voice held a gentle warning when he said, "Abby."

She pulled in a deep breath and let it out in a heavy sigh before she came up on an elbow, lifted a hand and pulled her hair from her face.

He noticed that he hadn't thought to take her jewellery off last night and he felt a powerful sensation strike him at the vision of her in bed, hair dishevelled, face grumpy and sleepy, wearing the silk and diamonds he'd given her.

"All right," she gave in, cutting in to his thoughts.

Cash stood. She threw back the covers and he walked to the turret. He decided if she didn't notice he'd not remind her that she was walking around barefoot in a nightgown, wearing tens of thousands of pounds worth of diamonds.

Instead he poured coffee in delicate china cups, adding milk to Abby's, taking his black with a sugar.

She'd donned her cashmere dressing gown and had her hair pulled back in a ponytail when he turned and handed her the cup and saucer. She sipped at it as he sipped at his. Then he sat in one of the chairs. Abby began to move to the other one, but he caught her wrist, leaned to the side, deposited his cup and saucer on the tray and carefully pulled her in his lap so as to not spill her coffee.

She held her body stiff, not a thing like the warm and pliant Abby who snuggled close to him two nights before.

Cash knew instantly, even after her avowals of love in front of her dead husband, his family and even her fucking cat, that this conversation was not going to go as he'd hoped.

"What do we need to talk about?" she asked guardedly, keeping her eyes on her cup as she sipped again.

"Our future," he replied, and at his words she choked and spluttered.

When she got herself under control, her gaze moved to his.

He watched her breathe looking like this wasn't an easy, natural task.

Finally she whispered, "Yes, I agree. We need to talk about our future."

"You start," Cash demanded, wanting to hear what he was up against right away so he could tear it apart, explain the way it actually was, take her straight back to bed and fuck her so hard she'd still feel him inside her on Thursday.

Maybe Friday.

She didn't argue as he expected.

She nodded, leaned forward, put her cup and saucer on the tray and sat back, folding her hands in her lap and continuing to hold her body stiffly.

Her attention turned to him.

"I'm sorry I fell in love with you."

Cash felt his lips part in surprise.

That, of all things, he did *not* expect to hear.

She had these last weeks, apologised for a number of bizarre things. But this was by far and away the most bizarre.

"Sorry?" he asked.

She waved her hand in the air and repeated, "I'm sorry I fell in love with you. I wasn't going to tell you, but I didn't want you to believe Vivianna. It was stupid. I should have let you believe what she was saying, but I didn't want you to. I don't know why."

"Abby—" he began, but she talked over him.

"Jenny told me last night about your talk." When he opened his mouth, she waved her hand in the air again and said, "It's okay. I'm okay with it. I mean, I'm *not*, like, *at all*, but I have to be, don't I?"

She didn't let him answer and went on.

"I like what we have. No, I *love* what we have and I'd be really happy to stay this way for as long as you want. But Jenny reminded me I'm kind of weird in that I get attached, as in *really* attached, and she's right."

She took a deep breath and Cash thought he had his chance to speak, but she got there before him.

"Even though, you know, I love you and everything, I think it's best if we just move on. End it. Now. I don't want it to be messy for you and I'm sure you don't want that either. I mean, it's better for you this way. Trust me."

Cash's arms moved around her and he pulled her closer to his chest, deeper into his lap.

She didn't notice this and kept right on talking.

"And I'm being kind of selfish. I don't want it to be messy either and I don't want to get *more* attached, if you know what I mean."

He tried to cut in. "Abby—"

He failed as she rattled on.

"So a clean break now would be good. I mean, not *good*, but better for all concerned. You've got your castle and Alistair got what he deserved and Vivianna is in hell so all's well in the world of Cash. Which will make me feel a bit, you know, more okay with everything, knowing it's all good for you."

She stopped on a sharp breath that hitched in the middle and he realised she was close to tears, her body stiff and tight. Her eyes not meeting his were bright and she was, lastly but most importantly, completely full of shit with this whole act.

He wanted to laugh.

He didn't.

He also wanted to kiss her.

Something else he didn't do.

Instead, he said softly, "Darling, look at me."

Her gaze came to his face but not to his eyes.

"Look at me, Abby," he repeated.

He watched her teeth clench, then her eyes lifted to his.

When their eyes caught, he asked, "Are you finished?"

She bit her lip.

He felt his own lips twitch then she nodded and said, "I think so."

"Good, I'm talking now," he declared.

Her eyes went funny, guarded and surprised and something else, something he couldn't read.

"Oh...kay," she replied hesitantly.

Cash didn't delay.

"I'm in love with you," he announced, and her mouth dropped open but he went on, "We're not over. We're never going *to be* over. There isn't going to be an end. This is it, you and me, in Penmort, you wearing diamonds and silk and having coffee delivered to our bedroom every morning."

"Cash—" she whispered, eyes wide, face pale, expressions clashing between shock and awe.

"I'm not done," Cash stated and pressed on, "I know you still love Ben. I'm not going to pretend I like it but I will try to live with it."

"Cash—"

"Abby, stop interrupting me."

"Okay," she whispered, and he felt her body start to soften in his arms and he knew he was getting somewhere.

"You were right last night, it's early. We'll take some time, learn more about each other. Not much, but we'll do it. Then we'll get married, have children and live happily ever after, if you don't annoy me too much." She gasped, but he ignored it and continued, "I've spoken to Nicola this morning and she and her daughters are going to give us a few months. They'll stay in Bath then move back here. I'm sure you'll agree they'll be welcome here for as long as they wish to stay."

"Of course," Abby mumbled.

Cash kept going.

"I want you to know I'm not only fine with you becoming more attached to me, I want it and you're going to give it to me. I want you so attached you can't imagine a life without me. I don't give a fuck if that's selfish, that's what I want because, Abby, you must know, I already can't imagine life without you."

He stopped talking and watched as the brightness in her eyes became wetness shimmering at their edges. One tear dropped to her cheek and slid down her face.

Cash watched its progress.

Finally she whispered, "Are you done?"

Cash's eyes went from her lone tear back to hers.

"Yes," he replied.

She was still whispering, nearly breathless, when she asked, "Are you sure? About what you said?"

"Yes," he answered instantly.

"I thought—" Her breath caught audibly, it sounded painful and Cash drew her yielding body closer, tucking her deep into the protective fold of his arms as another tear slid down her cheek. She sucked in air, her hands coming up to rest on his chest, and with visible effort she continued, "I thought it was stupid to hope."

"Hope for what?" he asked softly, even though he knew the answer.

She didn't give him that answer.

Instead she whispered, "I thought it was selfish."

"What was selfish, darling?"

"To have something so good, so wonderful, with Ben." His body grew tight but her hand moved to rest on his face and she admitted, "It was stupid to hope, selfish to want something even better. Something that felt *magical*. Something I thought I had with you."

An overwhelming sense of triumph coursed through him and Cash again wanted to kiss her. This time it felt like a need rather than a desire.

Instead he confirmed decisively, "You have it."

Her face came close.

She rested her forehead against his, her nose alongside his, her eyes open and looking deeply into his, she whispered, "I know."

It was then Cash surged out of the chair.

Taking her with him, he carried her to bed.

There, he fucked her so hard it was likely she still felt him inside her on Thursday.

However, he'd never know, since he fucked her Wednesday night as well as every night in between.

And some mornings besides.

EPILOGUE
EDITH'S MENTAL SNAPSHOTS

"It's too early," Abby, pacing the waiting room in severe agitation, announced for the seventeenth time.

Cash's eyes went from the papers in his hands to his wife.

He knew it was the seventeenth time because after she'd said it five times in the car on the way to hospital, he'd started counting.

"Abigail, calm down," Mrs. Truman, sitting and knitting in a chair next to Cash, demanded imperiously.

Abby whirled on Mrs. Truman, narrowed her eyes and planted her hands on her hips.

"Calm?" she asked in a deceptively light tone.

"Yes, dear, *calm*," Mrs. Truman answered, her voice gentling. "Let nature take its course."

"Nature," Abby declared, her voice beginning to tremble, exposing her not-very-controlled fear, "demands a gestation period of nine months. Jenny's baby has only had seven."

This wasn't, Cash knew, exactly true.

Jenny's baby had seven and three-quarter months of gestation.

Cash's eyes swept Abby's body in her form-fitting, very elegant, demurely sexy, plum-coloured dress complemented by rich suede, charcoal-grey, spike-heeled boots.

She was also wearing the diamond bracelet he'd given her, which she wore daily. A modest (but not too modest) diamond pendant hung from a delicate platinum chain and lay in the indentation of her throat and double-diamond drop earrings hung from her ears.

The necklace he'd bought her in France during their first holiday together on the Riviera. The earrings he'd given her during a dinner they'd shared when she'd been on a business trip with him in Rome six months previously.

Cash should probably diversify into giving her different precious jewels, but he found he liked her wearing his diamonds.

His eyes stopped at her boots and distractedly he wished, as usual (however at that present time most especially, considering his wife's condition), that she wouldn't wear those fucking high heels.

He let go of this wish, knowing it was in vain, and finally his gaze moved up and settled on the small, but becoming more noticeable by the day, baby bump at her belly.

Cash, after copious amounts of research once Abby told him she was pregnant, knew the extra three weeks Abby wasn't declaring of Jenny's pregnancy meant a great deal to the outcome of that afternoon's events.

Cash also knew that for the first time in decades Abby and Jenny's relationship had turned on its head.

Jenny's pregnancy had been difficult from the start. She'd been tremendously ill in the beginning, incapacitated with morning sickness, crippling migraines and terrified by intermittent cramping and spotting.

These symptoms lasted well into the second trimester and there were two very legitimate scares when she'd stopped spotting and started bleeding.

Both times it was Abby who had rushed her to the hospital.

Absolute bed rest was prescribed during the last trimester. This, under Abby's edict and Nicola's urging, both firm and forceful which brought about Kieran's acceptance, happened at Penmort and was accompanied by Abby's and Nicola's near constant companionship.

It was also a strategy that obviously didn't work.

Jenny had gone into labour four hours ago.

Even though labour had begun at Penmort, Kieran had called Cash to ask for him to return from his Saturday morning in his new office in Exeter instead of telling Abby this news.

This was a kindness for which Cash was grateful. Cash didn't want Abby anywhere near the steering wheel of a car in her present state.

As Cash watched his wife, his mind wandered over the last several months.

Jenny had been used to taking care of Abby through her many dramas. Abby had been used to being taken care of. This change in the state of affairs had altered their relationship in a way Cash didn't quite understand.

Women, he'd decided some time ago, were baffling to the point where it was futile for a man even to attempt to comprehend.

So he didn't.

What he did understand was that Jenny was a strong and capable woman who didn't like having to be taken care of.

Cash had grown to admire this greatly.

Abby, on the other hand, was beside herself with glee that she had an opportunity to pay Jenny back for all her care and attention. And this she did with an enthusiasm akin to religion.

They clashed frequently, more than likely because Jenny was frightened and trying to hide it and Abby even more so.

Cash and Kieran steered well clear. They often found themselves together, in the beginning in Kieran's office in his home, in the end in the billiards room at Penmort drinking whisky and letting their wives (more often than not *loudly*, in another room) sort through their relationship turmoil.

Abby was not beside herself with glee at the circumstances. For seven and three-quarter months she had been functioning on adrenaline and very slim hope, and not succeeding by any stretch of the imagination at keeping her fear at bay.

His wife unfortunately had been conditioned to the fact that if something bad could happen, it would.

"Darling," Cash called, putting aside his papers and making an effort at controlling her fear. An effort he knew was doomed to fail but he made it all the same. "Sit down."

"No," was her swift, sharp retort.

Mrs. Truman chuckled.

Cash tried not to smile.

At that moment, Nicola walked in bearing a cardboard tray of gourmet coffees.

"Any news?" she asked.

"No," Abby repeated just as swiftly and sharply, and Nicola's eyes flew to Cash.

Cash gave a short shake of his head and Nicola pressed her lips together.

She handed out the coffees she'd gone to a local shop to purchase after Mrs. Truman declared that hospital coffee would *simply* not do. When she was done with the coffees, she approached Abby, putting her hand on his wife's arm.

"My dear, you really must try to relax. You're not doing your own baby any favours by getting upset," Nicola advised.

"How do you propose I do that, Nicci? She's my best friend!" Abby ended on a cry.

Cash watched Nicola's hand squeeze Abby's arm comfortingly.

It still amused him that Abby called Nicola "Nicci." Nicola was *not* a Nicci. However, Nicola didn't seem to mind in the slightest.

Over the last several months, Nicola's daughters had moved out of the castle one by one.

They'd all had jobs since Cash had been reunited with the family, Fenella's part-time. However Fenella found a new, higher paid, full-time job in Plymouth and was the first to go.

Suzanne had received a promotion and a transfer to Bristol. She was the second to leave and was renting Abby's long since fully restored grandmother's home in Clevedon, an idea Cash had suggested to Abby, which she'd adored, thrilled to have a "family member" residing in her beloved home.

Honor moved out only the month before. She was now sharing a flat in Exeter with her boyfriend.

Cash decided they did this because they were free, finally, to leave their mother and live their lives because Nicola was now safe.

Coming to this understanding caused Cash no small amount of guilt that for a year he had entirely misread the Fitzhugh women. He had been so wrapped up in his retribution against Alistair that he had not caught on to what was happening and moved far more swiftly to end their mistreatment.

Although he shared this with Abby, who urged him to let go of his blame (which he did not), he did not share it with the others nor, at his request, did Abby.

He would, as was his nature, demonstrate his remorse by making certain Nicola Fitzhugh was safe, protected and happy for the rest of her days.

Nicola had taken a part-time job in a local shop but she had, Cash knew, no intention of leaving the castle. It had finally become her home, something which Cash made clear and Abby made clearer.

But also she seemed intent on raining love and affection on Cash and Abby, the kind Cash never had and Abby had lost.

He decided this was likely her way of paying for what Alistair had stolen from Cash, a responsibility she did not bear, but assumed all the same.

Cash also decided she just simply loved Abby.

As this fit in with his plan, he let Nicola continue her endeavours unhindered.

Abby and Nicola had offered Penmort to the National Trust, opening it to the public for six months of the year on Tuesday and Thursday afternoons and alternating weekends.

Cash had not liked this decision and had only been cursorily involved in it.

He found, somewhat to his annoyance, but mostly to his amusement, that his wife and aunt regularly teamed up to steamroll him with some rather bizarre capers. These capers, Cash knew, were likely *always* instigated by Abby, and she simply took Nicola along for the ride.

However Cash also knew Nicola was having the time of her life.

Therefore he didn't resist.

Much.

He found to his surprise that he not only didn't mind his home being open to the public, he liked it. The castle was so popular due to its beauty, history, and the "myth" of Vivianna, made stronger by the many reports of her appearance at the anniversary dinner—some of which were printed in newspapers and magazines—that the National Trust had to do viewings by appointment only.

That meant his family was not overwhelmed with visitors. Anyone who came had a genuine desire to see the property and was thus utterly respectful.

He enjoyed their interest. His legacy was rather extraordinary and he found he liked sharing it.

When he confided this to Abby, she didn't say she told him so but she gave him a look that said it.

Cash's attention moved to the door as Suzanne sauntered in looking stylish in a tailored black wool overcoat.

James followed her looking peeved.

Mrs. Truman glanced at them, her eyes turned to Cash and they shared a smile.

Suzanne and James had met during the planning of Abby and Cash's small, but elaborate (the latter, at Cash's command), family-and-close-friends-only wedding.

Suzanne had found a way to leave the bitch behind.

She had, however, retained a certain coolness and cynicism which was not in the least unattractive.

His friend James immediately found this intriguing and had begun his pursuit just as immediately.

James was used to success. *Rapid* success.

Therefore James was surprised then frustrated then annoyed, albeit not deterred, when his aims had not been achieved after months of concentrated effort.

Cash knew, because Suzanne had confided in Abby who had confided in him, that Suzanne was in love with his best friend.

He did not share this with James, however.

He didn't because he didn't want to break Suzanne's confidence with Abby.

He also didn't because Suzanne's reasons for keeping her love from James were a test James would have to pass unaided.

Suzanne had been cruelly abused and mishandled for twenty-five years by Alistair, something else she confided in Abby, who then told Cash, sharing that Alistair had been verbally abusive to all the Fitzhugh women, but for some reason he saved his worst for Suzanne and dished it out with heartbreaking regularity.

Therefore James would have to win her trust on his own.

Cash had no doubt this would happen.

Suzanne, who, to Cash's surprise, had formed the closest of the three sisters' very close bonds with his wife, took one look at Abby and her face grew pale. Then her eyes moved to Cash.

They were soft and filled with concern and Cash thought, not for the first time since that night at Penmort, that he was quite happy Alistair was in prison for being behind the now proven murder of his father (the investigation was again opened) and his attempt on Cash's life. Suzanne had confessed her love to him, but had been unable to share her true self when he'd entered her life.

If she had he might have been tempted.

Then again, that would have meant he wouldn't have met Abby.

As lovely and interesting as Suzanne was now, Cash knew without a doubt he'd still have a hole in his life if Abby wasn't in it, even if he'd never met her.

They were simply meant to be.

He understood this was a ludicrously romantic notion.

And he didn't give a fuck.

"Please don't ask how things are going," Abby, standing with her arm around Nicola as well as in the curve of Nicola's arm, begged Suzanne.

"I wouldn't dream of it, love," Suzanne murmured, took off her coat and threw it on a chair. She sat beside Mrs. Truman and mumbled under her breath, "Abby's obviously in a state. I sincerely hope you're behaving yourself."

Mrs. Truman's eyebrows shot up, her hand came to her chest, and she mouthed the word, "Me?" as if she was at all times the soul of kindness, affection and love.

It took a great effort of will for Cash not to burst out laughing.

"Yes, you," Suzanne returned.

Mrs. Truman made a "pah" noise, but said no more and Suzanne rolled her eyes at Cash.

With great energy and dedication, Mrs. Truman had insinuated herself in the lives of all of Cash and Abby's family.

With alarming frequency, she was domineering, cantankerous and interfering.

With complete consistency, she was also unwaveringly loyal.

James threw his overcoat on a chair and sat beside Cash.

Cash turned his head to his friend and took off his reading glasses.

"How are things?" he asked.

James knew to what, or more precisely, to whom he was referring.

"Last night, I made progress," James answered.

"Good," Cash murmured.

"This morning, I lost it," James went on.

Cash chuckled.

James's voice dropped low. "Last night she told me some of what Alistair did to her. I'm guessing not all. Do you know what he did? The things he *said*?"

Cash regarded his friend and remained silent. James accurately read and deferred to Cash's unspoken demonstration of loyalty to Suzanne.

"I'd like to know how, *exactly*, you stopped yourself from hunting that bastard down and committing murder," James inquired, his voice still low and quiet, but now it was vibrating with a barely controlled but understandable fury.

"His punishment is longer this way," Cash replied.

James nodded though, Cash guessed, he didn't entirely agree.

Cash had to admit he often wondered what the use was of Alistair's continued existence on the planet. However, he usually had these thoughts late at night while listening to Abby breathing in her sleep at his side and Zee's purring as Cash stroked him at his other and found he didn't often dwell on them long enough to come to any conclusion.

Suddenly Cash's gaze sliced to Abby, his senses so attuned to her that he didn't need to see her to know her change in mood.

She was smiling tentatively at something as she called, "Well?"

Cash's eyes moved to the door and he saw Cassandra, dressed somewhat normally for once, strolling in.

Although no longer having to work her questionable talents on their behalf, Cassandra had also become a fixture in their lives. Mostly at the many dinner parties Abby and Nicola, Jenny or Mrs. Truman held but often simply coming 'round to the castle to drink herbal tea or, before Abby's pregnancy, margaritas with Abby where they would cackle loudly about whatever it was women found to cackle about.

Cash did not have a good feeling about Cassandra's arrival.

"Abby," he muttered warningly, but his wife either didn't hear him or she ignored him.

He was guessing the latter.

Cassandra shook her head and approached Abby.

Cash stood, dropped his glasses on the chair he'd vacated and walked to his wife.

"Someone came up to me, mate. Asked me what I was doing. I had to abort the mission," Cassandra said.

"What mission?" Cash asked a question to which he, to his intense frustration, already knew the answer.

Abby looked up at Cash. "I called Cassandra and asked her to come, make her way to the delivery room and send some pixie dust Jenny's way."

Yes, he was correct. He knew the answer.

"You asked Cassandra to send some pixie dust Jenny's way," Cash repeated with no small amount of consternation at his wife's antics.

Abby looked up at him and jerked her head, shaking back her hair in a now-familiar act that announced her defiance.

"Yes," she declared.

"Fucking hell," Cash muttered.

"I hope you stop saying the F-word after our baby comes along," Abby snapped.

"I hope you stop doing wild and ridiculous things so I won't feel the need to curse after our baby comes along," Cash returned.

Nicola emitted a stifled giggle.

Cassandra grinned.

"I am who I am," Abby shot back, and at her words Cash relaxed.

Then he smiled.

"Yes, you are," he murmured, and he watched his wife's face take on a look of surprise at his easy capitulation.

Then she smiled back.

He pulled her in his arms, she melted into his body and he felt the usual sense of peace having her in his arms gave him.

After all this time, nearly two years together, he'd never gotten used to the ease she brought to his life.

He also hoped he never did. If he did, he'd lose the understanding of just what a precious gift it was.

There was a commotion at the door and Angus stormed in, his kilt awhirl.

"What'd I miss?" he shouted.

"Nothing, McPherson. We don't have any news. Sit down and don't be so loud!" Mrs. Truman demanded tartly (as well as loudly).

"How many times do I have to tell you, woman, stop ordering me about!" Angus retorted.

"You keep behaving like a man with a dozen screws loose, I'll stop telling you what to do when they're shovelling dirt on my coffin," Mrs. Truman replied.

They entered a glaring contest.

Unsurprisingly Mrs. Truman won.

Angus stomped to Cash and Abby's circle, and Cash dropped one arm, holding Abby to him with the other.

Angus's face had gentled when he looked at Abby. "How're things, lass?"

"Not good," Abby replied softly, and Angus's worried eyes moved to Cash.

Angus was not exactly a fixture in their lives. He'd come and he'd go. He was, he explained to them, quite busy with expunging the vast number of malevolent spirits that infected the British Isles. Nevertheless his visits, although not common, were regular.

Fortunately for Abby and Jenny, who at that present time needed their friends close, Angus was working "a job" in the vicinity and using Penmort as what he referred to as his "headquarters."

He'd told them over dinner the night before, the job was proving difficult.

"Well, I'll give you something else to think about." Angus moved close to Abby and his voice had grown quietly conspiratorial. "See, my new wee ghosty has a thing against blondes. She doesn't like anyone particularly, but she *really* doesn't like blondes. I thought you could—"

Cash, his voice firm and inflexible, cut in with one word.

"No."

Angus's gaze came to him. "She'll no' be in any danger."

"No," Cash repeated.

"You know I know what I'm doing," Angus kept trying.

Cash clenched his jaw then repeated yet again, but even more firm and far more inflexible, "No."

"Fraser—" Angus started, but Cash interrupted.

"First, Abby's pregnant. Second, even if she wasn't, there is no fucking way in *hell* I'd allow her to get caught up in another of your hunts."

"Cash," Abby murmured soothingly, but it was Cash's turn to ignore her.

Angus took a step back, muttering, "No harm asking."

"Except for the fact you sent my blood pressure through the roof. I'd rather not suffer a stroke five months before my child is born," Cash clipped.

Abby went rigid at his side and Cash realised his mistake instantly.

His head tilted down to her. "Darling—"

She curled into him and her hand came to his stomach. "It's okay. I'm sorry. It's the circumstances. I'm just being stupid."

"Don't apologise," Cash bit out with irritation at himself. "What I said was thoughtless."

"What you said was in anger," she told him, leaned in, tipped her head back and gave him a small smile. "Cash, you can't guard against everything you say just because I'm an overly-sensitive idiot."

"I can try," Cash returned, and she gave it to him. The look he saw often. The look he had mistaken as awe the first time he saw it.

Then, it was her burgeoning understanding that she loved him and what they had growing between them was what she deemed "magical."

Now, it was the shining knowledge of the same thing.

He dipped his head and touched his mouth to hers as her arms stole around him. When he was done, he brushed his nose alongside hers and he watched close up the brightness of love turn to the warmth of contentedness.

She could wear his diamonds and the seven hundred pound boots his money bought her.

But Cash knew the best thing he'd ever given her was the same peace she'd given him.

"Conner!" He heard Mrs. Truman call (once she'd learned his real name, she never used anything but, and also when she was annoyed, which meant quite frequently, she addressed him by all three of his names).

Cash's head came up and he looked at the door.

Angus moved out of the way and in his arms he felt Abby's body grow solid.

Kieran stood there looking alarmingly haggard.

Then he grinned.

"It's a boy. Ten fingers, ten toes, and thankfully breathing on his own." His relieved eyes moved to Abby, "Jenny's fine."

Cash took the entirety of Abby's weight as she sagged against him.

She then buried her face in his chest and he felt her body tremble with silent tears.

Angus let out what could only be described as a very loud "whoop."

Cassandra shouted, "Hurrah!"

"I need to call Fenella and Honor," Nicola mumbled, moving to the chair that held her purse.

Suzanne, Mrs. Truman and James were all standing. Mrs. Truman, to Cash's surprise, allowed Suzanne to hug her. Then Suzanne walked into James's arms which closed around her tight and she pressed her face in his neck. James turned his head and kissed Suzanne's temple.

Cash's own arms tightened around his wife.

She leaned back and looked at him, tears wet on her cheeks. She came to her toes and touched her mouth to his, her arms giving him a squeeze. After doing that, she gently pulled away, swiping at her face, and moved to Kieran who was disengaging from his own surprising hug from Mrs. Truman.

Abby stood by Kieran's side as he accepted congratulations.

Then she walked with him hand in hand, gracefully moving away in her elegant high-heeled boots to go see her friend.

Cash watched his wife's departure, his eyes riveted openly and without even a hint of shame, on her exquisite ass.

※ ※ ※

Edith Truman sat in the corner of Jennifer's hospital room, her arms curved protectively about a tiny, blanketed bundle. Her head was tilted low, her eyes on the scrunched-up, sleeping face, her mind marvelling at the miracle.

Conner was sitting by Jennifer's bedside. Abigail had somewhat forcefully declared that she was taking Kieran to get him some dinner. Kieran had not wanted to leave and only did so when Conner assured him he'd look after his wife.

And that was precisely what Conner did, not leaving her side for an instant.

"Cash." Edith's sharp ears heard Jennifer whisper softly.

Edith didn't move anything but her eyes. They'd never know she was watching them. She saw that Conner's head was turned to Jennifer. His hand was resting on the bed beside hers.

From the beginning Edith had liked Conner's hands. They had long, tapered fingers and were nicely veined. You could tell a lot by a man's hands and his were strong, capable and handsome. Three words, Edith thought, that quite aptly defined Conner Ewan Fraser.

"Yes?" Conner murmured in reply to Jennifer's call.

"I want to tell you before I tell Abby because—" Jennifer started then stopped and Edith watched her bite her lips.

Edith was always telling her to stop doing that, but did Jennifer listen?

No.

"What is it, Jenny?" Conner urged softly, his words held a kindly invitation which stated without him having to explain that she was safe to say whatever she pleased to him.

Their relationship had not started well. This was something, to Edith's annoyance, which had never been fully explained to her.

However Edith wasn't born yesterday and she reckoned (astutely) it had to do with Jennifer not wanting to let go of her grief for her best friend's first husband and Conner's determination to be his replacement.

Over the years that had changed. Mainly because Jennifer adored Abigail, and Conner made Abigail blissfully happy.

Not to mention, although Edith would never tell anyone this, Conner was a highly likable fellow.

"We've named him Benjamin," Jennifer announced carefully, and Edith guarded her astounded reaction to this news.

Benjamin, Edith thought, was a good enough name.

She preferred Mortimer, but that was just her.

However it was also clear why Jennifer and Kieran had named their child thus. Both had been close with Abigail's first husband.

This was meant to be a posthumous honour.

It would also be a constant reminder to Conner of Abigail's past blind devotion to her dead husband, which, Edith thought irritably, wasn't very considerate of Jennifer and Kieran.

Edith watched Conner, who, gallantly Edith thought, didn't show even the slightest reaction.

However he said with honesty and genuine warmth, as well as demonstrated it when his hand closed around Jennifer's, "Abby will be pleased."

"Um," Jennifer went on cautiously then quickly, "Actually, we've named him Benjamin Conner."

Edith felt the air in the room go still.

She lifted her head and didn't even pretend not to watch openly as Conner held his body rigid for a moment. Then he came partially out of his chair, bent to Jennifer's forehead and kissed her there, never taking his hand from hers.

He sat back down and said in a rough, low voice that explicitly betrayed intense emotion, "Now *I'm* pleased."

Jennifer, face still wan and tired, smiled at him.

Edith dropped her head to look at the baby, again blinking rapidly to quell the tears that were pricking at the backs of her eyes.

With iron determination she succeeded in this effort.

The door opened and Abigail and Kieran walked in.

Kieran went directly to his wife.

Abigail smiled at her friend then her husband, but she walked to Edith.

She lifted her hands and wriggled her fingers. "Come on, Mrs. Truman, give him up."

Reluctantly, with an irate glare at Abigail to show irritation was exactly how she felt, Edith did as she was told.

Abigail walked slightly away, cuddled the baby close, and cooed to him in a soft voice.

Conner approached his wife and slid his arms loosely about her body.

Kieran sat on Jennifer's bed and held her hand with one of his as the other stroked her cheek.

Edith took a mental snapshot of Kieran and Jennifer, something she'd learned to do a long time ago in order to pull them out and savour them in her far-less-frequent-now lonely times.

She looked back at Conner and Abigail and saw his tall head bent to look at the baby, only one arm now around his wife, the other hand was curled tenderly and protectively at her neck.

Abigail's eyes went from the baby to her husband's and she grinned.

Conner grinned back.

Edith Truman took another mental snapshot and filed it happily away.

She gave them all a long moment.

Then she snapped loudly, "Conner Ewan Fraser! I need tea!"

The End

Next in the Ghosts and Reincarnation Series is
Fairytale Come Alive

AUTHOR'S NOTE

Penmort Castle, Cash and Abby's home in the book, is loosely based on Dunster Castle, a National Trust property. Dunster Castle, located in Minehead, Somerset, UK is a glorious and imposing building with history dating back to Norman times.

The National Trust is a UK charity dedicated to conserving and opening to visitors historic houses, gardens and large parts of the countryside and coastline.

I highly recommend, if you live in the UK or are just visiting, that you plan a trip to Dunster Castle or the many National Trust properties open to the public: www.nationaltrust.org.uk.

A stand alone tale of a deceased wife who's love reaches from the afterlife in the **Ghosts and Reincarnation Series.**

Fairytale Come Alive
the story of Isabella and Prentice.

In Isabella Austin Evangelista's life miracles never happen…she knows she's destined to be the princess who's stuck in the middle of a fairytale where there will be no happily ever after.

Once upon a time, Prentice Cameron loved Isabella Austin. Until he discovered she was a spoiled rich girl who spent her summers toying with his heart.

Life led Prentice to his own fairytale, the love of the full-of-life Fiona Sawyer. That being so, that fairytale was torn away when Fiona died leaving Prentice with a house to keep clean, piles of laundry to be done, a business to run and two children who were getting tired of takeaway.

But Isabella comes back to Prentice's tiny fishing town and she sweeps into his children's lives like a beautiful, well-dressed fairy godmother who bakes exquisite chocolate cakes and gives the perfect manicure to six-year-old girls. Then Prentice finds out Isabella's soul-destroying secrets, secrets that explain why she left him so many years ago.

Fiona, stuck in her village and forced to haunt her family and watch Prentice and Isabella's crazy dance, finds the impossible happening. She's cheering for Bella and Prentice to rekindle their love. Then she finds out why she's caught in her heartbreaking haunting and discovers she must embrace her magic and keep Bella safe or Bella's fairytale will never come true.

FAIRYTALE COME ALIVE
PROLOGUE

The Destruction
Prentice

"You're a fisherman," Carver Austin said, his voice filled with derision, even his lip was curled.

Prentice Cameron could not believe this bloke.

His eyes moved from Austin to Elle.

The minute he'd walked into Fergus McFadden's home in answer to Elle's father's summons and laid eyes on Elle, Prentice knew something was wrong.

She wasn't wearing shorts and a T-shirt. Her lustrous, light-brown hair wasn't falling free down her back or pulled to the top of her head in a haphazard knot. Her hazel eyes weren't shining with mischief or humor or happiness.

Instead, her usually thick, wavy hair was smoothed back in a neat ponytail at the nape of her neck and falling in a long sleek column down her back. Not a wild, riotous wave in sight.

Prentice loved her soft, beautiful, unruly hair. He thought it defined her perfectly.

She was also, he had noticed immediately, wearing makeup, which she never did because she didn't need it.

Lastly, she was wearing a sophisticated light-blue dress, which Prentice had to admit looked sweet on her, but he also noted its obvious style and expense.

He knew she was rich but she never acted it, nor did she dress the part.

Never as in *never*.

And Elle was usually chatty and energetic. Unbelievably chatty and energetic. It was difficult to keep her focused and in one place. Even when they were drinking at a pub, she shifted on her stool and chattered away. It was as if she had so much energy, if she didn't fidget and talk to release some of it, she would explode. Prentice was often forced to haul her into his body and pin her to his side or kiss her to shut her up, neither of which he minded in the slightest.

Now, she seemed frozen.

Not as if today's shift from the unusually hot weather they were having to gray and drizzling had caused her to have a chill. It was as if she was frozen from the inside. She'd barely said a word since he'd arrived and she hadn't fidgeted once.

In fact, she'd hardly looked at him at all.

"Elle, are you all right?" Prentice asked and her eyes, which were studying the carpet, flitted to his briefly then slid away.

"Perfectly fine," she replied, her voice strong, cultured, controlled, a voice that he'd never heard before.

Elle was an open, friendly person, everything about her screamed it. The last two summers she spent in the village, she'd charmed every soul there with her nearly pathological sociability. By the end of her first summer, she knew every man, woman and child *and* their pets, and they all adored her (even the pets).

But most especially Prentice.

Now, she sounded like an entirely different person.

Prentice's vague sense of alarm intensified.

"Elle," he repeated, preparing to move toward her. She was seated in an armchair. He was standing, facing off against her father who, from the very beginning of this meeting, made no bones about the fact he didn't like the idea of a lowly Scottish fisherman marrying his wealthy, educated daughter.

Before he could move, however, Austin spoke.

"Isabella has had a change of heart about your proposal."

As Prentice's eyes were still on Elle, he saw her body give a small jolt before he watched her fingers curl into tight fists in her lap.

Prentice's alarm turned to anger.

His gaze moved back to Austin.

"That's surprising," now Prentice's voice was filled with derision, "Elle seemed pretty excited about it when I put the ring on her finger."

This was not a lie. She'd been so excited, she'd tackled him with such force they'd both fallen to the floor, which at first, considering she'd knocked the wind out of him, he thought was disadvantageous. Then, as he got his breath back and realized she was kissing and touching every inch of him she could get her hands and mouth on, *and* they were horizontal, Prentice saw the advantages of the situation.

Austin interrupted Prentice's train of thought. "Isabella and I are leaving today, going back to Chicago. She'll finish her senior year at Northwestern and she won't return."

Prentice glared at him.

No, he could not believe this bloke.

"It's my understanding her plans have changed," Prentice replied.

"I'm quite certain you'll eventually be happy with a woman who has not accomplished a higher education, however, my daughter—" Austin went on.

Prentice cut him off. "No, I'll be quite happy with whatever Elle wants to do. And she's decided she'll finish uni, but after she graduates she'll come back here."

Austin smiled a humorless, condescending smile. "And what, for the sake of curiosity, could she possibly do *here*?"

Prentice's anger escalated.

He'd been born in his village, as had his father and mother and their parents and their parents, for as far back as anyone could remember. It wasn't cosmopolitan by a long shot, but it had charm and it was filled with good people who looked out for each other.

Furthermore, Elle loved it there. He knew that not only because she acted like she loved it but because she'd told him she loved it, about ten thousand times.

Prentice didn't like anything about this discussion and he was beginning to like it even less.

"We're in Scotland, not the wilds of the Serengeti," Prentice returned. "We have trains. We even have cars. She can do whatever she wants."

"It would be quite a commute to any worthwhile employment," Austin retorted disdainfully.

"That depends on your definition of 'worthwhile,'" Prentice shot back.

Austin rocked back on his heels, crossing his arms on his chest.

"It does, indeed," he replied as if he'd made a point.

Prentice was done.

He looked back at Elle.

She was again studying the carpet.

"You want to jump in here, baby?" Prentice asked softly, and he felt Austin's mood shift dangerously at his tone and, likely, his endearment.

Prentice ignored it.

Her eyes lifted to his.

Prentice felt a chill slide through him when her gaze locked on his.

She stood, slowly, lithely, the graceful way she moved was one of the things that first attracted Prentice to her. Even her incessant fidgeting looked like a beautiful dance.

She walked the four feet to where he stood in front of the fireplace and stopped not far but also not close.

She tipped her head back to look at him.

"This was a mistake," she said in that cultured, controlled voice.

Prentice thought she was not wrong.

He'd spent every moment he could with her for two summers. When she was back at home at uni they talked on the phone as often as they could, considering the time difference and the expense (which wasn't often enough for either of them). She wrote him letters and he did the same. She sent him packages filled with cookies she'd baked (at first these had arrived in crumbles and she'd made it her mission to find a way to get them to him with the cookies intact, eventually wrapping each cookie, dozens of them, tightly in cling film) and mad, ridiculous gifts she'd pick up here and there that she told him he "had to have" because they reminded her of him. Prentice had seven Northwestern T-shirts and three sweatshirts and even a pair of sweatpants that had a small Northwestern insignia on the hip.

It was safe to say Elle thought of him often.

They had, essentially, been "together" for fifteen months, unfortunately only six of those being in the same location.

In all that time, she rarely talked about her family, but of course, after he proposed she'd said it was time he meet her father.

She didn't seem excited about this, she seemed worried and Prentice put it down to normal, everyday nerves. Her mother died when she was young and she had no siblings. He assumed she and her father had formed a necessary bond because of this but any father would be cautious about the man to whom he was giving his daughter.

However now he understood her nerves were caused by something entirely different.

"Yes, baby," Prentice took a step toward her, "this was definitely a mistake."

Something flashed in her eyes, something he couldn't read, before they froze again.

Then she lifted her hand and put her fingers to his ring.

It wasn't much, he couldn't afford much. He'd taken three years after school working on his father's fishing boats and saving so he could afford university. Finally, he went, reading to be an architect. His mother told him, since he was a kid he never drew anything but houses and buildings, and when he wasn't drawing he was building with anything he could get his hands on. He built massive structures in the garden, in trees, in the lounge. It drove his mother daft since half the time he was nicking whatever he could, even to the point of dismantling furniture (and their shed), so he'd have building materials.

He went back to the boats in the summers because he needed the money.

The ring he'd given Elle wasn't what he wanted to give her, neither was it what she deserved, it was what he could afford. He'd vowed to himself (although he hadn't told her) that he'd eventually replace it with something that suited her, something bigger, shinier and worth the moon.

He'd been shocked when she'd loved the ring, tears filling her eyes as she examined it after they'd finished their horizontal celebration on the floor.

Her hand close to her face, her eyes glittering with tears, she'd whispered, "It's absolutely *perfect*, Pren. The most beautiful thing I've ever seen in my life."

Now she was sliding it off her finger.

Prentice felt his gut twist as the alarm returned, sharp and vicious.

"Elle."

"This was a mistake. I'm sorry," she said, her voice still strong, controlled. "I got caught up in the whole..." she hesitated, and with his ring between her thumb and forefinger she twirled her hand between them in a dismissive way, "Scotland thing."

The gut twist tore upwards, slicing through his innards.

Who was this girl?

"The whole 'Scotland thing?'" Prentice repeated, his eyes narrowing.

"Yes. American girls have a thing for boys with accents," she replied calmly as if her words weren't a verbal knife thrust to his heart.

"You have got to be fucking joking," Prentice hissed.

And if she was, it wasn't fucking funny.

"Mind your language around my daughter," Austin warned, but Prentice didn't even look at him.

His eyes stayed locked on Elle.

"We need to talk," he demanded. "Alone."

"I see no reason to draw this out, Prentice. As I explained, I made a mistake."

He took a step closer. She took a step back.

He stopped.

She'd never retreated from him.

Never.

Even when they were arguing, something that happened often. Elle could be annoyingly if adorably stubborn.

"Don't you see?" Elle asked. "This was a lark. Annie and me—"

Prentice's body jerked. "Don't you fucking tell me Annie and Dougal—"

Her best friend Annie had hooked up with his best friend Dougal the same night he and Elle met. They'd been just as inseparable and had fallen just as deeply in love.

Quickly, she shook her head in a frantic way that was far more Elle than anything he'd encountered that morning, and he watched panic flash through her eyes before she hid it.

"No, no...Annie and Dougal are something else," she said swiftly and firmly.

"But you and I are a lark?" Prentice asked, his voice ugly and dangerous in a way it had never sounded before and it surprised even him.

"Well...yes," she replied then continued. "I took it too far. Got caught up in it. I'm so sorry, Prentice."

She rarely called him Prentice and he didn't like it, especially not now.

She called him Pren. She was the only one in his life that did so and he liked it when she did.

And furthermore, she didn't look sorry.

She didn't look anything.

She didn't look even a little bit like the girl who tore into town with her crazy antics, her abandoned laughter, her outgoing, fun-loving American cheerfulness, stealing his and everyone's hearts.

She looked like a girl he wouldn't glance at twice.

And she acted like a girl he'd detest.

He couldn't believe he'd been so deceived.

"We need to talk," he repeated.

"There's nothing to talk about," she replied.

He got close and she stood her ground. He tipped his chin down and stared in her eyes.

They were cold.

"Something's happened."

"Yes, my father arrived and gave me a wakeup call," she threw her hands out to her sides. "This isn't my life. I wouldn't be happy here.

Honestly, Prentice, the idea is ridiculous. I don't know what I was thinking."

Prentice felt like shaking her.

He also felt like picking her up and carrying her away from Fergus McFadden's posh house and Elle's despicable father and doing everything in his power to bring back his Elle.

He didn't do either.

"I don't know what he said to you—" Prentice started.

She interrupted, "He gave me a few home truths."

"And they were?"

"It doesn't matter."

Prentice lost control of his temper and shouted, "It fucking well does!"

Austin materialized at their side. "Calm down, son."

Prentice turned only his head to Austin. "Don't call me son."

"Prentice, really, don't make a scene," Elle put in sounding, if he could believe his ears, *bored*.

Prentice turned back to Elle. "We weren't a lark."

"Prentice—"

It was his turn to interrupt and his voice held an edge of steel coated with a sheen of deep emotion, which as much as he hated showing the weakness he couldn't quite control. "At least for me it wasn't a lark."

He wasn't sure but he could have sworn Elle flinched.

He decided he was wrong when she calmly held his ring up between them.

Prentice didn't take it.

Instead, he said, "When you're away from him and you realize this is madness, you find me, you call me, you write me, I don't give a fuck what you do." He leaned into her and took her head in both hands feeling her body go solid when he moved an inch away from her face. His voice dipped low when he continued, "I'll be pissed off, baby, and I'll make you work for it. But I love you enough to get over it and take you back. I promise you that."

"Prentice—" she said softly, but he cut her off in the way he always stopped her from chattering.

He touched his mouth to hers.

Without a choice, as usual, Elle went quiet.

Prentice pulled away and looked into her eyes.

"I've had a good life, you know that," he whispered. "Even so, you're the best thing that's been in it."

He watched, up close, as she slowly closed her eyes, emotion washing over her face making her radiant.

That was his Elle.

Whatever this was, he'd made it through.

Thank Christ.

He kissed her forehead, let her go, and without a backward glance at her or her father Prentice walked away.

Fairytale Come Alive
is available for purchase in all formats.

NEWSLETTER

Would you like advanced notification about Upcoming Releases? Access to exclusive content? Access to exclusive giveaways? The first to see a new cover reveal? Sign up for my newsletter to keep up-to-date with the latest from Kristen Ashley!

Sign up at <u>kristenashley.net</u>

ABOUT THE AUTHOR

Kristen Ashley is the *New York Times* bestselling author of over one hundred romance novels. She's a hybrid author, publishing titles independently and traditionally, with books translated into fourteen languages and millions of copies sold.

Kristen's novel, *Law Man*, won the *RT Book Reviews* Reviewer's Choice Award for best Romantic Suspense, her independently published title, *Hold On*, was nominated for *RT Book Reviews* best Independent Contemporary Romance, and her traditionally published title, *Breathe*, was nominated for best Contemporary Romance. Her titles *Motorcycle Man*, *The Will*, *The Hookup* and *Ride Steady* (which won the Reader's Choice award from *Romance Reviews*) all made the final rounds for Goodreads Choice Awards in the Romance category.

Although Kristen is super proud of all those accolades, she's just happy that—after years of writing with no publisher or agent interested in what she did—she now has a loyal readership who, on social media, she can share recipes with and regale with stories of her bent toward being a klutz.

Kristen was born in Gary and raised in Brownsburg, Indiana, but since leaving her home state (Hoosier by birth, Boilermaker by the grace of God!), she's lived in Denver and the West Country of England. All of these places were home, and she's put them in her books with all the love she still has for them.

Now, after years of cold, misty days in the UK (that she still misses, along with cream teas, custard and battered sausages), Kristen resides in almost constant sun. She writes at her desk in Phoenix or among the deer and javelina in her little cabin up in the Arizona mountains, regretting often that she forgets to put the sunshade over her windshield, thus her car often doubles as a human oven. Even so, she loves calling all the sun, saguaro and beautiful mountains home.

You can read more about Kristen and her books at KristenAshley.net.

facebook.com/kristenashleybooks

instagram.com/kristenashleybooks

pinterest.com/KristenAshleyBooks

goodreads.com/kristenashleybooks

bookbub.com/authors/kristen-ashley

tiktok.com/@kristenashleybooks

The Chaos Series:

Own the Wind

Fire Inside

Ride Steady

Walk Through Fire

A Christmas to Remember

Rough Ride

Wild Like the Wind

Free

Wild Fire

Wild Wind

The Colorado Mountain Series:

The Gamble

Sweet Dreams

Lady Luck

Breathe

Jagged

Kaleidoscope

Bounty

Dream Man Series:

Mystery Man

Wild Man

Law Man

Motorcycle Man

Quiet Man

Dream Team Series:

Dream Maker

Dream Chaser

Dream Bites Cookbook

Dream Spinner

Dream Keeper

The Fantasyland Series:

Wildest Dreams

The Golden Dynasty

Fantastical

Broken Dove

Midnight Soul

Gossamer in the Darkness

Four Realms Series:

Night's Fall

Ghosts and Reincarnation Series:

Sommersgate House

Lacybourne Manor

Penmort Castle

Fairytale Come Alive

Lucky Stars

The Honey Series:

The Deep End

The Farthest Edge

The Greatest Risk

The Magdalene Series:

The Will

Soaring

The Time in Between

Manor and Mysteries Series:

Too Good to Be True

Mathilda, SuperWitch:

Mathilda's Book of Shadows

The Rise of the Dark Lord

Misted Pines Series

The Girl in the Mist

The Girl in the Woods

The Woman by the Lake

The Woman Left Behind

Moonlight and Motor Oil Series:

The Hookup

The Slow Burn

The Rising Series:

The Beginning of Everything

The Plan Commences

The Dawn of the End

The Rising

River Rain Series:

After the Climb

After the Climb Special Edition

Chasing Serenity

Taking the Leap

Making the Match

Fighting the Pull

Sharing the Miracle

Embracing the Change

Finding the One

The Three Series:

Until the Sun Falls from the Sky

With Everything I Am

Wild and Free

The Unfinished Hero Series:

Knight

Creed

Raid

Deacon

Sebring

Wild West MC Series:

Still Standing

Smoke and Steel

Smooth Sailing

Other Titles by Kristen Ashley:

Heaven and Hell

Play It Safe

Three Wishes

Complicated

Loose Ends

Fast Lane

Perfect Together

Rock Chick Series:

Rock Chick

Rock Chick Rescue

Rock Chick Redemption

Rock Chick Renegade

Rock Chick Revenge

Rock Chick Reckoning

Rock Chick Regret

Rock Chick Revolution

Rock Chick Reawakening

Rock Chick Reborn

Rock Chick Rematch

Rock Chick Bonus Tracks

Avenging Angels Series

Avenging Angel

Avenging Angels: Back in the Saddle

Avenging Angels: Tenderfoot

Avenging Angel: Bad Medicine

The 'Burg Series:

For You

At Peace

Golden Trail

Games of the Heart

The Promise

Hold On

The Chaos Series:

Own the Wind

Fire Inside

Ride Steady

Walk Through Fire

A Christmas to Remember

Rough Ride

Wild Like the Wind

Free

Wild Fire

Wild Wind

The Colorado Mountain Series:

The Gamble

Sweet Dreams

Lady Luck

Breathe

Jagged

Kaleidoscope

Bounty

Dream Man Series:

Mystery Man

Wild Man

Law Man

Motorcycle Man

Quiet Man

Dream Team Series:

Dream Maker

Dream Chaser

Manor and Mysteries Series:

Too Good to Be True

Mathilda, SuperWitch:

Mathilda's Book of Shadows

The Rise of the Dark Lord

Misted Pines Series

The Girl in the Mist

The Girl in the Woods

The Woman by the Lake

The Woman Left Behind

Moonlight and Motor Oil Series:

The Hookup

The Slow Burn

The Rising Series:

The Beginning of Everything

The Plan Commences

The Dawn of the End

The Rising

River Rain Series:

After the Climb

After the Climb Special Edition

Chasing Serenity

Taking the Leap

Making the Match

Fighting the Pull

Sharing the Miracle

Embracing the Change

Finding the One

The Three Series:

Until the Sun Falls from the Sky

With Everything I Am

Wild and Free

The Unfinished Hero Series:

Knight

Creed

Raid

Deacon

Sebring

Wild West MC Series:

Still Standing

Smoke and Steel

Smooth Sailing

Other Titles by Kristen Ashley:

Heaven and Hell

Play It Safe

Three Wishes

Complicated

Loose Ends

Fast Lane

Perfect Together

www.ingramcontent.com/pod-product-compliance
Lightning Source LLC
Chambersburg PA
CBHW051424190726
48289CB00001B/41